EMERGENCE

Siana Wineland

Publisher's Note: This is a work of fiction. Names, characters, places, and incidents are a product of the author's imagination. Locales and public names are sometimes used for atmospheric purposes. Any resemblance to actual people, living or dead, or to businesses, companies, events, institutions, or locales is completely coincidental.

Emergence/ Siana Wineland. -- 1st ed.
ISBN 978-0-6159531-7-5

Shivering barefoot in the darkness, Jessica hid in the bushes and watched the recovery team flip the lights on in her house. She bared her teeth at the invasion of her territory, a growl rumbling in her throat. The instinctive response brought her up short and fear flooded her, cutting off the animalistic sound. Panic tried to set its icy claws in her gut, but she pushed it away ruthlessly. Her unusual response and the arrival of the recovery team confirmed her worst fear: she must have started the change.

She had done her best to deny this possibility her whole life. But reality now walked through her home, leaving her in the cold and dark.

She took a deep breath and returned her attention to the house. Fear of what was to come had to take a backseat.

A large, lean man with shoulder-length blond hair had entered her bedroom. He moved with the grace of a predator, and her eyes widened when he turned, allowing her to see the suede of his wings fall gracefully down his back like a dark cloak.

Holy crap! They've sent a Hunter. Her mind froze in panic. Why is there a Hunter here? Recovery teams only have unchanged people in them.

She watched as the Valkyrie stopped and sniffed the air, scenting her, before walking over to the window and examining it. After a moment he spread his wings, the large fan covering the glass to block the light from behind him so he could scrutinize the dark yard. Fascinated, she stared, transfixed at the way the light shone through the membrane of his wings.

She felt her mind slowing again. Fruitlessly, she fought the lethargy that was her body's natural response to the changes taking place within it.

It wasn't long before the Hunter's eyes found hers, even in the dark, their intensity boring into her, and he smiled a slow feral smile.

Dedication

For Chas. Who believed in me enough to push me to get this done

Acknowledgments

There are so many people I wish I could thank. Too many to list here. This book is a long time coming, and so many listened to the dreams along the way. The biggest would be my husband, Chas. I would also like to thank my beta readers, especially Jen. And last, Keri. Thanks for all the help, and I'm so glad we found each other again.

Chapter One

"I've broken through the pass codes, and I'm initiating the virus," Jennifer whispered. She sat hunched in her chair, focused on the screen, her fingers stabbing at the keys. "There, it's running. I hope you coded this thing right, Andrew, or we're screwed."

She shifted in her seat. The compact fall of her skin-covered wings pressed tight to her spine and pulled where she sat upon them. One of their flexible struts dug in so she pulled them out from under her.

Her heartbeat thudded in her ears, and she glanced over her shoulder in the dim room, past the aisles of computer terminals, at the door leading to the hall.

"I'm almost in too, Jen," her husband murmured, drawing her attention back from the door. She could barely make out his dark-clad form across the room. The clatter of his fingers against the keys pounded in her head.

She took a deep breath and tried to relax. She hadn't been back to the Facility since she went through the change and her wings grew six years ago.

And I wish I wasn't now.

Jennifer looked back at her screen. Everything moved along fine, at least on the surface.

"Just relax, Jen. I do know how to do my job." Her husband chuckled. "Ok. I'm in."

His sudden hiss drew her attention.

"Oh my God..."

Andrew slammed disks into the computer, switching them out as fast as they filled. She glanced back at her own terminal. The virus she'd uploaded had reached the halfway point. Certain that it would continue on without her, she rose.

1

Her wingtips brushed the back of her knees through her leggings as she slipped around the closely packed computer stations to see what had caused his exclamation.

"How bad is it?" She leaned against the back of his chair.

"According to this file, they're preparing enclosures for those of us who've changed. The numbers of people infected are rising. The first building complex is ready for occupation. The bastards. Look at this."

He pressed a few more keys, then pointed to the screen. "They have Gabriel slated to run it."

"Gabriel..." Jennifer drew in an unsteady breath and scanned the document. The thought of Gabriel having control over anyone she knew... *It doesn't matter if he's one of us, he's insane.* "We need to get these disks out to Marcus. There's no way our people in the Facility know about this, or we would have gotten word about it in the last relay."

"Maybe he didn't want Marcus concerned. Could this be why they put such a rush on this job?"

"No." She ran her hand down the soft suede of his folded wing membrane, comforted by the contact. "Nickolas just completed the change."

"So, they're going to go ahead with the mule project after all? That still doesn't explain the rush."

"Something happened during Nickolas's change. I don't know what went wrong, but whatever happened caught Gabriel's interest. Marcus needed us to delete his son's file."

"Ah, got it. That's why you needed a broad spectrum wipe," he said as he reached for another disk. "So, do you think Marcus will move Nickolas and his brother out to the valley now? If Gabriel gets his hands on him..." He shook his head. "God, Nickolas is just a teenager."

Jennifer shivered at the thought. "Marcus doesn't see how. Nothing has changed. Nickolas and Christoff still have too much surveillance on them."

A beep echoed from her computer. She squeezed Andrew's shoulder then moved back over to check her work. "The virus just finished. I guess you did do your job right."

She smiled at his snort and got her computer shut down. "Are you almost done?"

"This is the last disk."

Jennifer slipped over to the door and cracked it open to look out on a deserted hallway, blinking in the light. She felt Andrew's body heat press into her back as his lips touched her ear, his whisper tickling across.

"No words outside of this room."

Fear jolted her, and a vision took shape behind her mind's eye. The sudden knowledge that Gabriel was *here*, at the Facility tonight when he shouldn't be, slammed into her. As the only other uninhibited Valkyrie present on the grounds, he could sense their telepathy. Damn it, why couldn't her clairvoyance have shown her this sooner? This was a piece of information she could have used, instead of all the numerous warnings of her death the last several months. At least this vision passed swiftly.

She turned her head to meet her husband's eyes over her shoulder. "No, An..."

His growl reverberated through her, and she swallowed the rest of her sentence. Andrew's gaze reinforced his order of silence. She turned back to look out at the hallway blindly.

I should have told them. I should have told them about my visions. She sucked in a wavering breath. Andrew reached around her and pushed the door wider. His body moved with the lethal grace of a Hunter around her. He snagged her hand and pulled her in his wake.

She moved on autopilot as she assimilated the information her vision brought. *But if I had told them, Marcus would have pulled the plug on the mission. And the files I wiped tonight were crucial. My visions were clear enough recently to know that this was the only way to succeed. I would never have convinced him of that.*

They reached an intersection and paused while Andrew determined if their exit route remained clear.

We're almost there, Jen. This is the last hallway. We take a left and the door to the outside is at the end. Then we meet Marcus in the woods on the other side of the compound.

Jennifer closed her eyes in dismay. She took a deep breath and grabbed his shoulder, stopping him before he could move on. The surprise in his eyes faded to a questioning look as she stared into them. Her hand trembled as she brushed a lock of hair away from his forehead. Then she rose up on tiptoe to kiss him. *I love you, Andrew. Now, let's go.*

Are you ok, Jen?

Her gaze slid away from his too perceptive one, and she shrugged reluctantly. *I have a bad feeling.*

He tensed under her hand. *You're the Seer, I'm just the Hunter. Do you have anything more substantial to help us?*

It was too late. Nothing she knew would make a difference. She had received the warning too late, even avoiding their telepathy probably wouldn't have made a difference anyway. Jennifer shook her head, but Andrew caught her chin. He searched her face.

The strength of his gaze held her pinned and stripped the truth from her. His eyes hardened and she shivered at the wildness that rose behind the facade. She understood it came from the need to protect her, but she had never reconciled herself to the violence that forever lurked just under their skin after fledging. She exhaled in relief when he turned back to the corner and glanced around it before taking her hand. They walked down the hall together.

Anxiety colored her perception, causing this last hall to stretch forever. She'd always hated this place. From the moment she started working there. Then when it became known that people were changing into something else, something that didn't seem quite human, she'd tried to leave, but it had been too late. Andrew had become infected.

They'd made it out alive, barely. Others hadn't been as fortunate. But it looked like she'd come full circle.

The bleak atmosphere of the Facility still gave her nightmares, and she had hoped to never step foot in it again. The desolate blank walls of a hospital were more inviting.

She slowed her shallow breath. A faint touch had brushed the edge of her mind. She swept her power out in a quick probe. The time for being careful had passed. Gabriel either knew they were here, or not. *Andrew, can you sense anything?* She felt the quick burst of power that he sent out.

No, I... His fluid movements held the barest hint of a jolt as he strained to detect what she sensed. *Wait.*

Jennifer stumbled as Andrew shoved her behind him. She looked up in time to see the door closest to them open and a guard step out. The surprised look on the grounded's face didn't last long. The man started to draw his gun and shout, but Andrew grabbed him by the throat and smashed his head into the door jamb, then yanked the limp body in front of them as a shield. Shots rang out. Thankfully the man wore a Kevlar vest, so the bullets didn't go through into Andrew.

There's too many of them, Jennifer, run!

Andrew slung the body into the room, tripping the others, and wrenched the door shut. He jerked a knife out of his boot and slammed it into the crack of the door to wedge it. He grabbed her hand, propelling her in front of him. She ran down the hall, focused on the exit. The sudden blaring of the Facility's alarms lashed through her. Her enhanced senses screamed in protest, and her knees buckled from the pain as the lights and sirens assaulted her. *Andrew?*

I'm fine. Just keep going. I'm right behind you.

Her breath hitched in her throat as her fear and relief fought. She crashed into the door at the end of the hall and burst through into the night. Outside, her relief dwindled as the compound lights came up like solar flares, illuminating the stark reality of their situation. Before her stood an avenue of trees with a walkway running under the intertwined branches. Another walkway followed the perimeter of the building. The booted stamp of a large contingent of guards echoed off it. And a dark, ominously winged shape that followed in their wake.

Andrew, we need to clear the trees before we can take off, Jennifer screamed mentally. *I think I saw Gabriel back there.*

Andrew's calm voice bored into her head. *Keep going down this avenue. There's a cleared perimeter at the end of it. The woods are on the other side of that fence.*

Breath rasping in her lungs, she pushed herself harder to clear the gauntlet of trees, Andrew's protective presence a wall at her back. Spreading her wings, she launched into the sky. She needed to make it across the cleared ground and get over that fence. Almost immediately, gunshots rang out from below and she heard Andrew grunt.

Looking back, she saw him hit the ground in a sprawl. "Andrew!"

A last, faint thought reached her. *Jen...love.*

Then he was gone.

She hovered in shock, the sound of more gunfire lost with the roaring in her head. Searing pain lanced through her as the bullets struck, causing her wings to give out. She fell twenty feet to the ground.

"Andrew! No..." She sobbed, her fingers raking at the gravel in an effort to pull her body around. She tried to crawl to him, but her injuries held her captive. Fire ate at her and she felt her blood pump out of her with every beat of her heart. The crunch of Gabriel's footsteps penetrated her grief and pain. Twisting her head, she caught sight of the insane Valkyrie's beautiful, expressionless face. He stood over Andrew for a moment before bending down to check for a pulse. Gabriel shook his head and looked up at the unfledged Facility guards, who stood with their guns drawn at the edge of the trees. Then he searched through her husband's vest and pulled out the disks. He rose and walked over to where she lay.

"Hello, Jennifer. So, you turned out to be a Seer. I must say, that is a bit of a surprise." He shook his head. "You shouldn't have come back. But rabid dogs usually return home. Marcus should have listened."

"We're not the rabid ones; you are," she rasped. "Just because we don't want to live our lives doped up..." She coughed, and blood droplets splattered Gabriel's boots.

"Well, it hardly matters now." A gentle smile touched the corners of his lips and he held up the disks. "Fortunately, you didn't accomplish what you came for."

Gabriel stared at her for a moment, an inscrutable look on his face before he asked, "Who let you in, Jennifer? You had to have inside help." He crouched and brushed the blood from her lips with his thumb. "Tell me, and I'll get you to the medics."

"Never." She spit in his face.

His eyes turned hard and cold, he wiped the bloody spittle, streaking his face into a ghastly mask. "Fine, bleed to death." Rising, he shook his blond hair over his shoulder. "It's not like I don't know who did it anyway. I will get proof in due course. At least you can act as bait. We both know Marcus won't want to leave you behind." Turning on his heel, he gestured to the guards, and they melted into the trees.

A sob escaping, Jennifer pressed her face into the gravel.

The echo of the alarms still reverberated through the dark woods. Marcus picked up the pace, a vise around his heart, and he pushed his Flight to slip faster through the bushes. *They'll make it. They'll be ok. Jen would have sensed something...* When they reached the edge of the wild land, and the fence to the Facility, he motioned his Hunters to a stop. They crouched down and peered through the greenery. The vise squeezed tighter and he moaned, "No."

Jennifer and Andrew lay sprawled, broken and bleeding on the ground like unwanted toys. Marcus silenced the rumble that rose around him with a gesture. He reached out with his mind, already knowing what he would find, hoping he was wrong.

The lance of power took him by surprise. Jennifer's mind latched onto his with surprising strength, sparking hope. But then the contact wavered in and out. **Marcus, go, while you have the chance. Escape.**

He clenched his teeth from the pain he could feel flood through the link. **Hold on, Jen. We'll come and get you. Take you home.**

No. I'm just bait. He knows you're close, and he's counting on you to show yourselves trying to save me. Please don't risk anyone. I'm not going to make it. She coughed and the contact faded then strengthened again. She turned her head toward them and Marcus could see the blood on her face. The tension emanating from the rest of his Flight soared. Marcus placed his hand on the arm of his Second to hold the Hunter back. Jennifer coughed again before she continued. **We succeeded, Marcus. We destroyed the old network. But...Andrew found something else.**

A convulsion ripped through her body, and this time Marcus found himself held back by restraining hands. He pulled against them halfheartedly. Tears filled his eyes. *Jennifer?*

I don't have much longer, she sent weakly. Extending her wings, she tried to flap them, but they sank to the ground. *Andrew had the disks, Marcus...but Gabriel found them. I don't know the details...worse, worse than anything imagined. Be careful.* The link faded and he held his breath, willing strength down it to support her. She coughed again, and he could see more blood trickle down her cheek to mingle with her tears. *Robin and Jessica. You have to watch out for them, Marcus. Please...promise me. Promise me you'll take care of them when their time comes. They will both change. I have Seen it.*

Bowing his head under the weight of his grief, he replied, *You know I will. We all will. I'll move them to Aurora tomorrow.* The fear that shot through the link when he said that surprised Marcus.

No! Don't. They need to stay where they are. Please. Her connection faded in and out again as she weakened. *Jessica...she's special, different. Watch out for her.* Helplessly, he watched her body twist, the movement exposing the pool of blood that had seeped out onto the rocks around her. *Marcus, I'm sorry. Tell them I'm sorry and that I love them.* Heaving a breath, she lay still.

Then there was only silence.

Chapter Two

Fifteen years later.

Nickolas Sinclair watched his brother, Christoff, shift his wing into a more comfortable position in the dimness of the van and wished he could do more than shift his. He took a couple of deep breaths and shoved the longing away. He needed the open air on his wings. The space was too cramped. He hated the van. Well, any vehicle really. *I guess I shouldn't complain. I get more free flight than any of the others.*

He settled deeper into the van's seat and took another breath in an effort to relax his back muscles. They were almost to their destination—finally.

"Nick, why didn't Ian send Gamma team out for this recovery? This is their territory," Christoff asked.

Nickolas had wondered the same thing. *Especially since I still have a boatload of paper work to contend with. He knows that.* And the retrieval documents fell short of normal. Maybe that counted as an explanation for their assignment? "Jules, have they sent any more details?"

The small, dark-haired communications technician didn't bother to turn away from his bank of monitors and equipment. The grounded just shook his head.

Nickolas sighed and turned back to Christoff. "I have no idea, Chris. We're the only fledged team members, that's my best guess. You're right that Jeff's team should be the one handling this recovery. They're already stationed out here. It's a six-hour drive for us."

"Well, other than being stuck in this van for hours, it is nice to get out of the Facility for a bit. I haven't gotten out for a few weeks." Christoff raked a hand across his head, tousling his blond hair before he shifted again.

"Hmmm," Nickolas returned. *Yes and no Chris. You know how much I hate recoveries.*

Christoff laughed. "Don't even try to pretend you aren't glad to be out for a bit. You need to loosen up and relax. Enjoy some free time. You're way too serious."

Nickolas scowled halfheartedly at his brother. Too serious? What else was there for him to do? Between the piles of paper work and responsibilities to his little clan of Valkyries, the schedule of tests and training they were always under. What was he supposed to do to have fun? The closest he got was sparring in the ring. But that only occupied his mind for a brief period of time. The others all had each other for companionship; he never quite fit in.

"See, there you go again, Nick. Stop thinking so much."

"Well, one of us has to, Chris."

"Oh, ow." Christoff gasped, dramatically clutching his heart. "That one was really uncalled for." He laughed.

Nickolas's lips twitched. He could always count on Christoff to be a clown. Somehow his little brother never failed to notice when he needed distracting.

"We have another couple of blocks before we arrive, Nickolas," Flynn called from the driver's seat.

Nickolas watched the levity leave his brother's face. Christoff was fully aware of how hard a trip like this was for him.

Hating his weakness, Nickolas looked out the window onto the darkened pavement. They wound their way down a rustic, residential street. Unlike most cities, where the houses were so close they were touching, these houses had large yards, lots of space. Huge, big-leaf maples lined the road, blocking out a majority of the light cast by the street lamps. Flynn pulled the van up behind a dark SUV.

Before the engine died, Nickolas had popped open the door and was climbing out. He stretched his wings to their full extension before folding them closed on a sigh of relief. He could finally breathe. The sound of Christoff's wings followed suit.

Jeff and Rick climbed out of the SUV and came over to join them. "What are we looking at, Jeff?" Nickolas asked.

The Gamma team leader smiled a greeting. "She was lethargic when she came home. She arrived about seven tonight. We haven't seen any movement for at least four hours."

"Good." Nickolas caught Flynn's attention when he came around the van. "Flynn, get the back ready for our guest. Jules, ready to get us inside?"

Smiling from ear to ear, Jules pulled a little black case out of his pocket and tossed it in the air. "I'm always ready, Nick."

Nickolas rolled his eyes at the wiry little man before turning to address the Gamma leader. "You want to join us, Jeff? This should be your retrieval."

The grounded snorted and shook his head. "No. It's your job. We'll wait out here."

Glad that Jeff and Rick didn't seem to be harboring any resentment, Nickolas turned to look at the old rambler across the street.

Blue paint, fading but not yet peeling, washed the walls. The yard had an overgrown quality to it that invited you to explore the paths and see what they hid. The effect appeared purposeful not neglectful.

Darkness shrouded the house. No lights shown from the windows or the shadow-filled porch. As Nickolas studied the house, the hair on the back of his neck rose. A feeling he couldn't describe lightly brushed across his mind, like a breeze ruffling his hair. Narrowing his eyes, he cocked his head.

"The van's ready, Nickolas."

His absorption shattered, he pulled his gaze away from the house. Flynn's greying red head popped out of the van.

Only a moment had passed, Jeff and Rick weren't even back in their car yet, but to him it felt like everything had slowed down. He glanced at his team then made an attempt to shake off the disconcerting feeling. "Let's get this over with."

He followed in the wake of the other three.

The closer he got to the house, the more he felt like he was walking through molasses. Something inside him felt like it stretched. Not like a rubber band, more like he pushed through a balloon. Then, to compound it, that strange feeling crawled across his mind once more. This time stronger. It wasn't repellant; in fact, it was the opposite.

He stumbled on the pavement. The desire for it twisted through him, quickly chased by fear. He repressed both ruthlessly.

Christoff's wings flipped nervously up ahead and drew Nickolas's attention to the porch. Vines wrapped around the pillar on the left, fading blossoms still clinging to the turning foliage.

Stepping over the curb, Nickolas crossed the sidewalk and passed down the plant-lined walkway. *Get a grip. Stop jumping at shadows.*

Shaking his wings out, Nickolas followed the others up the steps. The moment his foot touched the wood, he went blind. Power swept through him, burning channels in his mind, clearing a fog he hadn't realized existed. He opened his mouth to scream, but the fire seized his lungs and was gone. Instantly. Almost like it had never been. Shaking, Nickolas found himself clutching the pillar of the railing with one hand. A quick glance up showed the others still had their backs to him and were just gathering by the door. None of them seemed affected.

What the hell was that! Pulling himself together by sheer willpower, he finished climbing the steps, glad for the darkness. He didn't need the others noticing anything strange.

Christoff shot a quick glance at him when he joined them at the door, but then his brother went back to watching Jules pick the lock.

It didn't take long. Jules could get through pretty much any lock out there, so a house was simple. The door released and Jules pushed it open. The two unfledged and his brother stepped back away from the opening, giving Nickolas the space to enter first.

That was a routine he wished wasn't the case at the moment. Still uncertain about being fully in control, Nickolas swept past and entered the house.

Disoriented, Jessica clawed her way up out of the tangled images of her nightmare. A potent combination of adrenaline and panic made her heart race. Shoving a hand through her hair, her fingers tangled in the curls as she tried to push the mass out of her face. Tears stained her cheeks, and she wiped haphazardly at them. Her chest tightened with sorrow as the memories of the last night she saw her parents alive continued to circle through her head.

Angry, she squeezed her eyes shut and tried to push them away. She gained some distance, but that allowed her to realize the panic and adrenaline weren't fading. They were growing. Attempting to control her rapid breath, Jessica opened her eyes and stared at the ceiling, but the urge to move overpowered her. She threw back her covers and swung her legs out of bed. The pounding in her head briefly masked everything else.

Tim's right, I'm getting sick. She laid her forehead on her knees, confused. It was hard to think.

Goose bumps rose all over her body. It felt like a cloud of static electricity had passed through her. That was the only warning she had before a blinding pain punched through her head. Her breath seized as her body tried to react—move, scream, anything. It was over instantly, but in the wake of it, the fog that had clouded her mind swept away.

She slowly sat up on her bed, taking stock. Her mind raced. The surety that she was catching a cold suddenly faltered. *What is going on with me?*

A soft sound reached her ears, interrupting her contemplation. *That's the front door. What is May doing back already?* A quick glance at her clock showed that it was just after midnight. *That can't be May. She wouldn't come home at this hour.* Already the clarity faded and the fog drifted back across her mind.

She reached out and switched on her bedside lamp. The light stabbed daggers into her head and she slapped her hand over her eyes.

What the hell? Panic blossomed in her chest, momentarily superseding the adrenaline. "No," she moaned. "No, I can't be."

♦ ♦ ♦

Once over the threshold, Nickolas crossed the entryway and stepped into the living room. He kept his back to the others and pretended to study the titles on a bookshelf. He needed a moment to regain a calm façade to present to the rest of his team. The surge of energy that had mentally rocked him back on his heels on the porch had yet to completely dissipate. A slight tremor still shook his fingers.

Get a grip, boyo. You don't need to attract Chris's attention. His brother could be annoyingly overprotective. It was an admirable quality, unless you were the one being subjected to it. *All I need is for him to decide something's wrong and sic the rest of our Flight on me when we get home. I'll never get a moment's peace.* He ran his fingers through his hair. He was pretty sure he had the shock hidden now, even though he still reeled inside.

Flynn had just found the light switch with his flashlight and had turned the foyer light on. The grounded showed no indication that he was aware of what had happened on the porch. *Now, if I can just be so lucky with Chris.*

As if his thoughts had called him, Christoff pulled his blond head out of the entryway closet. His brother's boyish grin didn't hide his intelligence, or his searching look, when he met Nickolas's eyes.

Damn, he noticed. Or... he felt it too, maybe?

He thought about that for a second, but irritation washed it away when he saw worry enter Christoff's green eyes.

We're working, Chris, back off. He hoped his body language would convey his thoughts to his Second. He didn't need Christoff nursemaiding him.

Chris snorted a laugh and threw a salute in the air before he gave in and looked away.

A momentary reprieve, Nickolas sighed. *He takes Ian's dictates way too seriously.* He watched his brother search through the rest of the hall closet for a moment, just to make sure that Chris had actually dropped the subject. *I suppose I can't really blame him. I would do anything to protect him.*

He gave himself a shake and turned back to the job. A fledgling often ended up in strange locations in their houses when they finally passed out. Once he'd found one had managed to stuff himself into his dryer.

Their target had a beautiful home. Open and inviting, filled with well cared for antique furniture. Definitely not the sort of home he would expect to find from a woman in her twenties. His unease grew the more he looked around.

The pristine state of the rooms also didn't match what he expected from a fledgling entering stage two. "What's missing?"

The other three members of his team went still as his question sank in.

"Where's the mess?"

Christoff's face grew serious and he snapped his wings tight from their relaxed state. Quick efficiency replaced his more standard, relaxed surfer dude façade. "Are we sure she's here? Jules?" He strode through the archway on their left. "Kitchen, dining area. Both intact."

Nickolas folded his arms and watched his team go to work. Jules reached up to his ear and spoke quietly into his mic. Flynn closed the front door then went to search the cabinets in the living room.

"Jeff swears that she didn't go out the front." Jules took his finger away from the button on his earpiece. "He said she could have gone out a back door, but why? It's nothing but woods there."

"She has to be somewhere." Cocking his head, Nickolas listened. Everything felt different tonight. It was almost like that surge of power had triggered something. Detecting possible movement from the rear of the house, he motioned everyone to spread out.

♦ ♦ ♦

The distinctive rattle of her front door closing snapped Jessica out of her stunned disbelief. *Someone's in the house.* Pushing the pain away, she jumped to her feet. Her thoughts swirled in chaos. She wasn't normally prone to panic, but her reactions were not all her own tonight. If what she feared was correct...well, it was only going to get worse.

Damn it, where are you, May? I need you. Why'd you have to up and leave town and not tell me where you are?

She grabbed her sweats and thrust her legs into them, wishing her shoes weren't out by the front door.

Run, Jessica.

The sound of her mother's voice echoed through her head, slamming home the remembered images from her dream.

"Mommy, will I ever have wings like you?"

Her mother squeezed her hard before she answered. "You will, one day. But not for several years yet, and Robin will get his first."

"Robin! He always gets to go first."

Her mother's voice laughed quietly, the sound filling her. "He's older than you."

"That's not fair."

"True, but life's not fair." Her mother grew serious. "You need to do your best to avoid the Facility, Jessica. Remember."

Remember.

Panting, Jessica shook her head, forcing the cobwebs to clear. The sound of feet stepping quietly on her hardwood floors galvanized her. *Leave, I have to leave.*

Run, run, run. Her mother's voice beat a staccato that matched her racing heart. She slid her bedroom window to the side and slipped out into the cold October night.

Christoff swept down the hall to the last bedroom. He was sure that he'd heard someone in that room. All Valkyries had their strengths and weaknesses. Nickolas was a decent tracker... *But he's not as good as me. His Hunter abilities are just not as strong as mine.* Christoff thought, perplexed. But, there *was* something, something that couldn't be defined, about Nickolas that had all of the Valkyries baring their throats to him. His strengths lay in a different arena.

He was Alpha.

Christoff grimaced. *Nick may be Alpha, but this is one captain who won't be allowed to go down with the ship. I can't trust him to watch out for his own well-being. If something's wrong, he'll confront it. With no regard to how important he is to the rest of us. Whatever that energy surge was affected him more than me.* Christoff felt his worry resurface.

There was a dim light shining from under the door on the left. He paused to listen for a moment before he reached out and quietly turned the knob. It wouldn't do to surprise the new fledgling. Those who were just starting the change were usually unaware of what was happening to them. Unfortunately, they were also volatile and prone to attack. *Which could make life really interesting. Good thing I like interesting.*

Peering around the door, he saw no one. A breath hissed between his teeth, and he shoved the door wide, looking the room over more thoroughly.

It was a decent-sized bedroom, but the pale purple and white walls made him cringe. This room, unlike the rest of the house, looked more like what they expected to find. Possessions were strewn around the room, but it still was not as messy as it should be. With a second glance, he decided that it just looked lived in. It was not the sort of destruction associated with the onset of the second stage of the change. Surprised, Christoff flipped his wings to settle them more comfortably then crossed the room to look inside the closet. Shoving the hangers over revealed nothing, and the shelves were too small for anyone to hide on.

I know I heard you. Chris ran his hand through his hair and looked at the rest of the room. The only other place to hide was the bed, but it really didn't feel like she was here in the room anymore. Still, just to be on the safe side, he walked over and flipped up the skirt to look under the bed. Sighing, he straightened up then felt the bed coverings. Heat under the down blanket.

She hadn't been gone long.

The only way out, besides going past them, was the window. Walking over, he studied it. *Yes*, he thought, looking at the slightly open window. *I knew you were here. Now the million dollar question is, why did you leave? Or, better yet, how did you manage it?*

Shivering in the darkness, Jessica watched the recovery team flip the lights on as they searched the whole structure looking for her. The invasion of her territory made her mad, and she bared her teeth, a growl rumbling in her throat. The instinctive response brought her up short. Fear flooded her system, cutting off the animalistic sound. Panic once more tried to set icy claws into her, but she pushed it away ruthlessly. Her response and the arrival of the recovery team confirmed her worst fear: she must have started the change.

Just what I needed. This sucks! At least the cold air is helping to clear my thoughts. I think.

She had done her best to deny this possibility her whole life. But huddled out in the woods barefoot, wearing only an oversized T-shirt and sweatpants, she couldn't pretend any longer.

She was changing.

It's just not fair, she thought mutinously, shaking her head as she tried to clear her vision. Now was not the time to let her fears of what was to come control her. She returned her attention to the house.

A large, lean man with shoulder-length blond hair had entered her bedroom. He moved with the grace of a predator, and her eyes widened when he turned, allowing her to see his wings fall gracefully down his back like a dark cloak.

Holy crap! They've sent a Hunter. Her mind froze in panic. *Why is there a Hunter here?*

She watched as the Valkyrie stopped and sniffed the air before walking over to the window and examining it. After a moment he spread his wings, covering the glass to block the light from behind him so he could scrutinize the dark yard. Fascinated, she stared, transfixed at the way the light shone through the membrane of his wings.

She felt her mind slowing again. Fruitlessly, she fought the lethargy that was her body's natural response to the changes taking place within it. It wasn't long before the Hunter's eyes found hers, even in the dark, their intensity boring into her, and he smiled a slow feral smile. Backing away in fear, the last thing she saw was the Hunter turning. Feeling like a fox with the hounds about to be released, Jessica slipped farther into the bushes and fled into the night.

They expected no resistance. Not this early in the change.

Nickolas swept down the hall in response to Christoff's call and considered options. This should have been a simple retrieval. The timing for the recovery of a stage two fledgling was orchestrated carefully. It centered on several stages of behavior.

An emerging Valkyrie needed a lot of sleep. But before they succumbed to that need and passed out, they were extremely volatile. The signs tended to be obvious to those around the new fledgling but not, thankfully, to the person experiencing it. *Or we would have one heck of a time keeping people safe*, Nickolas thought.

Jessica Reuther should have been sound asleep by now. She also should have destroyed everything in sight before instinct drove her to find a safe place. *Damn it, there should have been no resistance!*

Not that it was unheard of in someone who'd been feral for a while, someone who had been alone during the first part of stage two and hadn't been reported to the Facility in time. But the call had just come in today. By all rights, she had just started to change, and she shouldn't even be *capable* of running right now.

But she had. That much was obvious.

Walking into her bedroom, Nickolas pulled his hair over his shoulders, securing it with a hair tie. "So what have you found?"

Christoff turned from the window to face him. "She must have felt us coming. Which is odd; she shouldn't be able to sense us yet. She left through here." Christoff indicated the window.

Sliding it open more, Nickolas leaned out, looking at the bushes along the base of the house. "How long?"

"I just watched her slip into the woods."

"Good. She can't get very far. Come on." He turned, pulling his wings in tight, and swept out of the room with Christoff on his heels. "Jeff must have miscalculated how far along she was. She's still in the active phase."

Yelling for Flynn and Jules, Nickolas led Christoff out of the house, pausing on the porch to wait for the other two members of the team to join them.

"Well, Flynn, she's not here, but Chris just saw her take off into the woods. Send Jeff and Rick home. There's nothing more for them to do at the moment, other than get yelled at for calling us in early. Chris and I will go and fetch her."

"Right-O, Nick," Flynn replied.

Descending the steps, Nickolas waved at them as he and his brother slipped around the side of the house. None of them noticed the van parked in the shadows at the end of the street.

◆ ◆ ◆

"Damn it, too slow. They got here ahead of us." The female Hunter slammed the palm of her hand against the steering wheel. "Marcus and Robin are going to be ticked that we didn't get to her in time." Kelley turned to look at the other occupant of the car. "Now we're going to have to face Robin and tell him the bad news."

Leslie chewed her thumbnail and shook her head. "Where's May? She should have warned us. We shouldn't have gotten an emergency communication from Dustin for this retrieval. It's too much of a risk for Ian to pass us information that way. The mule is much safer for them."

Kelley shrugged. "I don't know where she is, Les." Kelley shifted her wings out from under her a little and turned back to wait for the recovery team to bring Jessica out. She hated the inaction.

"It's Jessica." Leslie shook her head, bewildered. "Robin and Marcus only left her on her own because she had May to protect her. Why wouldn't she come in like Robin did?"

"Who knows? She's stubborn. Besides, you know she never would have stayed. She hates Aurora." Kelley paused as a thought struck her. "Maybe we should try and snatch her. There's only the four of them." Kelley winced at the punch Leslie slammed into her shoulder.

"Don't be stupid, Kel. There may only be four of them, but two of them are Nickolas and Christoff. We wouldn't stand a chance. So get that thought right out of your head. Robin would skin me if I let you do something like that."

"Yeah, well, I'm not too keen on bringing this news home to him." Kelley rubbed her arm, discouraged at their failure, when movement on the porch focused their attention. "Wait...what's this?"

The two Hunters watched the recovery team leave the house empty-handed. "They lost her? I don't believe this. Maybe we have a shot after all. And the evening isn't a total loss, there's Nickolas." Kelley snagged a little device lying between the seats and pointed it at the recovery team. She pressed a sequence of buttons. Smiling, she watched the screen as it flashed. "Good, transfer complete."

"Good luck on your hunt, Nick." Les laughed. "Hope she gives you a run for your money."

Nickolas walked beside his brother to the backyard and stopped near the window. It didn't take long to find her traces.

"Chris, here," Nickolas called. He gently touched some broken branches on an azalea before he squatted down to look at the footprints in the flower bed. "Where did you say you saw her?"

"Somewhere close to here," Christoff said, parting the bushes at the edge of the yard. "This is where I saw her hiding."

Joining Christoff, Nickolas could see the scuffmarks where she had crouched in the dirt to watch the house. "It looks like she ran deeper into the woods."

A branch snapped, and they looked at each other, slow grins settling on their faces before they turned and tracked off after the sound.

Adrenaline surged through Jessica's body, clearing the fuzziness that had taken over her mind again, clouding her thoughts. Jogging through the woods, she looked back over her shoulder as she felt a quick burst of...something...aimed at her, and she shivered. She knew the two Valkyrie Hunters were trying to narrow down their search. She had spent too much time as a child in Aurora not to be aware of the special mental abilities Valkyries had.

Hunters! Gods, what did I do? Why did they send two Hunters after me? I can't get away from them.

She blocked some branches with her forearm, picking her way barefoot across the cold, muddy ground. She stumbled and stepped on a stick, wincing at the loud crack it made more than at the pain it caused to her numbing feet. *I'm so screwed.*

It was hard to ignore the pain the forest floor inflicted on her feet, but she picked up the pace anyway, flinching every now and then as she encountered more stones or sticks. She wracked her brain for the distant memories of the Hunters she'd known in her childhood. Working to remember what they were capable of. She'd tried to forget them, but now she welcomed every half-forgotten scrap. Her gait slowed as the fogginess in her mind swelled once more and eroded her reasoning ability. She shook her head to clear it. Second guessing what the two following her might do would get her nowhere. Fear swirled through her again like the rising of the tide. Her emotions and thoughts surged and receded, mixing together like sand and surf. With each lapping wave something changed inside her. One moment the sand would be smooth and her thoughts were her own, the waters calm and ordered. The next, a wave would swamp everything and fear and confusion would reign.

She barely noticed when she tripped in a hole, she was so focused on her internal struggle. She just scrambled back to her feet, brushed the dirt off her knees and hands, and kept going.

Vague memories from when she and Robin had been kids, and had played in these woods, filtered through her eroding mind, pushing her deeper into the forest. Recklessly forcing her way through the ferns and bushes, she ignored the cost to herself, hoping her memory was true and not gilded by childhood. She needed to find a secure hiding spot where the Hunters wouldn't be able to find her. Jumping a log, she found herself skidding out of control down a hill. She grabbed at bushes and tree trunks to try to slow her descent then rolled to land head first at the bottom with a thump, her face plastered in the dead leaves and loam. Sitting up, she brushed the debris from her face, spitting out dirt. With a grimy hand, she wiped the grit out of her eyes and took a look around her. Tears blurred her vision. A meadow opened up at the base of the hill. She had a choice. Spend more time pushing through the bushes, or leave the relative safety of cover and cross the meadow.

She rose stiffly, brushing the rest of the leaves off, and tried to calm her labored breathing as indecision swamped her. Her mind whirled. The task of wrangling her thoughts into some order and forcing herself to focus continued to get harder. She stared out across the clearing. *Where can I go? I need to break my trail. The river?* She shuddered, and her thoughts immediately shied away from that possibility. She looked back up the wooded hillside and winced at the obvious trail she'd made. *I've been lucky. The only reason I've gotten this far is because of the tree canopy.*

Reluctance over leaving the safety of the forest paralyzed her, and she turned back to the meadow, rocking from foot to foot.

Snap.

She whipped a look over her shoulder then plunged without further thought into the field.

The soft grass felt much better on her bruised and battered feet than the forest floor. "I'm almost there, I'm almost there," she chanted in time with her labored breathing and pounding feet. A distant yell spurred her on. She risked a glance back. The two Hunters emerged from the edge of the woods and spread their dark wings, taking flight. Turning, she bowed her head and burst into the cover at the edge of the woods before they were more than a quarter of the way across.

Nickolas landed at the far edge of the field, his brother on his heels. They'd have to resume their hunt on foot where their quarry had ripped through the bushes. Nickolas beat his way into the dense plant life, swearing when he fouled his wings for what seemed like the millionth time on the thorny twigs.

"Damn it, where is she getting the energy for this?" he muttered under his breath. Once he got to a more open space, he started casting around looking for tracks.

Snapping branches, Christoff broke free of the thicket and shook his wings. "That's a good question, Nick. Why hasn't she passed out yet?" Crouching down, Christoff ran his hand lightly over the dirt. "Even if Jeff did miscalculate the timing, and I'm inclined to think that he didn't, she should have moved from the active phase into unconsciousness by now at least."

Christoff paused for a moment, and Nickolas froze when he felt the surge of uncivilized wildness course through his brother and color his voice. "Though, it is kind of nice to have a challenge. It's not like we get to really utilize our abilities at the Facility. Games aside, being out here in the wild, so to speak, is extremely liberating. Here, I found something."

Nickolas quit his search and joined Chris. He crouched down and looked at the smudge his brother indicated. There was a dark smear in the center of the impression. He reached out to pick up a pinch of the dirt, intending to sniff it, and froze. His eyes flared as something slammed into his awareness too fast for him to comprehend.

The sound of Christoff snapping his fingers in front of his face brought him back to earth. "Nick! Hey, what is it?"

Nickolas shook his head and frowned. *I don't know.* "She's lacerated her feet. We should be able to track the blood." Rising, Nickolas dusted the bloody dirt off his fingers and caught a worried frown from Christoff.

"Nick, seriously, how is she doing this? Even if Jeff *had* miscalculated, there is no way he was off by this much. He's too experienced."

"I don't know, Chris. Let's get her contained. Then we'll worry about the how." Setting off at a lope, Nickolas wished that he could follow his own advice.

Gasping for breath, Jessica pushed her way through sticker bushes and other undergrowth, heedless of the clinging tendrils that grabbed her clothing and tore her skin. She was barely keeping a lid on her panic. It felt like the whole world was reaching out and trying to slow her down. She ripped her clothes free and kept running, fear skittering up and down her spine.

She hit a path and made better time on it, sighing in relief. Her bare feet pounded rhythmically against the dirt. *Don't look back. You know they haven't given up.*

A sudden, splitting pain ricocheted through her head. She slammed her hands to her temples and fell to the ground, biting off a scream.

Panting in agony, she felt like everything she had ever eaten in her whole life wanted to revisit her. A moan escaped and she opened her eyes. *I can't see. What happened? Why can't I see?* She rolled to her hands and knees then sat back on her heels and wiped at the blood running from her nose. As she calmed her breathing, Jessica started to notice the softer grey shadows where the moonlight reached through the tree canopy and touched the ground. *The moon is out. But I could see almost as well as if it were day before. I knew Valkyrie vision was better but wow. So what happened? It just turned off? I guess I shouldn't have been thankful for the path. Well, I'm not going to just sit here waiting for them to find me.*

It still took her a moment to adjust to the change. At first the dark was stifling, but then Jessica cocked her head, noticing the riot of sound all around her. The forest creatures made a lot of noise shuffling around in the fallen leaves. Not to mention how loud the leaves themselves were, rustling and rattling as they danced from their branches to the ground. Way behind her, though as far as she was concerned not far enough, she could hear the Hunters tracking her. *First I can see in the dark, and now I can hear like a wolf. Well, this is peachy. I would really prefer being able to see right now. Actually, I would prefer to be home in my nice warm bed and not dealing with this right now.*

She climbed unsteadily to her feet and turned, trying to pinpoint different sounds. A rushing came from her right, and she spun toward it. *Is that water? I must be closer than I thought.* She couldn't see it, but she could hear it.

Tentatively she stepped out, feeling each step with her toes. When nothing happened, she moved with a bit more confidence, heading in the direction of the river. She thought she was stressed before, but using her hearing to navigate was hard work—and slow. Her tension built, and every step she gained down the path she could hear her Hunters gaining on her. She picked up the pace, moving into a jog. The rumble grew to the point that it drowned out most of the other sounds of the forest. *This is your last chance. What'll it be, it or them?*

She reached the bank of the river. The rushing filled her ears and the scent of the cold water made her pause. The moon glinted dully on the swirling current as it raced past. She couldn't hear the sound of her pursuers over the roar, but she knew they were just moments behind her. Angry at this whole situation, she waffled for a moment. The thought of entering that freezing water was almost too much, but then she thought about what would happen when the Hunters caught up to her. Resolved, she searched for a slope down to the water's edge, but the high bank crumbled under her feet and sent her tumbling into the river. She hit the frigid water and went under, the current carrying her downstream.

"Nickolas, come take a look at this. Something happened here."

Nickolas looked down the trail at his brother and saw Christoff studying the woman's tracks. He left his own search and joined him.

"See, Nick, it looks like she stumbled and fell, but when she got up again, her gait changed."

Nickolas reached out and lightly touched the scuffmarks the fledgling had left when she fell. Blood from her feet was mixed in with the dirt, and he hissed at the unusual response he had. The contact with her blood shoved a slide show of pictures into his head. It moved too fast for him to catch, but a couple of things stuck with him. Quickly rubbing the dirt off of his fingers, he sat back, shaking his head. *Gods, she is strong.* He couldn't help but admire her strength of will and her ability to keep going. He cleared his throat. "It looks like she got hit with a dazzle headache. She was running too well to have unchanged vision. There's nothing for her to trip over in the path. She just stumbled and fell. My guess is she got dazzled, lost her sight, and probably had her hearing come in." He looked ahead down the path then up at Christoff.

"That would account for the gait change. Navigating by sound is slower and more difficult."

Surprise plain on his face, Christoff moved down the path a little, examining a wider area. "Dazzle headaches? I didn't even consider that. Those aren't supposed to start for at least a week or so."

Nickolas felt his expression freeze and he shrugged. "That's the way it usually works, but not always. Personally, I'm amazed she could compensate for the sudden change and keep going, especially with the pain. She's one determined fledge. When the senses change like that, it can be excruciating, remember? She's going to make one magnificent Valkyrie." He glanced up. "Might even give you some competition, Chris," he teased. Rising, Nickolas continued to rub every speck of dirt off of his fingers then stretched his wings. "I don't like this. We need to get her in custody soon."

"That shouldn't be too hard. We're on a trail now, and with her sight dimmed, we should be able to catch up to her."

They moved off at a brisk pace, and Nickolas laughed mirthlessly at his brother's back. "Don't count on it, Chris. Has she done anything you would expect? I have a bad feeling about this whole situation."

They ran in silence for a few moments, the sounds of the forest surrounding them, giving them valuable information—the hush of the creatures a telling track in her trail. A steady rumble had grown to deafening proportion, and Nickolas quickened his pace more.

The trail came out at the edge of the river bank. The water swirled in a dark seething mass below him.

"Nick..." Christoff's voice dropped. "It doesn't look like she turned aside."

His heart in his throat, Nickolas scanned the ground. The breadth was too wide for him to believe she could swim across. She had to have gone one way or the other.

It was only a matter of moments before they found the collapsed segment of bank.

"Nick," Christoff whispered.

"I know, Chris," Nickolas snapped. He crouched down as close as he dared to the crumbling edge. His mind warred with some other part of himself that he'd never been aware of before. It didn't stand to reason that she could survive a fall into the river, in October, in the state that she was in, but Nickolas was sure that she wasn't dead yet. He didn't know how he knew, but he did. "Christoff, take the opposite bank."

"What's the point, Nick?"

"Don't question me, Second."

The sound of Christoff's wings beating the air reached Nickolas. He stared for a moment more into the water. Hoping that the dark, turbulent rush would offer up some answer to what was happening. Rising carefully, so he wouldn't end up sliding down the bank as well, Nickolas spread his wings and launched out over the water.

He studied the river for the fledgling's body, but the current was swift. It would have carried her away quickly. The moon set and he had trouble seeing. Both the water and the bank had taken on a one-dimensional, grey hue. Yet still he searched, too focused to give up.

The silhouette of his brother ghosted by, pulling his attention from the fruitless search. Christoff signaled a desire to land. Growling in frustration, Nickolas angled his wings and followed Chris to a rocky beach.

They touched down, and Nickolas snapped his wings shut.

"Nick, it's too dark. With the moon setting, we're going to have to wait until daylight to locate where her trail comes out." Then more quietly, he added, "If it comes out."

"It'll come out, Chris."

"Nickolas, look at the facts, man. It's October, she's barefoot and hardly dressed. Getting submerged, in perfect health, in the summer would be hard to overcome. But now? While her body is changing?"

Nickolas spun, sending rocks tumbling out from under his feet, and paced away. "No, you look at the facts. She *is* changing. And she's managed to elude us. *Us!* What does that tell you? Don't write her off. She's tough. She'll get out of the water. Watch."

His brother pursed his lips and nodded his head uncertainly.

Nickolas understood his Second's hesitation. She'd done some pretty unbelievable things so far. He rubbed his eyes with a finger and thumb. "You're right. It's too dark to search more tonight. We'll have to wait till first light." Frustrated, Nickolas pulled his phone out of his pocket, punching Flynn's number.

"You've got her?"

Nickolas ground his teeth. He'd been butting heads with Flynn more and more recently. The grounded was becoming difficult. The constant vying for supremacy was getting old. "No. She went into the river. It's too dark now; we'll have to wait until daybreak. Do you have a fix on my location?"

"Yes. There's a forest service road northeast of your position. We'll meet you there in fifteen minutes."

"Got it." Nickolas hung up then slipped his cell back into his pocket before spreading his wings and launching out over the river.

Chapter Three

The water was freezing. Breaking the surface with a gasp, Jessica tried to shake the hair out of her eyes with limited success. The swift current swirled her around like a kitten that had been tossed in to drown.

What the hell was I thinking?

With her mind the clearest it had been in days, unfortunately, it was a little too late to make use of it. Jagged rocks rose up from nowhere and she bashed into them, blindly scrabbling to hold onto their slimy coating. The river ripped her away, spinning her farther downstream. Attempting to get her bearings, she made an effort to slow her passage by swimming diagonally across the rapids, but a log loomed up in front of her. Franticly she dove, but a submerged branch sliced into her thigh and another one ripped her calf. She surfaced, gasping in pain and coughing up river water.

I've got to get out. I hope I've managed to lose them. She forced her leaden limbs to function and pushed her exhausted body toward the shore. For each stroke she made across, the current sent her quadruple that downstream. It wasn't until she hit a more placid stretch of water that she made any progress. After what seemed an eternity, she reached the edge and dragged herself onto the muddy bank, coughing up half the river. She collapsed, gasping in pain and shivering with the cold.

I need to keep moving or I'll freeze to death. She took a deep breath and tried to gain her feet, but her numb body wouldn't cooperate. *Come on, damn it. You can do it.*

Trying again, she finally managed to rise. A whimper of pain choked out of her. Now that she was out of the water, feeling quickly returned to her extremities, causing the gashes in her leg to burn and throb. It felt like someone held her leg in a vat of acid. She pushed aside the pain as best she could and looked around. *Ok, where am I? Looks like I came out on my side of the river. Yes! And I can see again. That's good news at least.*

She plucked at her sopping clothing, squeezing the water out. *I can't go on like this; I've got to get dry or I'll still freeze.* She reached around and scratched her back absently, shivers racing across her skin. *I've lost them, at least for the moment. But if I want to stay free, I need a few things. They'll spend time searching the river for me, so with any luck no one will be at my house.* Thankful that her mind was her own, however briefly, Jessica climbed the hillside and trudged her way through the bushes, leaving the river behind. It wasn't hard to find a trail where she could pick up her pace to a jog. Her mind wandered as she ran. *What does a normal recovery team consist of? I think May said that it's four men. Not usually Hunters though...I think. If I'm right, I left at least two of them behind at the river, which leaves two unaccounted for. Hopefully they followed the Hunters.*

Because of how the river bent, she wasn't as far from her house as she had feared, and she started to recognize the area fairly quickly. She slowed down when she neared her home, approaching it as quietly as she could. Though she knew that if the Hunters were around, it wouldn't matter how quiet she was. They'd hear her anyway. Skirting the boundary of her property, she watched the house for any sign of someone waiting. Finally, cold drove her in. She hadn't seen any movement inside, or other signs of recovery people outside, in the several minutes that she spent observing. Holding her breath, she slipped up to the back door and peered through the window. She couldn't believe her luck when she saw the building truly was deserted.

Dawn was just a couple hours away now; the hunt would pick up momentum then. With fingers shaking from the cold, she pulled the corner of the door mat up and grabbed her spare key. *Daylight will be on their side; they'll have many more eyes working for them.*

She kicked the door shut then stripped off her torn, sodden, muddy clothes, leaving them in a trail on her way to the bathroom. Once there, she fumbled with the knobs on the shower until she got the water going. Her body was so stiff she could barely climb into the tub. She moaned as the hot spray cascaded over her chilled and battered body, and she fought the overwhelming need to sleep. The tears she'd repressed during her escape started to leak out as she watched the filthy water swirl down the drain. She allowed herself a couple of minutes before telling herself to get a grip. Dredging up more energy, she washed her hair then ruthlessly scrubbed her newly acquired cuts, scrapes, and bruises. With those tended to, the discomfort along her shoulder blades asserted itself. She reached for the bath brush. Vigorous scouring gave temporary relief to the itching and burning on her back.

She stood there for a few minutes letting the water wash over her. It no longer ran muddy but a fading pink as her injuries washed clean. *So what now? I won't have much of a head start. Maybe I should try to go to Marcus. Robin did.*

But that option didn't sit well with her. Slicking her wet hair back, she shut the water off. *No, I made my decision about that a long time ago. Well, first things first, get doctored up then grab a few things and leave.*

She pushed the curtain aside and made her stiff body get out of the tub. She groaned as she reached for a towel to dry off with, but when she wrapped it around herself it didn't rest flat across her back.

Craning her head to look in the mirror, she could just make out a couple of lumps that had risen to the surface of her back between her shoulder blades. She stared at them in amazed, almost horrified, fascination and realized that her wings had started to grow.

The blisters were not too big yet, about the size of a baby's fist each. *Well, that certainly explains why my back itches.* She stared at this first definitive evidence of her transformation. *You'd think I would have noticed two huge zits growing on my back a little sooner. Granted, I guess I have been a bit busy.*

She shook off the amazement and pulled her medical supplies out of the cabinet, sitting down to doctor her injuries while she thought about where to go.

I need money first. My options are kind of limited, since May took the car. The nearest ATM is at the mall.

She picked the last splinter out of her left foot and slathered numbing antibiotic ointment on them both, before wrapping them with a layer of gauze. Next, she examined the gashes on her calf and thigh and frowned. They both needed more attention than she could give them in the short time she had. So she settled for squeezing half the tube of ointment into them, then pulled each closed with butterfly bandages. She taped over the more severe one on her thigh, hoping to give it extra support. The last of the antibiotic went to whatever scratches seemed to need it the most before she tossed the tube and grabbed a handful of bandages on her way out of the room. Once in her bedroom, she started tossing things quickly out of her closet. She pulled on the first warm clothes she found and stuffed a few more changes into a backpack that sat on the floor.

Twisting her mass of chestnut curls in a fist, Jessica looked in the mirror. *I should cut this,* she thought reluctantly, but then she saw reflected from the window that it was getting lighter. *Dawn. Not much more time. I'll leave it for now.* Securing the length into a ponytail, she finished her packing.

She threw in her hairbrush then dumped the first aid supplies on top. Sitting down on her bed, she squeezed her favorite shoes, a pair of red sneakers, on over her gauze-swathed feet then headed to the kitchen.

She looked longingly at the stove but moved past it to her pantry cupboards. *What I wouldn't give for some bacon and eggs. Or maybe some prime rib, or a nice juicy ham. Where are you, May, when I really need one of your home-cooked meals?* Instead, she grabbed a couple bottles of water, some granola bars and trail mix, and tossed them into the knapsack. That's all she had in the pantry that was instantly portable. Her sense of urgency screamed at her. Walking into the living room, she threw her wallet into the bag then looked around once more. Time to go.

She slung the bag over her shoulder and walked out the front door, then grabbing her bicycle from its customary spot on the porch, she headed off into the stream of morning traffic.

♦ ♦ ♦

"Hey, boyos, wake up. It's getting light enough to move," Flynn spoke quietly.

Sitting up, Nickolas rubbed his eyes then put his shoes on. "I sure hope she made it," he murmured.

"Don't worry, Nick, she led us a good chase last night. She's strong."

Nickolas looked at his brother, absently accepting an energy bar from Jules before replying, "I hope so. She couldn't have stayed in the water too long. Flynn, we'll call as soon as we have any information."

Outside the van the woods resounded with the dawn chorus of bird song. The mist from the river snaked through the trees, leaving a chill in the air. Nickolas stepped out and stretched, reaching above his head, then extended his wings to their full span, slowly flapping them as he woke up. Turning as Christoff walked up to him, he settled them with a snap. "You ready to go?"

"Yes, let's get this over with."

Nickolas could tell that Chris hadn't actually believed his own encouragement. His brother didn't really think Jessica still lived. But the more he focused his thoughts on her, the more Nickolas was sure she was still alive. His heart a little lighter, he spread his wings and took off into the brightening sky.

They flew low over the river, each scanning a side until they reached the point where she'd fallen in. Alighting on the precipice, Nickolas looked at the twenty foot drop.

Disturbed dirt marred the vegetation below them. Fortunately, there weren't any large boulders on the water's edge here. "All right, Chris, same as last night, you take the far bank."

They took off. Sweeping his wings in powerful strokes, Nickolas followed the river down its course looking for any sign that she left the water. Strange certainty aside, he really wanted to see a muddy bank. He wasn't thrilled at the thought of finding scraps of her clothing...or her body.

What was it about this recovery? Granted, she had pulled off the unexpected in getting away from them, but something about this situation pulled at him. He didn't know this woman, yet he found himself really worried about her, and the depth of his emotional involvement surprised him. *It's bloody freezing in there. If she managed to get out of the river, it had to be fairly quick or she would have succumbed to hypothermia. That's still a worry anyway; her tracks are barefoot. And the glimpse I caught of her showed that she wasn't dressed for outside. The only thing in our favor is that her metabolism will be running on high, so it should help keep her warm. But that's a double-edged sword. It also means she's going to need food—and soon.*

Scuff marks at the water's edge caught his attention. He dropped down and landed. *Well I'll be damned. She made it out.* Breathing a huge sigh of relief, Nickolas quickly examined her trail. The tracks clearly showed where she'd pulled herself out of the river and onto the bank before continuing her flight into the woods. He drew his phone out of his pocket and texted his brother.

Christoff landed in a flurry of wing beats and crouched down to take a look at the ground himself. That didn't surprise Nickolas, since his brother was the better tracker.

"Well, at least we know she made it out," Chris said, looking up at him. "Now, if she hasn't succumbed to hypothermia and blood loss, then we'll be in luck." He swiped a spot in the mud then held up his red-coated finger. "She's still losing blood. This much can't be from the lacerations on her feet."

Frowning, Nickolas punched Flynn's number on his phone. "Flynn, she made it out of the river and is, incredibly, still on the move. Get back on the main road and wait for my call."

"Right, Nickolas."

"Well at least it's an easy trail, Nick. Look at all the debris she's leaving behind." Christoff waved his hand up the hill, showing the torn-up ground and broken branches she had left in her wake. "She's definitely not trying to hide which direction she went in, is she?"

Something about his brother's comment nagged at him. It circled through his head as he ran at Christoff's heels. The direction of the morning sun as it slanted through the trees gave him the clue he needed. He stopped suddenly and looked around to get his bearings then back down the trail. "Damn. I don't believe this." He shook his head and smiled slightly. She certainly had her wits about her. Nickolas looked at his brother, waiting a few feet ahead of him. "No, Chris, she's not wasting any time on hiding. Clever, very clever."

Nickolas pulled his phone out. "Flynn, return to her house immediately. Her trail is heading straight back home. Be careful. If she has any weapons, she could be dangerous. It's time to raise priority on this. Alert the Facility, and let them know this is no longer a simple retrieval. She's gone feral."

"Copy that, Nickolas, we're on the way."

"Come on, Chris. Let's find a space clear enough to get into the air."

The two Valkyries dropped down into her backyard. From the outside, the house looked no different than when they had left several hours ago. Nickolas followed his brother as they approached the back porch, waiting tensely while Christoff checked the door. The knob turned easily, and Chris cast a quick look back at him before he pushed the door open and leaned inside to listen. A second later they walked into the kitchen.

"Well, you were right, Nicky. She did come back." Christoff gestured at the muddy, bloodstained clothes that trailed out of the room.

"She came back, but where is she now? This house feels empty." Nickolas shook his head.

"Maybe she's finally passed out?"

"Uh huh. Somehow I don't believe that, Chris. Why don't you check the rest of the house? I'm going to go and have a look at her bedroom."

Nickolas walked out of the kitchen. The lights were all still on throughout the building. Nickolas was sure Jessica was no longer here. He couldn't feel her presence. When the team had first arrived, he could feel her, even when she had been outside watching them. This time there was just a faint echo.

Her bedroom door was open. Nickolas stopped on the threshold. The room was not how he had left it last night. Clothing was strewn across the bed and other possessions were knocked to the floor or upturned that had been in their proper places before.

"Well, Nick," Christoff called from the other room. "The shower's wet, and empty med supplies are scattered about."

"She ransacked her clothes as well." Nickolas looked into her closet. *Ok, little fox, where to now?*

He paced the room, sifting through her possessions. A damp towel hanging over the back of a chair drew his attention. He brushed his fingers across the nappy surface and a jolt tingled in his fingertips. The amount of blood on the fabric bothered him. He picked it up and rubbed at a spot, then hissed. Suddenly, he was no longer looking at the towel but a vision of its owner. The sight was so real he felt like he could reach out and touch her, talk to her. She sat on the bed, awake, fear etched into her sleep-clouded eyes. Her emotions blasted into him. He felt her fear and uncertainty, her desperation...her determination.

Her pain.

Overwhelmed by the stimuli, Nickolas lost his balance and fell against the bed, dropping the towel in the process. The image vanished along with the feelings.

What the hell?

"Hey, Nicky, you all right?"

Jerking around, Nickolas stared at Christoff. His brother stood in the doorway watching him.

Disoriented, Nickolas rubbed his bloody fingers against his jeans. "Yeah, I'm fine." He looked back down at the towel then cleared his throat. "Did you find anything else?" He skirted past Christoff, ignoring his brother's look of concern.

Chris didn't answer until they were in the hall. "Not really. It looks like she might have grabbed some stuff from the kitchen, but if so, it was in a hurry. She couldn't have been here for that long. I'm surprised she got out before us, actually."

"She does seem to have a knack for staying one step ahead so far, doesn't she?" Nickolas followed his Second out the front door, but he stopped on the steps to the porch and turned back. His mind drifted to the image he'd seen in her room. The surge of sympathy he felt for her took him by surprise, and he quickly tamped it back down as useless. It really didn't matter if he understood her feelings. It didn't change what he had to do.

"Nickolas?" his brother said behind him.

Something about the porch seemed different. He pulled his wits together and tried to place it. Christoff took a step back up the stairs to stand next to him. "Something's missing, Chris. Wasn't there a bicycle tucked behind that planter?"

"Yes, I think you're right."

Christoff turned and followed his brother back down the steps. He watched Nick closely as they joined Flynn at the van. His Alpha was hiding something.

Flynn pushed away from the vehicle and opened the door for them.

"Well?" the older man questioned.

"She was here all right," Christoff said. "She got cleaned up, packed a bag, and took off." He followed Nickolas into the van. Folding his wings in tight to his body, he took his seat. Ian had drilled into all of them over the years to be alert for changes in Nickolas's demeanor. So far there had been three breaks in his Alpha's normally self-contained and controlled manner. The coincidence of it starting right after that strange surge he felt when they entered her house put him on edge. At first he shrugged it off to both of them being tired and worried, but it was too much.

"And she's no longer on foot," Nickolas added. "A bicycle is missing from the porch."

Christoff reached back and pulled his seat belt across his body. Pinning his wings down grated on him. Normally it didn't bother him too badly, but this morning he could barely tolerate it. He took a deep breath. Maybe he shouldn't be worried just about Nickolas. *I hadn't realized how fuzzy my mind has been.* He felt like he was waking up after a long sleep. He hadn't felt like this since...

Before I changed.

The thought surprised him, and he looked again at his brother. Neither of them had taken their pills this morning. That could account for Nickolas's odd behavior, though it was a little early to consider that. Nick sat so still that it gave him the impression that his Alpha could shatter at any moment. No matter how false the impression, it still worried him. He hadn't seen behavior like this from his brother in years, not since he came out of the Hub.

Christoff felt his protective instincts continue to rise. Nick hadn't buckled his belt, which didn't surprise him. *If I can't take the feeling, he must be going crazy. At least he's controlling his claustrophobia.*

His thoughts continued to circle while he picked apart Nick's behavior. Finally he shook his head. *This is silly. I'm just overreacting. Normally by this time I would have made at least two sarcastic remarks. Instead I'm inventing issues for Nick.* But the nebulous feeling made the rationalizations difficult to stick. The feeling that something wasn't quite right wouldn't go away.

This is just an unusual situation. They'd broken off of their normal routine, and no one had thought about what that meant...yet. *Well, I'm certainly not going to remind anyone. I can't stand those pills.*

"Boss, HQ has been calling for an update on the situation here," Jules announced, drawing Christoff's mind back to the here and now.

"That doesn't surprise me," Nickolas replied. "What started as a standard retrieval has turned into a potentially deadly, feral manhunt. We haven't had one of those in a long time." His brother closed his eyes, letting his head fall back into the seat.

Jules tapped a button on the earphone in his ear and turned to look at one of the screens on his bank of equipment. Then he punched a few keys before swiveling away from the console to face them again.

"Actually, Nickolas," Flynn commented from the driver's seat, "I don't think there has ever been a situation quite like this one. The hunts you're thinking of were all for fully fledged Valkyries, not one who had just started the change. Any fledge who has managed to slip by a recovery team has always been apprehended within a couple of hours. Miss Reuther has been running for close to eight now. Definitely a record."

"Why hasn't she passed out of the active phase? That's what I'd like to know. She should be so tired she can't keep her eyes open. I don't know what to expect from her. She shouldn't have been able to escape us like she has." Sighing, Nickolas opened his eyes and sat up. "Well, I'd better get it over with." Nickolas took the headset Jules held out to him and settled it over his head. "Ok, Jules."

Christoff could hear static from where he was sitting, so he wasn't surprised to see Nickolas wince before a voice came on too softly for him to make out the conversation.

"Yes, this is Nickolas. There have been some difficulties. She's gone feral." Pause. "No, tell the doctors I have no idea. Ian will just have to wait until we get her back because I haven't a clue." Pause. "I do know she has injuries, but to what extent is still unclear. Yes, that's probably a good idea. I need more information than what the retrieval documents contain. A picture would be nice, yes." Nickolas rolled his eyes in exasperation. "Yes, I agree." Pause. "Tell them I don't know that either. Good. We'll let you know if anything changes. Yes, fine."

Nickolas yanked the headset off and flung it onto Jules's console before he turned back to them. "They are sending more teams out to help. The doctors are amazed at what she's done. She is now a level one priority. Ian wants her caught before she kills herself or makes it out to the mountains, where the feral colony is. She's too strong to let fall into their hands."

Christoff caught Nickolas's eyes and raised an eyebrow, calling attention to his brother's unusual behavior, but Nickolas just glared at him, telling him silently to shut up. He smiled, relieved at something so normal as annoying his older brother, and sat back to watch Jules swivel around to grab the new printout he was receiving. The comm tech handed the sheaf to Nickolas.

His brother shuffled through them for a moment. "They've given us more to go on to track her now. Her name is Jessica Reuther. She's twenty-five years old. Weighs about one hundred twenty-five pounds, five foot one inch tall. Slender, hazel eyes and chestnut hair. Worn long. She works in a bookstore at the mall a couple of miles from here. Easy biking distance...so I think that's the direction we should take; she'll likely stay to familiar paths. They faxed over her driver's license."

Christoff took the page and examined her picture. The dry description the Facility supplied didn't do the woman justice. There was intelligence in her eyes that even the grainy bureaucratic photo couldn't hide. Handing it on, Christoff watched Nickolas's reaction as the other two looked at it. It was subtle. Chris didn't think Flynn or Jules noticed anything different in his brother's behavior; he probably wouldn't either if he wasn't already watching so closely. Something about their quarry was getting to him.

"Nickolas," Jules said. "The Facility sent out five more teams last night just in case; they're waiting for a destination."

"Let's start with the mall. Regardless of how erratic she's responding, her thinking is still going to be compromised. She'll find it easier to stick to familiar routes."

"Nickolas, her bike was bright red. It shouldn't be too hard to find," Flynn called out from the driver's seat.

Jessica merged her bike into the stream of morning traffic and smiled tiredly at the sun that rose over the water in the distance. *What a beautiful morning. I love sunrises. Especially in the Northwest.* Almost on autopilot, she jockeyed with the cars on the road, taking a route that had become second nature to her over the years she'd worked in the area. Two cars honked crankily at her as she dodged between them. She waved then veered off into the parking lot of the mall.

Wheeling up to the bike rack, she dismounted and hauled the bike in, securing it. A quick scan of the nearly deserted lot showed no sign of the Hunters in the vicinity. "Good, maybe I'm still one step ahead of them."

Jessica stretched her injured leg a moment before she crossed the two lanes of disabled parking that separated the bike rack from the door and entered the mall. *Too many people.* Her skin crawled with their nearness. *There shouldn't be that many here yet. We only opened a half hour ago.* She kept her face turned away from the people she passed, hitched her backpack higher up her shoulder, and worked to avoid the familiar faces. Her regular shift started later in the day, so an early sighting could cause questions.

The effort it took to keep her mind from wandering sapped her already tested energy reserves. She slid around a knot of window admirers and entered the food court, the far end of which housed the location of the nearest ATM. Her stomach growled aggressively at the scents of cooking food, and Jessica had to pause, grinding her teeth at the sudden nausea that accompanied the hunger pains. She looked across the gauntlet of food venders and saw the machine she needed.

Averting her face from the food handlers who knew her by sight, she walked over to the ATM and breathed a shaky sigh of relief for making it this far. Going through the motions, she punched in her pin number.

"I'm sorry, access to this account has been denied. Please try again later," The screen stated, refusing the transaction.

Jessica stared at the machine. It wouldn't recognize her. *But I have money.* Her card popped back out, and her sluggish mind tried to work through what had just happened. *I have money, I don't...*

Crap, they got here first. That's the only explanation. Now what am I going to do? I need money.

Dismayed and in shock, she looked furtively at the people around her for any sign one of them might be part of a recovery team. She stuffed her card and wallet back into her bag and slung it over her shoulder. Her focus narrowed. She was prey. And now the Hunters would have a fix on her. *I have to get out of here. They've shut my account down. They have to know I've tried to access it.* Her heart beat heavily in her throat as she retraced her steps to retrieve her bike. Hyper aware of every person she passed.

She reached the glass wall of doors and had already pushed one open when she looked out across the concrete and stopped cold. Surrounding her bike were the two Hunters who had pursued her last night, along with at least eight other people. More men with radios converged on them from different parts of the parking lot.

"Crap," she muttered under her breath. "This really is turning out to not be my day, isn't it?" *There goes my bike, damn it. Why did May have to take the car this week?*

Letting the door swing shut, she turned and ran back into the mall, not caring anymore if she was noticed. *Ok, what's the best way out of here? Can't hide in any of the stores, they'll sniff me out. There's no doubt those two Hunters have my scent. They have enough people with them to close off all the exits. I need to get out an unwatched door.* Racing back through the food court, she ran out the doors on the other side and stopped abruptly on the sidewalk. *If I only knew how to hot-wire a car.* She stared longingly at all the locked vehicles. *I need transportation; I can't outrun them here. It's too open. If those two take to the air, I'm toast.* Hoping for some means of escape, she grinned when a bus pulled up. *Perfect. That will work nicely.*

Fidgeting, she waited impatiently for the passengers to disembark and tried not to look around too much and draw attention to herself. Once clear, she climbed the steps and reached a hand into her pants pocket, pulling out the last of her change. With only the slightest hesitation, she dropped it in the meter. She flashed a tentative smile at the driver then moved to a seat in the back and hunched down.

Come on, bus, get a move on before they think to stop you.

"I'd bet anything that's it, Nickolas," Flynn said.

The van cruised to a stop next to a bicycle rack and Nickolas jumped out. He examined the bicycle chained to the bars. "I think you're right, Flynn." He started to run his hand over the metal but jerked away as if it burned him, blinking at the flash of vision that wasn't his own. Christoff joined him and cocked his head, raising an eyebrow at the odd movement. Nickolas blanked his eyes to hide his confusion.

His brother shrugged and knelt down near the bicycle. "Her scent is definitely on it. Do you want me to do an aerial search?"

Nickolas scanned the pedestrians in the parking lot and shook his head. "No, hold off a minute. Here comes Beta team." The door to the van opened and Jules stuck his head out as the newcomers arrived.

"Nick, command reports that someone just tried to access Miss Reuther's bank account from an ATM inside the mall."

A jolt of excitement shot through him and Nickolas smiled as he turned to Everett, the Beta team's leader.

"We got the same call, Nick." Everett looked at his team. "We left Epsilon, Theta, and Gamma on the other side of the mall."

"Good. Everett, you coordinate with them and make sure all exits are controlled. You have her picture, but don't make contact unless there's no other choice. Radio me as soon as she's located. Delta, you're with us. We search the interior. Let's go flush the quarry."

They crossed the last bit of parking lot and swept into the mall, pausing just inside the entrance. Nickolas watched Beta team secure the doors then turned to the leader of Delta. "Danny, take your team and search the north side of the complex, we'll take the south."

Nodding, Danny led his people off at a brisk pace, taking a left at the main corridor. "Flynn, you and Jules start here. Chris and I will go find the ATM she tried to use."

"Right," Flynn said. The two quickly disappeared into the nearest shop.

Nickolas paced down the corridor with Christoff. He regulated his breathing, letting the fear the shoppers projected pass through him. His brother was already suspicious. He didn't need Chris gaining more ammo from his reactions and then feel the need to inform Ian. This recovery mission kept throwing surprises in his path. *I have to figure out what is going on. Why am I suddenly having outside feelings shoved down my throat? And what does Jessica Reuther have to do with it?*

He strengthened his stride and focused on trying not to show his internal struggle. So he looked for a distraction.

"You know, Chris? I really hate feeling like a leper. Look at them recoil from us. It's not like we're going to eat them or something."

"They recognize a recovery team, that's all, Nick. And when two Hunters are obviously involved, they really don't want to get in the way. It scares them, not knowing who we've come for. Not knowing if they'll be next."

"I know." He sighed, scanning the crowd. "But I don't think I'll ever get used to the fear, the avoidance." He ignored the hushed conversations around him. The tide of humanity parted before the two Valkyries. They walked into the food court atrium, side by side. Across the room, Nickolas spotted the ATM next to the doors. "There it is. I'll go check it out. You take her picture around to the vendors."

"Right, sounds good."

He dismissed Chris from his thoughts, his attention immediately zeroing in on the cash machine. A tight knot formed in his gut as he crossed the atrium.

He stared at the ATM. A pattern of events settled in his mind. Each time the visions had come upon him unawares. This time he knew he courted them.

He really didn't want to touch the ATM. He braced himself then slowly reached out and placed his palm on the keypad of the machine. Similar to the episode in her bedroom, only not nearly as strong, he received a wave of feeling. His fingers smoothed over the keys.

The spike of fear was first. *That must be when she realized we'd closed down access to her accounts.* This time Nickolas made an attempt to control what he received. Closing his eyes, he concentrated and was rewarded with a jumbled vision to supplement the wash of feelings. Opening his eyes, Nickolas removed his hand. "Well that didn't help much."

"What didn't help?" Christoff asked as he walked up. "I believe this is the only ATM in the mall, so it has to be the one she used. The food vendors I showed her picture to all recognized her of course, since she works here, but none of them had seen her today."

"Oh she was definitely here. Just not long enough for me to get a fix on where she went after trying to get money out of the machine. Why don't we show her picture some more and ask the shopkeepers between here and the door where her bike was parked."

"Tracing her scent from such a brief encounter was chancy at best, you know that, Nick."

Nickolas shrugged his shoulders and started to walk back the way they'd come. He caught Christoff's shrewd gaze assessing him. His eyes full of questions that Nickolas didn't want to deal with. *I guess I didn't hide it as well as I'd hoped.*

The arrival of Flynn and Jules served as a good distraction. He waved them over and said quietly to his brother, "I'll find out what they've discovered, Chris. You start with the vendors on the aisle. I'll catch up."

Irritation poured off Christoff. Refusal formed in his eyes and Nickolas sighed. "Go, Chris."

Christoff's wings flared, but he turned without a word to go attend the task given to him.

I'm not going to be able to hold him off. Nickolas closed his eyes, then blanking his expression, he turned to greet the other two members of his team.

"So? Any sign?"

"Nothing yet, Nickolas. Nobody remembers seeing her today. And she isn't hiding out in any of the stores we checked either. Though maybe your better nose could sniff her out?"

"Not likely, Flynn. We may have a better sense of smell, but the trail is thin here and there are a lot of other people around."

"Nick," Christoff snapped. "Over here."

Nickolas felt a growl form in his throat, but he suppressed it. Instead, they all walked over to where Christoff stood next to a man who sold baseball caps from a free-standing stall.

"Yeah, I saw her," The man said when Nickolas and the others arrived. "Bright red shoes caught my eye, besides I thought she was pretty hot." He flushed and looked away briefly. "All that hair, wow. Anyway, she walked over to the teller down there, did her thing, and then walked back past me. When she got to the doors," he jerked his chin at the entrance nearest the bike rack, "she just stood in the open door for a moment before turning around and running across the mall like all the hounds of hell were after her. Which, I guess they are." The man cleared his throat nervously when Nickolas narrowed his eyes at him and Christoff growled low in his throat. "Well, she ran out the far entrance nearest the food court. Then you guys came in."

"Nick, I saw a bus through the glass leaving just as the door was secured," Jules said.

"That pretty girl is regressing, just like you guys?" The man asked tactlessly. "What a shame."

A savage growl erupted from his brother a second before Christoff slammed his hands down on the counter of the kiosk to lean in toward the man. "You should watch it. You might be next. You never know." The Hunter growled into the man's pale face.

"Christoff!" Flynn snapped.

Nickolas placed a restraining hand on his brother's tense arm and spoke quietly, "Not now, Chris. Leash it. All right, Jules get me the bus routes. I want that bus stopped and searched. Flynn, coordinate with the other teams, I need a group in here to finish the search. Just because we think she left, we shouldn't leave it to chance that she hasn't circled back." Flynn and Jules ran off, and Nickolas turned back to the vendor, giving the man a cold stare. "Beware what you say to a Hunter. For you might live to become one. Thank you for your help."

Nickolas tugged on Christoff's arm, pulling him away from the frightened vendor, giving his brother a growl of his own when he resisted briefly. "You feeling ok, Chris?"

"Yes, just a little irritable. Sorry," His brother replied curtly.

When they reached the van, Jules popped out. "Hey, boss, the bus route was sixteen. Gamma team is on its way to stop it now."

"Tell them to secure it but to wait for our arrival before boarding."

They pulled up next to the county bus. Nickolas got out of the van and looked the situation over. The bus had pulled over to the side of the road, its hazard lights flashing, the four members of Gamma team surrounding it like statues, tranquilizer rifles at rest. The pinched faces of the passengers looked out of the windows. "Any trouble, Jeff?"

"Nope. No one has tried to leave."

Nodding, Nickolas walked over to the bus and knocked on it. The frightened bus driver opened the door, and Nickolas stepped up to the platform. He rocked back on his heels from the fear rolling out of the vehicle. He had to clear his voice before words would come out. "We just need to check for a passenger," he reassured the driver before waving Christoff by. Nickolas pulled out the photo of Jessica and handed it to the driver. "Have you seen this woman?"

The driver nodded his head. "I let her off a couple of stops ago," he said quietly, handing the picture back.

"Where?"

The driver swallowed then said faintly, "The corner of main and thirty-second."

"She's not here, Nick," Christoff called from the back.

"I know, come on."

Stepping off the bus, Nickolas walked up to Jeff. "Get your team and follow us. She got off a few stops ago."

Back in the van, Nickolas gave Flynn the directions as he flopped down into his seat, Christoff following suit. Jules turned to look at him, his hand pressed to his ear as he listened to the reports coming in. Nickolas caught a flash of something indefinable from the tech, but in a blink it was gone. "Danny reports that they have finished searching the mall and she isn't there," he said.

Not really surprised, Nickolas replied, "Tell all teams to meet us at the corner of main and thirty-second. We're going to need to go door to door and canvas the neighborhood. Also, have the Facility send out Jays and the med unit. She's been on the run for..." He looked at his watch. "Twelve hours now. By the time we finally get her in custody, she's going to need his tender mercies."

"How long do you think she can keep this up, Nick? I doubt if she's had much food. No sleep. She's injured from the run and the swim last night, and she's only started to change. That requires great quantities of both sleep and meat. Red meat." Christoff sighed.

Nickolas shook his head. "I just don't know, Chris. I'm amazed she's made it this far. I don't know what to expect next."

Chapter Four

Jessica got off the bus at the first stop and looked around. Cars whizzed by on the arterial, their passing causing her hair to whip wildly around her head. Brushing it out of her eyes, she pulled the ineffectual band the rest of the way out of her hair and stared out across the street.

Tall fences lined the sidewalk on the other side. They stretched for blocks in either direction. *Maybe I should have stayed on the bus for another stop or two...* But something told her that it wouldn't take them long to figure out where she'd gone.

She looked behind her and saw her only other option, a suburban pocket neighborhood. It wasn't great, but better than being a sitting duck on the bus. *At least out in the open I have a chance. I wish they'd just leave me alone.*

She limped down the sidewalk into the neighborhood. Once off the main thoroughfare, she breathed a little easier. Now she just needed to figure out a way to put some distance between her and the Hunters. Unfortunately, the neighborhood was all but deserted at this time of the day. There didn't appear to be anyone she could ask for a ride or to use their phone. No point in even trying her phone. If they shut down her bank card, they would have her cell traced also. She walked for a while aimlessly, hunger gnawing at her.

The neighborhood was one of those twisting, convoluted types, with lots of cul-de-sacs and dead ends and houses that all looked the same, except for which pastel shade they were painted.

Grinding her teeth, she turned around, yet again, as she found herself in another dead end. If the stakes weren't so high, she'd have given up already. Fire consumed her leg and the fatigue ate at her. Sheer stubbornness kept her going, forcing her to move farther into the labyrinth and hope an opportunity would present itself.

The sound of a car approached. Uncertainty seized her. A possible opportunity? Or the Hunters trolling the neighborhood? She gripped her injured thigh while her mind dithered. *On the road? Off the road?* The car rounded the corner before she could decide, so she raised her hand, waving. The soccer mom just waved back and continued on her way. Jessica's hand fell to her side. She closed her eyes and suppressed tears of frustration and pain. Taking a deep breath, she looked up at the sky, then squeezing her leg tighter, she continued on.

How do I get out of this place? She thought a while later as she turned around in another dead end. The neighborhood was worse than a carnival maze. She was lucky that the recovery teams hadn't found her yet.

Something caught her eye. She hurried her pace, her leg dragging slightly. Ahead there was a paved walkway, nearly hidden between two of the houses. She ducked down it, hoping to just get off of the road and rest. Instead, she discovered a park. The ribbon wound through a manicured, grassy field enclosed by the backyards of the houses that surrounded it. Following the path, she limped along looking at her surroundings. It curved around a tennis court then on up past an empty playground. Other branches connected into the main walkway, showing where additional entrances to the park lay.

She sank down to rest on a bench and listened to dogs bark in the nearby houses, while birds picked worms out of the grass under the midday sun.

It was all she could do not to stretch out on the bench and fall asleep in the sun. Her stomach growled, distracting her. A quick glance around the park showed that she was still alone, so she pulled her backpack onto her lap. Opening it, she grabbed a handful of trail mix. A majority of the first bite scattered to the ground as she convulsively clenched it in her fist. Her stomach cramped viciously. She had to let the spasm ease before she tried again to eat it. The smell of the grain made her wrinkle her nose, but she forced herself to start crunching. All she could manage to ingest were two small handfuls before her stomach rebelled. Gagging, she shoved the trail mix back into the bag, dreaming of prime rib for dinner. With a sigh, she ignored the hunger pains and wriggled her sore feet before pulling her pant leg up enough to look at her calf. The butterflies seemed to be mostly holding the gash together so she let the material fall. There wasn't a good way to inspect the wound on her thigh, so she twisted to the side and tried to feel through the denim how the bandaging was holding up. Not as good as she could hope. Blood seeped through the layers.

Rubbing her face in her hands, she rested her elbows on her knees and hung her head. Her exhausted body craved sleep, and now that she had finally stopped, she was close to giving in to it. *No, wake up. You can't give in now.* She pulled one of her water bottles out and splashed some on her face. *Come on, get up.*

She zipped up her backpack then stood and started to sling it over her shoulder when some unknown inner alarm made her freeze. Cocking her head, she listened, and like a vixen that had heard the horn and the belling of the pack nearby, she shivered.

Too close.

That same unfamiliar feeling, that inner awareness that had warned her when the recovery team had come for her last night, started screaming at her again. Adrenaline jacked her system. Alert, she looked around. *They must have picked up my trail. Now what?* Scanning all the available cover, she noticed a large evergreen tree standing alone by the playground near one of the park entrances. *That just might work.* Ignoring her leg, she pushed it into a run, and slipping both her arms through the straps on her backpack, she cinched them up tight. She reached the tree and, without pausing, crouched and leapt to the lowest branch, stifling a scream as her thigh tore open. Climbing limb over limb, heedless of the pitch sticking to her hands and clothes, or the way the gashes in her leg pulled, she could feel the blood trickling down her leg. The branches grew smaller. She stopped. If she went any higher, the branches wouldn't conceal her. She just hoped the Hunters didn't notice the tree swaying.

Just in time. She peered through the needles and watched the recovery teams enter the park.

Thank you, she thought fervently. Squeezing her thigh, her hand grew sticky from the wetness soaking through. Guards were left at every entrance she could see. And more people swarmed throughout the park and perimeter of it, but the two Hunters who had tracked her last night were still with them, unfortunately. *Damn, they just aren't going to give up, are they?*

In the daylight, she had the opportunity to admire them from her hiding place. Her tired mind started to drift again, scraps of memory resurfacing. *I had forgotten just how beautiful their wings can be. Mom and Dad died so long ago, and I've only seen Robin once since he changed.*

The Hunters were both fully fledged Valkyries. Their supple wings swept from the middle of their shoulder blades down to their knees; the membranes were dusky in color like a good suntan. Moving with an unconscious animal grace that set them apart from the rest of the people, they quartered the park, searching for her. Alone, as their handlers watched from the paths, they gave the impression of wildness…but not quite. *She* knew wild Valkyries, and these two were tame; you could almost see the leashes that held them back, stopping them from being what they could be.

She watched as they circled through the park stalking her, trying to catch her scent and flush her out. Her heart pounded in her chest and she clung to the tree. They paused near her bench. The dark-haired one dropped to his knees and brushed his fingers over the seat. The blond one stiffened, but then both turned to look toward her hiding place. *Oh no.*

Her breathing suspended. Then she swallowed convulsively. She couldn't take her eyes off the slowly approaching figures. The two continuously scanned the bushes they passed, but their gazes always returned to the tree she was in. Pressure built in her head. The vise squeezed and she gasped. The two Hunters heads jerked in her direction.

It's them. They're doing this. She shivered. The sudden desire to go to them shook her. Something about them called to her, pulled at her, demanded she respond to them. *No. Leave me alone.*

She whimpered as she fought the pull. Something her mother once said gave her an idea. She pushed back with her mind, focused all her thoughts into a visual, built every minute detail until it was real in her head. The perfect hiding place to keep her safe. A wall for her mind to hide behind.

Nickolas entered the park and looked around, using all of his senses to actively search for her. He barely noticed the teams that secured the exits, responding to their signals almost absentmindedly. He could feel that she was near, but he couldn't see any obvious sign of her presence in the park. He looked around more slowly, his intensity sharpening.

"She's nearby, Nick," Christoff confirmed next to him.

Nickolas nodded agreement. Every Valkyrie, once they had reached a certain stage in their emergence, could feel when another of their kind was nearby. He wasn't even going to consider why he could feel her so strongly already. Strolling with his brother along the paths, he concentrated, trying to pinpoint her location. *Though, this is different. I've always felt the other Hunters, but now, even Chris feels different; clearer, stronger, with more layers and a lot more depth. It's almost like a blindfold has been removed and now I can see. But I have no idea what I'm looking at, since I've never seen anything like this before in my entire life.*

An elusive whiff caught his attention and he stopped. Christoff looked at him. "She was near here."

"The bench." His brother stalked over to it.

They both circled it, then Nickolas saw the stain. He dropped to his knees and reached out. A gasp escaped his control.

"Nickolas," Christoff snapped.

"She felt us and fled." He pinned his brother with a glare. "In that direction." They both turned toward the west entrance to the park.

Now with a direction, they resumed their hunt.

"Can you pinpoint her location, Nick? I can still feel her, but that's about it."

"She's definitely in this direction. Close. But I don't know how close."

She felt like a loadstone pulling him. He had to find her. All his concentration turned inward in an attempt to interpret this new broadening of his senses. The bright beacon of her presence flared in his mind's eye, then blackness.

Stunned, Nickolas froze for a second, his mental balance thrown by the sudden shift. "She's blocked me!" Nickolas swore incredulously and turned to look at Christoff.

"I lost her too. That shouldn't be possible. How could she hide her presence?" Christoff asked in a whisper.

"How has she done *anything* so far?" Nickolas growled, frustrated. He snapped his wings open and closed then motioned the teams over to him. "She's close. Finish searching the park then go door to door starting with all the houses bordering the park." Turning to Christoff, he worked on reining in his temper. "Come on, Chris, let's see if we can't break the block she's raised and pick up her trail."

Up in the tree, Jessica watched the teams disperse and start checking the nearest houses. She could still feel the dark-haired Hunter pushing occasionally, but as he and his wingmate got farther away, it lessened. Finally, the teams had all moved on, and she slowly let her guard down, relaxing her mental muscles. As soon as she did, exhaustion hit and she swayed, nearly pitching out of the tree. She just barely managed to catch herself in time.

How long have I been at this? Gods, I almost can't remember when I slept last. She rested her head against the tree trunk, weeping quietly and wishing she could just lie down and sleep. *I am so tired.*

But that's not going to stop them, is it? The insistent little voice inside her prodded. Sniffling, she gathered her wits, wiping her face on her shoulder, and started to climb down. Hanging from the last branch, she dropped to the ground. Her injured leg buckled underneath her and she stifled a cry, hoping the noise didn't alert any of the recovery team. Limping, she tried to rub the pitch off of her hands as she made her way to the edge of the park. Keeping an eye out for any stray searchers, she skirted the shrubbery near the houses.

Ducking between two buildings that were well away from any of the paved entrances, she used their plantings as cover to hide and look out onto the activity on the street. *A lot more going on now than there was a few hours ago. It's going to be nearly impossible to walk by unnoticed. At this rate I'm going to become the ten o'clock news.*

The hope that had been sustaining her waned rapidly as she watched the numbers of people moving about. In her condition, she wouldn't be able to pass unnoticed. Jessica crouched underneath the rhododendron, trying to figure a way out. A loud clang drew her attention to a work truck parked in front of a house three doors down. A painter had just finished loading his ladder onto the roof rack, after which he threw a tarp over the contents in the bed of the truck. Tension thrummed through her and a small spark of hope rekindled. Now if only the workman would move away... *Yes!* She hissed gleefully as he went back into the house. Slinking out from under the bush, she quickly slipped up to the truck, and lifting the tarp, crawled under it. Squirming around, she tried to quietly make a place among the paint cans and other paraphernalia, planting her hand straight into a wet paint tray in the process. "Ugh...man." She grabbed a cloth and wiped most of it off before she finished shoving things out of her way. Easing down on her uninjured side, she felt blood trickle down the back of her thigh. She clamped her hand on it again. Finally able to rest her head, she fought the need to sleep.

The truck rocked, jerking Jessica awake. The door slammed and the workman started the car. Closing her eyes, she sighed and relaxed when the vehicle started wending its way through the twisting streets. But too quickly, it slowed to a halt. *Why have we stopped? We only just started. They can't know I'm here, can they?* Full blown panic a hairs breadth away, she held her breath and waited for the tarp to be pulled off the truck. But instead, she heard voices. Straining her ears, she could just make out what they said.

"I'm sorry for the inconvenience, ma'am, but we must ask you to get out," a deep, masculine voice asked.

"What is going on?" She heard a woman reply nervously as car doors opened and closed.

"We need to search all vehicles leaving the area."

"Sir, this one is clean, a different voice called out.

"Thank you for your cooperation, ma'am. You may go," the first voice said courteously, and Jessica shivered as it seeped into her.

There was a softly mumbled reply and the car door closed. The truck rolled forward a car length.

"I'm sorry for the inconvenience, ma'am, but we must ask you and your children to please get out of the car."

Hearing that deep voice recite the same litany, Jessica peeked out from under the canvas. Nothing. She couldn't lift the tarp enough to see beyond the ground at the edge of the truck. Her hearing, though, had become acute enough for her to tell that the speaker wasn't close to the truck yet. Slowly worming her way around so she didn't rock the vehicle and alert the driver to his stowaway, she reached the end of the tarp and peeked out the back of the truck. No cars were lined up behind them yet. Carefully, she eased to the ground behind the tailgate and crouched down by the bumper, looking around the driver's side. Three other cars were lined up in front of the painter's truck. All stopped and waiting.

A woman stood in the middle of the road, watching the first car, trepidation on her face. The reason for her fear became apparent when another Valkyrie Hunter paced around the front of the vehicle to join her.

Groaning, Jessica dropped her head.

Great. Another Hunter. Just what I needed. Wearily, she raised her head and watched the scene unfold. The recovery team efficiently searched the interior of the van, followed by the roof and undercarriage. *No way am I getting out in a vehicle.* She scuttled over to the passenger side of the truck and looked around that side. Four kids stood on the sidewalk watching their car being swarmed over.

It was only a matter of time before another car came up behind, so taking a deep breath and praying to any deity who might care to listen, she pushed her leg and quickly ran, crouched, across the sidewalk to fall behind a hedge. Biting her lip to keep from crying out, Jessica squeezed her thigh and felt the blood drip off her fingers. Her breath hissed between her teeth, but she regained her feet and turned back to check and see if she had been observed. The youngest child looked in her direction, but he turned away after a moment, apparently uninterested in her. Jessica closed her eyes for a second then grimly turned and slipped into the backyard.

"Good afternoon, sir. I'm sorry for the delay, but we need to ask you to allow us access to your truck." Donald stepped back so the workman could open his door and get out.

The man looked pointedly at Donald's wings. "Sure, why not. Who believes in the constitution these days? Search warrants are just a waste of paper, anyway," he grumbled. "Here, let me get that." The painter quickly moved to the side of his truck and folded up the tarp. "So, what's going on?"

Donald cast a brief glance at the workman before returning to overseeing the search. "We have a young woman who escaped the recovery teams trapped in this neighborhood. We just need to make sure she doesn't hitch any rides past the checkpoints."

"Donald, I think you should see this," one of the searchers called from the other side of the truck.

A note in the searcher's voice focused his attention, and Donald saw that the man looked intently at something in the back. Walking over, he saw what could possibly be blood in the back of the truck, along with a small handprint in some spilled paint. He glanced at the painter and asked, "Were you using any red paint?"

The workman shook his head no as he looked at the blood and the spilled paint. "I didn't spill any."

"Donald, can you tell anything more in here?" the searcher asked.

They lowered the tailgate and he carefully crawled through the stuff in the truck. He gently touched the red puddle, rubbing the wetness between his fingers before raising it to his nose, inhaling. "Definitely blood. And the print is way too small to belong to the workman." Donald blinked slowly, a strange surge running through him with the blood scent. "Stephen, call Nickolas, tell him we've found sign of her." He shivered then worked his way out of the truck, trying not to disturb what sign she left. *Nickolas is going to want to have a look at this.*

As his feet touched the ground, he could hear Stephen on the radio. "Sir, you need to come over to checkpoint C; we're at the northern exit. We have found sign of her." The radio crackled and they heard the reply.

"Right. We're on the way."

Arriving at checkpoint C, Nickolas and Christoff dropped down to land in the road. Giving his wings a shake to settle them in place, Nickolas walked over to where Donald and his team had the work truck detained.

"Nick. Chris." The burly Valkyrie nodded his dark head in greeting. "We've got blood and a handprint in the bed of the truck. I figured you should take a closer look. Her scent is all over the back."

Nickolas looked at the truck then at Christoff. *Too risky for Chris to see. With this much blood involved, I'm bound to get hit hard.* His brother had enough ammunition already. "Chris, you and Donald look around and see if you can find where her tracks start again. I'll take the truck."

"Sure thing, Nick. Donald, did you see or sense anything from her?"

"'Fraid not. I was focused on the cars in front of me."

Nickolas listened to their conversation absently as he circled the truck. He could see her blood smeared in places all over the back. They were like hot spots on a thermal reading to his developing senses. Though so far, nothing pointed to where her injuries were, or how severe. That she was still losing blood was another worry to add on top of everything else. He stopped at the lowered tailgate where he bent down and inhaled. The scent pulled at him, stirring something inside that he couldn't identify.

He crawled in and studied the cleared place she'd so recently occupied. *Ok. Let's try this again, shall we?* Nickolas took a deep breath before he hesitantly placed his hand into the largest spot of blood. He stiffened as a jumble of images assaulted his mind, stronger for having such a large quantity to act as a carrier. Nickolas hissed as everything she felt cascaded through him. Unconsciously, he clenched his thigh with his hand, holding the same spot as her wound, as the vision started. He could see her curled up in the truck, then hiding in the bushes watching Donald, then vaguely, a girl and some house. As the images flipped by, her emotional state flavored the knowledge he received, her fear and anxiety, how tired she really was. The true essence of her mind seeped into him, just how demoralized and disordered her thoughts were becoming. A feeling of kinship rose, and Nickolas regretted not being able to give her what she craved so badly, to be left alone. He understood that feeling all too well. He pulled away and quickly wiped his hand with a rag to break the images.

"Humm..." *Something really is happening to me; it's not just my imagination.* He continued to absently wipe his hand. *Some of what I saw seemed to happen after she left the truck. I wonder what that means?* He stared vacantly out over the cab of the truck into the setting sun. *How am I doing this? I've never been able to before.*

"Nick...Nick, are you all right?" The hand flapping in front of his face and the question from Donald pulled Nickolas out of his trance.

He glanced at the other Hunter and responded absently, his mind still working over his questions. "Yes, sorry, just lost in thought for a moment. She only left a few minutes ago, probably because the truck was stopped. She's weakening from hunger and blood loss, I don't know how much longer she can go on without fatally harming herself. She ran off that way."

Surprise flashed across Donald's face and he asked, "Um, really? That's a lot more detail than I expected."

Realizing what he had just said and done, Nickolas was brought back to himself, and he looked into Donald's eyes. The Hunter stared at him strangely. Unbidden, energy surged through Nickolas, filling him, stirring the hair at the nape of his neck, marking the Hunter in front of him.

Donald shifted uneasily, his attention riveting on Nickolas. Nickolas felt something pass between them; a thread of awareness, like a snake's questing tongue, fed him knowledge. The Hunter's presence was muted somehow. Blocked. Definitely fuzzier than how Christoff felt at the moment. Emotions flooded Donald's eyes.

Nickolas tried to pull back, reining in the flow of energy. The subordinate Hunter looked away but not before Nickolas saw the heightened concern aimed at him.

"Nickolas..."

"Later, Hunter."

Donald's eyes shuttered, but not before Nickolas saw the concern etch itself deep. The Hunter nodded. "Sorry, Alpha."

Nickolas sighed at the formality that he'd induced with his clipped comment and climbed out of the truck. He wished he could redirect both of the other Hunters' concerns, leaving him free to explore this new territory without hindrance. *Ha, not likely. They'll both be glued to me now.* Disgusted, Nickolas waved in the direction Christoff searched. "Has he found anything, Donald?"

"We think so. He sent me over here to fetch you."

Nickolas paused to look back into the truck at the spot where she had hidden. Questions floated through his mind, but then he gave himself a shake and followed Donald over to join Christoff. "So what did you find, Chris?"

"Take a look at this and tell me what you think." His brother led him a few houses down the road. Behind some bushes in a front yard, Christoff pointed to the ground.

Crouching down, Nickolas examined the skid in the dirt. "Yes, this is her. She's bleeding much more." He stirred the dirt with a finger. "We need this ended."

"Nickolas, Christoff, I found a print over here," Donald called from the fence to the backyard.

Moving to examine the print with Christoff, Nickolas nodded. "Donald, keep the search going at the road. Come on, Chris, let's track her to ground."

He stood and stretched his wings then leapt up and grabbed the top of the fence, pulling himself up. He crouched on the top rail for a moment before spreading his wings; he drifted down in the gathering twilight. Christoff flowed over the fence immediately after.

Her eyes wary and on the lookout for more searchers, Jessica slunk from yard to yard like a feral cat, hiding in the fringes, constantly on the alert. For several hours, she'd managed to stay out of sight by going through the network of suburban yards, but her fragmenting mind made coping difficult. Fatigue, pain, and the change itself took their toll. She put her hand to her head as she swayed to a stop. A moment later she sank into a crouch and fisted her hands in her hair.

"Can't think anymore," she mumbled, pressing her hands into her temples and scrunching up her eyes. "Gotta think, gotta think, gotta think," she chanted then scrubbed her hands over her face. They came away wet. "I can't take much more of this."

Her hands fell. She looked up and stared unseeing into the distance. *I'm losing. I can't do this anymore. Even if I get away from them, I can't escape myself.*

The sound and scent of someone nearing snapped her out of her daze, and she jumped up, startled. A young, teenage girl approached her. Jessica backed up, baring her teeth and growling deep in her throat like a feral dog. The vicious sound helped to bring her a little ways back from the brink, and she cut it off abruptly.

The girl held out a hand fearlessly and took a step closer. "Shhh. It's all right, it's ok, shh." Another step. "They've already been here."

Jessica's eyes flicked from side to side searching for a way out...or for a trap.

"The recovery team has already searched my house. They shouldn't come back, and my parents work late. My name is Lisa." The girl took another step. "I want to help you. I don't like the recovery people. They came and took my brother away, and I haven't seen him since."

The girl's steady progress pushed Jess against a fence as she backed away. Trapped, she started to tremble; the part of her that wanted to defend warred with the sane part. "I'm so tired," she whispered.

Lisa slowly advanced. "Come inside. I'll keep watch while you rest. Please, I really do want to help you."

Confused, she stood there trapped by the teen's eyes as she drew closer. Finally, Lisa slowly laid a hand on her arm. She flinched violently at the touch, but Lisa firmly took her hand. Pulling lightly, the girl was able to coax her into the house. Numb, with her brain all slow and fuzzy, she allowed Lisa to lead her up a half flight of stairs to a bedroom on the front side of the house. At the sight of the bed, Jessica groaned and pulled her hand free. She stumbled toward it, falling down on the soft mattress.

The girl giggled. "Wait, you need to take your backpack off." With Lisa's help, Jessica managed to struggle out of it and her sweatshirt. But that was as far as she could manage with her exhaustion. She fell back over onto her stomach, sighing deeply. The last thing she was aware of was Lisa pulling her shoes off and covering her with a blanket.

Christoff raised his water bottle to his lips and took a long drink, though he didn't take his eyes off his brother. Nickolas paced the length of a fence, looking for some trace of the fledgling. Christoff felt his temper surge, so he wrapped another line around it in an attempt to keep it contained and focused his attention on Nickolas. Just like him, his brother was showing increased signs of missing yesterday's dose of the aggression stabilizer. But it was more than that. It wasn't like this was the first time any of them had been late with their pills, but Nickolas's responses, and if he wanted to be truthful, his own also, were different. Nickolas was doing his best to hide what was happening but... *I'm too attuned to him for him to be successful in hiding it. And I'm sure Donald noticed as well. At least everyone else still seems unaware.* For the moment, it was up to him to protect Nickolas. Somehow. Twitching his wings, he took another drink.

"We're missing something, Chris. We've spent the last couple of hours looking through half a dozen backyards. It's dark, and we haven't seen another trace of her."

"We know she's still here somewhere, Nick. We've both caught her scent. You don't think someone would be insane enough to hide her from us, do you?"

Muttering something about some girl, Nickolas launched into the sky. He sailed over the house, leaving Christoff cursing. Slamming the water bottle back into his leg pocket, Christoff followed him, wondering what girl he was talking about. His brother's silhouette dropped down to land a couple of blocks away, and Chris circled once, watching Nickolas stalk up to Flynn, who stood near the van.

"Flynn, get me the printouts of the houses already searched," Christoff heard his brother demand as he landed next to the van. After folding his wings, he settled back against it and watched Nickolas start pacing, running his hand through his hair restlessly as he waited for Flynn to bring him the reports. The door to the van opened and Jules handed them out with a flourish. Nickolas grabbed them, flipping through, obviously looking for something specific. Part way through the stack, he stopped and looked at an entry with more detail before he held the whole thing out to him. "What do you think?"

Reading it, Christoff looked back up at Nickolas, nodding his head. "There was a young girl home when we searched. Since her brother fledged, she might not have been afraid of Jessica."

"Look at the address."

"That's not far from where we lost her trail."

"Bingo. Flynn, I want all teams to converge on this address." He handed the papers over to their teammate. "I believe Jessica is hiding there."

A rough shake to her shoulder pulled Jessica out of a deep sleep. "Hurry, get up. The Hunters are coming back."

Jessica blinked in the sudden light and sat up, shaking her head to clear the cobwebs from her mind. The girl was gone already, and the sound of raised voices in the entryway pushed her into movement. She ignored the stiffness of her overworked body and grabbed her shoes, putting them on. It took a moment for her injured leg to support her when she tried to stand. One labored step and she reached for her sweatshirt thrown over a chair. The moment her hand touched the fabric; a shiver went up her spine and she froze. Her fist clenched in her shirt and she closed her eyes, knowing her worst fear had just been realized. Straightening up, she slowly turned toward the doorway.

Standing there filling the door and blocking her escape was one of the Hunters. The dark one she had heard someone call Nickolas. He was tall, not as broad as the other one, lean with a dancer's sinuous grace. His dark hair flowed down past his shoulders. He radiated an aura of controlled power that frightened Jessica more than any other Hunter in her memory. Meeting his eyes warily, she waited for him to make the first move.

Nickolas watched her assess him while he did the same. She was favoring her right leg. He could see where the blood had soaked through the material of her jeans, and he was amazed that she could stand on it to face him. Something inside of him started to relax now that he had her cornered. She looked exhausted. He wasn't sure how the kid had managed to wake her, or how the fledgling was managing to be coherent enough to function.

Her eyes flicked around the room, and he focused on them. They were the key. Nickolas folded his arms across his chest and her body tensed like a deer about to spring. Cocking his head, he realized that he could feel her presence again. *Either she's not blocking me anymore or it's the proximity. But it's more than just her presence...I can feel her emotion.* Waves of fear and pain poured off of her and into Nickolas, splintering his normal control and level of concentration.

Is this her? Or me? He continued to maintain eye contact as he spoke softly, hoping not to startle her. "Jessica, you need to come with me. It's all right; we aren't here to hurt you. We're here to take you somewhere safe. To help you get through this."

Her eyes flashed in annoyance and she let out a snort. "Yeah right, bucko. Not a chance. I know who you're with. Just keep away from me."

Surprised by her response, Nickolas took a step into the room without thinking. Her eyes widened in alarm and she backed up, looking wildly around. Annoyed with himself, Nickolas sighed as he loosened his wings, spreading them slightly to keep the door blocked, and watched her closely. She kept darting panicked glances at him while easing back as far away from him as she could manage in the room.

"Please, don't make this so hard. You'll not win. There's nowhere left for you to go," he stated calmly. Something, some sense he couldn't name, hit him as her face cleared of all emotion. Nickolas shifted nervously.

She straightened her spine and put weight on her injured leg; a feverish, desperate light filled her eyes. "There is still one place," she said softly.

With a sudden burst of understanding, he realized what she intended, and he lunged forward, forgetting about keeping the door blocked. He tripped on the table she knocked into his path, yelling, "No, Jessica, wait."

She turned, a chair from the table in her hands, and she threw it through the window glass, diving out on its heels.

Untangling himself, Nickolas reached the window too late. Through the lights of the street lamps, he watched her crash through the interlaced branches of the trees. She was able to slow her descent by grabbing branches, but she still landed hard in the fallen oak leaves littering the ground. Nickolas held his breath until she shifted. *Come on, come on.* He shook his head in worry and leaned out the window. He almost couldn't believe what lengths she was willing to go to.

Was I any less desperate? He remembered.

His brother approached her carefully, stopping just in front of her, leaves swirling to a stop at his feet. She struggled to her hands and knees, gasping for breath.

Christoff's voice floated up to Nickolas. "Impressive exit. You've certainly led us a merry chase," Christoff commented then looked up at the window. "She's all right, Nickolas."

"Leave me alone," Nickolas heard her growl just before she plunged her shoulder into his brother's stomach, taking him by surprise, then punching him in the groin. Christoff doubled over and fell to the ground, gasping for breath. She scrambled to her feet, but her leg gave out and she fell over Christoff with a scream.

Nickolas watched in amazement as she forced her body to her command, rolling off of Christoff and disappearing through the trees into the dark.

He growled viciously at the tree branches that stopped him from being able to give chase, settling instead for yelling down at his brother. "Damn it, Christoff, that was incredibly stupid." Nickolas pushed away from the window and took his radio off of his belt, snapping into it, "Flynn, do you copy? Please help Chris out front. Over."

"I'm on it, Nick. Over."

"All units, she escaped. Repeat, she escaped. I want a perimeter around this section of neighborhood that she *cannot* slip through. Over."

Frustrated, and not a little scared for her, Nickolas turned to the rest of the room. He picked up her sweatshirt, finding her knapsack underneath. Grabbing it, he rummaged through the bag as he walked out of the room then stuffed the sweatshirt into it. Stalking out of the house, he headed over to Flynn and Christoff.

"There, laddybuck, you got your breath back?" Flynn asked as he helped Christoff to his feet.

"Are you all right?" Nickolas asked grimly.

"Yeah. She just broke my balls and knocked the wind out of me." Straightening up, he took a deep breath. "Sorry, Nickolas."

"Hey, she jumped through the window on me." He turned to Flynn. "Coordinate with all the teams. I want this part of the neighborhood closed off. Let's keep her squeezed into as small an area as possible. Tell them to watch out. She could do anything." Shaking his head, Nickolas muttered, "She jumped through the damn window. This woman has a death wish."

"We should have her location pinned down soon, Nickolas," Flynn responded soothingly before walking off through the leaves, talking into his radio.

"Well, Nick, what's the plan? It's obvious that she isn't going to come quietly if we get her cornered again. Are we going to dart her?"

Nickolas looked up into the branches of the oak and sighed. "Only if we have to. She needs to eat or her metabolism is going to become unstable." He tossed the knapsack to Christoff, before he continued. "All she had with her was trail mix. If we knock her out long enough to get her back to the Facility, it might be too long for her body to be without food. So we'll try and kill two birds with one stone. We'll set a trap and bait it with drugged meat. Hopefully her hunger will override her better judgment and she'll take the bait. Then she'll get the food to tide her over, and we'll be able to take her back without a fight."

Christoff nodded his head. "Sounds like a good plan to me. What's my part?"

"I want you to set the bait. Everyone else is to stay out of sight. I'll be the only one who will get close to her. I'm pretty sure I can stay off her radar, and that way I can be sure of how much she ingests. And if she doesn't take the bait, I'll be in a position to trank her before she can get away again." Nickolas's radio crackled.

"Nickolas, we have her sighted in a tree about four blocks from where you are. Over."

"Copy that, Jules. Flynn, pull all teams back. I don't want her spooked. Under no circumstances is she to realize we know her location. I have an idea, but for it to work, I can't have her running again. Over." Turning his attention back to Christoff, Nickolas hooked his radio back on his belt. "Take Gamma team and get that trap set."

Christoff snapped to attention, giving a quick salute. "Aye aye, mon Capitan."

Shaking his head, Nick smiled and waved Christoff away.

Grinning, Christoff turned and gestured at Jeff, the Gamma team's leader, to get his group and follow. He strode through the shadows cast by the trees over to the medic van and poked his head in, calling to the youthful-looking man inside. "Jays, I need some sort of tranquilizer that can be mixed into meat. Nick has sent me on a mission to set a trap."

The lithe, blond-haired doctor turned toward the door, relief in his soft blue eyes. "That's an excellent idea! I've been worried about her health, since it's taking so long."

"Yeah, tell me about it," Christoff replied quietly. The sight of her, how hurt she had looked right before she had floored him, left him sober. The only other person he knew who could push themselves to the limit like this was Nickolas. Something about this whole scenario didn't smell right. Jays's muttering to himself brought Christoff's attention back from where it had wandered.

He watched the deceptively fragile form of his grounded friend as the doctor walked his fingers over the bottles in one of the cabinets. He pulled one out, looking at the label.

Shaking his head, he put it back and took out a different one. "This, I think, would be best," Jays said. The doctor turned back toward him and asked, "How much does she weigh?"

"About a hundred and twenty-five pounds."

"It'll take me a minute to measure out the proper dosage. I'll bring it out."

"Thanks, Jays." He pushed the door shut and turned to find Gamma team assembled and waiting for him. Bracing his back against a tree, he looked the four men over. "Ok, guys, here's the scoop. We have her located, and we're to set the trap."

He pulled a scrap of paper out of his pocket and wrote down the address of the house then handed it to the Gamma leader. "Jeff, I need you to quickly get a pound of hamburger and meet us at that house."

"Sure thing, Chris."

The van door opened, spilling light onto the pavement as Jays stepped out. "Here you go, Chris." Jays handed him a small bottle full of a thick liquid. "This should be enough even if she doesn't eat all of it. It's pretty fast acting. Make sure whoever mixes it in wears gloves, unless they want to take a nap. And be sure to mix it thoroughly, I've calculated extra since it will have an unknown level of cooking. With this much, she should start to go under in just a couple of minutes."

Holding the bottle up and swirling the contents, Christoff replied, "With any luck, Jays, you'll have a passenger in half an hour."

"I'll keep my fingers crossed."

Chapter Five

The car pulled to a stop in front of the house that Jessica hid behind. Christoff got out of the car, carefully disentangling his wings in the process. He stretched, extending his wings out, then snapped them back into place. "Tell me again why we had to take your car instead of our van?"

He looked around. Their destination seemed no different than any of the houses he'd seen all day long. Typical middle class suburban neighborhood, small manicured yard, SUV parked out front. The only difference seemed to be what color they painted their front door and whether or not their porch light was on.

"Poor baby. Get all rumpled?" Gavin laughed.

Christoff bared his teeth in a semblance of a smile. "You want to ride in the trunk?" The rest of Gamma team gathered on the sidewalk. Gavin shook his head, still smiling.

Christoff snorted then resettled his wings. "Rick, you wait out here for Jeff."

He led them up to the house then paused on the porch and took a deep breath to prepare himself for the homeowner's reaction. *Nick's right. I can't let their fear of us get to me.* He needed to make sure his temper had a leash on it. The ravening beast inside him bit at the bars of the cage and seemed to have worked a paw out. He slapped it back, then with a soft growl, he knocked on the door. Footsteps tapped the tiles and a man who appeared to be in his late forties opened it.

The homeowner's eyes went wide when he saw them standing on his porch, and the man's fingers trembled slightly on the door. After a hesitation he finally got out in a shaky voice, "Hello, um, what can I do for you?"

"I am sorry to bother you, sir, but we have a situation we must inform you of. May we please come in?"

"Yes, yes of course," he responded in a whisper, then opening the door further, he gestured them inside. He led them through the foyer to the formal living room on the left, where he offered them a seat. Christoff spotted a footstool and pulled it closer to the couch, leaving Gavin and Matt to position themselves where they would have the best view and maneuverability. The homeowner gingerly sat on the edge of the couch trying not to stare at his unexpected visitors.

Chris rested his forearms on his knees and licked his lips before he started. "Please, sir, relax. My name is Christoff. We are on a recovery operation." The man winced as he said that, and Chris rushed on to reassure him. "We are not here for you, or anyone else from your family."

For the first time the man looked him directly in the eyes, and the dawning hope made Chris sad. Continuing on, he held his feelings to himself. "We need your cooperation. We're in the process of trying to apprehend a woman who has succeeded in eluding the recovery teams. At the moment, she's in your backyard."

A startled exclamation came from the man, "What do you need?"

Before he could respond, there was another knock at the door. The homeowner started to rise, but Christoff held up his hand to stop him. "Matt, please get that." Sitting back down, the man looked at Christoff in confusion.

"I have two more team members arriving."

A moment later, Matt led Rick and Jeff into the room, the latter holding up a plastic bag in silent answer to the success of his errand. Returning his focus back to the homeowner, Christoff finally answered his question. "As far as what we need, I assume you have a barbecue?"

"Of course. It's on the back deck."

"Perfect. We will need to borrow your kitchen and a change of clothes." Christoff turned to look at Gavin, sizing him up and down, a wolfish grin twisting his lips. "You look to be of a comparable size, Gavin. Guess you get the acting job."

Gavin rolled his eyes but followed the homeowner from the room. The rest of them waited, ill at ease in the pristine space. Afraid to touch anything, he examined the show-room perfect layout.

Christoff racked his brain. He compared the place to what he had known growing up. His memories of living in a real home were so faded that he couldn't tell if they were actually genuine or something made up from TV and pictures. Life in a lab didn't offer this sort of environment. Beautiful white walls that somehow managed to not appear stark like those in the Facility. A real fireplace took up a corner. He wondered what the wood smelled like as it burned. Furniture that looked like you could sink into it and never find your way out. "Boy this place would pass for a picture in a magazine," Christoff commented.

"You should see their taste in music," Matt said.

Christoff walked over to where Matt stood by a state of the art stereo system that was set up on shelves against one of the walls. Perusing the selection, he was surprised by how eclectic a collection it was. It didn't seem to fit in with the perfect-looking house. At the sound of footsteps, Chris turned, and Gavin walked back into the room wearing slacks and a pull over and looking very much like a suburbanite. The homeowner hovered uncertainly in the doorway, waiting.

Christoff gave Gavin the once-over with a look as well as extending his other senses. "Very nice. I don't think she'll sense anything from you. We need to stay out of sight. So it's up to you to pull the rest of this off." He pulled the bottle of tranquilizer out of his pocket and handed it to Gavin. "Remember what Jays said. Do not use your bare hands, and mix it in thoroughly."

Gavin took the meat from Jeff and gave them a cocky smile. "Yes, Mom. You'd better hope this works, Chris. I don't want to be stuck out there with a rabid wolf," he said and cast a quick glance at Chris's groin before he turned toward the kitchen.

Chris growled, realizing that everyone knew what had happened. "Smartass. Nick is out there with the trank rifle. This time she isn't going anywhere," Christoff replied to his retreating back.

♦ ♦ ♦

Nickolas watched Christoff and his team enter the house from the shadows. After the door shut, he took a moment to survey the surrounding street and yards. No sign of the men that he knew waited for his signal. *Good. If I can't find them, she shouldn't be able to either. You are not slipping out of this one, Jessica. You have my word on it.*

With a quick check of his radio to make sure it was off, he pulled the rifle off of his shoulder. His hands were quick as he checked that the darts were loaded correctly and the air cartridge pressurized properly. Just in case. He slung it back over his shoulder. The weight of the weapon was an irritant, fouling his wings.

Nickolas took a deep breath and closed his eyes, trying to quiet his mind. The difference in this recovery staggered him. Something about the quarry really struck a nerve. *And I don't think it's just a result of not taking my pills last night.* He started to relax with effort. *How did you hide your presence from us, Jessica? I don't want to alert you when I get close.*

His breath whooshed in and out. The feel was almost hypnotic. As his mind fell into a trance state, it felt too tight, like his brain was caged in a box that had become too small. Instinct prodded him and he followed.

Light exploded behind his closed eyes when he breached the barrier, mentally blinding him. When he could think again, he found himself surrounded by unfamiliar energy. Wispy tendrils floated in the blackness, like the tentacles on a jellyfish. Tentatively, he reached out with a thought, touching the threads. Warmth flowed through them. They clung to his mental hand and Nickolas shook it lightly, but that just gathered more. They pulled and stretched like taffy as he tried to get rid of it, but they still floated no matter how thick they became. He hadn't felt this boyish sense of wonder for years. Smiling, he pulled more to himself and started to shape it into a wall then a dome. Anywhere that looked thin in his barrier, he just pulled a chunk off of his hand and patted it into place. It disappeared seamlessly into the opaque barrier. When he was done concentrating on his work, Nick noticed a definite distancing of everything around him. He smiled grimly and opened his eyes. *Let's see if that does it.*

He crept up to the fence surrounding the yard she hid in and paused by the gate to search through a crack for her location. She crouched in the crotch of a maple tree toward the back of the yard. *Why are you affecting me so strongly? You're just another assignment. I shouldn't care if you kill yourself being stubborn.* Unaware of her audience, her face showed all the strain she had been under. He remembered what it was like to have control wrested from him, and his heart ached. *Please take the bait. You need this more than you know.*

I just need a place to hide. That was much too close. All sound of pursuit had vanished behind her some time ago. She could barely stay on her feet anymore. Jessica numbly slipped from yard to yard in the shadows until she found what she was looking for. *Ah, that should do.* A tree. With a gnarled old trunk. A perfect tree for a tree house. She scaled it easily and hid among the branches, trying not to fall asleep. She didn't trust the silence.

Now what? They almost had me that time. Remembering the look in Nickolas's eyes, she shivered. *What does he want from me? God, my head hurts. I can't think straight anymore.* She peered out from her hiding place and scanned the house and yard. Clipped grass extended from the base of the tree, right up to the low deck that protruded from the house. Enclosing the whole was a tall wooden privacy fence with flowerbeds at its base. If need be, she could leap the fence from the tree and gain a head start.

A noise drew her attention back from the fugue she had fallen into from the pain and fatigue. A man had pulled the shades up on the kitchen door.

She froze.

He fumbled with the catch and slid the glass door open with his elbow. The sounds of music followed him out. He set a plate down on the table then turned to fiddle with his barbecue. Once it was going to his satisfaction, he put four hamburgers on to grill. Singing along with the music, he fiddled with their placement for a moment then headed back into the kitchen, shutting the door against the chill.

The aroma of cooking meat wafted across the yard and made her stomach growl. She licked her lips and considered her options. *Should I? I'm so hungry.* Her mouth filled with saliva. No sign of anyone watching. The hiss of the grease as it dripped down into the flames battered her ears, and her stomach clenched. The scent filled her mind. She slowly lowered herself to the ground and waited.

No movement.

Furtively she made her way across the yard, pausing now and then to listen and praying that the man wouldn't return before she got the meat. She reached the grill and paused to stare at the feast. A little corner of her mind surfaced, screaming that this was too easy. She looked around one more time for any sign of a trap, but the cooking meat proved too much of a temptation. The hunger wouldn't abate. Quick as thought, she scooped the food onto the plate and scurried back to the shelter of the fence and tree trunk.

Crouched in the shadows of the tree with her back against the fence, she devoured the rare meat. Bolting it like a dog with a juicy bone. In a matter of moments, she was done, wiping the blood and grease off of her hands on the grass in front of her. She leaned back against the fence, sighing.

The wave of dizziness took her by surprise.

She caught herself with one hand on the ground and raised the other to her forehead. "I can't believe I was so *stupid*," she berated herself.

The gate across the yard opened with a soft creak and she looked up. The dark-haired Hunter, Nickolas, stood there watching her for a moment, a rifle held loosely in his hand. He stalked her, never taking his gaze from hers. Something in his eyes scared her more than the reality of the Facility. She tried to rise and back away, but whatever they had put in the hamburger hit fast. She lost her balance and toppled over. Shivers ran across her skin, and she cowered away from him then pressed her face into the cold ground. Her thoughts spun out of control. *Go away*, her mind gibbered.

Heedless of her misery, Nickolas continued to her side. When he stood a foot away, he slung the rifle over his shoulder and crouched down, reaching a hand out to lift her face, trying to make eye contact. Her pupils were already dilating and refused to rest for any length of time. He brushed his thumb across her cheek, catching her tears. She flinched away.

"Please, won't you just leave me alone?"

"You know I can't do that. It'll be easier on you if you don't fight the tranquilizer. Just try to be calm."

A wave of dizziness overcame her and she swayed in his grip. He continued to hold her gaze locked with his, and he reached down, pulling his radio off of his belt. "Chris, call up Jays. She's taken the bait."

Noise erupted everywhere. Portable flood lights flashed on, illuminating the yard brighter than day. Jessica's eyes flew wide at all the sudden activity, and she managed to pull her head away from his hand. She turned toward the house and he saw panic settle on her face. Out of the corner of his eye, he saw why. His brother had just descended the steps. Nick carefully set the trank rifle aside. Her body language screamed her intentions, and when her muscles tensed to spring, he lunged forward, tackling her.

An ear-piercing wail of terror, like you would only hear from a trapped animal, rent the air.

"Chris, get over here!" He fought for control, losing ground.

Christoff threw himself into the fray, trying to pin her legs, but even drugged, she was making them work for it.

"My god, she's strong." Chris groaned, then looking up, he yelled, "Jays, hurry up. Get that thing over here!"

"Nooo!" she wailed. "Let me go, let me go." She got one leg free and kicked at Christoff, who grunted in pain. But he dove back for it again, this time managing to secure them both.

"Hush, just relax. Try to sleep," Nickolas soothed. He had managed to get her wrapped up in a bear hug, her back to his chest, his hands shackling both her wrists. They had her pinned for the moment. Nickolas looked up into Christoff's eyes as the stretcher was finally rushed up. Taking a breath he asked, "You ready?"

Nodding, Christoff shifted his grip on her legs, and together they forced her writhing body onto the stretcher. Flynn secured her feet and legs while Jules took one arm at a time from Nick and strapped them down. Nickolas backed up. She still wouldn't give up. He shook his head in amazement. Flynn fought with her to secure the chest straps on the stretcher.

"Nick, didn't she eat all of the meat?" Christoff asked from the other side of the stretcher.

Nickolas pulled his eyes away from her. She still pulled at the straps, trying to wriggle out in any way she could. He understood the look on his brother's face. "Yes, actually, she did eat all of it."

Nickolas ran his hands through his loose hair and watched Jays as the doctor worked on his patient over the moving stretcher. "She should be out cold by now. Let's get her back to the Facility."

They followed in the wake of the stretcher. Nickolas jumped into the med unit behind Christoff and pulled the doors shut. The click of the latches resounded and he pulled his wings in tight, sidling along the wall to join Christoff on the bench seat. His breath turned shallow. He looked about at all the medical gadgetry and gave himself a stern talking to. *Plenty of air. Look, Jays can even walk around to do all his doctor things. There's lots of room.*

Really, there was.

"Jules, tell the driver she is secured, we can go," Flynn called out.

Nickolas watched Jules slide into the front passenger seat, then the vehicle accelerated rapidly. He braced himself against the sudden momentum. His shoulder brushed his brother's as the van rocked. Jays reached up, absentmindedly grabbing a bar that ran the length of the ceiling with one hand while he rummaged around in one of the cabinets with the other, pulling out a pressure cuff. The doctor squatted down next to Jessica to keep from tumbling about with the momentum of the van. Even with her arm strapped to the stretcher, Jessica still made it difficult for Jays to secure the Velcro around her upper arm.

The young doctor growled in exasperation, turning to Nickolas. "Nick, could I get you to hold her arm still. She's making this extremely difficult. I'm not going to get an accurate reading at this rate."

"Personally I think that's her purpose in life, Jays. To make things difficult." Nickolas slid off the bench and crouched down next to Jays. His worry over the tight space retreated to the back of his mind when his hand clamped down on her bare forearm. Her skin shivered at his touch.

Pumping the bulb, Jays placed his stethoscope against the inside of her elbow then slowly released the pressure. "She's too high."

Jays dropped his stethoscope around his neck and pulled the Velcro free, discarding the cuff in a bin at the head of the stretcher. He pulled a clipboard off the wall to record his readings on. "Hold her head, Nick," the medic instructed quietly.

Nickolas captured her head between his hands and immobilized it. Jays flashed a light across her eyes while Nickolas stared into her face. The soft brown of her irises were almost completely gone, her pupils were so expanded. Her unfocused gaze roamed over him, and Nickolas held his breath as memories swamped him. Flashes of being in her position ripped through his mind, and gritting his teeth, he let go of her as soon as Jays had finished. It was too much, too similar, to his time in the Hub.

Jays made more notations on the chart then asked softly, "How much of the tranquilizer did she take?"

A fast turn sent the van rocking and Nickolas grabbed at the stretcher before he answered. "She took the whole dose, barely cooked." He sat back and watched her fight the drug. Her eyes would droop, then jerking awake, she would pull at the straps and look around with a dazed expression, not really focusing on anything.

"That's enough to drop an elephant." Jays shot him a startled look. "She should be out cold. Her body is burning it up at an incredible rate. No wonder she's running a fever. She'll probably have flushed it all out of her system by the time we arrive at the Facility." Jays shook his head and resumed his writing.

Nick sucked in a breath as a wave of fear swamped him. It took a second for him to sort through and realize that the fear came from Jessica, not himself. He reached over, brushing a curl out of her eyes and smoothing a hand over her head. The tactile contact gave her something to focus on, and she looked up at him with fuzzy, muddled eyes. He could see the effort it cost her to collect enough wits to form coherent speech.

"Don't...give me...to them," she finally managed to whisper. The quiet plea gave Nickolas shivers, making him uneasy with a vague feeling of presentiment.

"Hush. There's nothing to worry about. I'll keep you safe. You're one of us now," he whispered back and continued to caress her hair until she closed her eyes with a sigh. A quiet noise snapped his attention back to the rest of the passengers in the vehicle. He raised his head and caught a stunned look on Christoff's face, quickly hidden, but Flynn's expression prodded his instincts. Aggression flooded to the surface. Not sure what it represented, Nickolas resumed his seat at the foot of her stretcher, holding himself in check.

Christoff coughed then glanced at the others before he asked, "So, Nick...why is she doing this? It's not like she has a choice. Where does she think she's going to go?"

"I have no idea. But I doubt that she's given up." His gaze strayed back to her. He was having a hard time keeping his attention off of her. "Whatever has her freaked is pretty strong."

Jays placed the chart back in its holder then took a seat on the bench at the head of the stretcher. "You know it could just be the effects of her changing system. Both of you would understand better than anyone else here how the experience makes you more paranoid and volatile."

Surprised, Nick looked at Jays. "You don't truly believe that, do you, Jays? This isn't within any normal parameters that I'm aware of. Paranoid and volatile, yes, but what she has done is beyond belief. Besides, from things she said to me when we captured her, she knew exactly what she was doing and why. It's the why that I want to know."

"We may have ideas about what is normal, Nick, but that doesn't preclude occasional individuals who are different. We are still studying the mutation. And new differences are cropping up all the time," the doctor said.

"Besides, Nickolas," Flynn added sternly, "the why is not your concern. Only the capture."

He shot a look of disbelief at Flynn. He couldn't fathom that the man would say anything like that. His temper started to simmer and he narrowed his eyes. The van slowed to a stop, and Nick shifted his attention out the front window instead of ripping into his teammate. His acute hearing let him pick out the conversation of the driver as he bantered with the ferry attendant at the tollbooth for a moment. Emotions cascaded through Nickolas, and he ground his teeth in frustration. The van moved to the head of the carpool lane as the ferry slowly pulled into the dock, and Nickolas noted how few cars there were to unload. *I guess Kingston isn't a big destination at this time of night. This shouldn't take too long.* His mind circled back to Flynn's comment. Unfortunately his temper hadn't cooled any. Nick pulled his attention away from the window. Only a few moments had passed. He noted Jays's preoccupied face before turning back to Flynn.

The older man held his gaze. Nick felt a growl try to form, so he took a deep breath. Shoving his temper down, he tried to bottle it before he addressed Flynn's statement. "Since when?"

His brother's wings rustled as he shifted uneasily. "Nick...," Christoff murmured.

"No, Chris. Since when have we been forbidden to question? Flynn?"

"It's not your job, Nickolas. Leave it to those whose it is."

"Since when?" he asked again. This time the menace in his voice showed enough for everyone in the van to notice.

"Since always," Flynn said hotly. "It just never needed to be mentioned since you showed no interest beyond the capture before."

"What are we, trained dogs? Here, boy, sit, fetch, good boy. Now go lie down, we don't need you right now." The van rocked as it started to move again. Anger and betrayal pulsed in Nick. He turned to glare at Jays, who hurriedly found something else to do, obviously trying to stay out of the argument. His brother sat quietly, trying not to draw attention to himself, but watched the byplay avidly. Nick exerted control on his breathing, slowing it down, and thought about the implications of what Flynn ordered. He stared out the window as it sank in. The growl rumbled low in his throat.

"What don't they want us to know, Flynn?" he asked softly.

He waited for an answer from behind him. Through the window, he watched the ferry attendant motion them on with a bored hand gesture. They pulled to a stop overlooking the water at the front of the ship. The tense silence inside the van fed his fears, and he turned to meet Flynn's eyes.

"What don't they want us to know?"

The older man held his gaze unflinchingly.

Standoff.

An emerging predator and the one who thought he had been holding the leash.

The loud blaring of the ships horn interrupted their contest of wills. Jessica screamed. She renewed her panicked struggling. Nickolas leaned forward, intending to get Jessica's attention to calm her, but he froze instead. He blinked, not sure he could believe his eyes at first. A glow had started to form around the fledgling.

"Oh fuck," Jays snapped.

Nickolas tore his eyes away to see the usually calm medic in a mad rush. He rummaged through several different cupboards, tossing out vials, needles, and syringes.

Nickolas's attention jumped back to Jessica. There was most definitely a glow brightening around her. Trusting Jays's reaction to the bizarre situation, he didn't wait to see what the doctor had in store. He caught her face in his hands and held her still, forcing her to meet his eyes. Whimpering, she tried to break eye contact with him, but he wouldn't allow it. The glow around her grew brighter and a tingle formed in his fingers where he touched her. He reacted on instinct. Mentally fighting her, he pushed out, insistently probing at the barrier she had wrapped about herself.

Stalemate.

He shifted his grip and wrapped a hand in her hair to maintain control then slid the other down her side until he reached her injured thigh. He squeezed. Pain flared in her eyes as he clutched the fresh blood, soaking through the fabric. He used the blood as a way through to her. Pouring more energy into the unfamiliar exercise, he felt a chink appear, so he narrowed his attack. An inexperienced surgeon with a new scalpel. *I hope this works.*

Boring through her shield, Nickolas struggled silently. He could feel her determination, but his was just as strong and hadn't been tested as hers had been in the last twenty-four hours. It felt like forever before he broke through the barrier, but the glow suddenly flared, and Nickolas ordered, "No. Let it go. Now."

Her eyes opened wide in surprise as he succeeded in mentally overpowering her. Once inside, he could feel everything, her uncertainty, her anger, but most of all, her fear *of him* as he drained the power away from her somehow and the glow faded. He could understand her fear, he felt it himself. *What have I done?*

He took his bloody hand away from her leg and let go of her hair. Now wasn't the time to dwell on it, and he looked up. Very little time had passed; Jays had only just finished drawing his syringe and was tapping it to raise any air bubbles.

"Flynn, shut that door. Get back here and hold her arm," the medic snapped. He quickly found a vein and injected the contents of his syringe. Nick sat back on his heels and overheard him say to Flynn, "It's not like you could have gotten far enough away to make a difference."

Jays stared at her for a moment then shook his head and turned to dump the syringe and needle into the sharps box on the wall.

Nickolas's mind raced. He slid his palm down his leg, trying to rid it of the blood. When the doctor looked at him, their eyes met.

He can't know. I don't even know. What the hell is going on?

Jays held his gaze for a moment and, for the first time in a long time, Nick backed down. He looked away. The feeling that Jays judged him somehow swamped him.

"It was an anesthetic," the doctor said softly.

Nickolas shrugged and brushed his hand down Jessica's cheek then over her hair in a soothing motion. She had stopped fighting the straps, and clouds gathered in her eyes as the second anesthetic pushed through her system. He leaned over, his lips brushing her ear. "Sleep."

The wetness of a tear slid between their faces. He caressed his cheek along hers, drying the trail. A soft sob escaped, and she shuddered, but finally with the help of the second drug, she passed out.

Nick continued to pet her hair, watching her relax in sleep. His emotions rode a rollercoaster, and every dip and turn, a new feeling vied for supremacy. Anger finally topped out all of the others. His face hardened, and he pinned Flynn to his seat with a look. "I'm going out on deck."

Damn it. Nick, don't... Christoff held his hand out, but Nick pulled away. With a last glance at Jessica, his brother opened the rear doors and jumped out.

Damage control. I need to get him home and checked out. Christoff watched him stalk away. When he was out of sight, he turned his attention back to the others.

"What just happened?" Jules asked as he joined them from the front. The communications tech looked around in bewilderment.

Flynn got up and pulled the doors shut. "Nick got pissy and started asking too many questions. Or do you mean her?"

Christoff narrowed his eyes at Flynn's attitude. The jerk had pushed Nick's buttons on purpose. *And now he's blaming Nick?* Jules slipped past to take a seat at the foot of the stretcher. Chris turned to Jules. "Jessica had some sort of reaction, but Nick calmed her down. He's on edge from the recovery, and Flynn pissed him off. He stormed out. I haven't seen him show his feelings this strongly in a long time."

"Nickolas?" Jules asked, surprised. "That man has been working to perfect the art of *control* for fifteen years now."

Jules shot a look at their other team member. Flynn shrugged and slouched down onto the bench near the doors.

Christoff suppressed a growl and turned away from them. His temper danced dangerously close to the surface. Jays stood, contemplating Jessica as she slept, an odd expression on his unguarded face.

"She's a Caster," the medic murmured. "Damn, Jess, why did you have to do this to me? We don't have enough research on that subset here," he said under his breath. He obviously didn't realize that he was thinking out loud.

Christoff froze, staring at Jays. "Subset?" he finally managed to ask. "What the hell is a Caster?"

The unfocused quality in Jays's eyes caught his attention. It reminded him of someone in a trance. "Jays? What the hell are you talking about?"

The doctor blinked and his eyes cleared. "Um..." He cast a helpless look at the other two grounded.

Christoff swiveled in his seat. Jules looked uncomfortable, but Flynn wore a mulish expression.

God damn it. What is going on? "Nick's right. What are you hiding?" He stood up and shook out his wings. "What did she do to have you so upset?"

He zeroed in on Jays. The doctor stepped back nervously.

"And, I repeat, what is a Caster?"

Jays flicked his eyes to Jessica's still form before locking back on him. He took a step, and Jays swallowed. "You are a Hunter. She is a Caster."

"And that means what?"

"Jays. Shut up," Flynn barked.

Christoff spun, his wings flaring slightly in the small space. "Excuse me, Flynn?"

"Need to know, Hunter. And you don't need to know."

"Really? Sounds like it's about us. That sure makes me think I need to know." He clamped his wings down and turned his back on Flynn. Another step brought him up to Jays. The grounded pressed his back into the cabinets of the wall. Christoff wrapped his hand gently around the base of the doctor's throat. "What was that glow, Jays?"

"Death."

"How?" Jays's pulse thundered under his palm, the only sign of the fear his friend had of him at the moment.

"You see, hear, smell, and move differently, yes? Well that isn't all that got unlocked in some of you."

Chris glanced down at the fledgling's sleeping face and thought about how she had eluded them. Then there was Nick's odd behavior. *I really need to talk to Ian.*

The metallic crunch of a trank pistol chambering a dart echoed in the confines of the med unit.

"When's the last time you took your pills, boyo?" Flynn asked.

A growl rumbled in Chris's chest, and he turned his head to look over his shoulder at Flynn. His teammate stood at the foot of the stretcher, a gun pointed at him. "Does it matter?"

"You have Jays by the throat. I think it matters. I'm sure he does too." Flynn's hand didn't so much as waver. "You know your aggression will become uncontrollable if you don't take them, Chris."

He turned back to Jays. The eyes that met his contained pity and compassion. And something else the doctor quickly hid. His fingers twitched. "I want answers, Jays."

"Take the pills, or I'll shoot your ass, and you can ride back with her, Chris."

Jays's gaze flicked to Flynn then back. "He's going to shoot you, Chris. Do you want to leave Nick alone right now?"

Snarling, Chris pried his hand away from Jays's neck. The doctor slid to the side, keeping an eye on him, and fished around in one of the cupboards.

"How was she going to kill herself, Jays?"

He pulled out a bottle and shook two pills into the palm of his hand. "Not just her, all of us. I suppose if we were lucky, she wouldn't have sunk the boat."

Chris froze.

Jays snagged a bottle of water and held it and the pills out to him. He shook his head and backed up a step. "I'm fine."

"Chris, you need to take them now." Jays held his stare. "We've never needed to worry about a Caster manifesting during recovery before. It's something that Ian and I watch for, usually a week into the change."

"Why haven't we ever been told about this?" He reluctantly held out his hand. Jays dropped the pills into his palm. He swallowed them then downed half the bottle of water.

"I can't answer that, Chris."

"Can't? Or won't?"

"Does it matter?"

Chris growled. He drained the rest of the bottle and looked over at Flynn and Jules. Flynn put the gun away and sat back down. Jules stared at his feet, his hand pressed to his earpiece, listening to the comm chatter.

"How does this affect the rest of us?"

"You are the same Hunter you were before, Chris."

He turned back and something in Jays's eyes caught his attention. He looked back down at Jessica. "So she's different? A Caster, whatever that means. What about Nick? Is he a Caster too?"

"Not exactly…," he said softly.

Jays shook his head. Chris looked over his shoulder at Flynn, who now talked quietly with Jules.

"As long as she stays asleep she'll be fine, Chris."

The drugs already wormed their way through his system. The crystal sharp clarity dulled slightly, just enough for him to notice. He slid around the stretcher and made his way to the door. "I need to go check on Nick."

"What are you going to tell him?"

His hand on the latch, he looked back over his shoulder at Jays. "Does it matter?"

♦ ♦ ♦

Nickolas stood out on deck at the front of the boat and leaned on the railing, looking out over the water. The brisk wind raised by the passage of the ship blew through his hair and made his wings flutter and ripple like a dark cloak billowing out behind him, reflecting his mood.

What pieces of the puzzle am I missing here? What are they hiding? And why do I feel as though I know her? All I have are questions without answers. And feelings, I can't forget the feelings. Especially not when they slam into me like a runaway freight train. Speaking of feeling...

Nickolas sensed Christoff watching from the window behind him. *It's interesting that I can sense him so strongly now. It's like a fog has been wiped off and the window is clear. The last twenty-four hours have really opened my eyes. What if the wild Valkyries aren't as out of control as we've been led to believe?*

Nickolas felt when his brother finally got up the nerve to approach him. The door opened and he came out to take a deceptively relaxed pose against the rail, watching him intently. Nickolas clenched his fist and continued to stare out over the water. He hoped that if he ignored Chris's scrutiny, his brother would take the hint and leave him alone. But a rustle of wings warned him that that hope was in vain; Chris wasn't going to leave him be.

"So, Nicky, what's going on?"

I'm ignoring you, Chris, that's what. Take the hint.

Christoff cleared his throat. "Come on, you're taking this assignment pretty personally. She's caught, and no one got seriously hurt in the process, at least."

"Chris, just leave it."

"Leave what, Nick? What you're doing? I don't think so. How'd we catch her, Nicky?"

"Chris. Not now," he whispered, feeling the edge teeter perilously close as his brother pushed. Much more and he wouldn't be able to control his temper. He could not lose control. Not ever again.

"No, Nick. I'm sorry, but it has to be now."

Nickolas spun and backed Christoff into the corner of the railing. Trapped, his brother watched him warily. Nick paced back and forth in front of him, pent up aggression vibrating through his body, and growled, "Why?"

Cocking his head, Christoff looked into his eyes. "You haven't had your pills today any more than I had, have you? If you don't relax, they'll force you to take them too."

Nickolas watched Christoff stand there and face him steadily. He took a deep breath and pulled his temper back under control. He yanked his hair back into a hair tie then rejoined Christoff at the rail.

His brother relaxed slightly and turned out toward the water. "So talk to me," he said quietly.

Nickolas watched the waves curl under the moon. The smell of rain was growing, and he wished that he could use it to wash away the memories. He took a deep breath. "You say no one got hurt? I don't know if that's true. Look at what she put herself through to avoid us. Are we right in what we do? Are the drugs they make us take really necessary? What was she running from? No one got hurt? Look at her Chris. She wanted to die instead of come with us. Her fear has to be based in something."

"Some new fledglings fight their fate more than others, Nick. You know that."

Nickolas studied his brother out of the corner of his eye. He could see the drugs having an effect. The aura of calmness that descended on him seemed painfully obvious now. "Chris, I have never felt so whole in my life. My mind is clear today. I've missed the pills before, but this is different."

There's more out here than you know, Nickolas.

"Exactly. That's what I'm starting to wonder about."

"What? I must have missed something. What are you wondering about?" Chris sounded confused.

Nickolas glanced at him. "You just told me that there's more out there than we know of."

"No I didn't."

"What do you mean? Yes you did." Frowning, Nickolas caught movement out of the corner of his eye; his attention shifted quickly and he looked out over the water. To his left, pacing them just out of range of the lights from the boat, flew a darker patch of night. Assaulted by a jumble of feelings he would rather *not* put a name to, he could just discern the silhouette of a Valkyrie in flight.

Yes, it was me.

"How?" Nickolas whispered and looked out at the Valkyrie. His own sharp desire to fly free assaulted him.

"Nickolas?" Christoff questioned.

He held up his hand and motioned him silent then pointed to the feral Valkyrie across the water.

The drugs have worn off enough that you are receptive. Just remember there is always more than one truth out there, Nickolas.

"The drugs are supposed to keep me from turning into an animal...like you're supposed to be..."

So, is that the lie they've spoon fed you? We're all animals on the inside, Nickolas. He could feel her laughter and revelry in flight through the link. *They are just the collar choking you.*

The feeling traveling down the link grew quiet.

I don't suppose that you would let us take Jessica off your hands?

"Of course not! She's mine," he replied without thinking.

Interesting. I didn't think you would notice yet.

"Notice what?"

Keep her safe, Nickolas. And with that, the other Valkyrie veered off, flashing through the moonlight briefly.

"Wait," he called.

"Nickolas, what's going on?" Christoff finally asked.

"I don't know. That other Valkyrie was speaking to me." This was just too much for one day. *Telepathy, the visions, what else do the drugs inhibit?* Nickolas wondered.

"Speaking to you? What did he want?"

"They wanted Jessica. When I told her no, she told us to protect her."

Chapter Six

Ian Sinclair, head doctor in charge of the Facility Valkyries, stood in the sliding glass doorway and stared out into the night. The promised rain sheeted off the overhang that protected the drive up to the door. He sighed, feeling every bit his age. The brisk October breeze laced with the rain smelled wonderful, and he took a moment to savor the calm before the storm. The sound of footsteps approaching down the hall reached him, and he turned to greet two of his junior doctors. "Good evening, boys. Are you ready for this? They should be coming down the drive any minute."

Michael peered out into the gloom disgustedly then tried to lean casually against the door; Ian shook his head.

"What do you think is going on with her, Ian? I was going through the files and there's only one recorded case that has any similarities, and those aren't precisely similar."

Ice ran down his spine, and Ian stilled. "I know. And that case isn't for discussion. Understood?" His voice left no room for argument.

"Yes, sir," Michael said quickly.

"Jack?" Ian turned a slow look at the other man. The other twenty-something doctor just returned his stare for a moment in speculation.

"Are you going to let Gabriel get her?"

Surprised by the question, Ian blinked. "Not if I can help it, I won't."

"Good. Then I won't talk about it either." The young man took a stance in the doorway with his arms folded over his chest and stared out into the rain.

Ian narrowed his eyes in speculation but turned away from Jack. The lights of the medical van brightened the bushes as it appeared down the drive and continued toward them at a steady clip. While he waited for the van to reach them, he took stock of the people around him. Michael was the same old didactic stickler, annoying and overly efficient. Jack though... *Humm, now that I'll need to keep an eye on. He may be changing.* The sandy-haired doctor stood in the doorway in what he thought of as a classic Hunter's stance. *Stage one, early signs,* he decided, sighing.

Ian widened his scan to note the people approaching in the van. *Now, that must be Jessica,* he thought, feeling the whirling maelstrom restrained in the van. *This should be fun.*

Another more subtle well of aggression took him by surprise. He hadn't felt that barely controlled energy signature, unveiled, for fifteen years. Ian closed his eyes and whispered, "Ah, Nicky, what have you done?"

As soon as the van stopped, the back doors opened and Christoff and his brother Nickolas jumped out, securing the doors to the sides of the van. The foot of the stretcher appeared a moment later. Jules hurried around the side, taking the end, and with Flynn they lowered it to the ground, giving Ian his first view of the changeling that had caused such an uproar.

Ian stepped out, with Michael and Jack flanking, and approached the new fledgling. He met Jays's eyes across the stretcher as his protégé attempted to keep her calm. He looked to be losing the battle, and Ian laughed to himself. The bright lights and sudden movement of her arrival were rousing her out of her stupor. He lifted her lids and looked at her eyes then put his fingers to her throat to check her pulse. "I don't like this. Her heart rate is too fast. What's her blood pressure, Jays?"

"One sixty-five over ninety-eight. It's gone up since my first measurement."

He paused and looked across the stretcher at Jays then puffed out a breath and placed his hand to her forehead. He brushed her sweat-soaked hair away. "So give me the details, you know how chatty the comm techs are."

His Second looked down at Jessica before answering, a worried frown on his face. "She took fifty cc of drexirethirin mixed into hamburger, and the trank only barely incapacitated her. It allowed us to get her into custody, but that was about it. I then had to administer a second dose of venous anesthetic once we were on the ferry. She started to go into overload on the boat, but Nick was able to distract her enough so I could knock her out before she killed us all. But as you can see, she's already burned most of that out of her system as well. After she was out, I gave her two units of fluids for dehydration; she's lost a lot of blood."

Ian glanced down at Jessica and caught wariness starting to replace the fog in her eyes. "She'll need a primer dose of inhibitor."

He waved at Jack and Michael to take the stretcher then gave Flynn and Jules a dismissive nod. "We can move her from here, you two should go get some rest."

Ian placed his hand on Jays's arm to stop him from following when Jessica was wheeled away. Once both the stretcher and Flynn and Jules were far enough away to not overhear his comment, Ian asked softly, "Distract her how, Jays?"

His subordinate glanced over to where Nickolas stood a few feet away, by the emergency vehicle. "He didn't distract her; he broke her shield, Ian."

Nodding, Jays had just confirmed his suspicions. "Don't mention this to Jack or Michael."

"Yes, sir," he replied then continued on after the stretcher.

Ian waited until they had all disappeared into the building before turning to look at the two Valkyries. Nickolas leaned against the back corner of the van staring at him, his arms crossed.

He ignored the challenge in his body language for the moment and turned first to Christoff, who was shutting the van doors.

The normally carefree and energetic Hunter slouched in exhaustion. "I need to debrief, Ian. Nick, you should head to bed."

"No."

"Nick." Chris sighed in exasperation.

"You go to bed, Chris."

Ian caught Christoff's gaze. "It's fine, Chris. Go on to bed. We can debrief later."

The Hunter shook his head, and after a last concerned glance at his brother, he left. Ian turned toward the building, expecting Nickolas to follow. He wasn't disappointed.

The situation would need careful handling to maintain dominance. Challenge oozed from the Valkyrie. "So, Nicky, what happened out there?"

Undisciplined power swirled and spiked. After a moment, Nickolas answered in a flat voice. "She managed to stay one step ahead of us the whole way. I don't know where she got the strength. I've never seen anything like it."

"I have, once before," Ian said quietly.

"What?" Nickolas glanced sharply at him.

Ian clucked his tongue. "Never mind, it doesn't matter. What else can you tell me?"

He ignored the stirrings of curiosity in Nickolas. *Let him wonder. That will let me stay one step ahead of him. And if he's done what I think he must have, I'm going to need every advantage.*

"Don't underestimate her. She's dangerous, and she very badly does *not* want to be here. She's already having dazzle headaches. And...she's different."

A larger spike of power accompanied Nickolas's puzzled look. Ian stopped dead in the hall and grabbed Nickolas's arm, forcing the Valkyrie to turn and face him. He captured Nick's startled gaze with his own and tried to impress on the stubborn Valkyrie the seriousness of the situation. With quiet aggression, Ian pushed dominance and stared him down. "Nick, do not mention what you did on the boat to anyone, under any circumstance. If you care for Jessica's well-being and yours, you will do this."

Blinking, Nickolas dropped his eyes and looked away, pulling his wings in tight. "All right, but why, what is she?"

Ian turned from him and continued on down the hall.

"What does that make me?" he heard Nickolas mutter to himself before he moved to catch up.

You're not ready for that yet, Nicky, Ian thought. They reached the end of the hall. He held the door open for Nickolas, who slid past with a tired air of uncertainty that vanished the moment he looked at Jessica. Relieved and pleased at Nickolas's response to the new fledgling, he followed him into the Hub. Ian glanced across the observation room. Nickolas skirted around the center island of computers and video monitors on his way to the treatment alcove on the right. Ian stopped for a moment at the island to bring one of the observation rooms online. He double checked the opposite wall of closely spaced doors before he typed in the entry code to one of the cells. The monitor lit up, showing the tiny room. After a few more commands, he turned to join the party he could hear taking place in the treatment area.

"God damn it, you bastards. Let me go."

A quick sweep took in the scene, and he chuckled. Jessica was aware and quite alert on the stretcher and kicking ineffectually with her bound legs. She growled in frustration while Jays looked on with amused resignation. Ian shook his head. About what he expected. Michael fussed at her uselessly, trying to get vitals that Jays had already supplied. Jack showed promise though; he was working quickly and quietly putting together the surgical trays.

Ian met Jays's laughing eyes across the table then rubbed the smile from his lips as he approached. He highly doubted that Jessica found any amusement in her current situation and probably wouldn't appreciate his reaction. Jays handed him the clipboard with her stats on it, but he only gave it a quick glance. He was too interested in observing her reactions. Jessica's eyes jumped around the room before they came to rest briefly on Nickolas in the corner. She flushed and looked away and jerked at the straps. Then her eyes landed on Ian at the foot of the stretcher. She froze. He smiled.

"We haven't been able to get much done, sir. She's too restive," Jays spoke quietly.

"That's putting it mildly," one of the others muttered softly, though Ian wasn't certain who.

A growl of challenge rumbled from her, but she still gave him the high position when she jerked her gaze away from him. Ian chuckled. He flipped through the pages of her chart, noting her blood pressure and respiration, heart rate and temperature. "Have you administered the inhibitor yet?"

"No, sir. I thought we should wait for you," Jays answered.

"Jack, get me 10 cc of type A inhibitor." He handed the chart back to Jays and walked over to the head of the stretcher. Looking down at her, he smiled gently. "Hi, I'm Dr. Sinclair, but you can call me Ian. You're going to be here for a while, so you need to get used to the idea. I know you're confused. I'll try to explain what is happening to you in more detail later, but right now I need your cooperation, all right?"

Her bright eyes looked straight into his, and she smiled back up at him. "Like hell."

Jays snorted and Ian sighed. "Well, it was worth a try."

"Here's the inhibitor, Ian."

He accepted the syringe then held it up and tapped it for air bubbles. A strangled noise was wrung out of her, and Ian flicked his gaze from his task. His feisty little fledgling suddenly looked terrified. Her eyes darted nervously from him to Nickolas, looking for an ally.

Nickolas kept his back to the corner and watched the proceedings with a blank look. This had to be bringing up unpleasant memories for him. *I hope he can hold it together.*

She struggled even harder against the restraints, if that were possible. Tremors ran through her body and she pleaded with them to let her go. "No needles, please? No needles..."

"Jessica," he kept his voice soft. "What I am about to give you is called an inhibitor. It will help keep you safe during your change."

Her fear radiated from her, and he shot a look at Nickolas to gauge his reaction before continuing. "Jays, please hold her still. Nick, if you would care to help, you could try to keep her attention away from what we are doing?"

If I direct his awakening protective instincts, maybe I can get him through this. Just the sight of her looking up into Nickolas's face reminded Ian of similar situations between himself and Nick in the past. Nickolas folded his wings in tight before he knelt down by her side. She locked onto his face in desperation as Jays clamped down on her arm, immobilizing it. Deftly inserting the needle, Ian administered the injection, watching her fingers twitch as she gasped with the pain.

Power slammed into Ian, and he looked up quickly at Nickolas. The Alpha Valkyrie ground his teeth, his eyes fixed on hers, and Ian could tell the remembered pain swam at the surface. He placed a hand on Nickolas's arm, offering support. "I'm through. Nicky. You can let go now."

Shaking his head, Nickolas reached out, brushing his knuckles lightly against her cheek, and Ian looked over to meet Jays's serious eyes. Nickolas's timing could be better, he thought, resigned to the developing situation. Ian turned his attention back to admitting Jessica.

"Were you able to catalogue her injuries during transit, Jays?"

"No broken bones that I could find, or internal injuries I could detect. Some massive bruising, though. Her feet are in bad shape. But the worst trauma is the two lacerations on her right leg."

"Ok, then, let's get started. Get gloves on, guys."

After Jays and the others gloved up, he turned to her shredded pant leg. He peeled back the slit-open denim and looked at the bandaging Jays had applied underneath. Blood had started to seep through in places. Jack placed scissors in his hand, and Ian cut the rest of the denim off, followed by the gauze.

He worked the blood-caked padding away from the two large tears in her flesh then probed the edges of the bigger one on her thigh. She flinched in pain. "Jays, I'll need a saline bottle and a suture kit and some local to dull the pain. Michael, take a look at the gash on her calf."

Jack brought over the surgical tray, and Ian started flushing the wound.

"She'll need stitches down here too, Ian," Michael murmured.

Jays finished drawing up the anesthetic, so he moved to give his Second room and turned to look over the gash in her calf. "Jays, when you're done there, give her some in her calf as well, then please tend her feet. Jack, you can do the stitching on her calf."

"Can you still feel this, Jessica?" he asked as he probed the wound on her thigh again. Her face set mulishly and he sighed. "I would like to cause you as little pain as possible, but I need your help for that."

She turned her face away, refusing to reply. He shrugged and picked up a threaded suture needle. "Right."

Drawing the wound closed, he started to make neat stitches in her thigh and wasn't surprised when he heard her draw in a breath through her teeth. "You are so stubborn, Jess," he whispered.

Nickolas's soft grunt of agreement caught Ian's attention. In his exhausted state, the young Valkyrie couldn't hide his emotional vulnerability. *Damn, and it's just going to get worse. Why now, Nickolas? This is going to need careful handling. I don't know how fast his behavior will deteriorate.* "Easy, Nicky, I'm almost done."

He tied off the last stitch then laid the needle down on the tray, watching Jack finish off her calf. "Looks good."

He picked up her chart and made a few notes as Jays finished cleaning up her feet. Her stiff posture started to relax when they had all finished.

He placed his hand on her averted forehead. "You will start to feel dizzy soon, which is normal; you'll also start to get hot flashes. These symptoms will pass in a few hours. Unfortunately, there are some more unpleasant side effects that will manifest then. You'll need another dose of inhibitor tomorrow morning, after that it will be every twenty-four hours. You have quite enough drugs coursing through your already taxed system as it is."

He pulled his hand away, and she turned her head; he locked eyes. "Just keep in mind. The more you fight, the harder it will be."

She chewed on her lip, and he could read the struggle on her face. She had a strong will. Just like the rest of her family. He chuckled; this was going to be a challenge. *Time for a prod.* "But having known your mother, I doubt that you'll let a few needles stop you."

He grinned at her dumbfounded expression and he turned away, walking to the monitors in the center of the room. "I think we have enough for now, let's get her settled into observation room four."

Jack and Michael each took an end of the stretcher, pushing it across the Hub to the door Jays held open. Ian tapped out commands on one of the keyboards, calibrating the room's sensors as Nickolas slipped up beside him. He kept only half his attention on the monitor and what was transpiring. He was more concerned with keeping a closer eye on Nickolas's reaction to the scene. The Valkyrie was riveted to the picture on the monitor. The three doctors maneuvered the stretcher into the small observation room, stopping alongside the tiny cot bolted to the wall. Jays backed up to the door as Jack and Michael started to undo the straps holding her down.

"Wait, Jess, don't do it," Nickolas whispered.

What does he see? He turned more of his focus on Jessica. Her hands tensed. The straps loosened, and she kicked out, hitting Michael in the stomach. Jack reacted quicker, and he managed to dodge her attack. Pulling the straps out, she rolled off the stretcher, backing to the wall looking for a way out.

Damn it, I just set those stitches.

Jack held his hands out at his sides getting into position to tackle her if necessary. Michael still lay on the floor wheezing. She turned and lunged for the door, but Jays casually raised a tranquilizer gun and pointed it at her, a soft smile flirting with the corners of his mouth. She froze.

"Jays," she sneered, but Ian could hear the betrayal underneath that she tried to hide.

"Hi, Jess. How've you been?" he asked softly.

"How've I...? Fuck you, Jays."

He sighed. "I'm sorry."

He waved at the other two then held Jessica at bay as they backed the stretcher out. Raising the gun to his forehead in a quick salute, he shut the door, sealing her in.

Ian crossed his arms and watched as she flung herself at the door. He turned the volume down to muffle her tirade.

Another surge of power washed across the room, and he glanced over to see Nickolas's clenched fists turn white, his attention fixed on the monitor.

"Nick, why don't you go to bed? You look pretty worn out." No response. "Nick."

He snapped his fingers in front of the young man's face. "Hey, are you ok?"

Nickolas's head turned in slow motion. Their eyes met. Remembered pain laced them.

"Yes, sorry, just thinking." His gaze started to drift back to the monitor showing Jessica.

"Oh no you don't, out. Go on, get. You need some rest." Reluctantly Nickolas turned to go, casting one last look at the monitor before he walked out of the Hub. Ian sank into a chair, smiling at Nick's attempt to hide from him. *Does he really think I'm that unobservant? With his history…this could get interesting. Oh well, time enough to consider Nick's actions later. Right now I have more important things to deal with.*

Returning his attention to his new charge, he leaned back and watched Jessica in the monitor. The room she had been placed in was a carbon copy of the other dozen or so to either side. It was small, with a cot on the wall, a toilet, a built-in folding table, the door, and the camera and other sensors in the ceiling.

He reached out and turned the camera's volume back up. Jessica hit the door one more time, then moaning, she slid down to the ground next to it in defeat, her head in her hands. *Ah, Jess, I wish you didn't have to be here*, he thought sadly, watching her huddled form against the wall. *Well, since you are here, I had better deal with the results.*

"Michael, order food for her," he directed then turned to Jays to discuss her retrieval in more detail. Ian flipped through his apprentice's notes. A few minutes later, Michael arrived with a tray of cubed rare steak. Jack looked up from where he was cleaning up the surgical supplies, but Ian waved him back to his task. "Jays, why don't you take it in?"

Wariness flashed through the young man's eyes, but he quickly shuttered them, nodding. With reluctance, he picked up the tray then walked over to the door where he swiped his card. Ian settled back in his chair as Jays took a breath before he pulled open the door.

He stepped through and pulled it shut with his foot, then looked down at Jessica's hunched form sadly before he placed the food down on the floor next to her.

Crouched in front of her, he tentatively reached out but pulled his hand back before he touched her. "Jess? Jessica, here's some food. You don't need to worry about it. It's not drugged like the last batch."

She didn't lift her head from her knees, just started to rock.

"I know you're starving, please eat," he said, almost too quietly for the mic to pick up, then he stood and slipped back out the door.

Ian continued to watch the monitor. She twitched when the door clicked shut. At first she didn't respond, but then she slowly lifted her head and looked at the food next to her, licking her lips. She glanced up at the camera before she pushed herself unsteadily to her feet. She stared down at the tray then deliberately raised her eyes straight into the camera. A flash of defiance crossed her face and she kicked the tray over.

Her hand shot out and she caught herself on the wall. He watched her fight the dizziness that descended on her, then she started to pace her cell. Crossing his arms over his chest, he watched, contemplating his next move.

Nickolas made his way down the barren hallways of the Facility and shook his head sadly. Jessica's defeated image replayed in his mind. It was like a sore tooth that he kept prodding. An echo of pain haunting him from his own memories. Memories he used an iron fist to repress at all times. *I can't regret this retrieval, I just can't. No one else I have ever brought in has made me second guess this system before. What I am doing is right. Isn't it?*

He slowly made his way to his suite. The sterility of the Facility complex had never really bothered him before. It was just there. A fact of life.

He remembered the flash of Jessica's bright red shoes and flinched. *Are we going to suck the life out of her too?* Somehow that prospect never reached his awareness before. He arrived at his suite and switched on the light in the small living room. A sigh escaped as he closed the door. He threw the lock and realized how silly it was, like it could really stop anything.

I suppose if I wanted safety, I wouldn't be considering throwing years of belief out the window.

He crossed the living room. It had a couch that faced an entertainment system, a few bookshelves and another door, which he passed through into his bedroom, then on into the bathroom.

His hand flipped the light switch on autopilot, and he braced his hands on the sink contemplating his reflection in the mirror. "I wish I understood what the hell happened today."

He searched the blue of his eyes but didn't receive any enlightenment. "Maybe I understand too much and just don't like the answers."

He pulled the tie out of his hair, so the black mass fell around his shoulders, and threw the band across the counter then turned on the faucet. He bent over, cupping water in his hands, and splashed it on his face a couple of times before reaching for a towel. He tossed the cloth on the counter carelessly when finished.

No longer able to ignore it, he reluctantly picked up the brown bottle of pills sitting behind the sink and turned it around and around in his hand.

The drugs have worn off enough that you are receptive.

The voice of the feral Valkyrie reverberated through his head. It stopped him from blindly following routine and made him wonder about things he had no right questioning. Shaking the pill bottle, he came to a decision. With exaggerated care, he set it back down behind the sink and turned his back on them, and what they represented, leaving the room.

Tired, he walked over to his bed, stripped, and just dumped his clothes in a pile on the floor, falling over onto the blankets. He bunched up a pillow and hugged it, wishing yet again that he had windows in his rooms. A fresh breeze would go a long way toward helping him relax. Restless, his thoughts returned to contemplating the bizarre events of the last twenty-four hours. *She runs unexpectedly, managing to stay one step ahead of us for a long enough stretch of time that we get off schedule and miss taking our meds. The results of that are that I start hearing and seeing things, which normally one would consider a bad thing, but in this case feels more right than I could ever have imagined. So why would they want to block these abilities?*

Well that's easy enough to answer—control. *I wonder who else knows about this?* The last thought he had as he drifted off to sleep was, *I wonder where this path will lead me?*

Nickolas groaned and rolled over, opening his eyes to look at the clock on the bedside table. *Three hours. Well, it's better than nothing. I don't know why, but I really have to go check on her.* He levered himself out of bed and rummaged in his closet for clean clothes. He pulled them on in the dark then left his bedroom.

Pausing at the door to the hall, he looked back across his apartment. Funny, but this room had never felt like a cage before. *I know what a cage feels like, and Jessica is the one in it at the moment, not me.*

Unfortunately, he couldn't seem to bring himself to believe it.

He pulled his door shut. The next door down the hall was Christoff's. He was drawn to stop at it when he tried to pass, and he reached his hand out, palm flat against the metal. *I can feel him,* Nickolas thought in awe. *This isn't the same sort of awareness we all have of each other's presence either. There's so much more depth to this. His mind is fuzzy, not sharp like the feral one, but he's there, asleep. Soon to wake, though. I wonder if he feels the same call I do?*

Preoccupied, Nickolas turned away and retraced his steps back to the Hub. *These new abilities are going to take some getting used to.* The door to the Hub loomed ahead. He shook his hair over his shoulders and took a breath.

He slipped through the doors, closing them silently behind him, and took stock of the room.

"Ian, I'm really concerned," Jack said.

"Yes, as am I. But it's still a last resort."

"Sir?" Michael chimed in. "How long do we have until there *is* no other choice? Is she in danger now?"

"It's close."

The three of them stood, watching Jessica on the monitor as she paced restlessly, like a cat caged in a zoo. Nickolas approached them, and Ian took his attention from the monitor to look at him. He didn't appear surprised by his return.

"What are you doing back here so soon? You should still be asleep." Ian waved the other two doctors away.

"I tried, but I just couldn't stay asleep."

"You and everyone else. Just about every Valkyrie who can come up with the flimsiest excuse has been sniffing around here. You'd think we had a new zoo exhibit or something."

"Speaking of which, how's she doing, Ian?" Nickolas looked around him at the monitor.

"Not as good as I would like." The head doctor looked back down at the video display with a worried expression.

"Her condition was reported two days ago about six o'clock in the evening." He turned, picking up some papers lying on the desk, and leafed through them. "That would be the point where she was transitioning from the first stage to the second. So, she's been in the second stage of transformation for thirty-three hours by my calculation. During that time, she should be passed out for three quarters of the time and ravenously hungry the rest."

He waved toward the screen showing Jessica pacing her cell. "Look at her. This is the third meal she has refused in as many hours. What few tests we were able to conduct so far are showing a much higher rate of change than normal."

Ian slapped the papers back down onto the desk and glanced at him. "From what I can account for, from you and your team's observations, she has had maybe six hours of sleep total and most of that was at least twenty-seven hours ago. And the only food she's had in that time was what you used to catch her. Her fatigue toxins are building up dangerously, and her metabolism *will* fail soon. Between the two, she'll go into a coma I probably won't be able to bring her out of. Add to that, she appears to be changing in a different way. Without the tests, I can't be sure, but it seems that not just the normal systems are changing. I have no idea what that means."

Ian turned, catching his gaze and trapping him with his own. "If she won't eat, we are going to have to make her, and I don't think that's a great idea. You of all people know how detrimental that can be." He turned away, throwing his hands in the air. "I don't know why she won't eat," he finished in exasperation.

"We caught her with tainted meat, remember. She probably doesn't trust it not to be drugged. Besides, she went to a lot of effort not to be here. Let me try. She'll hate herself, and us, if you give her Xanthar to make her eat. She might not recover from the experience," he finished flatly.

Dr. Sinclair gave him a sad look. "It's better than being dead. Which she will be if she won't eat soon."

"That's debatable," Nickolas replied.

Moments later, the door to cell number four clicked. Shaking off remembered helplessness, Nickolas pushed it open and entered the small room carrying a tray laden with rare meat. The shiver of fear that ran the length of his spine at the *kathunk* of the door latching behind him made him close his eyes and take a deep breath. He set the tray down on the table, then he sat on the cot next to it before examining the room. The new observation rooms felt even smaller than when he underwent the change. When they built the new section, they had replaced the windows with cameras that took away an illusion of space.

Jessica paced along the back wall, her arms wrapped tight around herself. She spoiled her attempt at ignoring him when he caught her casting sidelong glances his way.

"You need to eat."

She stopped and studied him, her face unreadable. After a moment, a growl rumbled in her throat and she returned to pacing. "No."

A sigh escaped and he picked up the knife and fork he'd brought in, against the wishes of the staff. As he carved the meat into slivers, the juices burst into the air. His mouth started to water as he watched her carefully for any reaction and smiled to himself when she licked her lips and started to pace faster. She cast a slashing look at him.

"Why can't you just leave me alone?"

"You need to eat," he repeated.

She looked at the camera before shaking her head no again, but Nickolas could feel the hunger beating at her.

"Don't worry, it's safe," he said quietly before taking a bite himself, slowly chewing and swallowing. Her attention locked on him, and he offered her a bite; she glanced down and turned away, back to pacing, but not before he saw her swallow convulsively. "I know you're hungry, I've been there."

He purposely seduced her, slowly cutting the meat. "The hunger gnaws away at you like a living thing until you feel like you're being eaten alive from the inside. You're not thinking clearly, Jessica. What are you trying to do, starve yourself?"

"If that's all I can do, I'll take it." She threw her long hair over her shoulder and surreptitiously rubbed her stomach.

"You know they won't allow that, don't you? If you don't eat, they are going to make you."

"No."

"Oh yes, they can." He continued, laughing without humor. "Xanthar. They plan to dose you with it if you don't eat. It suppresses your conscious control over your body. You become all instinct, only responding to basic needs like eating, sleeping, fighting—sex. You can't even make yourself speak coherently." He gripped the fork tightly, closing his eyes. "They don't need to get close to you to give it to you. Just shoot you with a dart from the door. Then any food they put in front of you, you would eat like a good little caged animal, because you're starving. Unfortunately, *you* are still in there, watching behind your own eyes, but you can do nothing."

He opened his eyes and captured her stare, and he could see the horror just starting to seep in. "But the worst thing is, when it wears off and you regain control of your own body, you remember everything. Every little detail of what it was like. What you did, how you behaved. It enhances your memory, you see, for its duration. Makes it photographic. It's just a side effect, they say."

His focus on her faded and he stared at nothing for a moment. Fear washed over him and he snapped back. The soft brown of her eyes showed the fear he felt, but underneath the fear lay sympathy.

"Why are you telling me this?" she asked softly. "It's because of you I'm here. Why should I listen to you?"

With great care, he forced his hand to relax and set the utensils down, staring blindly at the tray. "Because this is your last chance, your last chance to avoid a horrific experience."

Too many emotions to name churned in his gut. He wasn't sure where his ended and hers began. He raised his eyes, trying not to plead. "If you don't eat, they *are* going to do that to you. Turn you into an animal. And I wanted to spare you. No one deserves to go through that, trust me. You are changing too fast. Outside of the norm, and apparently there are some differences. Ian isn't going to take a chance on a lack of food and sleep causing you permanent harm."

The debate to trust him or not waged in her eyes. He held out another morsel, putting all of the truth he could into his eyes.

Her tongue flicked out, licking her lips, and she inched forward. He held perfectly still. It became painfully obvious the closer she got that her reserves were completely gone. He understood her better than anyone, except Ian, could know. He pushed that aside to stay focused on the task. She pulled the piece off the tip of the fork with a shaking hand.

Once in her possession she backed up to the wall, her nostrils flaring as she tested the meat's scent. Indecision poured from her. He held her eyes and took another bite, chewing unhurriedly to encourage her. Reluctantly she raised the bloody chunk of steak to her lips. Closing her eyes as she chewed slowly, her breath hitched when she swallowed. Finally, he could see she was caught by the lure of food. Her resistance shattered and she looked for him again, her focus centered on him.

He offered her another bite and she came forward more readily. Piece by piece he hand fed her until all the food he brought in was gone. With a relieved sigh, he sat back and patted the cot next to him.

A cloudy haze obscured her eyes, and Nickolas could tell she had finally run out of steam. She took the seat he offered and sighed quietly. "What am I going to do, Nickolas?"

Her raw emotions battered him and he clenched his teeth trying to block them. "You can't let yourself worry about that right now. Trust me."

A yawn escaped her and the clouds in her eyes broke apart for a second. "I don't know about that."

Very wise, I hate to admit. Self-loathing descended and he pushed his hair out of his face then rose from the cot. With a careful touch to her shoulder, he urged her to lie down. "Sleep is the best answer at the moment."

She curled up into a ball, her glassy eyes staring through him, and mumbled, "Thank you."

Then, on a long sigh, she finally passed out.

Tentatively, not even sure if he should, he reached out and brushed a lock of her hair off of her cheek. *I don't even have a blanket to cover you with,* he thought sadly. They wouldn't allow anything like that in here. Not with her. No blanket, no pillows, no furniture that could be moved. Even the toilet had its water reservoir in the wall. That's all the cell contained, nowhere to hide from the keepers or the cameras. The need to flex his wings crashed down on him, but he knew he couldn't get full extension in here without hitting the walls. *Out. I need out.* Nickolas picked up the tray, leaving Jessica to her sleep.

◆ ◆ ◆

Ian watched the monitor and observed Nickolas enter Jessica's room; at the same moment the door to the hall opened. He felt Christoff enter the Hub and sighed. The young Valkyrie joined him at the monitor and they watched Nickolas interact with Jessica. From the corner of his eye, he saw Chris's face fall from the pain Nickolas tried to hide in his voice.

"The drugs, Ian? I knew Nick had a hard time when he fledged, but what else? What else happened to him when he changed that you aren't telling us?"

Surprised, he shot a glance at Christoff, quickly looking around to see if anyone had overheard the question. "Now is not the time for this."

"When, then? I have several questions I want answers to."

"Later. We can discuss it when I have her stabilized."

Chris looked like he wanted to argue, but he made it clear to the Hunter that the subject was over. They continued to watch the monitor. "So what brings you back here in the middle of the night, Chris?"

He shrugged and chewed on his lip for a moment while watching the monitor before answering. "There's something different about her. I feel...very protective of her. I can't stop thinking about her. I've never had this reaction to a retrieval before. And it's not like she needs protecting. She's one of the strongest I have ever met."

"No more so than Nick needs protecting."

Christoff jerked his head to look at him. And Ian could see the wheels start to turn.

"Nickolas is the strongest of you in many ways, but also the most fragile." Ian met his eyes. Chris blinked then turned to stare at the two in the cell again.

Nickolas had succeeded in getting the entire meal into her. The relief he felt made him realize just how worried he really was.

"Good, Nicky," he said softly then turned to Chris. "We need to watch the two of them together. Look at the way they react to one another. She hasn't responded to any of our attempts to get her to eat, or let us come near her. Let alone touch her like that."

"Nick's behavior around her today surprised me. That's one of the things I wanted to talk to you about."

Ian glanced over his shoulder. "I'm sure you do. But it can still wait until later."

Michael filled out paper work on one of the other fledglings across the room. He probably wasn't close enough to overhear them.

"Ian," Chris snapped, jerking his attention back to the screen. "We have to get him out."

Ian took one look at Nickolas's strained face and keyed in the door release command. The Alpha Valkyrie pushed his way out. Christoff rushed over and got the door shut completely.

Nickolas extended his wings, just missing Michael's head. The other doctor glared and opened his mouth. Ian silenced him with a look.

"Good job, Nickolas. I would like you to be here for her next meal as well. I'll call you when she wakes up."

Not looking at any of them, Nickolas dropped the tray on a table. "Sure, whatever."

Exchanging a look with Christoff, Ian waved the Valkyrie Second after him.

Chapter Seven

"Hey, Nick, wait up."

Nickolas ignored Christoff's call and continued to jog through the halls. It didn't take his brother long to catch up.

"Do you want to talk about it?"

"No." He glanced over his shoulder to glare at him.

"Nick, stop. Where are you going?"

He spun in the corridor to face Chris and bared his teeth with a growl, his wings mantling. Christoff jerked to a stop, just out of reach. Thrown off by the resurgence of his memories, the desire to lash out was almost too strong for him to control. He advanced a step, challenge thrumming through his body.

Christoff backed up. His eyes widened at the display of aggression. "Whoa, relax."

The growl rumbled in his chest and he watched Christoff warily studying his face. "Nick, you can't let them catch you losing control like this. What's going on? This is more than a reaction to your claustrophobia."

He stared at the concern in Christoff's face then snapped his wings closed. "They were going to give her Xanthar," he said through clenched teeth.

A soft sigh escaped Chris, who nodded his head in understanding. "I'm sorry, Nick. You know they'd only do that if there were no other options. They know what it does as well as you do. At least you got her to eat."

"This time." He yanked his hair back in frustration, wishing he had a band on him for it. Exploding into movement, he stalked down the hall with Chris on his heels. "What about the next time. I don't know if she could survive the experience the way I did. That's exactly the kind of thing she's fighting against. She doesn't want to be caged up."

"There's no choice. You know that. Once the change is complete, and she is in full control of her faculties, she'll understand."

He threw his hands up and spun back to face Christoff, surprising his brother into jumping out of reach and narrowing his eyes at him in annoyance. So he exerted some control and took a breath, counting to five, then leaned back against the wall and looked at the ceiling. "Will she? I just don't know anymore, Chris."

Christoff took a couple of steps closer, taking a chance getting within his reach. "You know once she was turned in, the Facility would never have left her alone. They would have just sent more and more teams out to catch her if we had failed. It's too dangerous to change unsupervised."

"So we've been told." The ceiling tiles blurred, so he closed his eyes and took a deep breath. No amount of counting was calming the rollercoaster his reactions were riding. He rolled his head and met worry in Chris's eyes. "Look, I'm sorry, this just brought up bad memories. I need to fly, to feel free."

He pushed away from the wall and strode out of the building, not sure whether he wanted Christoff to follow or not.

As soon as he reached an open space in the compound, Nickolas flexed his knees and spread his wings. Leaping into the sky, his wings made a powerful down sweep, cupping air underneath them and giving him the momentum to take flight. The sound of Christoff's wings broke the night as he took off after him. Nick didn't look back; he just savored the feel of the cold night air across his wings and face, blowing through his hair. The wind washing through him gave him some solace from the anger and pain. Back and forth his wings pumped to gain altitude. When he reached about three hundred feet, he stretched his wings out into a glide, soaring over the trees and buildings toward the west.

Below him the moon silvered the trees and bushes, and lights twinkled in the occasional window. The far off sparkle of moonlight on water drew him and he banked slightly, heading toward Puget Sound. Finally starting to relax in the open air, Nickolas's mind cleared and the memory of the conversation he'd had on the ferry with the unknown Valkyrie drifted in. He decided to try an experiment. Concentrating his thoughts, forming them with precise care in his mind, he broadcast them out.

*Hello? Is anyone out here?** He paused, stretching this new strange sense, looking for an answer. A far off feeling of surprise drifted to him, and he turned his attention in that direction.

Christoff flew up beside him at that moment, yelling over the distance and the sound of air and their wings. "I'm sorry, Nick, what was that? I didn't quite hear what you said."

The distraction caused him to lose the tentative link, and Nick looked at Christoff thoughtfully. "Actually I didn't say anything. I thought it. I need to talk to you. Let's land over there." He pointed off to the right where a small park lay nestled in the trees.

They landed in the grass next to a playground. Nickolas walked over and sat down on the edge of one of the benches and stared off across the park. He studied the moonbeams flickering over the play equipment while he composed himself. Chris's watchful presence waited beside him. Finally, taking his courage in hand, he looked over at Chris. "I've decided to quit taking the drugs."

Christoff looked thoughtful but no surprise showed. "I kinda surmised that for myself, Nicky. Your lack of control has been waving big red flags announcing the fact. So, the question remains. Why?"

Too much energy surged through him, so he stood up and paced over to the merry-go-round. He set it spinning. "Why do we take them? Why do *they* want us to take them?"

He continued to prowl around, wandering through the toys as he watched his brother stand like a rock with his arms crossed at the edge of the playground.

"You know the drill, Nick. Our violent tendencies will take control and suppress our compassion and humanity. Impair our reasoning ability until we are little more than wild animals. That's why the feral recovery teams exist, to try and capture the wild ones. So they can bring them home to get help."

"Help them..." He ran his hand along some metal climbing bars. "Did you see that feral Valkyrie, Chris? She didn't appear to need any help to me."

Chris cocked his head and waited.

Nick shivered his wings and looked away. "She talked to me in my head. So I ask again, what do they suppress?"

"She wha...I didn't hear anything. So you heard her voice in your head?"

"Yes," he whispered and looked up into the stars. Chris shifted his wings and the quiet rustle echoed in Nick's ears. The crunch of gravel under Chris's feet came nearer until he stopped on the other side of the bars to stare at him. Nick pulled his eyes away from the sky and settled on Chris's face.

"So, you think they suppress psionics?" Chris asked.

"I don't know. But that's my theory at the moment. Do you really think they would want us able to talk among ourselves like that?"

Chris grimaced. "No."

The power swelled again and he needed to move. He started to turn away, but Chris caught his gaze, stopping him.

"What else happened, Nicky? More than just a strange Valkyrie talking to you happened. How did we catch Jessica?"

There it was. The knowledge shown in Chris's eyes. He knew he hadn't succeeded in hiding the strange occurrences yesterday. Now he was on borrowed time. Chris wouldn't hesitate to tell Ian.

"I..." He swallowed and backed away from the bars, his emotions cascading again. "I don't really know how to describe it. If I touched something that she had touched, especially if it had her blood on it, then I saw flashes of things. Pictures in my head. I used those to follow her.

"I don't know what's happening to me, Chris, but I don't want to go back on the drugs. I don't think I can. I think I would feel like I had been stuffed in a box." He shuddered and turned away. *Breathe in, out.*

A hand gently gripped his shoulder, and he stiffened. He hadn't heard Chris move.

"Nicky...," he said softly.

"I don't know how long this will take. Will you help me? I know it's asking a lot. If they find out...well, the least I can expect would be getting forced back on the drugs. I don't know what else they might do."

Christoff's hand slid across his shoulder to squeeze the back of his neck. The warm weight of his brother's palm held him still. "You never need to ask, Nicky. You know I will protect you. We all will."

Nick groaned and Chris laughed. "You don't think I can keep this quiet myself, do you?"

"I could hope."

He laughed again and let go. "You're too strong, Nick. And we're going to see the aggression surface at some point. No matter what the drug's true purpose is, you can't deny that the aggression isn't faked."

He growled and started pacing the playground again.

"See." He smiled. "After you're stabilized, I think we should start pulling the rest of us off."

Nickolas stopped and stretched his wings. Then he looked back at Chris. "What's really going on, Chris? If the feral Valkyries are sane and in control, why are we told otherwise?"

"I guess we'll find out. Won't we?"

Nick shook his head then looked back at the stars. "Morning will be here soon. We should get back."

That morning Christoff rolled out of bed groaning. He sat on the edge of the mattress and rested his head in his hands. *Man I need more sleep. But I need to watch Nick's back, which means getting to him before he commits some heinous act.* After a breath to fortify himself, he stumbled into the bathroom then into the shower. The hot water finished waking him up, and he stepped out, vigorously toweling himself dry. The bottle of pills sat on his counter and he studied it for a moment. *As much as I wish to not take these, I can't leave Nick undefended.* He sighed and popped two of the pills, swallowing them with a grimace. *Bleh. Well, guess it's time to wake the dragon.*

He dressed quickly and left his room, heading next door to Nickolas's. The suite was still shrouded in darkness when he opened the door. *Good, I did manage to wake up before him. This should be fun.* He chortled to himself. Tiptoeing across the living room, he peeked through the bedroom door. Nickolas lay sprawled across the bed in a tangled heap of sheets and blankets. Chris smiled and entered the bathroom, where he soaked one of the towels in cold water, wringing it out well. Then stepping up to the bed, he tossed the wet towel across Nickolas's body.

"Ahhhh! What the hell!"

Howling with laughter, Christoff watched Nickolas struggle to untangle himself from the clinging mess of the offending towel and sheets. When he got clear, Nickolas pushed his hair out of his eyes and gave Christoff a baleful look.

"Was that truly necessary?"

"Of course, what are little brothers for?"

Nickolas stood, shaking out his wings, and picked up the wet towel to deposit in the bathroom, all the while still glaring, causing Christoff's laughter to continue. After a moment the shower started. Still chuckling, Christoff picked up the sheets and blankets, throwing them back on the bed before returning to the living room. He grabbed a book and settled down to wait.

About half an hour later sounds of movement drifted out of the bedroom. "So how are you feeling today?" he called from the couch. Nickolas entered the room, still tying the wrap on his vest.

"I have certainly had better wake-up calls. That's for sure," he replied with a wry twist to his mouth. "You can hide, but be warned, retaliation will come when you least expect it."

"Yeah, right. You don't scare me," Chris said and started laughing again. "You really should have seen your face."

"No, that's all right. Someday I'll get to see yours." Nickolas smirked.

His laughter faded and Chris took a good look at his Alpha, searching for any telltale sign that would alert others to the fact that he hadn't taken his meds in two days.

"Don't worry, Chris, I'm Ok." Nick looked away, his expression serious.

Christoff nodded. "Good. Let's go get some breakfast."

They entered the cafeteria and wove their way through the tables toward the buffet counter. Christoff eyed the crowded room. There was a mix of fledged and unfledged people sharing the space. The presence of the grounded had his protective instincts teetering on the edge, so he watched everything with extra care.

Because of that, he noticed the wave of awareness flow across the Hunters scattered around the room. Nick was the rock thrown into the still pond and the ripples spread. The effect seemed unusually strong today. But considering his undrugged state, that shouldn't be too surprising. Heads snapped up and attention focused when they found Nickolas among them. The urge, no, *need*, that they all felt to protect Nickolas ran incredibly strong, and it was reflected in all the eyes that followed their progress across the room.

The grounded appeared to be oblivious to the silent call. At least most of them were. He met Jays's eyes and blinked when the doctor leaned back, watching everything. Chris reluctantly pulled his attention away from that particular grounded so he could nod to the Hunters he passed.

Once acknowledged, they returned to their meals, but he could see that a part of their attention stayed alert to their Alpha. *It's like all their focus suddenly centers on Nick. And you don't even see it, do you, Nicky? I've always noticed it, heck I feel it too, but I've always taken it for granted. Why? What is it?*

He swept the room again, avoided Jays's knowing stare, and crashed into Donald's. The other Hunter sent a questioning look his way, and Chris nodded ever so slightly. *Well, I think this sixth sense is going to come in handy now.*

He picked up a tray and followed Nick through the line, absently filling his plate with his usual farm-style breakfast. His brother's odd food choices caught his attention. He stopped sweeping the room for threats and nudged Nick.

"That's a bit unusual for you, isn't it? You don't usually like sweets much."

The first shiver of alarm started to run through Chris as he looked down at Nickolas's tray, piled with sweet fruit and pastries.

Nick shrugged and grinned self-consciously as he added another scoop of sugar to some strawberries. "It's just what I'm craving today."

"You're going to give me a toothache watching you eat all that. Here." Stabbing a hunk of steak, Christoff dropped it on his brother's plate. "That should at least balance out the sugar high."

Christoff shook his head and waved toward an empty table by the back wall. "Let's take that one."

Ian turned his wrist up and glanced at his watch. *Jays should be here soon.* Tiredly he leaned his elbows on the table and rested his face in his hands, rubbing his eyes. *I'm definitely too old for this. All-nighters are for the young.* A sigh escaped and he sat back before turning to look resignedly over at the cabinet on the wall. *Well, it's time. I should get it over with.*

He pushed away and stood. Every step was a battle to force himself over to the wall. With a viciousness he seldom showed to anyone other than Jays, he yanked the door to the cabinet open, revealing a pharmaceutical refrigerator along with shelves of supplies.

He pulled a vial out and then prepped a syringe before replacing the bottle in the fridge. He grabbed the rest of his supplies and set them down on the adjacent counter before closing the cabinet doors. Rolling up his sleeve, he used his teeth to tighten the tubing he wrapped around his arm and brought a vein to the surface. Then he picked up a needle and inserted it into his vein. A quick tug with his teeth and the tube released, and the vial started to fill with his blood. When it was full, he carefully changed it for the vial he had drawn from the bottle in the fridge, and he quickly gave himself the injection.

A hiss passed his teeth when the drug entered his system. He dropped the needle into the sharps box and dumped everything else into the cabinet. Then he closed his eyes at the brief wave of dizziness, grinding his teeth as he made his way back to his chair.

And Jessica doesn't like what she's given. He shook his head then focused on the monitor again, trying to ignore the pulse of the drug. Jessica was still lying on the bunk asleep, though her slight movements showed that her sleep was not as deep. *She should wake soon. I had better get this paper work done and my copies put away.*

The words on the page squirreled around and he rubbed his eyes. A few minutes later, the door opened and he smiled slightly. *Prompt, as usual Jays.*

He set his pen down then divided the papers and tucked half of them into his leather folder. The other half he clipped onto Jessica's chart. He smiled tiredly at Jays. "I hope you had a good night's sleep?"

His young protégée settled on the corner of the table and nodded. "Sound enough. Doesn't look like you've been to bed though?"

"Not yet. I sent the others off to sleep a few hours ago. But we can't leave her unmonitored yet. After her next meal, I'll get some rest. You should only have a few hours alone before the others return."

"How's she doing?"

He slid the chart over to Jays. The young man picked it up and started leafing through it. Ian rose out of his chair and stretched, rubbing the soreness in his arm.

"So, you were able to go in and get some of the tests done?"

He focused his eyes on the coffee pot that sat on the counter across the room then forced his feet to stay in line as he walked to it. He managed to pour himself a cup without incident. "Yes. After Nickolas got her to eat, her body couldn't sustain the outpouring of energy any longer. She fell into a deep enough sleep that we were able to take in some of the portable equipment. I wasn't comfortable taking her out of the room yet. We couldn't get all of the tests done of course, but we managed several. The results are there." He gestured with his cup at the chart Jays was holding. "Do you want a cup?" he asked, holding up an empty mug.

"No, thanks. I just came from the cafeteria." Jays looked up from the papers and over at him, smirking. "They're gathering already. You should have seen the response when Nick and Chris showed up."

"I'm not surprised. I've kicked them all out of here quite a few times since she arrived. They'll look to Nickolas for orders. They always have. Speaking of which, keep an eye on him for me, will you?"

"Why?"

"I noticed some odd behavior last night." He cradled his cup and walked back to the table where he sank into his chair, absentmindedly looking at the monitor. "Beyond your report of him stopping Jessica's suicide."

"Like what?"

"I think..." He trailed off as his mind slid pieces around on the mental game board that overlaid his world. Something was still missing. He looked up at his protégé and took a sip from his cup. "He wasn't as foggy as he should have been."

"Oh no. Chris hadn't taken his pills yesterday. Flynn had to force him."

"Chris I could see, it wouldn't be the first time. But, Nick? So what happened?"

Jays rose and started to pace. "I don't know where my brain went. I guess I got distracted by seeing Jessica again after so many years...and her condition.... Anyway I was still in shock that we succeeded in stopping her psychic suicide and I opened my big mouth. I used the word Caster in front of Chris. He picked up on it right away and nearly ripped my throat out. I couldn't talk to you last night 'cause the others were still here."

Ian pulled out the chair next to him. "Sit."

Jays slid into the chair but continued to bounce his legs agitatedly. "So, Flynn pulled a trank pistol on him. But the damage was done. He knows there are different types of Valkyries now and has already placed Nickolas as not a Hunter."

"Well that explains what Christoff wanted to talk to me about last night." He stared off into the distance and took a sip of his coffee.

"Do you think he'll tell Nick?"

"What do you think?" He set his mug down and leaned back in his chair studying his Second in command. "I think that is a definite, though he'll wait until he learns more, which he's already started trying to do. After which, I think we can count on him telling Nickolas."

They were both quiet for a moment, then Jays asked softly, "Is that such a bad thing?"

"It depends on the timing." He picked up his coffee and took a drink. "I guess we'll see what state Nick's in when he gets here."

"You don't think he'll take his pills? He was certainly edgy last night but not as aggressive as his brother."

"He wouldn't be. At least not yet."

Jays groaned, and he chuckled. "But it does mean that we might have a fledgling Seer practicing in our ranks. We're going to have to be alert. We can't let Gabriel find out if Nick is coming into his power. So, now, we have two to watch."

"Jessica and Nickolas. Speaking of which, she appears to be waking up," Jays commented, leaning forward to look at the readouts from a monitor in her room.

His gaze shifted to the video display and he watched her yawn, sitting up slowly, the confusion plain on her face. "Jays, go page Nickolas and get some food for her. Let's see how she responds today, shall we?"

Chris glanced around the table at the three Valkyries who had joined them. The dance of rank was a subtly fluid thing. Determined by strength and situation. But strength could mean so many things; physical, mental, or numbers. The one rank that never changed was Nickolas's Alpha. *But even that isn't quite true. He has to yield when enough of us push.*

Nick shoved the plate of steak to the side.

Donald caught his look and shoved the plate back then continued his conversation. "So, she fought through the tranks? I've never heard of that. Not even you did that, Kieran."

Kieran rubbed the Celtic knot around his neck and turned a glare on his cousin.

Nick shook his head, his eyes unfocused, and slathered a thick layer of honey on a piece of bread. "She did a lot of things I wouldn't have thought possible, Donald."

Chris shuddered at his sugar intake. "Eat the meat, Nicky."

"We've all been over to the Hub to try and get a look at her, but Ian keeps kicking us out." Kieran sat up and his pendant dropped to the end of its chain. "We were hoping you might be able to tell us anything?"

Swallowing his bite of bread, Nickolas pushed the steak aside with a bland look. "There's not much yet to tell. She's strong. But her metabolism's still unstable, so they're probably trying to stay on the safe side by keeping her isolated. She still isn't resigned to her fate and keeps fighting us. Give it some time. You'll all get a chance at her soon enough."

Irritated, Chris pulled the contested plate in front of himself and started to cut the steak up into strips. Nickolas continued to down an entire bakery in between answering the three Hunters' questions. Transferring some of the sliced meat back onto Nickolas's plate, he met his brother's exasperated look and locked stares.

Silence hit the table. Then, with a grimace, Nickolas looked down and stabbed a piece of the meat. He started to eat it and a collective breath released from the table's occupants. He and Donald exchanged a look, and his Second bridged the turbulence and engaged Nick with talk about the schedule for the day.

Such an obvious challenge had a better than even odds of turning physical. The fact that it hadn't caught attention. Chris scanned the room. Every clan member watched their table. Worry on their faces.

He smacked Nick's fingers when he started to reach for the honey again and pointed to the meat. Donald slipped the jar of honey to the other side of the table. Chris cast him a thankful look.

"Chris," Nick sighed. But before he could finish his sentence, Nickolas caught his breath; his body drew rigid and his face had turned pale as a sheet.

"Nick?" Christoff asked softly. He met Donald's eyes across the table. The same concern he felt reflected back at him. "Hey, Nick. Look at me."

Slowly, like he was moving through molasses, Nickolas turned toward him, and Chris could see the horror that filled his brother's eyes. Nick took a deep breath and his fork clattered to the table unnoticed when he unclenched his hands. "It's all right, Chris. I'm fine, it's passing," he said raggedly.

Not convinced, Christoff continued to watch him, trading worried looks with the others. About to demand an answer, Chris growled when the loud speaker interrupted him. "Nickolas, please report to the Hub. You are wanted in the observation Hub. Nickolas, please report to the Hub."

Nick pushed his plate away and stood. "Jess is awake, I guess my breakfast is over. I'll see you guys later."

Nickolas's hands shook, and Christoff reached out, but he stuffed his hands in his pockets and backed up, almost knocking his chair over. Kieran caught it and pulled it out of the way. Concerned, Chris rose to follow, but his brother shook his head.

"There's nothing you can do right now, Chris. Come find me later."

"Damn it, Nick."

"Later, Chris."

A growl escaped and he sank back into his chair when Nick walked away.

"What's going on, Chris?"

He met the solemn looks of the other Hunters then shook his head at Donald. "Not here. Kieran, why don't you get everyone together and we'll go out to the course. We could all use a good game. Dylan, you help him."

"Chris, we're not scheduled for the course today," Kieran said.

Something in the Beta Hunter's voice caught his attention. Kieran stared after Nick, pain fading from his eyes. He waited for Kieran to look back at him.

"Your point, Hunter?"

Kieran met his gaze. "Ian."

He sighed. "No choice. Do it."

"Yes, sir." He and Dylan pushed away from the table to start making the rounds and gather up the loitering Valkyries.

Chris pushed his chair back and stood. "Come on, Donald, let's get ourselves out to the obstacle course."

Side by side, they strode down the hall, and Christoff waited for Donald to break the silence. They stepped out into the fall sunshine, and he took a deep breath of the crisp air.

Donald stretched his wings. "We're not scheduled for drills today, Chris. Why the impromptu game?"

The Facility Valkyries flowed around them toward the practice field, so Chris slowed, allowing them to assemble on the grounds before he and Donald arrived. "Everybody's antsy from yesterday and the change in our schedules as a result. The new arrival last night is sending shock waves through our group, and I think a little exercise will do us all good."

Out in the open, between the buildings and the practice fields, Donald drew him to a halt.

"So what's going on? Is Nick all right?" Donald asked.

"I don't know. You saw him yesterday?"

"Yes."

"Come on. Kieran has the teams divided." He started walking. "I didn't want to draw attention to all of us gathering. We can do that on the field. Nick has stopped taking the anti-aggression medication."

"What!"

"Something happened to us at the start of the recovery. Before we entered the target house, I had a massive pain rip through my head. I think it was worse for Nick. After that, he started trying to hide something."

They reached the gathering at the edge of the course. All eyes turned toward him. "Kieran, set everyone up with full jewel harnesses. Then get them started on warm-ups. We're going to go all out, so prepare them for that. I really need the violence today."

"All out? But what about the medics?"

"What about them?"

"Right. I'll let the teams know. We'll organize some spotters."

"Just make sure the spotters are playing too." With the others occupied, he turned back to Donald and continued the conversation quietly. "Turns out he was tracking her through her blood somehow. He told me last night he could see pictures of her in his head. So he's decided he won't take the pills anymore."

"This must be the sort of thing Ian wanted us to watch out for. That means he knows what this drug is for."

"That thought had crossed my mind too."

"How do we keep him safe through this, Chris?"

He ran his hand through his hair. "I don't know. I'm playing it by ear. I need more information. I don't like it. I hate feeling like I can't trust Ian, but he's the only one who can give us answers."

"You handle that part. I'll get a discreet guard organized. We can't leave him alone."

"He's getting aggressive."

Donald looked out over the assembled Valkyries. "Right. Pairs, no one alone. Not that two would be able to stop him, but at least one can run for help."

"He's going to be vulnerable while he gets the drug out of his system and learns to cover up the fact."

"So what happened to him at breakfast?"

Chris shrugged and shook his head. He watched the teams warm up. The course was a challenging one, specially designed for the abilities of the Valkyries. It was comprised of ground and aerial obstacles. The "game" as they called it combined the different skills involved in capture the flag and laser tag with martial arts all played out on an obstacle course. There were different levels of play. *But today we're playing for keeps, when you get hit, it* hurts. *Better hope you're not in the air when that happens.*

He looked back at Donald. "Have you ever heard the term Caster?"

"No, why?"

"Jays called the new fledgling a Caster on the way home last night. She started to glow, and he freaked out. The nearest I've ever seen him to panicking. He said she could have killed all of us if Nick hadn't gotten her to stop."

"Killed you how?"

"Psychically."

Donald whistled. "Ian *and* Jays, huh? Damn."

They were both quiet for a moment. Donald started to stretch lightly.

Chris rubbed the bridge of his nose. "After we've gotten him stabilized, then it's our turn. We're going to quietly and systematically free ourselves a few at a time."

"Then what, Chris? How do we keep *that* a secret?"

He met Donald's eyes but didn't answer.

"Shit." Donald folded his arms and looked up at the sky. "You know he's just going to love having a shadow."

"Too bad. He may be Alpha, but when it comes to his own safety, he doesn't know squat. And on this matter, Donald, you answer to *me*, no one else, no matter what Nickolas says. Got it?"

"Understood." After a pause, Donald asked, "Are you going to tell him what you've learned?"

"Not until I have more information. He has too much on his shoulders as it is."

Kieran joined them, handing over two jewel harnesses. "The flags have been run up, Chris. I think we're ready to go as soon as everyone has finished warming up."

"Good."

Taking his harness, Donald looked at him. "Remind me again why we're going all out?"

"Because I want to hurt something," Christoff stated softly.

Donald moaned, but Chris caught the understanding glimmering in his eyes. "Fun. Chris is out for blood. This is just gonna suck."

A savage grin spread as he started strapping his harness on, making sure that his wings were free and not binding. The harness had sensor jewels in the front, back, and on both sides. There were also individual jewels to strap onto arms and legs for incapacitation shots. And last but not least, a thin band for the head. Looking over at Donald, his grin widened. "Make sure you're set for stun."

"Are you sure of this, Chris? There could be casualties at this level. If someone gets a fatal shot in the air, they'll drop like a lead balloon when they pass out from the stun," Donald said as he checked his laser pistol then holstered it on his thigh.

"Then make sure your team has emergency plans. You're leading red team, I'll take blue." And with that, he spread his wings and launched into the air like a rocket, slamming into a red team member midair, somersaulting with him. He punched the chest jewel and felt the other Valkyrie go slack in his arms, unconscious. The Hunter's weight pulled at his arms and he landed, setting him gently on the ground. He looked around at the surprised expressions on everyone's faces.

"Blue team to me. Let's get this game going."

Nickolas wove through the halls, everything a blur. The vision he just experienced more real, at the moment, than his physical location. He tried to snap out of it and hide how shaken the occurrence left him. *I know Chris spotted it. And Donald too, I think. This is going to be harder than I thought to keep quiet.*

The flash of vision was relentless. He shook his head and stumbled; his hand shot out to catch himself.

Chris strung up by chains on a wall. Donald dead.

"No," he whispered.

The blood seeping into the stone of the floor.

He pushed away from the wall, the hall he walked an odd overlay of the vision.

Chris staring blankly down at his Second's body, where he lay sprawled.

Nick fisted the hair at his temple and punched the other into the wall. "Go away."

Labored breathing echoed in his ears. He was afraid to close his eyes and have the pictures be even more vivid. Sweat ran down his cheek and he wiped it on his shoulder. After a few deep breaths, the visions faded into memories as opposed to photographs.

On shaky legs, he finished the walk to the Hub.

He paused at the door, and after a quick check to establish a firm mask in place, he opened the door into the medical facility.

Ian and Jays broke off their conversation to look up at him when he entered.

"Good morning, Nickolas. Did you get enough sleep?"

Nickolas had to work hard to keep his expression unchanged as Ian's gaze raked over him. Inside, he felt like a roller coaster. *He can't know what I've done. Can he?* "I'm fine. How's she doing?"

Ian cocked an eyebrow before he turned back to the files he had been leafing through. "She made it through the night. That's a good first step."

Nick stopped in front of the island that contained the bank of monitors. Five screens were lit. His eyes roamed them until he found Jessica's set.

Just like last night, she paced her tiny cubicle in agitation. Hunched, she had her arms wrapped around her. A shiver came and went. Sometime during the night, Ian had managed to remove her blood-stained and tattered clothes. She now had on the plain cotton shorts all fledglings wore. His thighs twitched in remembrance.

She also wore a triangular halter that tied around her neck and below her breasts that gave free access to her emerging wings. It was more for the illusion of modesty than anything else, since she didn't have privacy for even the most basic of functions.

"Has she been doing this long? She looks cold."

Ian walked up behind him. He couldn't keep from tensing slightly in memory, but Nickolas didn't look away from Jessica.

"No, she only just woke. She's going through her first cycle of stage two disorientation. From my experience with you, I expect the amnesia hit her hard."

Nick shot a look over his shoulder and met the green of Ian's eyes. So close. He shivered in reaction then pushed away from the screens and started to pace around the room, fanning his wings slightly.

"Are you all right, Nickolas?"

He realized what he was doing and clamped down on his emotions, forcing his wings to still. "Sorry, I'm fine."

"Memories can be a hard thing to control. Learning to shield from them in times of stress is a difficult ability to acquire. Be careful you don't get locked into them." Ian caught his eyes. "Focus is the key."

Just then, a trolley came banging through the door and broke the trance from Ian's eyes. He jumped. The cryptic message circled in his head. His eyes shot to the woman who started to unload several large plates, most with meat, some with a selection of various other tidbits.

And he remembered the reason he was here. He closed his eyes and took a deep breath. "Feeding time at the zoo, I guess."

Ian's disapproving gaze followed him as he walked over to the pile and started sorting plates. "There's no point in lying about it. I've been there, I know. Is there any order you want me to do this in? How much should I take in to start?"

Jays joined him at the trolley and helped sort the plates. "Start with the meat first, that's what she needs the most of. If we can get her to eat at least half of that before we give her any of the other items, that would be good. Her sugar intake needs to be kept really low until she's done with the final stage, or it will mess up her metabolism. She won't be able to take in the right balance of nutrients if she's trying to digest the sugar. So don't take any of the desserts in. I don't know why they even brought them. The fruit will be quite enough sugar."

"Take in what you can comfortably carry, Nick." He looked up and regarded Ian warily. "We'll be watching on the monitor, so as soon as she is done, we can bring more to you."

The challenge of maintaining an even keel looked to be harder than he had imagined. Nick nodded and pushed his memories, of being the one held against his will by Ian, to the back of his mind. He picked up two of the largest plates of meat and walked with Jays over to her door. The click as the lock disengaged resounded through Nickolas and he froze. It was only the pointed stare from Jays as the doctor held it open that got him moving.

Jessica stood near the back wall; surprise and fear chased across her face. The door closed behind him and he had to swallow before he managed a smile for her benefit. He set the plates on the table and, ignoring the fear, sat down. Patting the bed next to him, he watched her reactions closely.

"I...remember you," she said finally, slowly. "You...brought me here."

"Yes, that was necessary. What else do you remember?" he asked quietly.

Her arms wrapped around herself, and she leaned against the wall next to the sink. "No. I don't think so," she replied, furrowing her brow in concentration.

"No, what?"

"Necessary. I don't think it was necessary. But I can't remember why. Everything is all jumbled." She started pacing again, squeezing her injured thigh. "Can I go now? I don't think I like it here."

He closed his eyes briefly and shook his head. "No. I'm sorry. I wish I could say yes. You should come and eat breakfast. It will help clear your mind."

"I don't know. I am hungry, but..."

"Jessica, you need to eat."

"Jessica...that's my name." She took a couple of limping steps before she reached the corner then looked at him. "You're Nickolas?"

"Yes. You remember." An uncharacteristic urge to play swept over him and he stood, dropping her an elegant bow, at total odds with their situation. A smile pulled at the corners of his mouth. "We were never properly introduced. My name is Nickolas Sinclair."

He held out his hand. "Would you care to join me for breakfast?"

Amusement warred with wariness, but amusement eventually won out and she came forward, placing her hand in his. That small sign of trust made him want to kick himself. He tucked her into the space behind the table and sat down next to her, sliding a plate full of sliced steak in front of her.

She poked at the meat then took a tentative nibble. She cast a questioning glance at the other plate and he felt his stomach grind at the thought of his abandoned food, but he shook his head. "No, thank you. Actually I just came from breakfast. I thought I'd keep you company. You'll find you're going to be hungrier than you thought."

After the first slice of beef, she seemed to lose interest in him as her appetite asserted itself. Not wanting to distract her focus from the food, Nickolas sat quietly watching her move, his thoughts running through recent events. She finished the first plate and pulled the second one forward, digging into it with a single-mindedness that Nickolas remembered all too clearly.

He studied her face as she ate, and he could see her slowly working to put all of the pieces together. "So, are things becoming clearer now? Do you remember yesterday yet?"

"Mostly. Though I suppose I'm not in a position to remember things I've forgotten, now, am I?"

"Astute." He chuckled then sobered. "This is only the first of many cycles you're going to go through. Your degree of amnesia and confusion will lesson in each episode over the next week as your mind changes."

"Lucky me." An irritated look crossed her face and she continued to chew.

He watched her gaze dart around the small enclosure. And he knew she was taking in all details, anything that might help her to escape. It's what he would have done.

Had done.

He stretched his legs out and sighed. "So is there anyone we can let know about your condition? So they won't worry. No one else was home, but you obviously didn't live alone."

"I'm sure they already know. I'm surprised they didn't beat you to me, actually." She shoved the empty plate aside.

The door opened and she jumped, panic flaring between them. Her body tensed when she realized that she was trapped between the table and him.

"Jess, look at me." He grabbed her chin and pulled her head around, locking eyes. "It's just Jays bringing you more to eat."

She tried to jerk her head away, but he squeezed, eliciting a soft growl from her. Her eyes tracked Jays when he came within her periphery, shooting daggers.

The doctor switched the empty plates for full and cast Nick an apologetic look before leaving. Nick let Jessica pull away, and her head pivoted to follow Jays out the door, but he didn't miss the accusation lurking in her eyes, or the pain that flowed around him.

He ground his teeth against the pain and shifted slightly to the side so their thighs no longer touched. The pain lessened, but still swirled.

He reached out to one of the new plates and picked up a piece of pear, pressing it into her hand. "Here, try this."

Her fingers curled into the squishy fruit and she glanced down, away from the closed door. Her nose twitched and she took a nibble. The pain dissipated like fog in the sun and she reached out for more, but he pulled the plate away with a chuckle.

"Na. You need to finish the meat first. Then dessert."

With a glare, she pulled the other plate closer and started to eat.

"Your body needs the protein and iron for building. You'll crave sugar something fierce, but too much becomes a problem when you change."

She snorted and looked at him out of the corner of her eye, but she kept eating.

"So, who would know? It wasn't family who reported your condition according to the retrieval documents. Is there a phone number you want to give us to call someone?"

"No. And even if they did have one, I want to see Aurora and my brother about as much as I want to be here. The only person that'll miss me is my old guardian, May. But I have no idea how to get ahold of her. She had gone out of town unexpectedly the night you showed up."

"You have family in Colorado? We should still inform them. The rate of change is much higher within family groupings."

He trailed off. She stared at him like he had grown another head. He looked over his shoulder just to make sure nothing had popped out of the nonexistent woodwork.

"No, I don't have family in Colorado. Are you serious?"

Thrown by her response, he snagged a slice of pear.

"And I really don't think Robin needs to worry about the possibility of fledging, since he's had his wings for ten years now."

He nearly choked on the bite of pear. Ten years? "What? I know everyone who came through when Chris changed. And no one with the name Robin did."

"Of course not. He's free."

Free?

People are changing outside of the Facility? He blinked then turned to stare into the camera lens in the ceiling corner. Then, as if to rub his face in the lies, another wave of feeling pressed in on him. Despair, so similar to his that he almost missed that it came from her, clogged his throat. He pushed it back.

I opened this Pandora's box, I need to deal with it.

He picked up more of the pear and fought his silent battle.

After a few moments of quiet, she looked up at him. "May I have something to drink?"

"Right, sorry." He leaned his elbows on his knees and rubbed the heels of his hands against his eyes and called, "Jays?"

Still resting his head in his hands, he tipped it to look at her. "Are you going to attack him?"

"Can I?"

His lips twitched. "No."

"You're really no fun."

The door clicked and he felt her tense. A low growl rumbled in her throat. Jays crossed the distance, the doctor's gaze traveling between the two of them, and set a pitcher of milk and two glasses down on the table.

"Ian thought you might be thirsty as well, Nick."

Surprise flashed into wariness, but Nickolas nodded his thanks and Jays slipped out of the cell. Pouring each of them a glass of milk, he handed one to her and she took a sip.

"How long have you been a Valkyrie?" She picked up a slice of meat with her other hand and sat back.

His thoughts full of his own questions, he met her eyes and saw her understanding glimmer. Her answers would be bought with his. Biting back temper, he swirled the milk in his glass.

"Fifteen years." Temper to match his swelled in her gaze at his short answer. He downed the contents of his glass then cocked his head. "So, your brother is a Valkyrie?"

She slowly chewed her piece of meat. The white column of her throat rippled as she swallowed, fixing his gaze. He shivered his wings and broke the trance, a growl forming in his chest. She narrowed her eyes at him. "Yes. I just said that, didn't I? Why do you stay here? You could fly anywhere and be free."

This wasn't going to get either of them anywhere. One of them would have to give. Terse, untrusting answers wouldn't help either of them. He sighed and relaxed back again, taking several slices of pear with him. "Leaving never appeared to be an option before. Besides, this is all I've ever known. My parents got caught in the change near the beginning. So Chris and I were exposed young, I guess."

"Chris? He's the other Hunter with you yesterday? He's your brother?"

"Uh-uh, my turn. You said you were surprised that *they* hadn't come for you. Who else do you know?"

"That's two."

He smiled. This whole exchange felt oddly surreal. But that didn't stop the contentment that snaked through him from matching wits with her.

Her eyes had started to twinkle as well. She pushed the last couple of strips of meat around with her finger. "I was just surprised that Robin hadn't made sure that Hunters from Aurora got to me before the Facility did."

That gave him something to chew on. Before she could formulate her next question, he cut in. "And yes, Chris is my brother and was the other Hunter tracking you yesterday. Do you see your brother often?"

Snapping her mouth shut, she glared at him and took a bite. "That was hardly fair." But then she pushed the plate away and sighed. "No. I haven't seen him since he fledged."

"Then you don't actually know that he's all right." She was assuming. He relaxed slightly in relief.

"No, he's fine. There's no way Marcus wouldn't have let me know if something had happened to him. How did you end up here? You said your parents changed?"

The ground under his mental feet turned to quicksand. His view of the world, his beliefs had all taken a giant hit in the last forty-eight hours. What was one more really? But somehow the truth that people were safely completing the change outside of the Facility left him reeling. He answered her absently. "My family was in the second and third groups to change. I was eight when they all fledged. Ten when my parents died. I don't think Chris even remembers them. Something happened to send all of the early Valkyries insane. They hadn't developed the aggression inhibitor yet and everyone except my grandfather lost their humanity. They fought. During the struggle, most were killed, but some managed to escape into the mountains to form the wild pack up there."

He shook himself clear and met her eyes. "At least, that's what we've been taught."

"Aurora is in the mountains."

Silence descended as they stared at one another. Then Nick felt his gaze swing away to stare into the camera lens again. *There's no way Ian isn't watching us and listening.*

The unblinking eye stared at them mercilessly.

"What happened to the rest of your family?" He turned back to her. She had pulled the plate of pear closer. "Do you know how you got infected?"

She picked up a slice of fruit and sat back then absently rubbed her back against the wall.

With sympathy he remembered the incessant itching.

She pressed the bridge of her nose then rubbed between her eyes. "Both my parents turned when I was five. So I don't really remember much from before. I have no idea how they got infected. They died when I was nine, and Robin and I stayed with May. He left me when I was fourteen."

She ate the pear.

"She always seemed to know things. I remember that." She continued after a moment. "She knew they were going to die that night. She came in to say good-bye to Robin and I. I was too young to understand, but looking back, I can see that Robin knew."

"What happened?"

"I have no idea. No one ever gave me the details. But it's safe to assume it wasn't by natural means. They were both perfectly healthy."

She met his eyes and he could see how clear they were. It wouldn't last, he knew. But for the moment, she knew exactly where she was and what was happening.

"Why wouldn't you let me go?"

He couldn't maintain the eye contact so he shifted, folding his arms across his chest and staring at the blank wall. "It's not safe. You know that."

"You do realize that's a lie, don't you?"

He pushed to his feet and started to pace the small confines. Lies within lies. Which were the lies?

"You could help me get out."

He cast her a slashing look. "No. You would die. Changing unsupervised, without help, isn't possible. There is no doubt about the facts of that."

"Then come with me."

He stumbled a step. The quick snapshot of the two of them flying over craggy rocks flashed through his mind and he pushed it away, ruthlessly. Come with her? And where would they go?

"It's not safe," he repeated.

"I won't sta..." The high-pitched keening struck a familiar chord and his head whipped to look at her. She had curled up on her side, clutching her head. Blood ran freely from her nose. He took the few strides to the toilet and ripped off a handful of tissue.

Dropping to his knees next to her, he wadded the paper against her nose. His free hand stroked her hair back from her face. Shivers wracked her body, and remembered pain danced through his mind.

"Hush. It'll pass in a moment. Just breathe through it." A thin trickle of blood snaked down her cheek from her ear. He wiped it with his sleeve. "It's called a dazzle headache. They'll hit you in random moments for the next couple of weeks."

He continued to pet her hair. The soft springy strands slipped through his fingers. After a couple of deep breaths, she opened her eyes and groaned. The pupils of her eyes worked independently, adjusting at light speed to process incoming data. Unfortunately, her processor wasn't quite up to speed yet.

"I think I'm going to be sick."

"Keep your eyes closed for a few more minutes. Your eyes are trying to take in more than your brain can accept right now. The inside of your head's going to feel like a bruised melon for a while."

She tried to sit up, but he pressed back on her shoulder, keeping her down. "Relax, don't push it. There's nothing you can do to hurry the changing process, and it turns your brain into Swiss cheese as it remakes you."

"I should have paid more attention when they tried to teach me about this whole thing. After my parents died, I didn't want anything to do with Valkyries anymore. Guess I was a stubborn teen."

He laughed and checked the tissue. "Really? Only as a teen?"

A smile curved her lips.

"Looks like the blood has slowed. I would wait a few more minutes before opening your eyes though. But that's just my opinion. Your eyes should settle down pretty quick. Of all the senses coming in, sight is the most disorienting. When your hearing changes, it isn't as disruptive, since you're in a quiet cell."

"From what you said yesterday, I take it things were difficult for you during your time?"

He rubbed his fingertips across her scalp and through her hair. Echoes of her pain, or memories of his own, slowly faded. "You could say that. Conversely, you could say I was difficult for them. Even though they knew me, they didn't expect for me to react in the ways that I did. We have a lot in common in that department."

She snorted and cracked open her eyes. He saw and paused. "How is it?"

She blinked slowly and looked around. "Strange."

"Like looking through binoculars? Or a microscope?"

"At the same time." She gulped and tried to sit up.

He helped her. "Ah, those are the worst. Anyway, I was uncooperative. Caused a bunch of damage, gave them a few heart attacks, that sort of thing. Got hit with Xanthar a lot. Trust me when I say you want to avoid that experience."

"There's a lot of experiences I wish to avoid. Where I'm sitting for starters. You seem to have some level of power here, why won't you let me go? What is right about kidnapping and keeping someone against their will like this?"

He stood and tossed the bloody tissue into the toilet. "I've been where you are. I know exactly how much fun you're having. But the isolation laws are what they are. And they are there for good reason. How many early fledglings were hurt or killed by people out of ignorance?" He turned back to her, ruthlessly suppressing the memory that tried to surface. "And how many innocents were hurt or killed by fledges?"

She huffed out a breath, obviously not moved by his argument. "I think there were a lot fewer than we've been lead to believe."

"And maybe not. Either way, I don't have a choice. I'm not willing to put others at risk. And for some unfathomable reason, I'm not willing to let you be at risk either."

"We all have choices."

"Only if they are presented."

"Or created."

Like two wolves in a standoff, they stared at one another, neither willing to give ground.

Chapter Eight

"Good game, Donald. You had some superior tactics this time. We were pretty evenly matched." Christoff sat on the wooden bench at the sidelines of the obstacle course and worked at stripping off the harness and sensors from his arms and legs. He massaged his stunned left arm and looked up at Donald.

"Yeah, but it still wasn't enough to get your flag, now, was it?" Donald joined him on the bench, handed him a towel, then added his harness to the pile.

"You were close. You and Kieran working together almost brought me down." He wiped his face then draped the cloth around his neck. "With my arm stunned useless, getting the flag up the pole posed a challenge. If you had gotten there just a little quicker, you could have stopped me from raising your flag and taken ours. So, I would call that close."

Chris stared out over the field. Both teams worked together, stripping off harnesses and carrying the injured and those stunned unconscious off of the field. "Did you have a chance to talk to your team?"

"Yes, but not in great detail. Kieran and I will take the first watch. Since the two of us are in the best shape after the way you guys slaughtered us today."

"What are you talking about? I only had a couple people left standing, myself. Your team did some damage, let me tell you." He accepted the water bottle one of the Hunters passed out, nodding his thanks. "How many injuries did you get? I had a couple wrenched wings and a broken hand..."

"We had a broken arm and a sprained ankle, but it was better than I had feared. I expect the infirmary will have something to say about this, though."

"Probably. But it was fun, wasn't it?" He grinned and capped his water bottle before setting it down.

Laughing at him, Donald agreed. "Correct, as usual. We're going to take a shower and grab some lunch before we find Nickolas."

He stood and dropped his towel on the bench then stretched, shaking the arm that had taken the hit. He looked over at Donald. "Didn't you get hit?"

Donald grinned even wider and just shook his head. Then without any warning, his Second punched him in his stunned arm before replying, "Nope. And that was for knocking Dylan out before the game had even started."

Swearing, he shook his painfully tingling arm vigorously, then grumbled, "Where's Kieran?"

They took their time walking back toward the main building, trailing in the wake of the rest of the Hunters. Some turned in the direction of the Hub, to take friends to get patched up. "He's already gone to shower. We'll meet in the Hub."

"Nick should still be with Jessica. I'm going to head there and stay with him until you guys arrive." They parted at the door, and Christoff waved as he headed for the Hub.

Still rubbing his arm, he opened the door to the Hub and stopped on the threshold. Pandemonium reigned as Ian and Jays treated the injured Valkyries while prying the tale of how they received the injuries in the first place from them.

The sight gave him pause, and he started to back up and let the door close. Somehow, even facing away from the door, Ian still knew he was there.

"Not one more step, Christoff. Get in here."

Resigned, he stepped inside and let the door close. Then he walked over to Ian and nodded to the Valkyries still waiting for the doctor's attention before leaning against the wall. Dev, Flight leader for Third Flight, smiled at him while Jays patched him up. "That was a great game, Chris. We need to do that more often. It felt amazing to really let loose."

He gave Dev a matching grin that quickly faded at the look in Ian's pale green eyes.

"Chris, when I am done here, you and I are going for a walk."

"Yes, sir." He stared at the doctor's back for a moment then asked, "How's Jessica today? Is Nick still with her?"

Chris walked over to the monitoring station to look at the camera screen showing her cell. Jessica paced restlessly while Nickolas sat at ease on her bunk, the remains of several plates stacked on a tray next to him.

"She's doing better today. She still isn't cooperative, but Nickolas is making progress with her. He was able to get her to eat. And he's gotten her to talk as well. There," Ian said, patting the arm of the Valkyrie he had just bandaged. "We'll take a look at that tomorrow. Jays you can handle the rest. Come on, Christoff."

The doctor walked out of the Hub without a pause. With a sigh, he followed Ian's white-coated back into the corridor.

Trailing Ian in silence, he took a deep breath to settle his nerves. *Where in blazes are we going?* He wondered until, pushing through an outside door, Ian took a path that led all the way out to the edge of the Facility's grounds.

Gardens filled the strip of property between the working buildings and the river. Paths wound around lush flowerbeds, and the only sign of the control placed on them was the tall fence topped with razor wire that stood in the distance.

The path they walked opened up into a circular garden that contained a gazing ball resting on a pedestal. Ian stopped. Christoff stood at the edge of the garden and watched the man who controlled their lives stare out over the river.

The only movement to break his stillness was the clenching of his fists, and Chris shifted uneasily at this small sign of the doctor's feelings. He waited for Ian to break the silence.

He knew a reprimand was coming, and deserved, but it shouldn't have warranted this level of anger. A moment later, Ian spoke; the softness of his voice didn't deceive Chris. He was pissed.

"Just what did you think you were doing, having an all-out war without supervision?"

"It's not like we haven't drilled at those levels before, Ian."

"Yes, but not without medical staff overlooking," Ian replied harshly, looking over his shoulder and pinning him with his gaze.

Chris fought not to drop his eyes, but he couldn't hold out, and his sight dropped to the gravel. A soft growl escaped and he cut it off, instead he turned to pace around the circle.

"That's the problem, isn't it? We didn't have permission to do what we did. That's what it comes down to. What difference would it have made, Ian? It's not like you could have prevented anything from happening if something went wrong, or are you up to catching a falling Valkyrie and I don't know it?" He winced and took a breath before he said anything else he might regret.

Ian turned and crossed his arms, staring at him. Chris's wings twitched nervously, and he shot a glance at his face then dropped his look just as quickly. He broke a branch from the nearest bush and started shredding the leaves off of it, continuing his pacing.

"We're all adults here, Ian, well most of us are at least," he amended, thinking of sixteen-year-old Aiden. "We are skilled and know what we're doing. After the hunt yesterday, and bringing Jessica in, we needed something to vent the pressure that I saw building. This seemed like the best outlet to me. You, of all people, know how different we are from the unfledged. The fighting gives us a controlled outlet for the aggression."

Ian continued to stare. Chris's steps faltered to a stop.

"Are you finished?"

He dropped his eyes at the softly spoken question and straightened his spine. Ian moved. Even on the gravel, his step fell silent. "I did not need this today, Christoff. I have enough problems without needing to spend time patching up injuries. I'm sure if you had put your mind to it, you could have come up with a better solution."

"Not really," he muttered under his breath. A breeze swirled around them, lifting the ends of Ian's lab coat, reminding Chris of wings.

"What was that?"

Chris cleared his throat. "I'm sorry, Ian. I still think it was the best choice I could have made."

"And why is that?"

He didn't dare turn to follow Ian as the doctor circled him. He shrugged.

"What am I going to do with all of you?" Ian finally sighed.

"You won't be able to hold our hands forever."

"I know that, Chris. But you *are* my responsibility. I can't stand to see any of you get hurt. You have no idea what's at stake."

That caught his attention and he turned his head to look at the doctor. Most of the anger seemed to have drained out of him, and he stood studying him. Chris fidgeted.

"If we don't know the stakes, whose fault is that?"

Ian's shoulders slumped and he ran his hand through his short grey hair. "I can fight against it, but I can't change it. The time has come. I've done my best to keep as many of you safe as I could, but so many slipped through my fingers."

He crossed the circle and sank down onto a bench. "The group who set this virus loose continues to keep a close eye on everything. They're still tinkering, hoping that one day they'll figure out what went wrong. Or how they can use it. Some factions are still trying to work out how to stop it."

"We don't belong to them! We're victims."

"They don't care about that, Chris, and they never will. Thanks to Siobhan, we've managed to preserve most of your rights on paper, but in reality?" He shrugged. "I try to protect you as much as I can, Chris, but so many are taken from me."

"So it's true? We are just prisoners, a part of this sick experiment?"

"Prisoners? Compared to what? We all are prisoners of one kind or another. Some more so than others. You're the control group, Chris, there's nothing I can do for that." Across the circle, he caught the flash of pain that Ian tried to conceal. "I have seen enough people, family, friends, those I've been responsible for, die or worse in my lifetime. You don't even know your potential."

"Then tell me. What are they hiding from us?" Concerned at how old Ian suddenly looked, he came forward and crouched at his feet.

"They have no clue what they let loose. You know you were infected by a virus that mutated you. That's the cover story spread to everyone. And it's true to a certain extent. They think of it as a disease, something like AIDs, with the underlying hope that a cure for the virus can be found. What isn't told, what they don't want to acknowledge, is that it isn't a disease. The virus triggered a sudden jump in our species' evolution. They've managed to slow the spread slightly, but there's no stopping it.

"The species of Homo sapiens is changing to Homo valkyrius. And we did it to ourselves."

He looked up into Ian's lined face, his pale green eyes full of shadows.

"But, how?" Chris pulled away and looked out across the garden, trying not to let the surprise show. Birds dove over the flowers that still bloomed despite the cold of fall.

"The science is too complex to go into; you have the basics. There's more important information you need to know at the moment."

Ian's fingers lightly turned his head back to the conversation. "Chris, everything is changing. I need you to get everyone ready."

"But, Nick..."

"Will be too busy." Old, yet nimble, fingers gently brushed the bangs out of his eyes. "Your wings are the most obvious sign of your change, but they aren't the only. I've had twenty-five years to research this. Mentally, emotionally, you are different. How you form attachments, your social structure, is much more like a wolf pack. How you exhibit aggression or show affection with one another are prime examples of pack behavior. And a pecking order has developed. A system of rank. The strongest members act as leaders while the others continue to compete until they fall into Beta and Gamma positions.

"But there's a not quite so obvious change. The species has a caste structure."

"Caste?"

"Like insects, with specialized aspects, worker bees, drones, queens. You're a Hunter. That's the most prominent caste. The next level is Seers and Casters. If you think of it like a pyramid, the Hunters are the foundation, with roughly seventy-five percent of the population forming the base. The next level is divided in half, with Casters and Seers being roughly equal. They form twenty-four percent of the rest of the Valkyrie population."

Chris swallowed. His mind raced with the new knowledge. "Where does Nick fit in?"

"I should explain what the castes are first. You're familiar with Hunter attributes, better sight, smell, and hearing. But there are some other things you might not have noticed. You have a natural grasp of tactics and for working in teams. Just like a pack. Now, Casters and Seers have some different abilities.

"They usually don't have quite the improvement in senses as a Hunter, though they still far surpass those who are unfledged. Their skills lie more in the realm of the mind. Psychic ability. A Seer talent is any power that is worked within an individual and stays confined to the mind. Visions, dreams, that sort of thing. Caster talents are psychic power projected. Like telekinesis.

"Your question about Nick, that's a difficult one to answer. I don't exactly know where he fits in."

He stared into Ian's green eyes. "But...wouldn't he be a Seer?"

One eyebrow arched and he realized his mistake. He lurched to his feet and started to pace.

"Now why would you think that, I wonder?" the doctor asked too softly behind him.

He gave in to the need to move his wings and fanned them out. His pacing increased.

"Chris? Nickolas is not taking the drugs anymore, is he?" Chris froze, his wings half furled. "You forget who I am, Christoff. I could tell last night. So what happened?"

He snapped his wings closed and resumed his pacing while he thought furiously about what to tell Ian. Finally, he realized the truth was the only thing he could tell. He stopped and looked out over the river to the buildings and trees on the far side. "While we were out chasing down Jessica, we missed our pills. Flynn caught on to me pretty quick, but no one realized what was happening to Nick. He didn't exhibit the usual aggression, or at least not too badly. But he did start to behave oddly. Both Donald and I noticed it. Every time I was sure we had lost her for good, Nick suddenly hared off in an unexpected direction.

"Then, later when we were on the ferry, he had an argument with Flynn and stormed off to think. I followed him, and while we were standing out on the deck, a feral Valkyrie talked to him...in his head..."

"What!"

He spun around to look at Ian. He couldn't remember ever seeing him look so livid before. "He said she was asking for us to release Jessica."

The sight of Ian mastering his temper was a new experience, and he was unsure whether to go on or not, but then Ian waved at him irritably to continue. "He told me later, after we got home, that when he touched something Jessica had touched, he would get a picture, and feelings, I think, of what she had been doing and where she had gone. He decided after all that had happened yesterday to quit taking the pills and see where that led him. That's why I took everyone out to the course today. I couldn't think of a better place where we wouldn't draw attention so I could discuss this with them."

"You could try the gym. There'd be a bit less damage."

"Yes, sir." He looked at his feet. "We are forming a guard to protect him during the detox period."

"He'll need it," Ian said unhappily. "You have no idea what you're up against. There's nothing I can say to get you to change your minds, is there?"

"No."

"Do you have any idea how powerful he is? I have no clue how he's going to react to the changes yet. I'm not even sure what changes will take place. All I do know is that Gabriel will do anything to get his hands on Nick. I've spent the last fifteen years protecting him, from himself, and those who would like to dissect him like a lab rat. And if Gabriel finds out about this, he'll finally have the power to get what he has wanted since Nick's fledging. I don't know what Nick is, Chris, but he isn't just a Seer."

Walking slowly up to Ian, Christoff looked down at him for a moment before he crouched in the gravel.

"And what about Jessica?" he asked softly. Ian's sober gaze made Christoff swear.

"I don't know, Chris, but keeping both her and Nickolas hidden now may be beyond me. They are something more, that's all I can tell you, though I have my suspicions."

He trailed off, turning inward. Christoff waited for his attention to return. "Keep up with the guard on Nickolas. He's going to need to learn control on many different levels. Think of it as mental fine muscular control. Tell him he needs to learn to focus his awareness; visualize a spider in a web, and all the lines that radiate out from the center. If he plucks one, focuses on it, he'll learn things. Right now I suspect he is flailing around in his web and is randomly brushing all the threads. If he stays in the center and doesn't touch anything, he won't see more than he might want. Spin a cocoon of silk around himself, and he will stop most chance encounters also. With practice, he'll learn the best ways for himself."

Ian glanced at his wrist and stood. "Times up. We need to get back to the Hub."

They walked back in silence.

Chris's thoughts turned inward as he struggled with how the new information fit. Castes? The concept seemed surreal. But the knowledge fit into a place inside, he couldn't deny. He barely noticed their route back, but the snort of amusement from Ian when they walked through the doors into the Hub brought him out of his contemplation.

None of the Valkyries who had come in for medical attention had left yet. A seething mass of bodies jockeyed for position around the console containing the video monitors.

Ian shook his head then caught Chris's eye. Laughter, mixed with something he couldn't define, lit the green depths. Chris glanced away. Jays stood across the room with his arms up, drawing a syringe. He grinned at the two of them then laid the sharp down on a tray with some other items.

"I almost have everything ready, Ian."

"Good. Chris, I need you to stay. Please wait with Jays."

Chris's eyes raked across the items on the cart. Nothing unusual. *He must want me to stay because of Nick. He's more concerned than he let on.*

Across the room, Ian escorted the flight out the door.

"Go on now, I'm sure you have things that need doing."

"Aww, Ian, can't we stay for a little bit more? Please?"

"Come on, out. You heard me. There'll be visitations once she's settled in more. Have patience. Go and tell the others everything you've seen."

They dragged their feet, but he finally got them and their excited chatter out the door.

Ian paused by the monitors before he joined them.

Chris cleared his throat. "So, what do you need from me?"

The doctor picked up Jessica's chart and flipped through it. "I'm not sure, Chris. Nickolas has her calm, but I doubt that will last. And I can't trust your brother's reactions at the moment."

He slid the chart back into the slot. "Just be ready."

"I'm set, Ian."

He nodded at Jays. "You good, Chris?"

Taking a deep breath, he nodded.

Chris followed Ian to door number four, where the doctor swiped his card in the reader. The latch popped and he pulled the door out.

With a twitch of his wings, he followed Ian through the opening, the soft rattle of the cart on his heels. Jessica pressed into the far corner; fear chased across her features. His brother straightened into an upright position from where he had reclined on the foot of her bunk. They stopped next to the bed and Chris watched Nick's muscles tense.

Beside him Ian stared at Nick, and Chris realized where Nick's fear lay. He flicked his gaze back to Jessica. She had managed to conceal her emotions and now inched along the wall, keeping as much distance as possible from them.

A soft squeak sounded loud in the room as Jays kicked the break on the cart. She froze, and the intensity of her gaze shot to Jays behind him.

Nick still hadn't moved.

"Nicky?" Ian said.

The shifting of his eyes was the only indication that his brother tracked what happened around him.

"Nickolas?" Jessica whispered. "Please?"

Chris watched his brother. Nick quivered, but Ian's stare held him in place.

"Nicky," Ian coaxed, "I know you have a lot of memories surfacing right now. But you know this needs to be. Are you going to get in the way?"

Nick closed his eyes then looked at his feet.

"Nickolas?" Jessica echoed.

"We've been over this, Jess," Nick replied, his voice thick. "It wouldn't be safe."

Ian's shoulders relaxed slightly. Behind him, Chris heard Jays shuffle a few supplies around as he got ready for the exam, but he kept watch on Jessica. She stared at Ian and continued to inch along the wall.

"How are you feeling today, Jessica?" the doctor asked.

She shrugged a shoulder and took a step.

"I'm very glad you ate so much. That's important at this stage."

Chris shifted closer to the bunk to keep her from getting behind his back as she moved along the wall. He flicked a glance at the closed door she was nearing.

His moving brought Jays into her view. Her eyes narrowed and he thought he heard the beginning of a low growl. Next to him Jays froze.

"I see you remember Jays," Ian said. "I wasn't sure you would."

"Why wouldn't I? He spent enough time around my house." She turned a sneering look on Jays. "You know, Robin was devastated when your family left with no notice."

Pain laced her acidic comment, and Chris watched Jays set down his stethoscope with too much care for its placement.

"We were kids, Jess. It's not like I had a choice."

"No. But you do now."

"That's not fair, and you know it."

"When has anything ever been fair, Jays?" And faster than Chris could believe, she lunged at the cart. With one hand, she grabbed the syringe off the top of the cart, and the other fisted around the lanyard dangling from Jays's neck. A quick yank and she held the keycard to the door.

He took a step toward her, but the needle immediately trained on him. Her back hit the door.

Ian's voice murmured behind him and he spared a glance over his shoulder. Nick had risen to his feet, and Ian had his hands full talking his brother down.

Without lowering her weapon, she got the card up and swiped. The door popped behind her. He took another step.

"Where are you going, Jess? How do you plan to get there?"

This time he was sure he heard her growl. She kicked the door wide and started to back out. Through the open door, Chris saw Kieran leap over the monitor desk.

Now if he could just get her to back into his arms.

He took another couple of quick steps, focusing her attention on him. "How do you think you'll get out?"

"I managed for quite a while yesterday..."

Kieran's arms wrapped around her the moment she backed through the doorway. An ear-shattering shriek pierced the air. He lunged forward and grabbed her wrists. A feral snarl ripped through the room behind him, but he didn't have time to deal with Nickolas. Jessica writhed like a snake. Kieran held on, but Chris heard the grunt of pain when she slammed the back of her head into his face. He got in as close as he could to avoid her striking legs.

"Drop the needle, Jess."

"Go to hell."

He worked his thumb under her clenched fist and dug into her palm, hitting the nerve. With a gasp, her fingers convulsed open. Kieran squeezed tighter, and he let go of her wrists to grab her thrashing legs. Together, they manhandled her back into the room. Backing up, he saw Ian had his hand slapped to Nick's chest, somehow holding the vibrating Valkyrie at bay.

Even over all the noise Jessica was making, Chris could hear Ian's voice.

"Nicky, I want you out of this room. Now."

"They're going to hurt her!" his brother shouted.

"Nickolas Sinclair." The ice coating Ian's voice chilled Chris. "If you don't want me to knock you out for the next twelve hours, get your ass out of here."

He and Kieran had gotten her to the cot and were working on pinning her down. "Damn it, Nick. Shut up and obey," he snarled at his brother.

"Donald," Ian yelled.

Chris saw his Second dash in.

"Get him out and make sure that door gets shut and locked."

"I can help, Ian..."

Over Jessica's struggling body, Chris locked eyes with his brother. Emotion swam hot through the blue depths. Donald had a grip on the back of Nick's neck and his arm twisted up behind. He fought the lock halfheartedly as the subordinate Valkyrie forced him out of the room.

The door clanged shut.

He heard Ian softly reply, "Not this time, Nicky." Ian scrubbed his face with his hands then turned back to them.

Kieran lay across her chest with her arms pinned above her head. He leaned on her shins to immobilize her legs. His nose twitched and he looked down. *Damn.*

"Ian. There's blood running down her leg."

The doctor sighed. He walked over and crouched down by her head, waiting until she turned to look at him. "It's your choice to make this hard. If you want to enjoy the freedoms and privileges of the other fledglings, then you will need to cooperate."

She bared her teeth at him.

He shook his head then stood. Chris leaned to the side as much as possible to give Ian room to look at the blood.

"Jays, she's pulled her sutures and reopened the wound. Chris, I need you and Kieran to get her turned. I need that leg on the outside."

"Kieran?"

"When you say, Chris."

"On the count of three. One. Two." He slid down her legs and gripped her ankles. Kieran slid his hands down her arms to her shoulders, still pressing her to the bed. "Three."

Kieran lifted his weight and they both flipped her to her stomach as she took the same moment to try unsuccessfully to break free from them. She screamed her frustration into the mattress.

Chris got a better look at her thigh. Blood soaked the leg of her shorts and ran freely down her skin. Ian rolled her leg a bit to get a better view of her calf.

"These are fine. It's just her upper leg. Scissors please." With a couple snips, the doctor had the shorts off of her, much to her indignant complaints. "They were dripping in your blood, Jessica. It's not like you could continue wearing them."

Readjusting his grip, Chris watched Ian examine the laceration. Several stitches had popped, so the wound had an ugly gape to it, and bright red blood leaked in a trickle.

"Glove up, Jays. With this much blood, be super careful of exposure."

Jays slid an absorbent pad underneath and handed a bottle of saline to Ian. Chris firmed his grip when she flinched as the doctor started washing the wound. Then Jays rubbed numbing ointment around the edges so he could set new stitches while Ian held the tattered edges together.

Her whines of pain got to him, and Chris watched Kieran's head bow until it touched Jessica's temple. His Flight lieutenant's shoulders had grown tense, and Chris could hear Kieran's voice softly singing one of his old Gaelic ballads. Jays finished quickly then sprayed it with something. Ian washed down the rest of her leg.

"Here, Chris." Jays tossed him a wad of cloth. "Try and slip those on her."

The stitching seemed to take some of the fight out of her because she didn't try and struggle when he caught the cloth, so he got her feet threaded through, and then with Jays's help, worked up her legs and over the wound.

Ian wrote in her chart, scrawling quickly. "I think there's infection starting, so keep a close eye. Let's get the rest of her vitals. You'll need to draw up another dose of inhibitor since the first is on the floor."

Kieran's voice floated around them while the doctors continued the exam. Chris started to massage her feet and calf, careful to avoid her stitches, hoping to help her relax.

A sob sounded over Kieran's notes when Ian punctured the vein in her elbow. He quickly pulled the blood samples then took the syringe full of inhibitor Jays held and clicked it onto the waiting needle. Depressing the plunger, he injected the substance into her blood.

She groaned in pain.

With surprise, Chris noticed a slight tremble in Ian's fingers that he quickly controlled when he pulled the equipment from her arm and taped down a gauze pad to staunch the blood.

"Ok, boys, we're done here for now," Ian said. "Jays, get the cart out."

He continued to rub the tension from her legs and feet while Jays trundled the cart out. Kieran brushed her hair away from the side of her face that was visible and wiped her tears with unsteady fingers.

Ian knelt down by her head again, but she refused to open her eyes. "Jess, I'm sorry about the burn. It should fade soon, but then the rest of the affects you experienced yesterday will start. Try and get some rest. It'll help."

When Ian stood, Chris and Kieran released their holds and she curled up into a tight ball on the bunk. With a last look over his shoulder, Chris followed the others out of her cell.

Ian paused in the doorway to let Kieran and Chris pass and pressed the bridge of his nose, hoping to ward off the headache he felt threatening. *Not bloody likely*, he thought as his mind turned to Nickolas. He pulled the door shut, sealing her in. *The next few weeks are going to need some careful handling.*

He turned to face the Hub. Jays had taken the cart to the far side of the room to clean and prep it for the next exam. Kieran had already pulled an ice pack from the freezer and had it pressed to his cheek. Donald and Chris talked quietly near the monitors while they kept an eye on Nickolas. And Nickolas?

He moved.

The restless pacing along the wall was full of feral energy. Ian could almost see the spikes of power swirling around him with his naked eyes.

The Alpha Valkyrie flared his wings and pivoted on his heel at the end of his circuit. His hand raced through his tousled hair as he started the length again.

Ian nodded to Chris and Donald, who stepped aside to let him into the monitor island. A quick glance at her screen showed her still curled up and rocking. *Hopefully she'll pass out soon. One down, now to take care of the other.*

Cocking his hip on the edge of the desk, he folded his arms and watched the restive movements. It reminded him too much of fifteen years ago. He took a deep breath and plunged in.

"Do you want to tell me what the hell that was about?"

Nick's gait faltered and his back stiffened.

"Well?"

Nickolas spun and fire flamed in his eyes for a split second before confusion drowned it. His wings dropped. "I don't know."

He started pacing again, but slower this time.

"I know the memories are hard. But I need to believe that you know this must be done. Or I'll bar you."

Nickolas clamped his wings tight to his back and stopped to stare at him. After a moment he spoke. "That won't be a problem. I don't plan on helping again. I have enough work to do anyway."

"Damn it, Nicky." Blowing out a breath, Ian took in his stiff stance. "Go to the gym and log in thirty minutes on your cardio regimen."

Nick fell back a step. "But I'm not on schedule for that."

"Your brother already threw my schedule with what he pulled this morning. So I think an extra thirty minutes for you will hardly make a difference." He threw a glare over at Chris, who had the grace to look sheepish.

"Shut up, Beta," Chris snapped at a chuckling Kieran. Donald snorted.

"All right, all of you get out of my Hub. Take him to the gym, Chris."

Ian watched the three lieutenants escort their Alpha from the Hub. After the doors swung shut, he relaxed into a slump and rubbed his pounding head. He looked up at a soft touch to his shoulder and took the silently offered pills and cup of water from Jays.

"Thanks." He drained the glass and set it on the table. "The next few weeks aren't going to be fun."

"What happened in there, Ian? I've never seen Nick lose it like that before."

He pulled a chair out from under the desk that held the bank of monitors and sank into it. His thoughts turned back, and he examined the mental snapshots of what had happened. "Chris confirmed that Nickolas has stopped taking his pills. He's entered stage four."

"Great," the other doctor groaned. "We did think that was a possibility."

"Yes. But his symptoms are too advanced. He's acting like his system is clear of residual amounts. That shouldn't happen for at least a week after his last dose. It's only been forty-eight hours. I want a blood draw on him, today if possible."

"So the aggression shouldn't be a surprise then?"

"No. But the focus of it is. His aggression had a clearly defined source. He reacted to a perceived threat to Jessica and instinctively moved to defend. He was clearly shaken by his response, if his behavior out here afterward is any indication. I don't like his resolution, however. If not for his help, we would have needed to use Xanthar on her already."

"But he's just going to continue to deteriorate as he progresses through the last stage. How much longer would he really be able to help with her?"

"True. There would come a turning point. But until I'm forced to pull him, I would rather keep observing their interactions. It's an entirely new field we are witnessing."

Jays slid up to sit on the desk. "Do you know what we can expect from him?"

Ian shook his head. "No. I have some ideas based on how he was during his isolation. But who knows what a fifteen-year delay will do to the end of his change? And I have no idea what talents he will manifest."

"Exciting."

"You have an interesting definition of exciting, Jays."

His Second laughed and he returned a smile.

"Well Jessica has definitely thrown a monkey wrench into our calm, running machine," Jays said.

This time he laughed outright. "Another brilliant observation from you, Jays. I expect today's antics will only be the first of many surprises. And I recommend from now on that you wear your keycard inside your clothes."

"Duh."

Still smiling, he continued. "You will remain lead for the fledglings, except for Jessica. Continue your normal duties, but I don't want her handled alone. Jack and Michael should be able to deal with the daily schedule of appointments with the Valkyries. We might need to adjust their testing and checkup schedules if they can't. Between Jessica and Nick, I don't think I'll be free to handle my normal duties."

"No, I doubt it. And talking about schedules...what about Nick? Who's going to take over his duties, if he can't?"

"Let me talk to Chris, but I think Dev will be the best choice. The PR schedule is set for the next couple of months, so he wouldn't need to deal with that. Well, except for Kieran..."

A beep sounded and he absently swiveled his chair to look at the monitors. Jessica had finally fallen asleep.

"So, why Kieran? He's the most sought after of our PR unit."

"Yes, but as of now he's reassigned. So start trying to come up with a good excuse to give the team. His value in handling Jessica today supersedes his pretty face on TV or wherever they have him going next."

"I doubt you'll hear him complaining."

"No. Not likely. He hates the attention. Though, he might not thank me for putting him on fledgling duty. Especially since one of them is Nickolas."

"Speaking of fledglings, I need you to take a look at Denis. He's halfway through the coma, and I don't like the looks of his readings. Carlo looks like he's going to drop into the coma in a day, maybe two. Allison and Ron are both a week or so behind him. Then we'll hopefully have a break in fledglings."

"Right." Ian sighed then scrubbed his face. "Give me the chart. I'll see what I can, and then it's time for me to collapse."

Chapter Nine

Rolling over in the dim light of dawn, Marcus opened his eyes blearily to look at the clock on the bedside table. *Ugh, five hours of sleep.* He fell back over and threw his arm over his eyes. Focusing his mind, he called out, *Who? What's wrong?*

Sorry to wake you, sir, it's Robin. Kelley and Leslie just arrived back...they have bad news.

Suppressed emotion twined around Robin's sending, so Marcus had a good idea what that bad news likely was. *I'll meet them in the longhouse. Please get some coffee and muffins or something.*

Marcus groaned and rolled over to his sleeping wife, brushing the raven strands away from her face. "Beth, honey, wake up."

Stirring lightly, she opened her eyes to look up at him, smiling sleepily. "Is it morning already?"

"Almost. Les and Kelley just got back. I need to go meet with them."

"Jessica?"

"I don't know yet, but it doesn't look good."

His wife's smile dimmed and her grey eyes lowered. He bent over and kissed her on the forehead. "I'll let you know later," he said softly.

She nodded then opened her eyes again. "I'll be up at the lake with Raven Sept today if you need me."

"Right. I expect I'll be in meetings most of the day now." He threw back the covers and got up, shaking out his wings and stretching them. Then he walked into the closet, grabbed the first clothes to hand, and put them on. "Whose turn is it for dinner?" he called over his shoulder.

"Puma. I believe their sept is planning on cooking venison pot roast, but if Robin isn't up to it...?"

"Don't worry. The activity will be good for him." He walked back into the room to slip his shoes on then ran his hands through the short strands of his hair, trying to put it in some semblance of order. The light coming in the window strengthened; the sun must have just started to rise up over the peaks of the mountains surrounding them. "Looks like it's going to be another nice Indian summer day today. Why aren't you up with the fishers now? This is the best time for catching."

Beth sat up and pulled the sheet higher, yawning. "I'm not catching, I'm just selecting for tomorrow night's dinner. It's my sept's turn tomorrow, so we thought some nice pan-fried trout would be good."

"Sounds good to me too. I'll see you at lunch, love." He bent down to give her a quick kiss.

He walked through their small living room to the plank door and stepped out onto the gravel path that led away from the front of their little cottage. The trail wound a short distance past fern-draped maples and the silent sentinels of dark coniferous trees before reaching the edge of the meadow. He took a deep breath of the early morning air then stretched his wings out to their fullest extent and gave them a flap. Settling them back into place, he looked around at the little village they had managed to carve out of the forested mountains of the Cascades.

To his left, he could just make out in the distance a waterfall that rushed down the rocky cliff face of the valley. It filled a pool at its base before running off in a wide tumbling creek that cut its way through the small valley. Autumn flowers still bloomed in profusion in the unexpected warmth of the season to spill over the rocks along its course. The cheerful color and scent filled the morning. Small footbridges spanned its length periodically. *Not that we have to use the bridges, but unless the livestock starts to grow wings too, they're still necessary.*

He stared out across the length of the meadow toward the south village. Other early risers made their way sleepily on the paths that defined the boundary of the grassland and trees. The trickle of humanity flowed toward the longhouse, and Marcus stepped out of the tree cover to join them. The longhouse had been the first building they had built after their escape from the Facility. It still housed all the communal cooking and other offices. Though, once it had been their only living space.

Now everyone had small cottages of their own located either in the southern part of the meadow, or more and more now, in the surrounding forest. They kept the buildings small. Most only consisted of a bedroom or two and a living room, grouped around a shared bathhouse. Someday, maybe their time and resources would be enough to give everyone private bath and cooking space, but not yet.

He took a shortcut through the vegetable garden; the thin mist hugging the ground swirled around his feet and through the few fresh vegetables they had left to harvest. *I'll have to ask Beth how the storing went this year. Hopefully we won't be short again. Every time we need to bring in outside resources is a risk.*

A bald eagle chuckled and he scanned the cliff as he let himself out the garden gate. The bird rested in the sun-gilded top of one of the fir trees at the edge of the cliff face. It called again then launched out of the tree. Its wings briefly flashed in the sunlight before it dove into the shadows of the cliff. Not sure whether to take it as a good or bad sign, he locked the gate, then finished walking the short distance to the door of the longhouse. The smells of breakfast cooking and the quiet murmur of voices invaded his senses. After a quick fortifying breath, he walked straight to his office.

Inside, he nodded to the two Valkyries seated before his desk. Then spying the cup and plate of biscuits already placed before his chair, he smiled over at Robin, who sat perched on the corner of his desk. Marcus took his seat and picked up the mug, inhaling the scent before he looked to Kelley. "Well, I take it the news isn't good?"

Grimacing, Leslie shook her blond head. "I'm afraid not. We didn't get there in time. Alpha team got to her first. We had hope briefly, when she gave them the slip. There was a slight chance we could get her while she was on the run. Unfortunately, Nickolas never gave us an opening. He managed to stay right on her heels the whole time. But we did succeed in downloading the latest data."

She set a tiny computer disk on the desk and slid it across to him. He looked at it and took a sip of his coffee before picking it up and putting it in the top drawer of his desk. He returned his gaze to the two Hunters and said, "Continue."

"Nickolas is the very best at recoveries, so imagine our surprise when she escaped him. I wish you could have seen his face, Marcus. He looked absolutely disgusted. It was a hoot."

He leaned back in his chair, surprised at her forced levity. He glanced at the silent Kelley. As the superior of the two, she should have been giving the report.

Leslie continued. "Well, she eluded them through the night, and us as well, though we had to avoid the recovery team more often than not. They must have emptied the Facility to capture her. I have never seen so many teams sent to one location before. They finally trapped her in a neighborhood with sheer manpower. She managed to elude them for nearly twenty-four hours before Nickolas wised up and set a trap that she would fall for."

A knock at the door interrupted them, and Marcus held his hand up to stop Leslie's report. "Robin."

His Hunter Prime jumped off the desk and crossed to the door. After a moment of quiet conversation, he admitted another older male Valkyrie. The older man stumped up to the desk, stopping between the two seated females, clearly waiting for Marcus's permission to speak.

"Good morning, Nathan. I assume from the interruption that the Seers have something to report immediately?"

"Yes, sir. The watch last night had a strange incident occur. My Second decided we didn't have an immediate danger, so they reported it to me this morning." He cleared his throat and fixed his gaze over Marcus's shoulder. "Apparently an unknown Valkyrie tried to contact us last night. Telepathically."

Marcus's chair protested as he sat bolt upright. "Excuse me. What do you mean?"

"Julie was on duty. She said that she got the feeling someone was trying to reach out mentally, so she lowered her shields then got blasted when a strange male called out. There's only one person that could be Marcus. Julie swears it can't be Gabriel. But he's the only Valkyrie not on inhibitor who isn't in the valley."

"Why does she think it isn't Gabriel?"

"She said the sending felt too raw and undisciplined."

"Any idea how close?" Robin asked.

Nathan furrowed his brows and looked at the floor for a moment. "That's the thing...she thinks it could have come from as far away as the Sound."

Kelley gasped and looked at Leslie. Her face had blanched.

"Kel...?" Robin asked.

Kelley turned stricken eyes on Robin before she turned and faced him squarely. "We hadn't gotten to the end of our report yet, sir. Nickolas started using his talents yesterday. During the hunt we could feel him getting clearer, and it soon became obvious that he was using his abilities to track her. I don't think he'd have caught her otherwise, sir."

"Nickolas?" Marcus relaxed back into his chair in bewilderment. "That makes no sense. How could he? And the distance...? Nathan, did Julie answer him?"

"No. The communication was severed immediately. She didn't get the opportunity. She wasn't sure what procedure you wished us to take if there is another try."

He picked up a biscuit and took a bite, thinking. "How did he figure out to try the first time? Let me find out what the latest communication from the Facility says before we make any final decisions. I'll get back to you by tonight, but as it stands for now, monitor for any signs of more communications but don't answer immediately."

"Yes, sir." Nathan nodded to the others present then walked heavily back to the door, closing it quietly behind him.

Eyes turning inward, Marcus absently took another bite of his biscuit, thinking about this new development. Then Kelley cleared her throat and drew his attention back to the meeting. Marcus took in the blush staining her cheeks and the hesitant way she sat. Slowly setting his biscuit down, he grew cold, his eyes boring into her. "What else happened?"

She looked at Les, then took a deep breath. "Um, well, sir. They had finally gotten her into custody and were on the ferry when..." She trailed off, hanging her head.

"When what?" He leaned forward so he could hear her quiet reply.

"When I...talked...to him."

Frozen for a split second, staring at her, Marcus couldn't quite believe what he had heard, but then he surged up out of his chair and slammed his hands down on the desk. "You what! What the hell did you think you were doing?"

He shoved himself away from the desk and started around it, his eyes locked on hers. "That was the last thing we needed. We did not need Nickolas becoming curious."

Robin lunged in front of him and snapped his wings wide to block his view of Kelley. "Marcus. There's no point. What's done is done."

Hard, hazel eyes pinned him and the warmth of Robin's hand on his chest brought him down. He took a deep breath and the Hunter Prime said softly, "She is mine to discipline, Alpha."

Nodding curtly, he returned to his chair. Robin slowly lowered his wings then looked over his shoulder at Kelley. Without another word, he too returned to his place on the left of the desk.

Marcus gripped the back of his chair and stared at his white knuckles until he felt that he had his temper under control again, then resumed his seat. He still needed a sip of his coffee before he could trust himself and look at Kelley again. "You do realize the danger Nickolas is now in, do you not? If Gabriel finds out..."

"Sir," Leslie made eye contact with him, which was no small feat on her part. "I don't think the communication we had with him made that much of a difference. From what we had observed of his behavior, he had already made the decision to stop taking the inhibitor. Something else triggered his choice. We decided to take the chance that maybe he had learned enough of the truth that he would actually let her go."

"No, Les. I made the choice. Let's be clear here. You wanted to stop me."

"Kel," she growled.

"No. This is on me."

"As Robin said, what's done is done. She's in their hands now. We can only hope that my father can protect both of them. Is there anything more to report?"

"No, sir."

"Good, then you two are dismissed. Robin, you stay." He swiveled his chair to look out the window.

"Kelley. You will wait for me at the practice ground." The edge of steel beneath Robin's voice almost made Marcus smile. After the door closed, he felt Robin approach his chair and stop. "It was only a matter of time before he figured it out, Marcus."

The mist was rising in wisps from the grass and water of the creek, but Marcus barely saw it as memories swam through his mind.

"I know. The games we play are always dangerous, but now...now the stakes are higher, and the players don't even know they are in play." He paused and rubbed his eyes. *Oh, Nick, I sure hope you know what you're doing. It's up to you to take care of the others. Be careful.* The comforting weight of Robin's hand came to rest on his shoulder, and he looked out of the corner of his eye at him. "I'm sorry about your sister."

Robin squeezed his shoulder. "You know how stubborn she is. She's always blamed you for Mom and Dad."

He shook his head, closing his eyes. "I wish there had been some other way. I wish Jennifer had *told* me."

Robin pulled away to pace back to the other side of the desk. He cleared his throat. "She hadn't even told Dad. She told us, but I think that was so we would know she chose to go and then I could tell you. And she knew there wasn't a way we could stop her. We were only children."

The comforting murmur of voices drifted through the closed door from the dining hall. "That's why I rarely allow Seers to go on missions."

He opened his eyes and turned back to face Robin, trying to give him a reassuring smile, but he could tell Robin didn't buy it, so he changed the subject. "So how are the Hunters doing? I meet with the Primes of the other two castes later today, and since I hear your sept is making pot roast tonight, I figure I might as well get the Hunters' report now."

He leaned back, smiling to himself, as he watched the young man who'd been his surrogate son pace the room. Robin's desire to press him for the truth of his well-being was written all over his face. As was the moment he decided not to press. *I've taught him well.*

Robin flicked his wings and shifted back to lean against the wall, pushing his hands into his pockets. The Hunter Prime stared at him a moment more before answering. "Well, I've divided up the three new fledges among the Lynx, Raven, and Wolf Septs. They are getting their flights all sorted out and seem to be adjusting well enough. Only had a few minor scuffles, easily sorted out. They should be ready to work soon. We'll then be able to get back to our normal hunting and sentry rotation. The hunting is going well this year. The larder is already half full for the winter, and game is still plentiful nearby. I've focused on sending the hunting parties farther afield since they've had the added protection of a Caster in each group. Thanks, by the way. The Facility's had a lot more people out searching."

"I don't think most of them are from the Facility proper. I think we have Gabriel to thank for the increase in activity. Be careful, we haven't lost anyone for over a year. I'd like to keep it that way."

Nodding his head, Robin pushed a stray curl of his shoulder-length chestnut hair out of his eye in irritation. "Other than that, things go smoothly within the Hunter caste."

Marcus leaned back in his chair and smiled at Robin's inherent gesture. "Good, I'm glad to hear that. So, on to new business. I suspect word is starting to spread throughout the valley. As soon as Kelley enters the penitition circle, people will start gathering to wait."

Sighing, Robin concurred. "This will be the first formal discipline action in quite a while."

"Yes. How much status do you think she's going to lose?"

"I don't know. That depends on how well she fights. And she is going to be facing *me* in the circle today."

Marcus blinked and just stared at him for a moment. "Are you sure you're ready for this? Rendering judgment is never easy, but when it's someone so close..."

A growl escaped him and he pushed his hair back again. "I can't let friendship get in the way of my responsibilities or duty. She's my Second, and I know she's no match for me, but what she's done is inexcusable. The risk to my sister, and every other Valkyrie in the Facility, has gone up exponentially. She, and everyone else, needs to know that this is not something that luck or skill can absolve. If she fought someone else, that would be a possibility; but by fighting me, they know it's serious. Besides," Robin added, snorting with the lightning change of mood Valkyries were known for, his eyes twinkling. "That's not the worst of it. She will also be removed from active hunting details. Once she heals, that is."

"Oh, ouch. Just remember a bored Valkyrie is trouble. Well, if you have nothing else to report, I should see what is on that chip."

"Right, I'll be at the circle in one hour. I think that will be long enough for her to contemplate her actions. Besides, she's going to have enough to concentrate on afterward. I doubt she'll be bored." He pushed himself away from the wall and sauntered to the door. "Oh, and tell Jessica she's an idiot for me."

Marcus stared at the door for a moment after Robin had left and considered his surrogate son. *You have matured well. I only wish I could have been there for your sister and my own children too.*

A sigh escaped him and he reached into the drawer to get the disk Leslie had brought back. He set it on the blotter then swiveled around, pulling out another drawer behind him and removing a laptop computer. The chip went into an adapter, which he then slipped into a slot of the machine he had placed on the desk.

He worked his way through the multiple levels of passwords until he got the chip activated. The screen flashed and the data started to scroll by. Impatient to get to the message, he only caught key words from the data stream. He could come back later; right now he wanted to hear his father's voice. After the data transfer, the screen lit up and Marcus leaned forward to watch and listen.

"Hello, Marcus. I hope this message finds you and Beth well. The data I've sent you is the latest research from the Facility's medical staff. It should keep you and your doctors busy for a while. As you should now know, Jessica has entered stage two. Nickolas's team is already gearing up to go get her; my hope is that they will return empty-handed of course, but if not, we'll have to make the best of it. Remember what Jennifer said, we have to protect her. We can't let Gabriel get his hands on her. Speaking of the devil, he was here again and removed two more from my protection. They have, of course, disappeared into the camps. My hope for them wanes as Gabriel relocates more and more from my custody. I don't envy those he has control over. I've reached another dead end in my search for the location of his camp. All I can do for the moment is hope another lead breaks or more data trickles in to give me insight on where to look. I fear Gabriel suspects my true allegiance and is purposely blocking my actions.

"My talent is pushing me strongly, Marcus. I don't think we'll have much longer. Toward that end, I'm starting to get things in order here in case we need a change of leadership. I'll go over that in more detail in a later sending, and once we know where Jessica is.

"On to the new research. It's all pretty self-explanatory, but there are a few things I should mention. Some of the material has come from Gabriel's compound. It's worth going through and expanding on, just don't look too closely at how it may have come about; you won't like the sources. I have clearly marked those portions. The rest of the research I oversaw. In your last message, you mentioned how long it took your fledglings to get to the coma. It's still taking us about twice as long from beginning to end. We also have higher aggression rates and a lot more incidences of mental breakdown. I'm not given a lot of opportunity to try and help the ones afflicted. Gabriel doesn't care what shape they are in when he takes them. Some of them haven't even made it to the stage three coma yet when he has received permission to remove them. Speaking of which, how long are your comas lasting on average?

"Now for some new orders. Send Robin out to the warehouse in Marysville on Sunday. I'll have a shipment waiting for him. We've managed the normal supplies, but I've also gathered a bunch of medicines requiring refrigeration, so tell him to come prepared.

"I also have finally managed to get the last of Jillian's assets freed. Dustin has the paper work to get it transferred into the Auroran accounts. She'll need to go and sign them to get the ball rolling. Dustin can get word to me if things don't go smoothly, otherwise the next communication from me will be Tuesday. I'll have more for you then. As always, I wish I had more time and that we could talk in person. Clear skies."

The screen went dark and Marcus drummed his fingers on the desk for a moment, then reaching for pen and paper, he wrote down the questions his father had asked and organized his own thoughts. From the desk drawer, he took out a blank disk and switched it for the one in the computer. He secured the disk from tampering then sat back, hitting the record button.

"Hello, Father. Two months? It takes your fledglings two months to complete the change? I suspect the pharmaceutical cocktail you feed them delays their rate of change. You might want to check their levels of B vitamins. Confined Valkyries get highly stressed, running through B's at an alarming rate. That could account for the breakdowns. Since our emerging Valkyries are not confined, this isn't a problem for us. We mostly run into bone stress and muscle damage from our fledges trying to fly too soon. Though, most of those injuries are usually all repairable. The trickiest part of the emergence for us, the part that gives us the most fatalities, is the coma. It lasts for us anywhere from five to seven days. Any insights you have would, as always, be greatly appreciated.

"Ok, now for my questions. How is Jessica doing? She sure seems to have led Nick on a merry chase, from what I understand.

"And speaking of Nick, what the hell is going on with him? The pair of Hunters I sent out to try and bring Jessica in reported that Nickolas was using his abilities to track her? And that she would have stayed free otherwise. I thought his abilities were locked down? This was not good timing for him to discover his other senses.

"Will this interfere with our current time plans? Unfortunately, my Hunter may have made things worse; she approached him telepathically in an attempt to get him to release Jess. She's being severely punished for endangering Nickolas with her actions. Robin is the Hunter Prime now, so it should be doubly effective. And it looks like we've already had some repercussions from her contacting Nickolas. Last night, which would be the night Jessica was brought to you, one of the Seers on the night watch reported that someone tried to mentally contact us. Could it possibly be Nickolas? My standing order, until I hear otherwise from you, is to not respond to any other communication attempts.

"I expect by the time you get this, you will already know Nicky is stretching himself, but I thought I would warn you just in case. I will heighten security, since things seem to be heating up, and keep a more wary eye out for unexpected occurrences. Beth sends her love, and Robin wishes you to tell Jessica she's an idiot. Please be careful, you have the more dangerous job. Clear skies."

He reached forward and switched off the recorder, sighing, then ejected the chip and closed the laptop. Idly spinning the chip between two fingers, he leaned back. *Jessica, this would have been so much easier if you had come to us freely.* He picked up his cold coffee and took a drink. *Well, love, has the news spread?*

Somewhat. No one knows the details yet, just that there'll be a discipline battle. Though there is speculation. Everyone's already gathering on the field.

Then I guess it's time for me to put in an appearance. He put the computer away then grabbed his mug on the way out of the office. He crossed the deserted common room to the kitchen door. The soft sound of humming floated through as he walked in. "Morning, Chrissie, you should be getting over to the practice field."

"I will in a moment, Marcus. I just needed to finish this up." She placed a cloth over the bread dough she had just punched down then wiped the flour off of her hands. "There. I'm done. See you at the arena."

With a wave, she hurried out the door. Marcus located the coffee pot and poured himself a fresh cup. Opening the refrigerator, he splashed a little milk into the mug and replaced the jar. *I have to remember to call a meeting with the engineers; I need to know if we are still short on solar panels or wind generators.* He pushed the door shut then followed in Chrissie's wake. *It wouldn't do if our power ran out again like last year. We need the refrigerators. Cooking with wood is one thing, but it's pretty difficult to use it to keep the milk cold.*

Still making lists in his head, Marcus stepped outside of the longhouse and into the midmorning sun. He followed the path around the building toward the nearest footbridge, sipping his coffee. The practice grounds were a bare, earthen rectangle on the far side of the grassy area on the other side of the creek. They extended from the base of the rocky cliff, three quarters of the way to the creek. The ground had been dug flat, and a rise built up around the perimeter to act as a viewing space. He could already see what appeared to be the population of the entire valley surrounding the practice grounds.

It still amazed him to see several hundred fully fledged Valkyries in one place. Some lounged in the grass, while others flew in or stood talking in small groups. The largest concentration congregated at the creek side of the field, where they obscured his view of the grounds.

Once over the bridge, he followed the path that cut between a stand of trees and the fighting circles, that way avoiding the large crowd. Marcus chose a place on the rise where he could remain separated from the others and still get a clear view of the ring. He scanned the ranks of those waiting on the sidelines. A few caught his eye, and he nodded a greeting, but most politely kept their distance and continued on with their quiet conversations. He spotted Beth on the other side of the grounds. Smiling, he sent her a quiet caress. She lifted her wings in acknowledgment but otherwise kept on with her conversation.

Marcus studied the crowd for a minute then turned his attention away from those gathered to watch and focused on the circle of stones set against the cliff wall in the left corner of the field. Within it, Kelley sat motionless, meditating, as she prepared herself for the coming battle.

"Fight well, Kelley." He whispered a soft prayer for her strength.

The crowd continued to grow, showing surprise at who was to be disciplined; though mostly a wellspring of support emanated from them. Curiosity ran rampant, but even when in trouble, they still emotionally supported their wingmate. At least they were following the rules and not talking to her. Respect for the ritual, a fundamental that was just as important as knowing how to fight.

The quiet murmur of the crowd ceased, and Marcus saw that all eyes had turned to the southwest corner. The crowd parted and Robin strode onto the field, his wings rippling behind him, his face a blank mask.

Marcus absorbed the shocked silence as everyone took in the fact that Kelley would be facing Robin for her trial. Hushed whispers started from all over the grounds as the crowd started to respond to the unexpected.

"Good lord, it's Robin. What did she do?"

"Robin doesn't normally stand judgment; this must be pretty bad."

"No wonder she's been meditating so diligently. She must have known who she was facing."

"She can't hope to win."

"That's the point," Marcus replied to those nearest him in an even voice. Then, crossing his arms, he returned his attention to the field and called a halt to the unnecessary speculation by bringing the discipline to order.

"Let us begin," he called out, his voice reverberating from the walls of the valley, and he nodded to Robin to take over.

Robin raised his arms for silence. "Has everyone gathered?"

"We are here," resounded from several hundred voices.

Robin turned around to face the stone circle on the other side of the field and raised his voice, the strong sound eerie with an echo. "Kelley Ashborne, Beta Hunter of the First Flight of Puma Sept, do you stand in abeyance of your status until such time as you prove otherwise?"

Rising gracefully, Kelley shook out her wings, lifting her head. "I stand in abeyance." Then, sinking to one knee in the circle, she faced the gathering. "I kneel for judgment."

Robin turned around to slowly scan the waiting crowd then continued. "This Hunter has endangered our safety by revealing our skills to those who would question. She also endangered those we wish to protect outside by causing them to question. For this, she will be punished."

Robin caught his eye as he raised his hand into the air. "Marcus Sinclair, Alpha of our clan, will you stand witness to the validity of the accusation?"

Marcus stepped forward and mantled his wings. "I will stand witness."

"Kelley Ashborne, what is your choice? Will you relegate yourself to permanent Omega status within Puma, or will you fight for your standing? Know that if you choose to fight, you could be permanently hurt or killed."

She held her head high and replied with just the slightest quaver to her voice, "I will fight."

"Who will witness?"

"Witnessed." The affirmation thundered out from the surrounding crowd.

"From now until the end of the penance period, your status will be Omega. After which time how well you fought will determine your final status. Killing blows are to be avoided; the boundaries are the edges of the practice grounds and the immediate air space. Are you ready?"

Her face ashen, she stood and took a deep breath before answering her Flight leader. "I am ready."

He bowed to her and replied, "May you fight hard and well."

She slipped between the stones of the circle, loosening her wings as she paced the width of the grounds. A wary eye followed Robin. He circled her slowly, like a cat stalking prey.

Marcus settled down on the ground to watch the fight, worry niggling. Robin would show no mercy for her because she was his Second.

The two Hunters moved with lethal grace. Feinting toward her, Robin forced Kelley to jump back nervously, and he laughed, starting to taunt her. He circled, herding her farther into the center of the grounds. She kept backing, her reticence obvious. He toyed with her like a cat with a mouse, but he allowed her to stay just out of his reach.

Marcus was a little surprised at his tactics and her caution. Normally she loved to engage Robin, and while walking into a fight like this didn't qualify as normal practice, he'd expected her to rush forward in her normal brash way to get the reprimand over.

Then Marcus caught a glimpse of Robin's face and his blood ran cold. His eyes had gone completely feral.

Oh no, he's unleashed everything; no wonder she's so wary. Unless she can match him and bring her own predatory instincts up to the surface, she won't last long. And any hope for her status will be in the toilet. No wonder he's taking his time and pushing her.

"Come on, Kelley, changing your mind already? Don't wish to face me after all? You want to stay Omega for the rest of your life? I thought you were a good fighter." The grin on Robin's face gave Marcus chills. He feinted to the left then snapped out a wing, nearly clotheslining her as she dove under.

She rolled, then jumped, taking a wing beat into the air to turn back toward him. "Oh, I'll face you in my own time, Robin." Her voice wavered, and landing, she continued to back up.

He circled her lazily, herding her more and more toward the center of the grounds. She stayed on the defensive, not rising to his bait. Then she stumbled. Robin's laugh followed her as she jumped back, expecting him to take the opening and attack. He just stretched and yawned.

"Practicing for Omega status already, Kel?" Then he lunged, taking her off guard. Her reflexes slow, she dove out of the way, but he still landed a solid punch to her back as she rolled. Grunting, she whipped around and just managed to block his follow-up punch to her stomach. She brought her own leg up and planted a weak kick to his ribs.

He whirled away unfazed and laughed. "Boy you are a wuss today. Look at you; that kick didn't even wind me. You fight like a five-year-old girl." Slowly fanning his wings, he grinned as she started to growl low in her throat, finally having enough of his taunts.

"That's right," Robin said quietly. "That's it. Bring it up."

His smile faded and his face grew grim. "Time to get serious. Now, *fight* me."

Lunging for him, Kelley sent a flurry of kicks and punches at him; blocking them, Robin spun, raking her neck with his nails.

"First blood!" he yelled as red flowed down to stain the collar of her vest.

Her eyes flashed and she spun a kick into Robin's gut, doubling him over. Then she grabbed for one of his wings and started to pull the frame, but he lashed out, knocking her knees out from under her. They fell side by side, and he backhanded her in the mouth.

Rolling away, she looked up at him and slowly wiped the blood from her chin. Then, rising with a feline grace, she started to circle her Flight leader, keeping her eyes glued to his. Taking the initiative, she lunged straight for Robin's throat. He twisted and dodged, barely managing to block her knee, but she grabbed his hair with one hand, pulling back to expose his unprotected neck.

He seized her other wrist and pushed it away from his face, so she leaned forward and sank her teeth into the hollow of his neck, just missing the vein.

With a shout, he twisted his free hand in her hair and pried her off then slammed his knee into her gut, dropping her to the ground. Backing up, he slapped a hand to the bite and applied pressure.

Gasping for air, she scuttled back, and then with a feral smile, her tongue swept his blood from her lips. She slunk around him, her breathing ragged, blood dripping down her throat from the scratches. Robin growled, and with a laugh, she launched into the sky.

Only a wing beat behind her, he made a grab for her legs, but she tucked her wings, somersaulting. Then as he shot by, she uncurled, lashing out to strike him on the shoulder blades with the full thrust of her legs, sending him plummeting out of control.

He turned his plunge into a dive and soared down, skimming the practice grounds to gain momentum before angling into a sharp climb, driving straight toward Kelley.

Hovering, she waited for him. As he neared, she turned her hover into a stoop, but before she could strike, he turned the move against her. He clapped his wings to his side and spun in a barrel roll. She couldn't correct her flight fast enough. He snapped his wings out to stop and snagged her pinion struts in both fists as she shot by.

A scream ripped from her as her momentum was arrested and her wings were wrenched out of their sockets. She struggled, twisting, trying to get some hold on Robin behind her.

Flapping heavily as he descended, Robin dropped to the ground. One arm still clenched on a wing strut, he pressed into her back, his other arm snaking around her neck.

"Do you yield?" he growled into her ear.

"No," she gasped out. And bracing her feet, she dropped her hips and pushed into him, heedless of the damage to her neck or wings. She bent, throwing him over her shoulder.

Dust flew as he landed flat on his back, the breath knocked out of him. Dragging her wrenched wings, she tried to stomp him, but he rolled out of the way. He hooked his leg out and knocked her feet out from under her.

Off balance, she fell and tried to curl into a roll, but her spasming muscles wouldn't cooperate, and she landed heavily on her side instead, breathing hard.

Kicking her over onto her stomach, Robin walked up her splayed wings and knelt on her injured wing joints to hold her down. He wrapped his fist in her length of blond hair and lifted her face out of the dirt.

"Do you yield?"

"No," she rasped, and Marcus could see the blood that flowed down her neck glisten wetly in the sunlight.

Slamming her face into the ground, the Hunter asked again. "Do. You. Yield?"

"No."

The muffled reply reached Marcus and he watched Robin slam her head into the ground again.

"Yield, damn it!"

Come on, Kelley, enough is enough. Don't make him knock you out.

"I...yield..."

Robin's head dropped as she finally surrendered.

Robin. Are you ok?

His Second's mind voice sounded faint with fatigue. *I'll be fine, Marcus. This was just more difficult emotionally than I had anticipated. She did well though, don't you think?*

Yes, she held her own. I expect her rank will rise from this.

Robin released his grip on her hair and smoothed it out, then rested his hand on the back of her head for a moment. After a last caress, he lifted himself away and raised his arms.

"This judgment is over."

Marcus stood. The only movement around the grounds came from Beth and Leslie. They hurried across the field over to the two combatants; he moved to join them. Everyone waited to see if Robin's Second was all right.

"Beth, could you and Les get Kel over to the infirmary?" Robin asked softly. "I don't think she can make it on her own."

"You need to come too, Robin. Your neck looks like it might need some stitches." Beth peered at his wound. "Come on."

"I'll be fine, Beth, really." The Hunter sighed.

"Move it, Robin," she snapped.

"I'd do what she says, son, if I were you." Marcus laughed.

"Kelley needs help more than I do."

"And she'll get it, right alongside you," Beth replied starchily. "Marcus, can you carry Kelley alone?"

"I'm sure I can manage." He knelt down next to the prone Valkyrie and carefully folded her wings across her back. The joints were too loose. Gently he touched her shoulder and asked, "Kelley, are you aware? Can you roll over?"

"I don't think so, Marcus," he heard, the words faintly slurred.

"Brace yourself. I'm going to turn you." He worked his hands under her shoulder and hip then carefully rolled her to her back, wincing in sympathy when she yelled from the pain. Her face was a bloody mess, and he used his sleeve to wipe the worst of the blood and dirt from her eyes.

"I don't think I can stand. Everything's spinning," she got out between shallow, sobbing breaths.

"That's probably because you let Robin pound your head into the ground too many times. Don't worry. I'm going to carry you. Though I think your wings might be dislocated, so this isn't going to be too pleasant." He slipped his hands underneath her shoulders and legs and slowly lifted her into his arms. She bit her lip until it bled. Rising, he turned around to the others, but her wings dragged on the ground and she screamed.

"Hold on, Kel. Hold on," he whispered and gripped her tighter to him as Beth and the others rushed back over. "Beth, can you get her wings folded up? I should be able to hold them if you can."

His wife dropped to her knees and Marcus could feel movement as she gathered up Kelley's useless wings.

"I've almost got it. Leslie, if you would please hold that end? Ok, Marcus, now."

He closed his eyes, and reaching into his power well, he started to pull the energy out of himself, shaping it into a rope of light that he used to wind about the trembling Hunter in his arms. He lashed her wings tight to her body. A portion of his concentration went to maintaining the mental image, then he opened his eyes. A faint light engulfed Kelley's torso and he tested his control of it. "Ok, Beth, I've got it."

He felt the weight of her wings slowly come to rest against his rope; he put a little more power into the binding until he was sure all was secure. Brushing his lips against Kelley's temple, he said, "Let's go."

The small group set out, slowly crossing the practice grounds. The tide of Valkyries on the edge of the field parted, forming an avenue for the five of them to walk down. The corridor stretched all the way to the bridge as more and more of the populace came up to help line the way. All remained silent.

Well, Marcus, I think you were right. I believe her status has risen, Robin broadcast, his mind voice weary and pain filled.

This isn't just for her, Robin, Beth chimed in.

She's correct, Robin. You handled yourself well and they acknowledge that.

They crossed the bridge following the path that led to the longhouse. Gravel crunched underfoot until they reached the cobbled courtyard enclosed by the community buildings. The longhouse formed the eastern side of the courtyard. The infirmary occupied a section of the squat square structure that bordered the south.

Leslie and Beth rushed ahead and held the doors open so he could get Kelley inside. He paused in the small foyer so they could get the second set of double doors, then he crossed the short distance to carefully place her on one of the triage tables. He had to hold her upright when she swayed.

"How's she doing?" Beth called from the supply room as she gathered up her medical equipment.

"She's a bit wobbly." He waved his fingers in front of her face, trying to catch her focus. "How many fingers? Kel?"

Kelley's face scrunched up as she attempted to focus; she started to shake her head, but the move caused her to lose her balance. Marcus held her steady then stared into her eyes for a moment. He looked to the right, down the long narrow room; Beth almost had the gear ready. "It looks like she's got a concussion, Beth; her pupils are dilated. And I'm pretty certain her wings are dislocated. I don't know what else."

Beth pushed the triage cart across the room, looking pointedly at Robin as she passed him. "Sit down, Robin. You're dripping blood everywhere. Put pressure on that, this may take a bit. Ok, Kelley, how are you feeling? Any nausea?" She flashed a penlight in Kelley's eyes.

"A little, yes. And it hurts to breathe."

"Humm. Keep holding her up, Marcus." Beth gently palpated Kelley's neck and forehead. "Definitely a concussion. We can have Jillian double check to make sure there aren't any fractures or bleeding."

Bethany turned and took a moist towel waiting on the cart and gently wiped the blood and dirt from her face before she checked her nose. "Looks like you were lucky. It doesn't appear to be broken. But you'll be black and blue for a while. You ingested some of Robin's blood. Are you two blood bound? I need to know if I'm looking at any complications from a sudden bond."

"No. We did that a long time ago," Robin answered for her.

"Ok, good. A one-sided bond can be a hassle. Lift your arms up, please."

Kelley struggled to lift her arms, and Marcus helped her hold them aloft so his wife could probe her sides. Beth paused when the Hunter hissed.

"Cracked or broken ribs as well. Leslie, will you call Jillian? I need her to do a reading on these. Until she gets here, Marcus, let's take a look at those wings."

He helped her lower her arms, then shifting his hold on her, he drew her head to his chest and pulled her tangled hair over her shoulder so Beth could probe the base of each wing. Gently, she lifted one, then nodded when Kelley tensed, stifling a scream.

"Marcus, you're going to need to set these," she said and lowered the wing.

"I'll need you to get her to relax." He pushed Kelley upright, and Beth took her shoulders so she wouldn't fall. He shook his hands out, letting his power build up in his reservoir.

Beth placed her hands on the injured Hunter's face and stared intently into her eyes.

"Have you got her yet?"

"Almost. Kelley, look into my eyes. That's it. Let your barriers down. We need to set your wings. I can help you relax if you'll let me in. This is going to hurt, but it'll hurt worse if you don't relax. Ok, Marcus, I'm in."

He reached out and lightly rested his hands on her back muscles. The tense bands started to relax as Beth manipulated Kelley's mind. He couldn't wait long or the anticipation would cause the Hunter to tense up again. Sliding one hand up under the first wing, he placed the other on the joint above it. Heat gathered in the palms of his hands, and he took a breath.

"Now."

He pulled up from below, while pushing down and in with the other hand, and snapped it back into place. A scream ripped from her throat, which faded into shivering. Rubbing the joint, he waited for her to relax again before placing his hands in position on the second wing. Kelley whimpered, tensing slightly even through Beth's manipulation.

"Hush, Kel, don't push me out. Soon would be good, Marcus," Beth said. Marcus could hear the strain in her voice.

"Now." Forcing the second joint back into place was harder, and Marcus felt her swoon, nearly passing out from the pain. He focused his mind, drawing on his power, and sent heat down into the joints to relax the spasming muscles. Then he immobilized them with a thought. "There. They're back in place. And I have them stabilized for a short time. It won't last long though."

"Long enough for us to get the rest of her worked on," Beth said quietly.

He pulled Kelley's shivering weight out of Beth's hold so her head fell back on his shoulder. Beth picked up a bottle of saline and some gauze squares from the tray next to her and started to clean the blood from Kelley's neck.

"Well, these scratches don't look too bad. Some antibiotic and bandages should take care of them."

As Beth secured the tape on her neck, Marcus glanced up when the door opened. "Ah, here's our X-ray machine."

Jillian padded her way over to them. "So, what have we got?" she asked softly.

"We should do a quick check of her skull, but I'm mostly worried about her ribs," Beth replied, smoothing the tape on Kelley's neck a last time before she looked at Jillian.

Jill wasn't one to talk much, Marcus thought. The Seer cupped Kelley's face in her hands, and both of their faces went blank as she took them into a trance. "Link with me, Beth."

Beth reached out and rested her hand on the back of Jillian's neck, closing her eyes. After a moment, she said, "Good, nothing. I wasn't too worried about the head, Jill. It's Kelley's ribs that I think are the problem."

Marcus quickly opened Kelley's filthy shirt when he saw Jillian's hands seeking bare skin. Her hands stilled on Kelley's ribcage.

After a moment, both Seers hissed in unison. "That's what I thought," Beth said in a faraway voice. "Three cracked ribs and a broken one. Marcus, are you up to any bone knitting?"

"I'll see what I can do. I won't be able to heal it completely," he said. He laid his own hand over Jillian's and took a deep breath; relaxing his mind, he reached out to where he could feel both Beth's and Jillian's presence. Seeing them both in his mind as two bright sparks, he joined them. *Ok, Jillie, let me see what you see.* The image of Kelley's ribs started to appear in his mind's eye. As he watched the picture sharpen in focus, he noticed the network of fine lines indicating the cracks, and one with a jagged crevasse.

Focus mainly on the broken one, Marcus. Anything you have left can go to the others, Beth's voice whispered in his head. *I'll keep her mind steadied while you work.*

Sending a wordless affirmation, he directed his thoughts to the ground under his feet. He centered himself within then cast an anchor into the ground to hold himself steady and act as a conduit for power spikes should they arise. Ready, he returned his attention to the damaged bones and started pulling power from himself, like a spider spinning out a web, channeling it through his hands into the broken rib. Molding it, he used the power to pull the two pieces of bone together again.

His focus was so absolute that he barely registered Kelley's groan as the rib moved back into place. Once he had it set, he created a splint out of energy and wrapped it around the rib like clay, completely supporting the weakness. Then using the last of his reserves, he poured liquid light into the fine cracks of the other bones to fill them. Completely drained, Marcus disengaged himself, swaying unexpectedly into Robin.

His vision greyed out, and Robin whispered in his ear, "I thought you might do something stupid, like use too much of your power."

His eyes shut, Marcus nodded.

"We've got her, Robin. Please get Marcus into a chair," Beth ordered.

A tug on his arm had Marcus opening his eyes, and leaning heavily on Robin, he moved slowly over to a chair against the wall. He needed Robin's help lowering himself into it, and his Second commented, "Your blood sugar's diving; you know better than to drain yourself so fast. Sit tight. I'll get you a glass of milk."

Marcus didn't bother to answer; he just leaned his head against the wall and listened to Beth and Jillian finish up with Kelley. He accepted the glass when Robin returned, downing it quickly as they got Kelley moved into a room. A few moments later, he felt someone crouch in front of him. Opening his eyes, he noted the concern on Beth's face, and he smiled tiredly. "Don't worry so, Beth. I'll be fine. Just used a little too much power too fast, I guess."

Her lips curved up and she replied, "That's a big surprise. Let me get Robin stitched up, then we'll get you fed. Leslie is going to stay with Kelley for now. She shouldn't be alone yet." She patted his knee then stood up.

He watched her walk away, directing Robin to a table. The Hunter looked resigned to the administrations, and Marcus hid a smile, asking, "How bad is the bite, Beth?"

"It needs a few stitches, and I expect it's going to bruise gloriously. Quit fidgeting, Robin, or I won't use the anesthesia." She took a small syringe and drew a little liquid into it from a small bottle. Delicately, she poked it around the wound. "Give that a moment to numb up."

Marcus watched Beth's lithe hands work at threading needles and commented, "Kelley and Leslie brought in news. I was able to check the disk before the fight. There's a lot of new research data for you, Beth, though some of it's come from Gabriel. I was hoping you could get your teams on it soon?"

"Get it sent over to us and we'll start today. I have a new packet to send out to him as well." Bethany picked up a bottle of saline and started flushing out the wound. Once it was clean, she proceeded to make neat stitches in Robin's neck.

"He also has two assignments for you, Robin. The first involves Jillian." He smiled at Jillian's surprised and slightly hopeful look. "Yes, he's finally managed to finish freeing the last of your assets, Jillie. The paper work's at Dustin's. Robin can escort you there. While you two are up in Lynden, I'm sure Beth has a list of things she wants picked up in town. You can arrange with Dustin and his family for the shopping trip. Next, a shipment has been arranged in four days at the warehouse. Robin, bring me your team assignments tomorrow for preparation. We'll brief the day after."

"There, Robin, that should do it." Beth finished tying off her last suture, then cleansed the area, patting it dry. "Try not to get it wet for a bit. Come back and let me look at it in a couple of days."

"Thank you, Beth." He hopped off the table and turned back to Marcus. "Do you know what is in the shipment? What size team should I assemble?"

"He said there'll be perishables, but other than that, I have no idea what he's managed to acquire for us. But I would say take the normal number of people. It should be a routine drop, and the mule will be there, so I'll send you with the next report."

"Should Jill and I go to Dustin's before or after the shipment?"

"Before is fine with me, unless Beth needs more time to write up her list," Marcus answered, chuckling at the annoyed look his wife cast him.

Robin shared a look with him, smiling at Beth's disgruntlement. "Well if you're through with me here, I have a pot roast to prepare. Come find me when you're free, Jill."

Closing his eyes, Marcus leaned back into the chair. "That's all for now. See you at dinner."

Chapter Ten

Kieran walked his fingers through the tabs in the open file cabinet drawer until he got to the correct space, then slipped the sheet into the jacket. He took the next sheet to be filed from the stack on top of the cabinets and found its spot. *And repeat ad nauseam, or at least until someone comes and relieves me of Nick duty.*

The muttering behind the desk on Kieran's right rose again, and he glanced over at Nickolas.

His Alpha stared hard at the papers lying on the desktop, one hand clenched in his hair at his temple. Then he growled.

"You ok, Nick?" *'Cause you certainly don't look it. You look like crap.* Dark smudges ringed his eyes, and the constant fidgeting... *Well, what should I expect from how much sugar he's been eating?*

Nick's eyes rose to stare across the room at him. "You know what? I'm getting really sick of everyone asking me that. You know the answer already."

"Sorry. Just wanted to check in with you, encourage you to talk if you want." *See if I can't worm my way into that obstinate skull of yours.*

"Talk? Do you really want to know?"

"What's happening to you? Of course. We want to help you."

Nick shifted in his seat and leaned back, looking up at the ceiling. "I really miss my privacy. What help do you think you can give me, Kieran?"

He closed the file drawer and leaned against the cabinet. Nick's chest rose in a shallow breath, and Kieran watched him swallow. If he stopped and let his imagination go, he could almost feel his Alpha's desperation. "I don't know that I can help. But I'll sure try everything to do so."

Nickolas looked back down at him, and he waited for the Alpha to make his decision. After a moment, Nick sighed then rubbed the bridge of his nose. "There are moments, Kieran, where I want nothing more than to go and pop those pills again. But I can't pretend that something didn't happen to me when I missed them. And I'm not that much of a coward.... No matter how hard it is..."

He trailed off for a moment then continued, "The mental noise pollution becomes greater every hour it seems. It's like I'm surrounded by TVs. Hundreds. More than can be counted, all blaring at full volume and on different channels. Shoving their pictures in my eyes, their voices in my ears..."

Nick put his elbows on his desk and leaned his head into his hands. "Makes it almost impossible to concentrate. But then one TV will pick a moment to outshine all the others. And thrust me into the picture. Everything is gone...here, there...for a moment or more at least.

"The only time the TVs have been muted were..."

Nick shook his head then shot a look into Kieran's eyes for a split second before he picked up his pen and studied his paper work again.

"When, Nick?" he whispered.

Nickolas shook his head.

"It's Jessica, isn't it? Then why in God's name are you refusing to enter the Hub? If she's helped you..."

Nick slammed his pen down. "No, Kieran. Don't push me on that again. I've told all of you repeatedly for the last two days, I've got a lot of work to do and you know it. I recover them, but I don't sit in the Hub holding their hands, do I? Why should I this time?"

"Well, for starters, none of the other fledges have had an impact on you before." He probably could have shaved with the sharp glare Nick cast him. *Sorry, Ian, I don't think I'm going to have any better luck this time getting him in there.* "But more to the point, you helped *her* so much, Nick. Doesn't that matter?"

He picked up his pen and acted like he was working.

"She's like a feral beast most of the time."

Nick's pen paused, so Kieran picked his words with the care of honing a weapon. "Her memory still fades in and out, but somewhere inside her, she knows. She sobs in her sleep."

Nickolas's fist clenched and he didn't even pretend to move the pen anymore. Kieran had his attention, even if he wouldn't look up. Pushing away from the file cabinet, Kieran took the steps to the desk. He placed his hands on the edge and leaned forward. "I've tried to help her, Nick, really I have. But she fights so hard. Getting her to eat..."

Nick's head snapped up and light flashed in his eyes, making Kieran uneasy.

"Did they hit her with Xanthar?"

The whispered words made him shiver. He shook his head. Nick closed his eyes and swallowed.

"But I don't know how much longer I'll be able to hold that off," he said softly.

"Damn it, Kieran, back off. Just...back off."

How far should I push you, Nick? Ian's right, you need to get back to the Hub. But his leader's body language told the story well enough, and Kieran let the subject drop. He returned to his paper filing. After a few moments, Nick's pen started moving again.

They worked in silence for a time.

Then Nickolas growled, followed by a scathing string of epithets. Kieran stopped in midfile to watch Nick shove a stack of paper over and pick up a new sheet.

"Christoff...you are so dead."

Kieran pressed his lips together to hide the smile that tried to form as he watched Nick shuffle more paper. *Guess he just found out about the game the other day.*

Nick scattered another stack and picked up the bottom sheet. "How much more..."

He fisted that sheet and then Kieran noticed the ends of Nickolas's hair rising in a breeze that couldn't be possible in the sealed room. A split second later, every sheet of loose paper in the room, including everything in the open drawer in front of Kieran, launched into the air like a tornado had caught them up, though Kieran never felt the driving breeze.

The paper exploded up and hit the ceiling, then started to flutter down around them like snow to cover every surface in the room.

In the midst of the gently falling paper, the door opened and Chris stopped in the opening.

Kieran heard Nick's growl and burst into laughter.

Chris stood in the doorway and met his eyes through the falling sheets before he turned his look on Nick. "Problem?"

Standing behind his desk, Nick pointed his finger. "Don't even start..."

Still snickering, Kieran mimicked, "Lucy, you've got some 'splainin' to do."

Chris shot him a look then shuffled through the paper to sit down at the other desk across from the filing cabinets. He started scraping the paper together to clear the desk top. "Nick, Ian wants you in the Hub."

"No."

"Come on, Nick. It's been forty-eight hours. You didn't do anything wrong, ok. Ian says you've had the most impact on her, and he wants your help."

Nick turned away and started to pick up the paper on his chair and the floor around it. "I said no, now drop it."

Chris sighed, and Kieran shrugged at him then started to pick up the floor.

"Ok, Kieran. Ian said if he wouldn't go then you would be needed."

"Right. Well, have fun sorting." He dropped the paper back to the floor. Christoff's snort followed him into the hall. He didn't pass anyone on the short walk to the Hub. He pushed open the doors and slipped inside. The room sounded unusually quiet. Everyone felt subdued after losing Denis. So no one sat visiting with the remaining fledges. *We all know it's a chance. Not that we have a choice in falling into the coma or anything.* But it still came as a shock when one of the fledges didn't make it. *There's usually more warning. I didn't realize that I'd started to feel safe about them when they dropped in, since if they're not going to make it, they usually go way before the coma.*

He joined Ian and Jays in the work alcove.

"Still no Nick, huh?" Jays asked. The doctor bent his head back to his microscope.

"Still refusing."

"I'm not really surprised," Ian said. He clipped his papers to the folder next to him then dropped it all into the wall holder above the counter.

"I think he's scared. But he's never let his claustrophobia inhibit him like this before. He jumps all over any scrap of news I pass on about Jessica."

Ian swiveled then leaned back in his chair to look at him. "Nick only *thinks* his worst fear is claustrophobia. He has no understanding that it's really loss of control. Like what happened to him in Jess's room when you and Chris restrained her. His instincts took control, and he responded to the perceived threat. It'll take time, or a large enough prod, to get him over the hump and back in here."

Kieran watched the doctor's eyes grow unfocused for a moment before they snapped back to him. "Anyway, moving on, I've waited as long as I can; I have to have some of the more complex tests done on Jessica now. I had hoped to have Nick's assistance with her, their rapport is phenomenal, but now it's up to you."

"Up to me?" He stiffened. "What do you mean?"

"I need a full MRI, an EEG, and whatever else we can manage." Ian raised an eyebrow and Kieran realized he had his medallion clasped between his fingers again. He dropped it and felt the weight tug on his neck. Ian continued. "You know she won't cooperate, Kieran. I don't want to traumatize her by darting her. And she's been taking food from you."

His wings rustled and he clamped them to his back. "Damn it, Ian. She barely trusts me. What then? After I betray her?"

"She won't even know, Kieran. You'll take in her lunch like normal, but hold off on giving her any milk until after she's eaten her food. Then give her the glass. She'll fall asleep after a few minutes. Then we can perform the tests and tuck her back into bed before she wakes up."

"I don't like this, Ian. I don't think it's a good idea."

"It needs to be done, Kieran."

He sighed and traced the lines on his medallion again. "Fine."

He carried the tray Jays handed him into her room. Like normal, she ignored him at first. Her limping gait paced restlessly at the end of the small room. He set her lunch down on the table and walked closer to her. She cocked her head as she passed and glared at him out of the corner of her eye.

"How's your leg today?"

She pushed her tangled hair out of her face. "It hurts."

"Then why are you on it?"

She passed him again.

"You don't have to cause yourself this pain." He absently rubbed his right thigh. "Come and sit down. Have lunch."

"Lunch? Is that what time it is? And what day is it, Kieran? I've already lost track of time, and I know it's only been a few days. Get me out of here. Please?"

She squeezed her thigh and turned at the corner to stare at him. Dark shadows ringed her eyes and her long hair hung in a snarled curtain. *And go where, Jessica? You'll understand, one day. I hope.* When he didn't answer her, she narrowed her eyes and looked all around the cell, her eyes stopping to rest on the vent in the ceiling, but then she moved into her pacing again, and he dismissed the uneasy thought.

"What is it with all of you? Are you all so into bondage? I figure you must be, since you like being on a leash so much." She growled, then stumbled slightly when she turned at the end of her circuit. "Don't you ever want to be free?"

Free? Like I could ever be free with giant wings on my back? "Free? What is free, Jessica? At least I have a job here and get fed and stuff. Do you really think normal people would just let us be out there? I mean, come on, they don't leave each other alone."

She stopped with her back to him. "You won't help me, will you?"

"I am helping you. You just don't believe me. We've all spent our time in here, Jess. We know what you're going through. It's not fun. Trust me, once you're fledged, you'll understand."

She turned back to him and something in her eyes made him look away.

"I've heard that a lot, Kieran. But it's all of you who don't understand. Except for Ian." She turned to stare into the camera, and Kieran felt a shiver run down his spine. "He understands completely."

He glanced at the slowly blinking light and tried to push the doubts finding fertile ground out of his mind. "Please, come and have lunch, Jess."

She cocked her head at him but then made her way over to the bed. He set the plate of food in front of her, making sure the tall glass of milk rested at the edge of the table. Outside of easy reach, so hopefully she'd eat more before drinking it.

He leaned against the opposite wall and found his fingers on his medallion again. Irritated, he dropped it. Jess ate quickly. Obviously her appetite was normal. Even if her attitude left a lot to be desired. "So why won't you take the easy route, Jess? Why fight so hard?"

She licked her fingers and stared at him a moment while she finished chewing. "A promise."

And that's all she'd say.

He let his hand stray to his medallion, the skin-warmed bronze smooth against his restless fingers. She finished the plate and reached for the milk. He held his breath as she downed the entire glass. She used the back of her hand to wipe her mouth, then rubbed it on the cotton of the bed pad. With a sigh, she leaned back against the wall and closed her eyes.

"You've been nice company, Kieran. But what happened to Nick? Ian's not let..." Her eyes snapped open and she sat up straight. Kieran could just make out the low growl from her chest. "What have you done?"

She pushed to her feet. Anger and fear chased across her features. She lunged at him, and he let her get her hands around his throat. This time, her unsteady gait was due to the sedatives and not her injury. He wrapped his hands around her wrists, but she didn't try and squeeze, just pressed him into the wall.

"Why?" broke from her lips.

"I'm sorry. You weren't supposed to know. They need some tests. And you won't cooperate..."

A tear slid from the corner of her eye.

"I'm sorry," he whispered.

She closed her eyes and her hands loosened around his neck. It felt like she tried to turn away, but her knees buckled and he caught her weight before she collapsed to the floor.

"Just leave...," she slurred.

Instead, he cradled her in his arms and crossed to the cot, where he laid her down. Wet streaks marred her skin, and he brushed her cheek with his thumb and decided today was a really sucky day.

Jays stood with the gurney as Ian swiped his card in the reader outside of Jessica's cell and pulled the steel door wide, holding it open for him. He swung the back of the gurney around and slid it through the door, then brought it to a halt alongside the cot. Kieran raised troubled eyes to his.

"You said she wouldn't know. You said she'd just go to sleep."

He glanced away from Kieran and looked at Ian. His superior lifted her lids and checked her pulse.

"I'm sorry, Kieran. She doesn't seem to respond to drugs in a normal manner. I would have warned you if I had realized. Jays, let's get her moved."

He moved to her feet, and at Ian's nod, he and Kieran lifted her onto the gurney then secured the Velcro. They slowly wheeled the table out into the Hub.

"Kieran, why don't you go and get some food. She's going to be out for some time. I have a lot of tests to catch up on."

Kieran nodded to Ian then cast a worried look across Jessica as he left.

Resigned to the situation himself, Jays wheeled his best friend's sister across the Hub and out the doors. Ian kept a guiding hand on the front corner as they made their way through the halls to the testing suite.

They entered the first room, where Ian gestured him to a stop. He locked the wheels and started to get her ready. While Jays brushed her hair back away from her face and pulled the electrode cap on, Ian got the wires laid out. After a few adjustments to make sure the sensors were aligned properly, he joined Ian at the machine as it whirred on.

The pattern on the screen jumped to life. EEG's were not his specialty, but he knew enough to know that what he was looking at was not normal. Ian grunted next to him and folded his arms as the activity on the monitor continued to scroll by. Her brain appeared to be in super drive, if he understood what he was looking at.

"Is it the sedatives?"

Ian shook his head. "No. They wouldn't cause this. Her mind is incredibly active. But as to what it's doing? I haven't a clue. Even Nickolas didn't have readings like this."

The test ended after forty minutes and her brain didn't slow for even a second of it. Ian shut down the machine while Jays went to remove the electrodes.

"Let's get her into the MRI. I want to see what's going on. We'll come back to the other tests after."

Jays nodded and carefully wound the wires under the cap then unlocked the wheels and pushed her through into the imaging room. Ian waited next to the MRI table. Together they lifted her over onto the sled. He tucked her hands to her sides and gently brushed her hair away from her face. His fingers lingered a moment, memories of her as a young girl flitting through his mind. He took a deep breath and pushed the slab into the tube, then turned to follow Ian into the control room.

The operations tech tapped away at the keyboard. The machine in the next room started up, and he could hear the loud banging, even through the thick observation glass. Ian winced. He joined him at the monitor when the results started to feed in. The tech had started at her feet. Nothing of interest appeared until he reached her pelvic area.

"What the..."

"Hum." Ian had leaned forward. "Theo, mark this. I want a more detailed scan of this area after the overall."

"Yes, Doctor."

The scan moved on. Jays caught a quick glimpse of her growing wing buds, enough to see their prematurely large state, then they were past and moving on toward her head. When the images of her skull started to come through, he stared, transfixed. The activity on the EEG had prepared them to expect something, but... *Wow*, he thought as he watched the image on the screen.

"I want a PET scan on her immediately. Jays, call the lab and get the radiotracer started." Ian looked down to a clipboard and scribbled notes across, flipping pages to continue. "Finish the primary scan, Theo. We'll come back for the detail later."

The image distorted. "Ian?"

The doctor looked up just as the image blurred again. "Theo?"

The tech punched some buttons and moved dials. The image got worse.

"She's moving," Theo barked.

"What?" Ian said.

Damn it. Nickolas scratched out the last line on the sheet he was filling out. His thoughts kept circling in his head, and between that and the mental riot, his concentration was a bust. He took a deep breath. He felt like he was going to fly apart.

I will control this.

He looked back at the form and reread it. Papers rustled. Donald had finished picking up the scattered files and now started the daunting task of sorting them back into order. His and Chris's voices filled the air. Chris sorted papers into various piles at the other desk. But Nick kept catching the fleeting looks both would turn on him when they thought he wasn't watching.

His thoughts circled back to the Hub again. The pull was strong, but he still pushed it away.

I am in control.

Donald and Christoff's banter got under his skin. He crumpled the paper and threw it at Chris with a growl. "What is taking him so long to feed her lunch?"

His brother froze then turned to stare at him. "Um, Nick. He wasn't just feeding her."

A chill swept him with those words. Chris threw a glance at Donald, who promptly set down his stack and turned to him as well. He didn't remember rising, but he found himself leaning on his desk, focused on his Second. Chris slowly rose also.

"What are they doing?" he said in a low voice.

Chris's eyes darted a look at Donald and back. "Ian needs to do an MRI."

"He's sent Kieran in there to drug her? Don't they have any idea what that's going to do?"

"She's just going to fall asleep."

He pushed away from the desk and stalked around it. "After our capture of her, you should know better..."

Halfway between his desk and the door, he was mentally blindsided. The pain of his knee as it contacted the floor was drowned out by Jessica's mental scream.

Pure animalistic fear, fight or flight, flooded his system.

The howl ripped from his throat, and he pressed his fists into his temples. He fought the wave back and his sight cleared. He staggered to his feet, focused on the door. It crashed into the wall and he was out it at a run. Chris and Donald shouted behind him, but he ignored them in favor of the line pulling at him.

"She's moving," Theo barked.

"What?" Ian said.

Then the faint echo of an animalistic scream reached them through the glass. Jays leapt for the window, his hands braced against the cool surface to stare in shock as Jessica crumpled to the floor at the foot of the pounding machine. Her hands plastered to her ears. She wobbled to her feet and looked around. Her eyes wild. She lurched at the only door in the room.

"What in God's name...," he heard Ian breathe. Then she was out the door. Ripping himself out of his shock—the tranquilizers should have kept her out for another six hours at least—he bolted for the door as Ian hit the alarms.

The door resounded on the wall as he surged through and the sirens blared on. He caught sight of Jessica's form as she staggered around the corner. His lab coat flapped behind him as he put on a burst of speed to catch up to her. *Robin's going to kill me.*

He slid around the corner as her drunken form raced down the corridor ahead. Ian's voice echoed the halls.

"Code red. Code red. Building in lockdown. Escape from the MRI room. Lockdown initiated."

Well, isn't this going to be fun to explain to Kratz. He timed his breath to match his racing feet, the distance between him and her closing. She took another hall and he slid around the corner, keeping her in sight. Pounding feet approached from behind, then his name was called. He looked away from her in time to catch the trank pistol Jack tossed him without missing a step. Racing shoulder to shoulder, they gained on her. She took another turn, and then he heard the loud bang as she body slammed into the locked door. They skidded around the corner and saw her frantically scrabbling at the sealed exit.

Their steps slowing, he raised his arm to sight down the length of his gun. Jack mirrored his action. But then a blur of motion summersaulted out of the corridor on the right. It resolved itself into Nickolas. His dusky wings spread wide, shielding Jessica from their weapons.

"Nick! Get down."

The Alpha Valkyrie made eye contact with him and growled. He kept his wings extended, covering Jessica's body as he flexed his knees.

"Nickolas. What the fuck are you doing?" Chris snapped as he slid to a stop, coming from the same corridor Nick had, Donald beside him. Nickolas shifted his gaze to his brother, and Jays heard an even more menacing growl rumble from him.

More footsteps arrived on the run, and both hallways started to fill as Valkyries crowded in.

"Damn, Jays. He's feral."

"No shit, Sherlock." He didn't dare look at Jack as he answered the other doctor.

"Should we shoot him?"

"I don't think we have enough to drop him. Chris?" he called across the hall.

"Don't, Jays. Give us a moment."

The rumble of Nick's menacing growl rolled through the hall. Jays could barely see Jessica, curled into a ball on the floor behind Nick's legs.

"Stand down, Jays." Ian passed between him and Jack. "Jack, get that damn siren off."

Jack passed him his pistol and slipped back down the hall.

"Nickolas, look at me." Ian clapped his hands and the snarling Valkyrie's head turned away from Chris and locked onto him. "Leash it, Nicky. Come on."

His wings quivered, but the growl faded.

"Come on, Nicky, come back to us."

The Alpha's gaze slid around the room. Jays watched him swallow, then he spoke in a gravelly voice. "She's terrified, Ian. Shooting her won't help with that. Let me try."

The two stared at each other for a moment. Then Ian swept the audience with his gaze. "All right, everyone, back up. Give them some space."

Jays stayed put with Ian, but the rest retreated down the two halls. Nickolas watched the movement warily, then he finally lowered his wings. After a last glance at Ian, Nick crouched down by her head.

The wail of the alarms died and Jessica's soft whimpered breaths sounded extremely loud in the sudden hush. Jays kept the trank guns ready but lowered.

"Hey, Jess." Nick's hand reached out and stroked her hair. "I'm here now. Let's get out of this hall, ok?"

She raised her head out of the protection of her arms. "I don't know what's happening."

"Don't worry. I'm here; I'll take care of you. Come to me now."

She uncurled and scooted into a sitting position, then flung her arms tightly about Nick's neck and buried her face into his chest. He cradled her in his arms and stood then turned to Ian.

Ian gestured Nick to precede him. The onlookers cleared an aisle so he could take her to the Hub.

Jays reached out and touched Ian's sleeve. "I'll stay and mop up."

He nodded, then followed the Valkyries.

As soon as they had disappeared around the corner, he turned to Christoff. "How the hell did he get here like that?"

Chris ran his hand through his hair and looked at Donald. The other Valkyries crowded near. "I don't know what happened, Jays. One minute he was complaining about you guys getting Kieran to drug her, then the next he's feral and running down the halls."

Jays shook his head and looked at the Valkyrie faces gathered round. "We'll have to deal with it later. Right now we need a head count. The lockdown won't release for a bit. Ian has to coordinate with Kratz to enter their codes before we'll be free of the wing. And anyone out there right now will be at Kratz's mercy."

Chris and Donald started calling out names and bodies shuffled. He shoved both trank guns into the pockets of his lab coat.

"Dev," Chris said. "Are all the lieutenants accounted for?"

"Kieran's not here."

"Damn. Ok, get everyone into the gym and do a full head count. Send a team to sweep the wing. Stay in the gym until released."

"Yes, Chris."

As the hall cleared, Jays turned to Chris. "Ian sent Kieran to get some food. He was probably still in the cafeteria."

Donald's face fell and Jays knew how he felt. Any Valkyrie outside of the lockdown zone probably wouldn't fare well with Kratz. "As soon as you have numbers, come to the Hub. Ian will need to know."

They nodded and took off after the rest of their clan, and Jays turned his feet toward the Hub.

Ian sat and watched the two on the monitor. The last four hours had been a nightmare. Not for Nick and Jessica. Nick had held a groggy Jessica, comforting and reassuring her, for most of that time. *They have no idea what repercussions I'm dealing with.* He shook his head. Jessica no longer clung to Nick but cuddled to his side. He had the volume down so he didn't know what they discussed. He could always replay the recording later. He pinched the bridge of his nose. Kratz had been stubborn about cancelling the lockdown with him. It had taken him nearly an hour to pin down the general on the phone and coordinate their code inputs.

Damn the man anyway. His excuse? Dangerous Valkyries were free on his side. He had to finish dealing with that first. *Bullshit. Just his normal excuse to mistreat my people.*

Chris's head count had come up five short, including Kieran. After the doors had been released, he'd had to find out what Kratz had done with them. After too much ferreting, he finally found them in a lockup on the other side of the Facility and had sent Jays to retrieve them.

At that moment, the doors to the Hub were kicked open, and Donald and Jays entered with Kieran slung between them. The Beta tried to walk with them, but it looked like he was mostly being dragged. They lowered him to a chair in the monitor island.

"The other four were fine," Jays said. "Looks like Kieran took the brunt of it to protect the others."

"Let's take a look at what they did to you, kiddo." He raised Kieran's face with his hand. The bruise that Jessica had given him had begun to fade to a sickly yellow, but now it had more black and purple on top of it. And black rung the eye now too. "Did they damage your wings?"

He started to shake his head no but seemed to think better of it. He licked his split lip and said, "No, I don't think so."

"Don't think so? We need to know so. Open up."

He stood, not quite as steady as Ian would have liked, and slowly unfurled his wings. He noted every wince. He ran his hands over the struts and rope muscles, flexing and pulling. He elicited a few groans, but nothing major.

"Looks like you've got some good bruising, but nothing that will keep you out of the air for long. I don't want you trying to fly for a few days, though. Let the bruising have a chance to heal a bit. Now get your shirt off."

As he thought, Kieran had some extensive bruises across his ribs and midsection. Thankfully, none of his ribs seemed to be cracked. "Jays, get him something for pain. Donald, after you get him to his room, go and bring back some dinner. I doubt he has any interest in going to the cafeteria right now anyway."

"No one does. Chris was already making arrangements to have a group go to the cafeteria and bring food for the whole clan back to the gym."

"Good. And Donald, tell Chris I'm keeping Nick for the next few hours, but he'll need to be escorted back to his room to sleep."

"Yes, sir. Come on, Kier, let's get you to bed."

Donald helped a subdued Kieran to his feet and out the door.

"Jays, please call the kitchen and see what's taking so long for dinner to get here. I want to prevent any more unexpected outbursts from our pair of fledges here. And if their blood sugar drops..."

He moved back to the screens and saw Nick laugh at something Jessica had said. Then he reached out and tucked a lock of her hair behind her ear. She smiled and leaned her shoulder against the wall and curled her feet up under her. Jays joined him.

"Did his blood tests come back yet?" he asked his protégé.

"Yes. Just before the hullaballoo. You were right. There's not a trace of the arresting inhibitor left in his system. That shouldn't be."

"No, no it shouldn't. But it does explain his accelerated responses. But all things considered, he's holding himself together well. Each instance of his loss of control was triggered by a threat to Jessica."

"Any clue why?"

"Not enough yet, but each piece is going on the grid. Soon I'll get a clear picture. I wonder if it's tied, somehow, to Jessica's drug responses? Could it have something to do with her talents?"

"Isn't it a little early for her to show psychic talents?"

"Playing it by ear here, Jays. Do you have a better theory? Didn't think so. I need that PET scan and the rest of the MRI. She isn't going to be happy about it, but those tests will happen tomorrow."

The rumble of the food cart reached them just before it bashed into the doors to the Hub. The woman pushed it just inside the door then left. Ian sighed.

"Ok, why don't you get Allison and Ron their dinners, and I'll take in Jess and Nick's."

With a nod, Jays pushed the trolley across the space, near to the isolation room doors, and picked up a tray. Ian followed suit but crowded on enough for both of his charges. Balancing the tray on one hand he swiped his card, then tucked it into his pocket and pulled the door open. Two sets of eyes turned in his direction when he entered. He set the heavy tray down on the table.

"Here you guys go. Sorry dinner's late tonight."

Jessica shook her head. "I'm not touching it. Not again."

Ian noticed Nickolas's face and realized he didn't trust it any more than she did. Irritation swelled and he suppressed his own growl. He took a deep breath. "Can either of you please face reality here? You will be eating, so a childish tantrum won't get you far. Obviously I won't let you starve yourselves, so deal with it."

Neither made a move toward the food, and Ian narrowed his eyes. "You know what will happen, Nicky. Think about it."

Nickolas shifted uncomfortably and looked at Jessica. She still wore a mulish expression.

With a sigh, Ian reached out and took a bite of everything on the tray. "There, happy? Now eat. Nick, you've got a few more hours and that's it."

He turned and stomped out of the room. He glared at Jays who pressed his lips together in an unsuccessful attempt to hide his smile.

"They are going to be the death of me," he muttered as he walked over to the monitor island where Jays had laid out their dinners. His Second snorted.

Chapter Eleven

Very early the next morning, Nickolas shoved the doors to the Hub open and hurried through. He'd managed a few hours of restless sleep, but the need to see Jessica drove him from his bed and back to the Hub. For two days he had succeeded in staying away, but after yesterday he wasn't strong enough to resist any longer. Overnight, alone in his room, the mental noise pollution inundated him. The respite while in her company had lowered his threshold.

She soothed him.

The doors swung shut, blocking out what little fresh air penetrated the building. The sterile, antiseptic burn clogged his nose. Jays turned to look at him and sighed. "Nick, what are you doing here? Ian told you he had to be here to supervise."

"Supervise what? Come on, Jays. What will happen in a locked room?"

"She's sleeping."

"I doubt that."

Jays flipped on her monitor as if to prove his point, then stopped. Nick looked over his shoulder. She sat on her bunk tapping her foot. He chuckled.

"It's still no, Nick. Go back to bed."

"You know I've never slept well. She's awake, I'm awake, it's better than going for a flight..."

"At this hour?" Jays cut in. "You should not be out flying alone, Nickolas. You know that."

"Give me a break, Jays. You sound as bad as Chris. Come on, let me in."

Jays swore under his breath then stomped over to the phone. "Ian? Yeah, sorry to wake you. Nick's back in here.

Yeah, I already did that. Well, what do you want me to do? No. That won't work."

Nickolas pulled up one of the chairs and sat to watch Jess. Already the proximity helped. Now if he could just get into her room.

"I did; the alternative wasn't good. Ok." Jays hung up the receiver.

Nick waited for him to join him at the consoles.

"Ian isn't happy with you right now."

Nick shrugged and turned back to watching Jessica. After a few minutes, the doors to the hall opened. He looked over his shoulder at an irritated Ian.

"I thought I told you to go back to your room and get some rest?"

"I did."

Ian leaned his hip against the desk next to him. "Five hours doesn't count as a night's sleep."

"Four," he muttered.

"And that makes it better?"

He turned back to the screen. Jessica had stood up and started to pace the room.

"Look, Nicky, we need to come to an understanding. There are things we have to do. Are you going to hinder us? I won't let you in then."

He shrugged, and Ian slapped his hand down over the controls, cutting the video. He took a breath and suppressed the growl that tried to crawl up his throat.

Ian leaned over and pressed into his space. "You know what to expect. I still need to get the tests that were interrupted yesterday, and I'll expect not just your compliance but your help to get them. Are you up for that? Because it won't do her any good to have to watch you get tranked and removed if you lose control."

They stared at one another for a moment. "What do you want from me?"

"Whatever it takes, Nicky. Can you do it?"

He pulled away from the intense green eyes and rested his head in his hands. *What choice do I have? Do what he wants, or not see Jessica anymore.* "I'll do what I must."

Ian stood, then squeezed his shoulder. "All right, come on."

He rose from the chair, then stretched and flapped his wings before following Ian to her cell. The doctor looked him in the eye for a moment, then swiped his keycard and pulled the door open.

Jessica spun when he entered, then he saw her exhale in relief.

"Couldn't sleep?" she asked.

He shook his head. The sound of the door lock engaging barely registered. "You either?"

She chuckled without much mirth and tried to run her fingers through her hair; they caught in the tangles. "I slept plenty yesterday."

"Here, let me help with that." He glanced up at the camera, then pulled the hairbrush he had tucked into the back of his waistband out. He moved over to the cot and sat, sliding back against the wall. He patted the space between his legs.

Her gaze flicked to the brush, and he watched the longing fill her eyes, then she paced the couple of feet separating them and sank to the mattress.

He ran his fingertips along the length of silk then gathered up the mass and teased out a lock before placing the rest over her left shoulder to keep it out of the way. He set the brush bristles to the ends and started to work his way up the lock, teasing the snarls out on the way, careful not to scratch the skin covering her emerging wings. Once the lock was clear, he tucked it over her right shoulder then freed another and started again.

They sat in silence for a long time while he worked on her hair. His fingers reveled in the slick softness, delving into the thickness and letting the strands slide through. He watched as they trailed along the skin of her neck and down her exposed back, over the swollen wing buds, before he started on another lock.

The pressure in his head from the absence of the drugs hovered in the background. A constant reminder of the unknown, of the lies...

He pushed the thoughts away.

Here and now. Concentrate on that.

Once all the knots had been worked free, he continued to run the brush through the length, along her scalp to the ends, rhythmically soothing.

The scent of summer air currents rose between them, and he bent his head to rest his cheek on her crown; his arms slipped around her waist. "You smell so good."

She relaxed into him and laughed. "Are you kidding? I stink. It's been how many days since I've had a shower?"

"Doesn't matter. Don't try and keep track. It'll drive you nuts. How's your memory been?"

"It comes and goes. The first few days seemed to be the worst. The headaches have been hitting with more frequency though."

"I'm sorry. I wish I could help you."

He felt her breathing pause, then she said softly, "You could get me out of here. That would help."

He closed his eyes and rubbed his cheek against her head. "We've talked about this. It's not safe. Where would you go? You need care, whether you want it or not."

"Then come with me."

She turned her shoulders to look up at him. He hadn't felt a desire like this to leave the Facility since his own isolation. But he shook his head. "Same question. Where would we go, Jess? And even if they left us alone, so we didn't have to constantly look over our shoulders, how would we get food? We don't have much money, and it's not like we're inconspicuous. Maybe if it were summer..."

He stared out across the room into nothing, then shook himself back to reality. "No. I protected you yesterday. I will again."

Sadness crept into her expression. "You can't. You don't have any more control than I."

She pulled her legs up and rested her head on his shoulder. He ran his hand up and down her spine. *You're more right than you know.*

His hand passed over a wing bud again and a rolling movement stilled his hand. He gently probed the swelling while he added up the days. Shocked at their size for how early it still was in her change, he could feel the full definition of a wing frame. An uneasy feeling crept over him.

He felt her yawn, and he pulled her tighter, leaning his head back against the wall.

The squeak of a wheel shocked them awake. Nick felt his emotional descent too late to suppress the growl that issued warning. Ian's face swam into view. The doctor crouched at eye level. At some point, he realized, he had slumped to the side with Jessica on the cot.

The sudden waking had triggered his body to react before his brain caught up. Ian's steady gaze bored into his as he sorted himself out. His arms braced over her, Jessica's tense form lay still, waiting, caged under his protective one.

He blinked, then his eyes shifted to look at the closed door, then at Jays, the cart, and the rest of the room, before meeting Ian's eyes again.

"Are you both fully awake now?"

He forced his muscles to relax so he wasn't about to spring. "Time?"

"Several hours."

Jessica's hand had slid out to rest on his wrist in front of her. He furled his right wing, which was draped over their bodies, and let himself ease back down to the bed, pressing into her back. Ian's green gaze never left him, and he waited for the doctor to make the first move.

"I let you two have as much time as I could, but we have a lot to get done today. First, let's look at those stitches, Jess."

He watched Ian stand and put the trank gun he had held concealed into his pocket. Then Ian crossed his arms, waiting. Nick buried his face in Jessica's hair and inhaled deeply before loosening his hold around her middle. She started to growl but let go of his arm. He didn't like it either. He pushed himself up into a sitting position; she remained on her side and stretched her leg across his lap. His fingers slid under the cuff of the shorts and worked it over the stitches.

Ian examined the two wounds closely. "Good. Jays, note down that the infection seems to have dissipated. And the lacerations are healing nicely."

Nick pulled the cloth back down and watched Ian steel himself. That didn't bode well.

"Ok, Jess," Ian addressed her, but Nick noticed that he stared into his eyes. "I need to check your wing growth."

The uneasy feeling he'd had earlier returned full force. His gaze shot to Jays's blank face then back to Ian. Why would they be so concerned... *They wouldn't...*

He turned his head and looked at the waterfall of hair that concealed her enlarged wing buds. One hand resting on her hip, he reached out with the other and brushed the strands to the side. Movement rolled beneath the surface again. His hand glided over the skin. Hot. And he felt the strut flex against the confinement.

Sliding his hand down farther, he pressed the small of her back, urging her to roll onto her stomach. He pulled her farther across his lap.

Ian stepped forward and after a swift glance at him, quickly palpated her emerging wings. A sigh escaped his lips. "Tape, Jays."

He stretched the cloth tape across her swollen skin and recited the various numbers from the measurements he made.

"So they *are* ready?" Jays said.

"Looks like."

"But it's too soon," Nick said.

"Tell that to her," Ian snapped, then took a calming breath. "Look, Nick, now's the time I warned you about; you have to decide."

"Decide what? You're just going to free her wings." He looked back and forth between the two doctors.

"I need you to hold her, Nicky," Ian said softly.

"Why would.... No. You wouldn't do that." He shook his head and stared at the truth in Ian's eyes.

"Nick?" Jessica whispered.

He rubbed the stiffened muscles in her back. "This isn't right."

"She has shown repeatedly that she doesn't react properly to drugs. Look at what happened yesterday. I can't have strange interactions from different meds popping up. And she has a heavy load today."

"Damn it, Ian, we're talking about a bit of local anesthetic. What's that going to interfere with?"

"She's felt it each time we've set stitches. Haven't you, Jess?"

Nick felt her starting to tremble, but she nodded her head to Ian's question. He ground his teeth and looked back at Ian.

"You've done worse to yourself in practice, Nicky."

"Something is better than nothing."

Losing his temper, Ian snapped, "We don't have a choice, Nickolas. If they aren't freed, they will be permanently misshapen and never bear weight. So which would you rather her have, Nick? Unavoidable pain now? Or the pain she'd have for the rest of her life because she would never fly? I know which I would choose."

Wanting to howl, he closed his eyes instead and took a deep breath. Her fear swirled around him, but she didn't try to struggle off his lap. She twisted her head and he looked down into her eyes. Tears glistened in them but had yet to fall. He gathered up her hair and tossed it over the other side to fall down toward the floor, then ran his thumb across her cheek.

"I'm sorry, Jess," he whispered.

She nodded her head.

He slid one leg out from underneath her and stretched it across the back of her knees then placed a hand in the small of her back to hold her steady. They locked eyes.

"I'll be as quick as I can, Jess," Ian said.

Only a portion of his awareness stayed on what Ian and Jays did. Instead, he sank into the hazel of her eyes. The rustle of an absorbent drape pushed between him and Jessica and the bed. Ian's shoulder brushed his arm as the doctor felt around the first swelling before he carefully incised a slit the length of the wing bud; fluid and blood gushed out, and Jays sopped it up with gauze.

Jessica shuddered and the tears glazing her eyes started to escape, but she didn't utter more than a gasp. His mind pushed out, wanting to help her somehow.

Ian had separated the skin encasing the fragile new appendage and gently pulled the mucus covered limb free of the pocket, laying it across her back, then turned to the second wing.

A flexible barrier stopped his mind. Light flickered in the hazel depths but then sputtered out. In contrast, his own eyes, reflected in the watery sheen, blazed. She shuddered and cried out when the scalpel bit in again; the coppery scent of her blood filled the sterile air and coated his tongue. He pushed harder and popped through the bubble. As fast as a thought could travel, he cocooned her, separating her from what her body felt. He stood between her and the pain. It washed around him, but pain was second nature to him.

Nicky, the thought whispered. *Come out.*

He pushed it away, but then a giant shove sent him mentally stumbling, and he ripped out of her mind.

He cracked the back of his head against the wall and saw stars. Jessica moaned. Ian hovered over Jessica's head and stared into his face. Jays had just finished flushing the pockets clear of the mucus and was spreading the membrane of the fragile new wings out to dry.

"Jess?" he whispered but couldn't tear himself away from the strange look on Ian's face.

"She's fine." The doctor's clipped words cut through the throb in his head. Ian stood and looked at Jays. "Let's get the rest of the exam done. We've got a busy day."

Nick looked down at Jessica's face. Her eyes were closed and tear tracks ran across her nose and down her cheek. His hand trembled slightly when he lifted it up to pet her head. He forced them to subside. Her back wasn't a pretty sight. The loose skin of the encasing pockets sagged, and the cut edges had been cauterized. The stench still hung in the air. A little surprised that he had missed that, he looked closer at her wings. They were the most well-defined wings he had ever seen at this stage. As her flight muscles bulked up, the loose skin would stretch a little and what wasn't needed would slough off. Eventually, her back would appear smooth and blemish-free. But for the moment, it looked like a battle wound. The new wings lay like a limp fan down her back. The rope muscles coiled along the twig-like pinion struts, the membrane so thin it was transparent. In a couple of days, the struts would solidify and take on the whip-like strength that allowed them to be so flexible, yet strong. It was amazing that a limb that looked so fragile and skeletal would develop into such a beautiful, strong body part.

The two doctors had finished taking her vitals, and Ian exchanged the last vial of blood for a syringe of amber liquid, which he clipped onto the needle and injected. That got a reaction from Jessica. She flinched violently and hissed, her eyes snapping open. His leg across her knees was the only thing that stopped her from leaping up.

"That was the inhibitor, Jessica," Ian said. He unclipped the syringe and took a second from Jays. "And this is a radio tracer."

"What?" they said in unison. Nick caught the fear in her eyes.

Ian slapped a gauze square on the vein inside her elbow and taped it down. Jays pushed the cart toward the door. The no-nonsense look Ian cast him put his hackles up.

"I must have those scans. You have one hour, Nickolas. The tracer will have penetrated all of her tissues by then. One hour to convince her to take a sedative willingly, or watch her get tranked from the door."

"Damn it, Ian!" he shouted at the doctor's back. He couldn't leap up like he wanted to, couldn't take the chance on damaging her drying wings. He slid out from underneath her, but the door sealed before he reached it. He slammed his fist into it.

"Now will you help me get out of here?" she asked softly.

He spun and raked a hand through his hair. She had sat up, her hair pulled over her shoulders to keep it out of her wet wings. He stalked the short length of room.

"I..." He stopped and stared at the corner. Silence fell heavy between them.

"I'm scared, Nick," she said in a voice so quiet and full of defeat he could barely hear her.

He turned back to her, his step leaden, then crouched down in front of her. His fingertips brushed the softness of her skin then cupped her cheek. "Please, Jess. Will you do as he asks? I can't watch them do that. He knows it. So they'll come in and take me out too. You're right. I can't stop them. But I can promise not to leave your side while you are out."

"I don't want this."

"Neither do I." He dropped his hand to the mattress and looked down.

A touch as soft as butterfly wings slid across his hair.

"Why do you stay here?"

"I don't know anymore." His forehead lowered to her knees. "I don't know."

Jays steered the cargo van through the gate, topped with razor wire, and stopped on the inside. He jumped out into the weak sunlight and pulled the tall gate shut, then laced the chain through the galvanized mesh. He hooked the padlock in place and twisted it so that it looked locked. His gaze raked the length of forest across the road.

Gravel crushed with each step back to the waiting vehicle. He swung up behind the wheel and looked at Nickolas in the passenger seat.

The Alpha Valkyrie lifted his nose and scented the new air currents that blew in from the opening and closing of the door. *I wonder what it smells like?* The crisp cool air, the brittle scattered leaves, damp underneath the sun-warmed top layer. *I hope Ian's right that Nick can hold it together for this trip out. He certainly wasn't pleased to have his routine altered.*

Oh no, definitely not. The snarling and snapping they'd had to deal with...

He had not wanted to leave Jessica.

The farther away from the Facility, the quieter he had gotten. And the more fey.

He met Chris's eyes in the mirror for the millionth time. Then he put the truck in gear and wound through the buildings until he got to the warehouse number he needed, backing up to the loading platform. Nickolas was out before he'd even gotten the engine off, Donald and Chris on his heels.

"Keep those wings furled, Nick," Chris growled.

"I was just going to stretch," he snapped back.

"There's plenty of room inside the warehouse."

Jays held his breath, but instead of attacking, Nick stalked up the steps. He stood, waiting, by the locked door, rubbing his forehead.

All three of them let out a sigh.

His hand brushed the soft cotton of the cargo pocket on his pants and felt the reassuring shape of the trank gun, then he hurried up the steps and unlocked the door. Mumbling to himself, Nick passed through.

Jays reached to the left of the doorway and flipped the row of switches. Lights flickered on high overhead, gilding the tops of the shelves and casting shadows into the aisles.

Let's get them busy so I can get on with my job. He pulled a list out of his pocket. After comparing it to the aisles and some of the boxes, he found what he needed in the middle of the warehouse and called the others over.

"We need all the boxes on this row of shelves, along with those over there." He pointed to another set an aisle over. "I need to go to the office to see if anything else got scheduled and to record the inventory list of what we take. I'll let you guys take care of loading."

A nebulous feeling, something like a brush of wind whispering by, startled Jays, and he whipped a look at Nickolas. The Alpha Valkyrie stood frozen, his face distant. Concerned, Jays snapped his fingers. "Nick?"

Chris and Donald surged up around him, worried frowns on their faces.

Nickolas shuddered, then his eyes cleared and he turned to him. "Is there anyone else here, Jays?"

"No. It's Sunday." The piercing blue eyes unnerved him, so he turned away. *At least no one you need to know about.*

"We've got this, Jays. Go deal with the paper work."

Trusting them to keep Nick contained, he left them to load the truck and made his way toward the office in the rear. After a quick look over his shoulder, he bypassed the stairs leading to the office and let himself out the back door quietly. Easing the door shut, he jumped down the stairs and entered the neighboring building, leaving that door ajar. He had just started to unlatch the loading gate when the door behind him squeaked. He looked up and smiled at the man who entered. The dark coat covering his wings billowed out behind him as he approached.

"Hello, Jays. How're you doing?"

"Not too bad, all things considered. A bit stressful though, since you guys failed."

"Yeah, well, she always did want to go her own way."

Clasping forearms with Robin, Jays laughed. "True, her temperament hasn't changed much. She's still a real pain in the ass."

Robin's brow wrinkled and his gaze locked on him. "Is she all right though?"

Jays squeezed the Hunter's arm then let go. "For the moment she is. But it's been touch and go. She's a fighter. She doesn't want to be in the Facility and refuses to cooperate."

"You know she wouldn't have if we'd gotten her to Aurora, either."

"That's what Ian said." He leaned back against the wall. "Really, it's thanks to Nick that she's doing as well as she is. Something's happening between them, but Ian doesn't know what it is yet. We managed to get in-depth scans on her, finally, a couple of days ago. He's still interpreting the results, and they are raising more questions. He's trying to figure out how to get the same scans done on Nick now. Nick's the only one who she'll listen to and will allow close to her. She ignores me and is skittish of Ian. He's the only reason we've gotten her condition stabilized. Her test results are off the charts. If Gabriel finds out..."

"She's exactly the sort that he'd dearly love to get his hands on."

"Yes. And he's been around the Hub a lot lately."

Robin looked up at the ceiling and sighed. "Damn. How're we going to get her out of this?"

"That's Ian's job."

"I know. But this is my baby sister we're talking about."

Robin's neck convulsed when he swallowed, which drew Jays's attention in the dim lighting of the warehouse. There was an immense purple black bruise and stitches on the Valkyrie's neck. "What happened to you? Aborted vampire attack?"

Robin snorted and dropped his chin. "Funny. The cost of failure, I guess. Souvenir from disciplining Kelley."

"She got you that bad?" he blurted.

Crossing his arms Robin smirked. "*She* didn't walk off the field."

He swallowed then replied softly, "Oh."

At the feral light in Robin's eyes, Jays ducked his head and turned back to the rest of the warehouse. *I have to remember he's not the friend I played with as a kid anymore.*

Robin's wings rustled beneath the fabric of his coat, then he spoke in a gentle tone. "You mentioned things happening between Jess and Nickolas? I need to know what's going on with him."

He looked back at the Valkyrie. Robin slipped the duster off and stretched his wings. "Nickolas took himself off the arresting inhibitor and has started experimenting with his talent. I don't know what he can do, but he's unpredictable and extremely volatile at the moment. So be on guard when you attempt the transfer. We don't know how much longer we can risk taking him out of the Facility, so this may be the last message we can pass for a bit. Ian has included a detailed report on it for Marcus in this data stream."

"We knew something was going on. Kelley reported that it looked like he'd been using talent during the hunt."

"Ian's confirmed that."

"So what now? How long can you guys keep this hidden? Especially if Gabriel's coming around."

Jays just shook his head.

The door creaked again, and Robin's Flight filed in. Robin closed his eyes for a moment. "Right," he exhaled.

The enormity of the situation was not lost on Jays. He felt the burden on his shoulders, and his wasn't as heavy as Ian's.

"Ian will tell us what to do."

Robin's Flight started poking around the stacks of crates and boxes.

"I know. You're all just in such a precarious position. I worry."

Jays coughed then cleared his throat. "Well, the stuff we've been able to misappropriate is all stacked over here."

He led Robin over to a large pile waiting against the wall and rested his hand on it. "There're some medicines in here that will need refrigeration as soon as possible. And be careful of the boxes with blue tape, they're fragile. It's all we've been able to manage so far, though we hope to have another drop ready in a few weeks."

"Anything is always appreciated. You know that, Jays. Just don't get yourselves in trouble right now."

"I don't know if there's any avoiding that, Robin." He chuckled mirthlessly. "And this may be the last shipment we can put together."

They stood silently for a moment.

"I should get back. The guys will be close to done loading the truck. We'll be out of your way in a few."

"We still need to make the data transfer," Robin said.

"Just watch it. Nick's really acting odd."

Robin snaked an arm around him and pulled him into a tight hug. "Thanks for the warning."

He stiffened before allowing his arms to slip around his friend's waist and return the hug, then stepped back. The physicality of the Valkyries still threw him at times.

"Thank you, Jays...for all you do."

Not sure what to say, he looked into Robin's hazel eyes, then shrugged and turned, walking to the door. He stopped when Robin called his name and looked over his shoulder at his old friend.

"Be careful, Jays. And please take care of Jessica."

Nodding, he raised his hand in farewell. "I'll do my best."

Bright sunlight struck his eyes when he exited. He squinted and jogged across the alley to slip back into the warehouse he had left his Valkyries in.

He eased the door closed, then made his way swiftly up the back stairs to the office. After riffling papers to make it look like he had been there for a while, he searched through a file drawer to locate the current requisition sheet. A quick glance showed him a few extras tacked on from what Ian sent him to bring back. He jotted down their location in the warehouse then made short work of the removed inventory sheet. He grabbed up his note and headed back out to find the others.

He took the stairs down from the office three at a time and nearly ran straight into Nickolas at the bottom. Skidding to a halt, he stepped back. "Whoa, sorry. Didn't mean to almost run you over."

Nickolas gave him a queer look then slowly paced a circle around him, sniffing. Jays stood straighter. The image of a feral dog examining him flashed across him mind...if he made one wrong move...

He cautiously met Nickolas's eyes. Ian's training kicked in. His voice echoed in his head. *Always maintain dominance. Never drop your eyes, for even a second. If it comes to a battle of wills, you have to come out on top or you'll lose control of the group. Redirect them. Because if it turns physical, you don't stand a chance. Not against their enhanced strength and speed.* Plastering a cocky self-assuredness across his face that he didn't feel, he raised his eyebrow at the Valkyrie.

Still staring at him, Nickolas spoke so softly Jays had trouble hearing him. "We're almost done, I came to find you and see if there was anything else?"

Jays took a step forward into Nick's space; the fey look in his eyes worried him, with Ian's warnings still loud and clear. "Are you all right, Nickolas?"

The Valkyrie lifted his head up, scenting the air again before he replied. "I feel like I'm being watched."

Startled, Jays responded. "Excuse me? Watched by whom?"

"I'm not sure."

Goose bumps rolled across his skin, and he walked past Nickolas, hoping to get the Alpha to follow him. "It's probably a side effect of all the time you've spent with Jessica this week. Her fear and paranoia rubbing off."

After a glance at his list, he turned down an aisle, scanning boxes as he went. "Try to ignore it."

"I feel..."

He looked over his shoulder at Nickolas and stopped to study the vagueness in his eyes. He watched a shiver ripple the length of his wings, then the vagueness faded.

"You feel what?"

"I feel like there's another Hunter around," he said, scanning the ceiling and surrounding aisles.

Damn it. He's one step away from going feral. So he snapped, "Don't be ridiculous, of course there are. They arrived with us." Then pointing to a box at random, he drew Nickolas's attention. "That box, Nick. Take it up to the truck and send the others back here. There are a few more I need to locate."

The Valkyrie hesitated, scanning the area, then shrugging, he picked up the box. Jays watched him turn the corner at the end of the aisle and his shoulders fell with the gust of breath that whistled past his teeth. *Close.* He searched out the other items on his list and set them on the floor for the rest to cart back. *The sooner we get out of here, the better.*

Chris and Donald arrived on the run. They loaded up, leaving one last box that Jays carried when he went to join the others at the loading bay doors. He handed his box off to Donald, then turned to lock up the doors and caught a glimpse of movement out of the corner of his eye. *No. You idiot!*

Growls erupted all around him. Jays whipped about and yelled at all of his mantling charges. "Everyone in the van now. Move it. In the vehicle," he snapped. Robin's Hunter had only been visible for a split second, but that had been enough to send his boys into an uproar. He pushed each of them, one by one, until he got them in the vehicle. As he slid into the driver's seat, he glanced at Nickolas.

"I told you there was a Hunter," he said.

Jays shivered. Nickolas's reactions really brought home how different a non-controlled Valkyrie behaved. The brief contacts he'd had with Robin over the years had given him warning, but Robin stayed on his best behavior when they met, Jays knew. He just wanted to get Nick back to the Facility—now—and without any more problems.

He started the engine and shot gravel into the concrete bulkhead. "Let's just get home."

Jessica paced the confines of her cell, her arms wrapped about her stomach. She stopped and took slow, shallow breaths to ease through the nausea. When the wave passed, she continued pacing and reflected while she could on the fragmentation of her mind. At the moment, she had a clear patch and could see her deterioration, but more importantly, she could see how the effects seemed minimized when Nickolas was near.

Where is he?

He hadn't brought in her breakfast like usual. And the change of routine left her unsettled. She gripped her stomach when a strong surge twisted it. Not a lot in there for the drug to work with.

Jays's face swam across her memory. Concern warred with exasperation when he had come in to clean up the breakfast tray she had refused.

That had been hours ago. Immediately on the heels of that, Ian had joined them and committed his exam on her. Now the side effects from the inhibitor pulsed through her system.

She steadied herself with a hand against the wall and hissed a breath through clenched teeth. Once she had it under control, she stood and stretched her miniscule wings.

The air pressure changed, and she looked up to see the door swing open. Kieran stepped through, a full tray in his hands. She gulped in a breath and held it. He set the tray down then shrugged a black canvas case off his shoulder and leaned it against the wall. He turned to her, his eyes downcast, his face a mottled yellow-green blotchy mess.

"What the hell happened to you?" Opening her mouth had been a mistake. The air, filled with the aroma of the food, hit her. "Oh god."

She slapped a hand over her mouth as her stomach rebelled. She couldn't force it back down this time and spun, dashing for the toilet. Muscles heaving, she retched over and over. Gentle hands held her hair out of the way, and he supported her straining body, murmuring how much he had hated this part of the change too.

Mortified, she shivered, still panting. Tears pricked her eyes. Kieran brushed a hand over her sweaty forehead. As soon as the tremors subsided enough to stand, she pushed away from the toilet and the Hunter. Leaning heavily on the sink, she cupped water in her hand and rinsed her face and mouth. She stood over the sink, water dripping off her face, for what felt like hours.

Eventually she turned to face him. The compassion emanating from his eyes struck her, and she turned away from it, pacing again.

He cleared his throat, and the slide of plates scraped across the table. "Look on the bright side, the worst of the day is over. You should be able to keep food down now."

She bared her teeth at him and kept pacing. A flush crept under the bruising and he looked down again.

"I'm sorry, Jess. I didn't want to do it. Ian insisted, and I..." He sighed. "Please..."

She glanced at his injured face again. "You didn't answer my question. What happened?"

His finger touched the half-healed split in his lip and he shrugged. "Nothing you need to worry about."

"Really?" The sudden upsurge of possessive anger caught her by surprise and she turned to stalk him. His eyes darted a look at her then turned down again. He stood his ground, but she noticed his wings slick tight to his back. "You drugged me last time, Kieran. You owe me something. Now, what happened? Who beat the crap out of you?"

She stopped in front of him and put her hands on her hips. He was only a few inches taller, but she could still look up into his downturned face. A sudden thought rushed in. "It wasn't Nick?"

His eyes widened and met hers squarely. "No."

Relief softened her spine. "You know I don't want to be here, but with how much time you've spent with me, I had thought we'd become friends."

Hope brightened his eyes and he bit his lip. "I'm a Wing leader. I have rank. And that means responsibility. I had to protect the others."

He turned away and fidgeted with the plates again. "I knew you wouldn't trust food I brought in, so I brought two plates. You pick and I'll eat the other. Ok?"

"What's to stop them from just knocking you out too?"

"Nothing, I guess. But I think Ian learned his lesson. I expect you'll see it coming from now on."

She grunted then picked a plate and sat on the floor opposite the bunk. "Go ahead and have the comfy seat. So, I'm still waiting to hear why your face is the color it is and who I'll have to look up when I'm out of here."

He grumbled under his breath while he got settled. "You're just not going to let it go, are you? It's not someone you can take on. And none of us would let you if you tried."

"No I won't let it go. I'm probably more stubborn than anyone you know."

"No one's more stubborn than Nick." He chuckled. "But so far you're giving him a run for his money."

"Speaking of? Where is he?" She started to pick at the food in her lap and ignored his pointed look. It took work to give the impression that she wasn't overly interested in his answer. *What's up with this, anyway? Why should I care? I need to focus on getting out of this trap while I can, not on how I feel about the one who put me here.*

"Ian sent him and a couple of the others on an errand with Jays. He should be back in a couple of hours."

Fog slithered through her thoughts, and she pushed it back. As meat juice slid down her finger, she licked it off, and then her nose twitched as the air currents shifted. She glanced up at the air register in the ceiling. *Maybe.* She left the thought to stew and turned her attention back to Kieran. "Errands, huh? That seems a little mundane. Valkyries aren't thick in the streets, after all. As I'm sure you know being the 'face of the Valkyries' as you are. You've been on all the major news programs, haven't you? How's it being famous?"

She leaned her head against the wall and chewed another bite of food. Kieran fidgeted on the bed and ducked his head to his plate but not fast enough to hide the red blotches that overtook his cheeks, even through the dark clouds marring them. He cleared his throat.

"Thank my sister Siobhan for that. Let's just say I'm glad Ian reassigned me for a bit. Not that I could have worked right now anyway."

"What? You don't think anyone would want to see your pretty face at PR events at the moment?" she said with sweet venom.

The look he cast her gave her some insight into why he was a lieutenant. The sharp edge he usually kept carefully contained showed through. "You're not the only one who gets to do things you don't want."

She smiled and his eyes narrowed. "Then why do it? I really don't get you guys. Are you kept prisoners? That wouldn't surprise me from what I've heard. Why stay? Why let them parade you around like a zoo exhibit? Or better yet, a prized pet. Yes, that's more accurate."

"I help people. The appearances, the talks, and yes, the gawking, all serve to teach. The change is loose. That's a fact of life. The ripples have only begun to spread, and there's no stopping them. Before Siobhan got the protection laws into place, a recovery was Russian roulette for the fledgling..." He trailed off, his eyes staring at something she couldn't see, then swallowed before continuing. "At least now the authorities have a framework in which to operate. And more and more the average person reacts from a base of knowledge instead of fear when a recovery is in process, because of the program."

With a sigh she set her plate on the floor next to her. "There's no way you'll help me get out of here, is there?"

His face grew blank. "Nothing's changed."

"I agree."

It was a stalemate as they stared at one another.

"Nothing will keep me here, Kieran."

He shook his head then set his empty plate on the table. "There's not that many of us, Jess. We don't get a lot of choices. There's here and then there's Gabriel. Here's a better choice. Trust me."

They don't tell them about Aurora. What a shocker. "So you are prisoners. I'm not really surprised."

"Not exactly prisoners. At least I've never made that comparison. I always felt more protected than imprisoned."

"Just like a prized pampered poodle. You even do their obedience trials. Can you please try and break out of your mindset? Remember what it was like to live before you changed. And compare the two. You can go anywhere. It's not a choice of here or there. And then there's Aurora. Not all Valkyries live under lock and key."

"Aurora?" Puzzlement warred with indignation on his face over being called a poodle.

The door unlocked and Ian strode in. His eyes flashed her a look that she easily interpreted as "shut up." She smiled at him, all teeth. As he bent to pick up her plate, his breath shivered across her skin. "There's some information better divulged in small doses."

He rose then stacked Kieran's dishes with hers on the tray. She watched his white back retreat out the door and mulled over his warning.

Kieran looked thoughtful as well. She pulled her knees to her chest and wrapped her arms around them. "I still want to know why you're beat up. Who were you protecting?"

He sighed and turned a slow look her way. After a moment, he reached down to the black canvas bag he had brought with him. He pulled it up onto his lap and started to unzip it. "I really didn't want to go into this with you, Jess. I was stuck outside the lockdown perimeter. There were four others brought in before me. The guards thought they could have some fun with them, but I occupied their minds instead."

He sent her a rueful grin and finished stripping the case off of a large flat drum. His long lean fingers caressed the skin in a circular motion. The harsh glare from the overhead fluorescents picked out the delicate silver inlay woven in a band around the wood side. "Someone I used to be very close to gave me this bodhran. Zach changed many years ago; before either Donald or I. I haven't seen him since."

He set the edge of the drum on his knee and slipped his left hand inside. She noticed that when he talked about his past, his accent picked up. The lilt grew stronger. He rummaged in a pocket of the bag. "They both made a habit of watching out for the young kid."

He pulled out a round-headed stick then shifted his wings and sat back more comfortably. "I was never as big or as strong as either one of them. Even now I still can't take Donald. I can only imagine Zach as a Valkyrie."

He tapped the beater lightly against the skin, testing the sound. "You seemed to like my singing the other day. And I know how boring it is in here, so I thought I'd play a bit for you."

She nodded and leaned her head back against the wall. A slow heartbeat rhythm started, and she closed her eyes. Soon his clear tenor twined softly with the drum.

She thought back over everything he'd said. *Great. It's my fault he got beat up. That's what he didn't want to tell me.* She sighed. *I've got to work a plan to get out of here. And not just for me.* She opened her eyes and watched Kieran sing. Purple shadowed his eye and the blue and green blotches shifted across his cheekbones as he moved. Anger pooled under the calm the music brought. She'd have no qualms snapping the necks of whoever had caused his pain. That realization shook her. *No strings, damn it. I won't take responsibility for anyone else. Why does this stupid change have to screw with me like this? It's bad enough that I feel so dependent on Nickolas, but now I want to take care of Kieran? Come on. Give me a break.*

None of them will help me. It's up to me. It's always been up to me. Why would I even try to trust anyone else? She rubbed her thigh. The stitches were healing nicely. At her last exam, Ian and Jays had discussed removing them soon. She glanced up to the ceiling and the vent caught her eye again. *Yes. That could work. Now I only need to figure out when it's night and when someone is actively watching me.*

Chapter Twelve

"Pheromones? Maybe I'm right." Ian reread the test results page a third time. "But why has it taken twenty-five years?"

He sat back and stared into Jessica's monitor. She slept curled on her side, facing the wall, her small wings tangled with her hair. She had fallen asleep to Kieran's singing a couple of hours ago. When he noticed Kieran moving her to the bed, he pulled the Beta out to go catch up on what he could with his weekly exertion tests. The bruises on his torso had healed enough. *His test scores might be a little out of normal for him, but I doubt it'll be much.*

A tremor rocked her body, and he leaned closer to turn up the sound. A soft keening filled the room and she covered her head with her arms. Dazzle headache.

At least she's sleeping through this one.

He turned the volume down and leaned back, picking up his notes again. Voices echoed from the hallway just before the doors pushed open.

"That's a real thin excuse, Jays."

"Well, I'm sorry. It's the best you're getting at the moment."

"Not acceptable."

Ian stacked up his papers and slid them into a folder, then watched the Alpha Valkyrie prowl toward him. Tentacles of power quested out, touching everything. Ian blinked and tuned down that part of his vision. Now the currents of energy didn't obscure his observations of Nickolas. Irritation mixed with the restless energy.

Nickolas stopped on the other side of the desk and stared. Ian met his eyes and held the blue gaze squarely.

"Why are we being lied to?"

He cocked a brow. "Hello, nice to see you too, Nicky. And how was your day? Here? Jessica refused to eat breakfast and threatened Kieran, but what else is new."

"How was my day? Why did I need to go on a pointless errand to move a few boxes around? And see? I told you I was needed here if she wouldn't eat breakfast."

"It wasn't a pointless errand, and I needed to see how she would do without you, Nick." *And you without her.*

The Valkyrie shoved away from the desk. Ian cast a glance at Jays, who cocked his hip against the desk and rolled his eyes. Nickolas walked around the center island then came in and stopped next to him, his attention riveted to Jessica's monitor.

She had uncurled, but her hands still clasped her ears. As they watched, she slowly sat up to rest her head in her hands. *Interesting. She must be able to feel Nickolas.*

A huge sigh escaped Nick and his shoulders relaxed their tension.

"Have you eaten, Nick?"

"Lunch. Some time ago," he replied absently. His wings rustled and he braced his hands on the desk, leaning forward, closer to the screen.

Ian tipped his head to Jays, who reached over to the phone and ordered an early dinner for the Hub's occupants. Including Nickolas.

"She seems to be waking up from her nap. Do you want to go in? It's close to dinnertime. You can join her if you want."

Nick shot a look out of the corner of his eye before returning his attention to the monitor. He pulled his wings still. "I...I should..."

"You need to eat. And you might as well make sure she does too. So come on." Ian rose from his chair and herded Nick toward her door.

After coaxing him inside, Ian returned to Jays at the monitors. Jessica wore a wary expression, and Nick paced the opposite wall. They watched the two metaphorically sniff around each other since their absence.

"So? What was that all about, Jays?"

The younger doctor snorted. "They caught sight of Robin's Hunter when they took the data."

"Ah. Yes, that's something I need to take up with Chris and Donald. There's no point in addressing it with Nick just now. He won't remember it soon. Other than that, how was he?"

Jessica stretched her leg then rubbed at the stitches. *They must be starting to itch. They might need to come out sooner,* Ian thought.

"Mentally? Not really with us. At first he fell into the expected aggression/anger cycle. Chris and Donald handled that without a problem, but the farther we got from the Facility, he became dissociative. Nothing like he is now." He waved at the screen where an animated conversation had erupted. "Now, he's holding a reasonable, rational conversation."

Ian crossed his arms and watched the two interact. "Jessica mirrored that. At least until Kieran went in. Then she became really clear. I would need to compare the tapes, but I would say it was the clearest I've seen her. Including any time she's spent with Nick."

Jays's head snapped to face him. "You're saying she's responding to Kieran the same as Nick?"

Ian shook his head. "No. Not quite. Though there is something…. She and Nick appear to be equals. She was most definitely Alpha to Kieran's Beta. She hasn't responded like that with Chris or Donald when they've been in with her. I think it had something to do with Kieran's injuries. But I feel like there's more to it."

"That's why everyone has kept Kieran out of Nick's sight, too."

"True, but…" He tipped his head and met Jays's gaze. "You're on the roster for weekly exams tomorrow. Make sure Kieran is in your group. I need you to get a couple of extra tests, discreetly. I have Nickolas's weekly tomorrow. I'll get the same then."

"What have you found out?"

He pulled the folder containing the test results out from under the monitor and handed it to Jays. They both settled into chairs. Ian propped his feet up while Jays started to leaf through the papers. "A few answers. But they just pose more questions. Jessica is releasing pheromones like crazy. We haven't run across this during any change I have been involved with. Male or female."

"Reproductive pheromones?" Jays exclaimed and flipped more pages. "But..."

"I know. There's not a single other Valkyrie whose reproductive tract has been functional after the change. Estrus ceased in the females, and most of the males contain no sperm in their ejaculate. Only a few have had nonmotile sperm counts. We had assumed that in those individuals the metamorphosis just hadn't wiped that part out completely. And effectively, it really didn't matter, since nonmotile sperm are sterile and none of the females could breed anyway."

Jays turned another page. "Well their change in reproductive properties certainly hasn't hampered their coital relations. They're like rabbits most of the time."

Sputtering a laugh, Ian dropped his feet to the floor. "That's an apt way to put it." He stood and stretched. "All except Nick that is. His original change file is in there too. I falsified the official document. He had too many abnormalities that I needed to keep out of Gabriel's hands."

"Right." Jays shuffled through the stack then started to read. "So Nick is one of those tested during the coma with sperm? Wait...it's almost like his reproductive system is prepubescent or on hold or something."

Jays's finger traced lines as he read quickly. Ian walked over to the minifridge in the corner, where they kept refreshments, and grabbed a soda.

"That was my interpretation as well," he said as he popped the top on the can. "He's not like the others that tested with a sperm count. Of which Kieran is one, by the way."

He made his way back to his chair and propped his feet back up, glancing at Jessica's screen. Nick was brushing Jessica's hair again. He sighed. "We're going to have to start frisking him if he keeps sneaking things into her room."

Jays looked up then laughed.

Ian studied them. "Jays? Look at the way Nick handles her."

"If I didn't know for a fact that Nickolas didn't have sexual relations with either males or females, I'd think he was courting her."

"And that brings us back to the start of the conversation. That's why I want tests done on both Nick and Kieran. She is releasing not only reproductive pheromones, in high quantities, but primer pheromones as well. I want to know what those primer pheromones are changing in the other Valkyries."

He took a drink of his soda and stared at the screen

"Because I think they have put *something* into motion."

He watched Nick's fingers slowly caress Jessica's hair before he bent his head and buried his nose in the locks.

"Full extension on your right wing please, Allison."

The fledgling stood against the blank wall of the Hub, her arms straight out and hands pressed into it. The wing unfurled while Jays picked up the tape measure. "Here, Jack. Since you're here, you can help me."

He handed one end to the other doctor and had him hold the pivot point at the ball joint of the wing so he could measure along each strut. He jotted them down on her chart.

"Looks like she's reached full growth," Jack said.

"Just about, I'd say. Other wing, Allison." They repeated the procedure on the other side. "I still don't like it, Jack."

The other doctor shrugged and continued to hold the point. "Sorry, Jays. But it'll work. You'll see. My transfer is complete in two more days. Neither you nor Ian has managed to get anyone in. We can't let this opportunity pass by."

Still not liking it, but knowing Jack was right, Jays finished her measurements and patted her wing. She folded it closed and turned around.

"All right, have a seat at the desk and let's go through your hearing." They all moved over to the island, and he got her set up with the headphones, turning the machine on. While she listened and pushed buttons, he turned back to Jack. "What do you have left today?"

"I have Third Flight exams. I finished the first wing this morning, so I just have their second wing to do still; so five more weekly physicals."

"Good luck with Aiden. He's been extremely teenagerish lately."

"Great. I haven't dealt with Third Flight in a couple of months." Jack crossed his arms and leaned into the desk. "Sorry to leave you shorthanded like this, Jays."

"Can't be helped. And with Michael being gone so much this week, it's not going to seem much different." He smiled at Jack to let him know he was joking.

He snorted. "True. The little prick. Sorry to leave you with him too. But thanks for the help this week. There's no way I would have gotten through all five Flights' physicals and their phys-ex tests by myself."

"No problem. I just have Chris's physical to do, then I'm done with First Flight. The rest of the afternoon I'll be in the gym with Second Flight doing their physical exertion tests."

"I'm done, Jays," Allison's tired voice interrupted.

"You ok, Allison? You seem awfully quiet today," Jack asked.

She rubbed between her eyes. "I'm just feeling really drained. Don't know."

He shared a look with Jack then asked her, "How's your appetite?"

"Actually, I'm starving. I was going to ask if I could have a snack after we were done?"

"No problem. I'll make sure you get plenty to eat." He looked up at the sound of the doors opening and watched Chris walk in. "I left your change of clothes in one of the shower stalls, Allison, so why don't you go get a shower, and when you're done, the food will be here."

"All right."

He waited until she had crossed the Hub and the door to the bathrooms had shut before he spoke to Chris. "She's going into the coma tonight."

The Hunter closed his eyes for a moment. "I'll let everyone know, thanks."

Jack straightened. "The second half of Third Flight should be arriving soon, so I'd better get over to the exam room. I'll catch up with you in the gym later, Jays."

"Sure. And can you please order Allison's last meal for me?"

"I'm on it," he called over his shoulder.

"I hate that term," Chris murmured.

Jays cocked his head at Chris then led him over to a stool in the triage alcove. "What would you call it then? It isn't a normal meal; it allows us to deal with the kitchen without too much fuss because they know the requirements, and it *is* their last meal. Whether she makes it through the coma or not, she won't eat or drink anything for the next week while she's unconscious. So we need to make sure she has enough food and water in her system to last her through. Dying of dehydration is the most common cause, you know that. I just wish hooking them up to an IV worked."

"Why doesn't it?"

Jays sat on a second stool then reached over to rummage around in a drawer and pulled out the pressure cuff he needed. "Ian told me that they had tried that at the start, but more often than not the fledge died. His theory is that when you are in the coma, your body is completely focused on the work it's doing. It uses up all stored energy and water, but the distraction of trying to take in extra is more than your bodies can handle."

He adjusted the cuff and took Chris's blood pressure. "That's also why we don't tell the fledglings about the coma. Historically, the knowledge has caused worry that has detrimentally interfered. And worrying about whether or not you will wake up has prevented some from eating and drinking enough. So it's just best all around if it isn't common knowledge."

He popped a thermometer into Chris's mouth, and while waiting, he got the blood draw equipment ready. After the beep, he recorded the reading in the Hunter's chart, then quickly took his weekly blood samples. "Ok, Chris, you know the drill. Anything to report?"

"Nope. Sight, hearing, smell are the same as always."

"Good. Go get on the scale." He scribbled on the chart, then recorded the weight Chris called over to him. "I went over your phys-ex chart and you seem to have lost some points in agility."

Chris sat back down and looked at his paper work with a frown.

"Sorry, dude. You know what that means."

"Come on, Jays..."

"No exceptions. Even Nick has had to deal with this one, and he gets out more than the rest of you for free flights."

"You know what's going to happen?" he growled.

Jays tried to suppress the grin, but he could tell he wasn't completely successful from the look on Chris's face. "I'm sure you're up for putting anyone in their place who teases you. Now, over to the wall. We need to see how much muscle we're looking at before I can see what sort of strengthening exercises you need."

With poor grace, Chris stomped over to the other side of the Hub and placed his hands on the wall, extending his wings. Starting at the rotator joint between his shoulder blades, Jays worked over the muscles in the right wing. He garnered a grunt of pain with how deep he probed, then he started following the rope muscle that spiraled down the pinion strut, testing for weak sections. The rope muscle was probably the most important muscle in the wing anatomy. It twisted the length of the front leading strut and enabled the person to extend and retract their wings and to trim them during flight. It was closely tied to the heavy flight muscle attached to the rotator joint, which allowed for the lifting of their body weight.

After examining those two major muscle groups, he moved on to test the flexibility of the secondary struts and fan muscles, then the anchor strut. If the anchor strut attachment had weakened, then that could certainly be a cause of loss of agility as the rest of his flight muscles tried to compensate for a weak foundation.

He wrote down his observations then repeated the procedure on Chris's left wing.

"All right, lower them and rest for a few minutes."

Christoff furled his wings and turned around. "Well?"

Jays finished writing before looking up into Chris's irritated face. "You haven't been doing all of your exercises, have you?"

"Damn it, Jays. You know how much I've been covering for Nick."

"And how's that an excuse to not spend ten to fifteen minutes doing them? Your anchor is weak and you're already starting to develop strain spots in the rope muscle."

"I don't feel it when I fly."

"You might not feel it yet, but it's showing in your numbers. None of you get enough flight time to allow you to skimp on the exercises, Chris, and you know it."

Irritated at his behavior, Jays stalked over to the cabinet that held the resistance bands for the strength gauge. Yanking the size he needed off the hook, he returned to Chris. He pressed the button to turn on the machine built into the wall, then lowered the cables and threaded them through the appropriate height hook for Chris's size.

With a sigh, Chris turned his back to the wall and extended his wings again before reaching up to take the bar that hung bolted to the ceiling in his hands.

After clipping the bands to the cables, he snugged the slip loop at the other end of the resistance band onto the digit at the base of Chris's anchor struts, then he typed on the keypad on the wall next to the power button. "Ok, feet off the floor. I want a steady extended pull."

He watched the numbers scroll by and made sure they were feeding over to the computer properly. It didn't take long before Jays could detect a tremor of overexertion from the weakened muscle set. "Relax."

Chris set his feet back to the floor and let his wings slump. Isolating the muscle like that really let the Hunter know how much he'd fucked up. He sighed and closed his eyes.

"Right. Let's check the rest of the struts. I won't be able to tell you how bad it is until tomorrow after I've gone over the numbers. But I expect you're up for more than just exercises. You'll likely have to spend time with the weights."

"Damn it."

Jays tsked at him and moved the band up to the next digit so they could repeat the test. The doors to the Hub opened and he glanced over.

"It's confirmed, Jays. I know what they are." Ian hustled inside and set his paper work down on the desk before joining them at the wall. He looked Christoff up and down, then turned to meet Jays's eyes and raised an eyebrow. "So how much are we looking at? I saw his phys-ex report too."

"Feet up, Chris." And Jays turned the machine on again. Chris pulled using only his wing muscles and held the resistance. Sweat started to bead his forehead. "Enough that he's going to need to use the weights it looks like. Ok, Chris, relax."

He moved up to the next digit and started again. Ian stepped over to look at the numbers scrolling by. "Yep. Boyo, you need to pay more attention. Especially now. I need everyone in top shape."

"What do you mean?" Chris asked, panting.

"Release," Jays said.

He continued to test each of Chris's struts while Ian paced over to the desk and leaned against it, looking at them. "Jessica's arrival has set certain things into motion. I highly doubt that Nick's decision to stop taking his pills isn't connected somehow. He wouldn't have any clue that he was being influenced, either."

"So I take it you just finished running the tests we took on Nick and Kieran the other day?" Jays asked.

"Yes. And I'm really glad we didn't chance sending them out to the lab. All three have active VNO organs at the base of their sinuses processing pheromones. What I don't know is if all the others have them too, since that hasn't ever been something we've tested previously. The VNO are either atrophied or nonexistent in humans. Anyway, the pertinent piece of information is that Nick is now producing reproductive hormones in his own right and Kieran has traces that I almost missed."

"What?" Chris dropped to the floor in the middle of an active phase, his wings sagging.

Jays slammed the stop button. "Chris."

"Sorry, Jays," he mumbled and reached up to take the bar again.

Ian grinned at him, and he shook his head at the old man, then started the test phase once more. Obviously, he'd really enjoyed dropping that bombshell. He tossed over his shoulder, "So we *are* looking at a new caste?"

"Yes. At least for Nick and Jessica. I don't think Kieran is, but we'll have to start checking the others to see. But I'm almost positive that we are looking at a new caste of Breeders. And it really makes sense; look at how everyone treats Nick. Yes, he's Alpha, but he's different. Not like the other Alphas that I've known. And that's how rank *and* caste work together."

Jays finished testing Chris's last wing strut then closed down the machine. Chris stretched and gave his abused wings a vigorous flap before folding them at rest on his back. After he put the equipment away, he joined the other two at the desks in the island.

"Nick has always been different, you know that, Chris," Ian said. "That's why I hid his change records to protect him. This helps explain so much from that time. What do you recall? How old were you? I don't remember. Eleven? Twelve?"

"Thirteen, actually." Chris hooked a stool with his foot and pulled it out to sit on.

Jays sank into a chair next to Ian and propped his feet up on the desk. "That was before the Hub here was active, wasn't it?"

"Yes. Actually it's because of Nick that we now have this set up. Nick's reactions to the change were much like Jessica's have been; completely out of control, aggressive, irrational, and extreme. They almost seem to be opposite from a normal fledglings change, but in reality, they are just at the far end of the spectrum. Their reactions take longer to down them and hit harder. A perfect example is how Jessica didn't pass out at the normal time for a second stage fledge, yet the amnesia wiped her out. So it's a safe bet that you can gauge either of their current responses to something in that light. Think about how an average fledge would react and swing it to one end of the spectrum or the other."

"Wait." Chris held up his hand. "Gauge *either* of their responses? You were comparing their isolation experiences, not..."

He trailed off when Ian shook his head. Jays watched the surprise and disbelief in the Hunter's reaction to the shoe Ian was dropping.

"Your assumption that the drugs just suppressed an active talent that Nick had already developed was incorrect. The pills are actually an arresting inhibitor. They halt the last stage of development after the coma. Stage four. That won't affect the Hunters much, there's very little mental development left for them. But anyone who's a Seer or a Caster will have a significant impact when they are taken off of the drugs. So Nick is actually completing his change now. Not just coming off the drugs and learning how to cope with hidden abilities. Those abilities are, in reality, developing now."

"Why?" Chris whispered.

"Why else? How would you be controlled if you could do these fantastical things with your mind? They couldn't allow it."

"You did this...to us..."

Ian gave a harsh bark of laughter. "You think I had a choice, Christoff?"

"Obviously you do. Since you're choosing to tell me this now. After all these years?"

"The situation has changed. Now you need to know."

Jays dropped his feet to the floor with a thud. "Worry about it later, Chris. Let's deal with the situation first. What about the rest, Ian? You're sure about them being Breeders?"

"As sure as I can be until I get a sperm sample and see if she still produces viable eggs; but why else have the active pheromones? The hope this brings leaves me giddy. I've lived in despair for years about the death of our species. The change is loose, and so far there's been no hope of stopping it. And I doubt the current live Valkyries would go for the extreme measures some would wish to go to in order to eradicate it. So given enough time, the number of people growing wings is going to overtake the grounded population. It's a death sentence if there's no hope of renewal."

"So what does all this mean?" Chris asked.

Jays pushed his chair back and swiveled to run a quick check over the room monitors while he listened to Ian.

"When Nick started the second stage, none of us thought much about it. Ten years of experience helping fledglings through the metamorphosis had made it pretty routine. But only hours into his change had us scrambling. A rabid feral wolf would have been easier to care for. The change completely overwhelmed him. He injured a number of people, flat out refused to cooperate or care for himself. Unhappily, I had to order Xanthar repeatedly. Just to get him to eat or sleep. And the test results I got back were almost more surreal than his behavior. There were moments when I was sure we'd lose him. I couldn't accept that."

Jays glanced away from the monitors to Ian's faraway look then to Christoff's grim face before turning back to the readings he needed to record.

Behind him, Ian cleared his throat then continued. "But one incident that happened, that has always bugged me, just got explained, I believe. Nick had had a particularly bad day. He'd been shot with Xanthar multiple times, and I was afraid of the drug reaction he might have if I tranked him. This is why we now have the Hub and cameras. He went through the observation window of his room. Even with the tempering, he still managed to slash himself up. The oddity about the situation was that he didn't try and escape. He'd made several escape attempts previously, but this time he damaged the exit door of the observation room so we couldn't get in right away. The screams through the door sounded like a wild animal was tearing the people apart. We finally got the door open. It took six darts to drop him, but the worst had been done. Blood dripped down the wall like condensation in several spots. Of the four people in there, two were severely injured, one dead, and the other...

"Well, he had attacked Jillian in a completely different way. I remember watching him crouched over her, like he wanted to defend her from us, as the darts finally took him down. The horror in his eyes because of what his instincts had pushed him to do.... Because of the Xanthar, he hadn't had any control over it."

Chris coughed before he asked in a rough voice, "Is this why he hasn't wanted to get physically intimate?"

"Maybe. But I don't think so. The most puzzling aspect of it all is that the vast majority of you no longer produce sperm, while a small percentage produce nonfertile sperm. Still, that doesn't stop you from having an incredibly active sex life. But Nickolas's tests showed that his system had gone backward. His reproductive system now mimicked that of a prepubescent. The factory was still there, but the conveyor belt wasn't moving so to speak. So the drive wasn't active. But now I have to wonder? Was Jillian's potential like Jessica in some way?"

Jays capped his pen and swung back to the other two. Ian had pulled out the paper work he'd brought with him and leafed through it. "And now it seems like Jessica turned a key in the lock."

He peered over Ian's arm to look at the test results. "So what are you saying? He's going through puberty?"

"Yeah. Accelerated. So expect the irrational. The emotional storms. The complete pain in the ass behavior all wrapped up into one month, at least that's my current estimate based on the last two weeks of observation on him."

"Fun." Chris sighed. "That, on top of developing psychic powers? What should we do differently?"

"Nothing for the moment. We have the best compromise going. It would be noticed if he suddenly quit walking the halls. Gabriel would get wind of it. And that's something we have to avoid at all costs. The discovery of a new caste must be kept hidden. I wouldn't tell you either, but because of the involvement you'll have in controlling Nick, there will be no hiding his differences. So I don't want this to go any further than Donald. Not even Nick, not that he'd understand right now, because he's the most at risk of falling into Gabriel's hands, and Gabriel would be able to strip it from his mind. He won't gain the skill to protect himself for a while. For now, until I have no other options about visitations with Jessica, he can spend the majority of time with her and the rest shadowed by the Flight and Wing leaders."

The rattle of wheels trundled through the doors from the hall, heralding the arrival of food. Looking bored, the young man pushed the cart up to them then without a word turned and left.

Jays rose and walked around Ian to inspect the cart. "Looks like they brought everyone's lunch early since they were bringing up Allison's last meal."

"It's a good thing Nick's taking most of his meals here, Ian. You should have seen what he piled his plate with in the cafeteria yesterday." Chris chewed his lip then asked, "When are you going to let Nick know?"

Wondering that too, Jays shifted a couple of plates then looked at Ian, who fidgeted around with the paper work.

"Not yet. I can predict what sort of reaction he'll have. His change wasn't a good time in his life."

Chris nodded and stood. "Is there anything else, Jays?"

He cast a quick look at Ian then back to the Hunter. "Not at the moment, Chris. We'll go over your test results. Tomorrow we need to get together and discuss what you'll need to do to fix your flight muscles."

"Right." Chris sighed but then hesitated before finally focusing on Ian. "What about Nick? If the last two weeks have had this much impact on my wings..."

"A valid worry, Chris. I'll see if I can't get him on the machine today."

The Hunter nodded and, resettling his wings with a flip, left the Hub.

Jays finished arranging the meals before breaking the quiet. "That was a lot to drop on him."

"We don't have much more time. They are all going to have to come to terms with a different world than they're used to."

Contemplating that exact inevitability, Jays pushed the food cart to the cell doors and started delivering lunch.

♦ ♦ ♦

Nickolas pushed the soggy, tangled covers from his body and sat on the edge of the bed. He rubbed the pain between his eyes then glanced at the red glare of the clock: 2:00 a.m.

About normal I guess. At least I got three hours straight this time.

He stood and stretched the muscles that still refused to relax. Like usual, the dreams felt more real than reality, and his body refused to believe. He grabbed the clothes he had dumped on the floor just a few hours previous and slipped them on. Then, without bothering to turn on a light, he left the bedroom and crossed the darkened suite to his door. A thin crack of light split the darkness as he checked the hallway. Typical at this hour, it was deserted.

He stepped out and pulled his door closed. He stood for a moment and fought the pull to walk in the direction of the Hub. The consequences for disrupting the Hub in the middle of the night anymore had been spelled out loud and clear for him. He most certainly didn't wish to be locked in at night for wandering, so now he just made sure no one knew. With a sigh, he turned away and walked with purpose down the hall. After navigating the maze of corridors, he reached an exterior door that he knew would lead out into the gardens. The military personnel up at that hour concentrated near the front of the complex and in their own wings, leaving him free to exit into the darkness. He tread a familiar path down to the water's edge and launched out over the river, staying low to avoid unwanted eyes.

With the start of November, the weather had turned cold and wet. The weedy smell of the river rushed through his nose, and after gaining enough distance from the Facility, he angled sharply up to the clouds. Through the scudding wisps he shot, the wet beading against his face, and he wiped it off when he leveled out. A powerful down sweep propelled him forward.

The dream remnants started to fade, but not quickly enough for his liking. The horrific images twined with his memories of when he was locked up during his isolation. The moon had yet to rise, so darkness covered the meadows and forest below him. He pushed his speed, and it started to rain in earnest, the stinging needles hot little sparks against his face.

His muscles warmed so that the chill air had little effect on his body. The pain in his head faded and a smile stretched his lips. He tucked his wings and did a barrel roll then snapped them open to pump higher in the sky. He started a complex aerial dance that pushed his agility and stamina. The memory of Ian's puzzlement that evening caused him to laugh out loud and the sound ricocheted off the quiet trees far below him.

Ian had pulled him from Jessica's company early and subjected him to a muscle isolation strength test, much to his irritation. With disbelief, Ian had him perform the test twice because the numbers didn't add up to his expected conclusion. Not only hadn't Nick lost any strength or agility in his wings, but he'd actually gained, stunning the doctor, who had looked at him with a calculating expression. So he'd been happy to quit the Hub and get away from any questions that might be forthcoming.

You have no concept of how much I'm out at night. Flying soothed him almost as much as visiting with Jessica. He pushed that thought aside and turned into a complex series of moves that took all of his focus. The burn in his flight muscles grounded him in reality when his mind wanted to slip into visions and dreams without his consent. He shook his head and pushed harder.

Why is this so hard? And taking so long to get control of?

The thought turned over in his mind, but the pace he pushed himself to quickly drowned out the troubled thoughts. Eventually his body screamed enough, and he settled down into a steady, restful glide. His chest heaved and sweat started to chill on his exposed skin, mixing with the spitting rain.

Reluctant to turn for home yet, he spiraled up higher to get above the clouds. His muscles ached. If he'd been flying with any of the others, they would have been all over him.

Shit. If I'd seen anyone pushing themselves like this, I'd have grounded them. He chuckled softly.

But the mirth died on the next wing beat as his thoughts descended back into the quagmire of his brain. He remembered the look in Ian's eyes and shivered. *He hasn't looked at me like that since...*

With a mental wrench, he thought of Jessica. She still hadn't settled and resigned herself to her circumstance. *But why should she? I never did. And she has almost as much reason as I.*

Maybe she's right. Why couldn't we leave? Obviously we don't need the drugs to safely change like I've been told. So the hardest part would be seeing her through the coma. But really, what do they do? They sit and watch. I can make sure she eats and drinks enough before, then keep her warm for the week. But I'd need to find somewhere safe for that time. I couldn't move her.

He pumped his cooling muscles to keep the blood flowing and prevent cramps. *So where could we go? The Facility wouldn't let us just walk away. And money? I need to figure this out.*

A slicing pain ripped through his head. His wings faltered, and he dropped several lengths before he regained control. He wiped blood from his nose on his forearm. *Damn. Time to head back I guess. At least I'll be able to sleep, finally.*

He adjusted his flight and started to drop down toward the river to make his way home.

"Jays, have you got that preliminary report yet?" Ian snapped. He quickly looked up from the computer terminal he was accessing to grab the clipboard that Jays sent careening down the table. Flipping through it, he called over to Jays, who came rushing back to the table to deposit more gear. "We need to get them out of here now. Time is short."

He swiveled around to the monitor on his left to check the status in Jessica's room.

"I've got the basic gear gathered. Do you think they'll need any specialties?"

"Not likely on this one, at least not for the fledge they're going after." Ian slid the report back down to Jays, then he reached under the table and pulled out a small bag, sending it after the report. "Pack that as well. Chris might need it."

A beep sounded from the console, and Ian returned his attention to Jessica's monitor. "She's stirring; Nickolas won't be far behind. Call in Chris, Jays. I think we'll need him."

Jays glanced at the clock and asked worriedly, "Will we make it before he arrives?"

Ian closed his eyes. "We can keep our fingers crossed."

The door to the hall opened, and Ian turned to watch Nickolas enter the Hub. He took a deep breath and prepared himself to handle Nick, not a task he looked forward to. His behavior had deteriorated rapidly over the last couple of days. *I really don't want him leaving the Facility...* Ian stood and beckoned him over, drawing him away from where Jays had picked up the phone.

"We've got a change in plans today, Nickolas." He caught the younger man's attention and gestured at the bag on the table.

Nick's breath hissed explosively when he saw the preparations laid out; he turned away, moving over to the monitoring station. "No. Not today, Ian."

Right on his heels, Ian said firmly, "There's a recovery that needs to be seen to. You are taking your team out."

Nickolas's gaze remained fixed on the screen. "I need to take care of Jessica."

"Not today, you don't." All of his muscles tensed from the tightrope he walked, and he pointed at the table. "The initial report is in the bag."

Nick shook his head, the only indication that he'd heard him. Ian studied him; the Alpha's instability had grown. The agitated Valkyrie ignored everything except Jessica, but that wouldn't last, Ian knew. His behavior would become increasingly erratic. Unfortunately, the need to push him overrode the safety of the move. *If there was any other choice...*

"She's awake. It's time for breakfast." His wings flared and he moved toward her door.

"I'm not unlocking it, Nickolas. I need you to handle this recovery more than Jessica needs you right now." He held his ground when Nickolas whipped around to face him. The barely restrained violence in his eyes turned the blue into seething clouds. Maintaining eye contact, Ian raised his hand to stop Jays, but his protégé still took a step toward them. Ian flexed his hand, ordering his Second to stay still and not provoke the man. "Nickolas..."

"I don't want to go, Ian. Send one of the other teams." He snarled and started to slowly stalk around the room. "Jessica needs me. You don't understand what it's like. She needs *me* to help... "

"I understand more than you think, Nick."

The door to the hall opened, and with relief Ian felt Chris enter. The Hunter paused and took a look at the situation before making a beeline for Ian. "What's going on, Ian?"

Not giving an inch, Ian retained dominance every time Nickolas met his eyes, but it took a toll. Nick was strong and he was getting stronger the more he came into his mental abilities. Ian didn't dare take his attention away from the pacing figure.

"I just got a call for a recovery that I need your team to handle. Everything is ready. You just need to get your team assembled." Folding his arms across his chest, he nodded at Nickolas. "That includes your leader."

When Nickolas's pacing had taken him to the far side of the room, Ian said under his breath, "Chris, I need you to get him loaded up and out of here. Now. He's deteriorated fast the last three days, and I just got a call that Gabriel's on his way. He can't be here with Nick like this."

"Shit. How long?"

"I don't know. Just get him out of here."

"Jays, call up Flynn and Jules," Chris said, turning to watch Nickolas himself. "Tell them to get the van ready; we'll be there in five. Nick, come on, we're going."

Christoff walked up to his brother, and Ian held his breath, waiting for Nickolas to lash out, but the younger Hunter held his ground, matching him stare for stare. "We don't have a lot of time, so don't waste any of it arguing with me. You're not going to win. I can get all the Flights to back me if necessary."

"Chris..." Nickolas growled in warning.

"Not now, Nicky. Trust me, we need to go."

A quiver ran through Nickolas, and Ian waited, praying that Chris had enough pull to get his brother to cooperate. With one last wistful look at the monitor, followed by a glare for Ian, Nickolas walked out of the Hub.

"Jays, grab the bag, we need to keep up with him. You can tell me what you know on the way to the garage," Chris said and raised his hand in a salute as he followed in Nickolas's wake. "See you tonight," he called over his shoulder.

His shoulders sagging when the door swung shut behind them, Ian turned back to the computer terminals and sank into one of the chairs, letting his breath out. He placed his elbows on the table and rested his head tiredly in his hands. *Close. They're not out of the woods yet though.* A beep echoed out of the consoles and he looked over to Jessica's monitor. She paced the length of her cell, her movements restless, and cast expectant glances at the door. *Sorry, Jess. You're going to be disappointed today.*

♦ ♦ ♦

You sent me on those stupid errands to the warehouse and now this? What is so important about this recovery that Ian couldn't send another team? Nickolas thought as he stormed through the corridors.

"Nick, stop. Wait," Donald snapped when he passed the Hunter.

He didn't respond and sensed a concerned Donald join up with Christoff behind him.

This is stupid. He slammed the double doors into the garage open. They bounced off the wall, making a satisfying crash. "Do they think I'm an idiot?" he growled out, then feeling Chris and Donald, and amazingly enough a nebulous Jays, warily flank him, he turned to face the group ranged against him.

"No, we don't think you're an idiot, Nicky, but you need help. You asked me to, remember?" his brother placated. "That means you need to listen and trust me. So get in the van."

He flipped his eyes to Jays and Donald, then looked back to a wary Chris.

"Nickolas, take our judgment on this. You know you can count on us to watch over her." Donald's eyes pleaded with him to cooperate.

He opened his mouth to argue, but Jays shushed him with a motion. "Now's not a good time, Nick, ask later. But be careful who you ask."

The doctor tossed the bag to Christoff, who caught it without removing his eyes from Nickolas. "Chris, the preliminary report is there with the basic gear. You've got a couple hour drive ahead of you, but even more wait time after that until the fledge passes out."

When Jays turned back to him, the fear and compassion contained in his eyes jolted him. "Stay quiet, Nick, now's not a good time to draw attention to yourself. Don't touch anything." And with that cryptic message, Jays turned on his heel and walked out of the garage.

The anger drained out of him as quickly as it had arisen, and Nick looked tiredly at his brother, who glared back at him, the exasperation radiating. "What's going on, Chris? Why do I feel like I'm being forced to run away?"

Christoff threw his hands up in the air and stalked away. "You're not, Nick, you're overreacting. Now, get in the damned van. Before I toss you in."

Footsteps rang on the concrete and Chris stiffened. Nickolas turned to see Flynn and Jules arrive.

Flynn looked Nickolas up and down distrustfully, then glanced over to Christoff. "Is he all right? Has he taken his pills?"

"Don't worry, Flynn. Ian says it's just the stress of dealing with Jessica lately and to be prepared for him to be edgy. Right, Donald?"

"That's right. Nick's been spending a lot of time helping in the Hub recently."

Nickolas felt his spirits plummet as he listened to the two cover for him. He turned and crossed over to the van, climbing in. *Am I ever going to get this under control?* He took his seat, wearily leaning his head back, and closed his eyes. The conversations of the others flowed by. Absently, his mind started to range out, and after a moment, he brushed against an abyss so dark and cold he instinctively recoiled. His eyes snapped open as a half-formed memory surfaced from the contact.

Fear, desperation, and pain, the key he didn't wish to turn to find out what that memory contained. Lack of air brought him back. He sat up with a deep inhale.

Shying away from the lock on his past, he gave his attention to his brother as the Hunter entered the van. Nickolas spoke more to hear a voice and block out the memory than out of any desire for the answer.

"Are we ready to go?" The relief that replaced the wariness in his brother's eyes made him look away and he smiled self-consciously. "I do trust you, Chris. You know that?"

"I know, Nick." Chris squeezed his shoulder as he passed then said, "Flynn and Jules are grabbing the last of the gear, then we're out of here. I was just giving Donald orders for the day."

"He called me when I passed him in the hallway. Did he tell you what he wanted?"

"Not specifically, but I suspect it might have had something to do with how you were snowplowing through the halls."

Uncomfortable, Nickolas looked at the floor. "I'm trying, Chris."

"I know, Nick, I know. We'll take it one step at a time. Here," Christoff threw the bag at him. "Jays said the folder was in there, along with a few other essentials. So what are we looking at today?"

He pulled the retrieval documents out and dropped the bag on the floor next to his seat. The van dipped as Jules climbed in, pulling the door shut. He felt his normal veneer of calm briefly return and asked, "We ready?"

"Yep," the comm tech answered, taking his seat at the communications station. Jules turned his chair to face them, buckling up.

Flipping open the folder, Nickolas started to scan the documents as the van pulled out of the parking space. "Well it looks like we're heading south, down to Chehalis. The target was reported an hour ago by his college librarian; apparently he was getting pretty surly over some books. They managed to get him settled and back in his dorm for the day to study. Our watcher is already on him." Nick turned in his chair to see if Flynn had heard the report or not. "Let's try and not have a repeat of the last recovery, shall we?"

Flynn piloted the van through the garage bay and called back, "What's the likelihood of that, do you reckon, Nick?"

"I wouldn't have thought it possible the first time, Flynn."

"Well, boys, sit back and relax. It'll be a couple of hours before we get there even with good traffic."

Nickolas closed his eyes and settled back to wait.

Ian spent the next half hour getting Jessica fed and recording the readouts from the monitors. Her cooperation had hinged on Nick's presence more than he had anticipated. *And here I thought she had started to settle in.* He sighed. It was becoming more apparent that a strong bond had started to form between the two.

A familiar wave of icy, emotionless energy washed across him, shattering his concentration. Like nails scratched across a blackboard. He stiffened then hit a few keys to blank out Jessica's screen, leaving the other three fledglings active. Standing, he turned to face the door.

The man who entered a moment later always left a chill residing in Ian's heart. When the council decided to play god and engineer the start of an evolution, the punctuated equilibrium, which brought about the first of the Valkyries, something went seriously wrong with Gabriel.

The first Alpha. The only surviving member of the original test group. The most tortured soul Ian had ever been in contact with.

And if I could put him down like a rabid dog, I would. That's the only mercy he'll ever see.

Silent, Ian watched as Gabriel slowly inspected his domain. The man prowled the perimeter of the room, ending the circuit in front of him.

"Hello, Ian. How are you today?"

Gabriel's voice had a hypnotic, melodic quality to it. Ian blinked and had to work to keep his face impassive as he fought the pull. "What do you want now, Gabriel? It's still a little early for these fledglings."

Laughing, Gabriel tossed his head and sauntered the perimeter of the monitor island. "Where's your manners? You should say 'fine' to my question, then ask me how my day is. That's the way conversations go."

Ian just stared at him.

Gabriel flexed his wings and shook his head. He prowled closer to the isolation room doors.

"You know why I'm here, Ian. Something's different." He sniffed and paused then turned his intense gaze toward him. "I came to see what."

Ian pivoted, keeping the rival Alpha in sight as he continued to move restlessly, then shrugged, subtly weaving his mental shields tighter. "Nothing I know of is different."

Gabriel stopped and pinned him with the unblinking stare of a reptile not sure whether it was hungry or not. After a moment, he resumed his pacing; the Valkyrie cocked his head. "Of course not. How would you know? In your pathetic, stunted glory."

He ignored Gabriel's slam and pressed, "So what did you sense, Gabriel?"

"Nice try old man." He tossed his head and smiled. "I'm not going to give you any more info on my abilities than you do me. The council can delude themselves all they want about you. I know they're wrong."

"I don't know what you're talking about. I'm just trying to determine baseline information."

"What, be the *doctor*? It's a little late for that, don't you think?" Fanning out his wings, the suddenly irate Valkyrie slammed his hands on the island. "You couldn't stop these; you couldn't stop *them* from doing this to me, and look at what they did to you? What makes you think you can do anything?"

Ian kept his surface thoughts blank and held Gabriel's probing look, though he couldn't suppress the shiver after Gabriel closed his eyes and took a deep breath. The insane Valkyrie smiled slowly before opening them again and resumed his stalk.

Ian cleared his throat. "You know I didn't have anything to do with the original experiment. I was only called in when it went bad. I did my best to save as many of you as I could."

"Yes, I should be grateful I survived, right? Well it's down to just you and me now, Ian. We're the only ones left."

Jessica's monitor beeped, and he suppressed his annoyance when Gabriel glanced over at it. His mind started running multiple scenarios on his best choice of action at lightning speed, something his strategic talent excelled at. It was his ace in the hole. No matter how much Gabriel suspected, the truth was so much stronger.

"What have we here?" Gabriel crooned, and over the back of the desk, he hit a few keys and brought up the visuals on Jessica's cell. "Well, well, something different."

Ian barely glanced at the screen, but he still noted that Jessica's agitation seemed more pronounced than even her first day here. The change in her routine had made a huge impact on her. Her wings, each about a foot long already, were in constant motion, the dark membrane rippling as she paced the miniscule confines of her cell. Irritation visibly poured off her, and Ian wished that she didn't have such a habit of talking to herself as he watched her muttering. Thankfully, the sound was muted.

Ian soaked in every nuance of Gabriel's reaction to her. Dismayed at the intensely fascinated look in his eyes, Ian moved to cut the visuals, but Gabriel got his hand over the keys. The proximity to the other unshielded Valkyrie battered at him. He turned his head and was pinned by the insanity in Gabriel's eyes.

"She is coming with me."

No asking, no doubt, just a demand.

"She stays. You have no jurisdiction over her yet, Gabriel."

"I want her."

"She is mine until her change is complete. Until that time, you cannot have access to her. You may run the camps, but the Facility is *mine*," Ian snarled softly, challenge written in every fiber of his being.

Surprise showed briefly on Gabriel's face, to be replaced immediately by his normal cocky self-assuredness. "Not all of it is yours, as you well know. By the way, how is Nickolas? She seems to be asking for him. As usual I notice he is absent. How do you manage that, I wonder?"

Gabriel removed his hand from the keyboard and started to pace again. Ian quickly blanked the monitor. "He's on a recovery, of course. His team is the best we have."

With a negligent wave of his hand in dismissal, Gabriel continued, completely ignoring his own previous statement. "You're right of course. She's in your purview."

He walked toward the door but stopped to look back, promise in his eyes. *But when she's done, I'll be back, Ian.*

"Stay out of my head, Gabriel."

Even after the door had closed behind him, Ian could still hear Gabriel's laughter echo through the room.

Chapter Thirteen

Gabriel ignored the sight of the patchwork ground as it sped by below. He shifted his wing out from underneath himself and settled more fully into the seat of the helicopter, returning to his introspection. Damping down his flare of irritation at the Facility's head doctor, he returned to his normal equipoise. *Soon, I'll catch him...soon. I know Ian is the hole the rebels keep slipping through. I just need to get the proof. If I keep batting him this way and that, eventually the mouse will break cover.*

But then what? The joy of the game he had been playing with Ian for years would be...gone? *They* loved pitting the two of them against each other. He chafed at their control.

Gabriel held out his hand, examining his nails predatorily. *Blocking Ian's search for information has been challenging. At least he's had as much success in his hunt as I've had in mine.*

He pulled his knife from his boot and started to clean his nails. *I don't know why the council trusts him so much. He's free to do anything he wants. It's obvious he's been blocking their attempts to maintain control of the Valkyries.*

The knife paused. *Ian, how do you stay one step ahead of me? You're too soft and weak. You don't have what it takes to do what is necessary; not like I do.* He shook his head and the knife started moving again. But this time, he turned it against his skin. The tip parted a delicate line along his palm. *Well, Ian, you've certainly managed to win with Nickolas. Your control there is absolute. Every attempt I've made in his direction has ended in an immediate brick wall.*

Blood welled up in a thin tracery along the path the knife took. The bright red against his skin was fascinating.

What I wouldn't love to do with you, Nickolas, my boy. If only I could get my hands on you. What I could learn...and the fun we would have.

He lifted his hand up. His tongue slid across his palm, gathering the salty wetness. The shock of his power, returned on itself, sent a shiver down his spine.

Well you may have managed to keep me from Nickolas so far, Ian, but this new fledgling is another matter entirely. Once she has completed her transformation, she is mine. There's nothing you can do to stop it either.

The vision of the woman pacing the length of her cell filled his mind, along with the feeling of the power she contained. She had drawn him from home, projecting her presence unknowingly...until he found her. *I could feel you, little one, calling to me all the way out here from the time you started to change. You're stronger than any other I've located besides Nickolas...or me.*

His headset crackled, and Gabriel looked up as the pilot's voice blasted out, making him wince. "Sir, we have almost arrived. The tower wishes to relay a message to you."

"Patch them through." He stared out the window and watched the compound speed toward them. It didn't look like much from the air. Several buildings set behind a large barbwire-topped fence standing in the open plains of the dry Eastern Washington landscape. There was nothing for miles around the compound. *Nowhere for anyone to run to,* he thought. *Not even me.*

The buildings on the surface were just a portion of what was there. The majority of the holdings lay underground.

"Gabriel. Boy, am I glad you're back. The general called. He's bringing VIPs out tonight and wants some entertainment," the tinny voice announced.

"Did he say how many?" Gabriel asked resignedly.

"About twenty, twenty-five, I think."

"That shouldn't be a problem. Let him know that I can't serve them any delicacies on this short of notice, but the entertainment should be on par. I'll deal with it after I land. Gabriel out."

"Sir," the pilot announced, "please buckle up, we're about to land."

He pulled his harness into place and stared out the window. The pilot maneuvered the helicopter over the landing pad between the fence and one of the buildings, slowly lowering it until it bumped the ground. Unbuckling, he popped the door open as the pilot flipped switches on the console, shutting the machine down. He didn't bother to wait for the blades to stop. He jumped out, staying in a crouch until he was clear, then made his way into the building.

At the reception desk, he leaned over the counter and grabbed a chart that hung from a hook. He propped his hip against the counter and scanned the paper work, smiling idly at the receptionist. "Hello, Mary. Have they finished yet?"

"No, sir," she whispered. Her hands shook slightly when she set her pen down. "They should still be in the middle of the experiment. I just updated the chart."

He flipped through the pages. "Good. I'll just go check on them. By the way, the arena is going to be open tonight. Please get some sort of refreshments set up for around thirty guests."

His smile widened when she gulped, and he handed the chart back. She pressed the button releasing the lock on the door.

He passed the checkpoint and walked down the hall, taking the elevator down two floors. Exiting into an unmarked hallway, he walked confidently through the maze. He eventually pushed open one of the many plain doors he had passed and entered a small office. A guard sat at a desk just inside. The man sat up, but when he recognized who had entered, he went back to his work. Ignoring the guard at the desk, Gabriel approached a set of glass observation windows that flanked the main laboratory entrance.

Looking out over the laboratory through the glass, he watched the scientists conduct their current experiment. Five Valkyries, in various stages of consciousness, were strapped to tables or tethered to the wall. Fredrick, the team lead, was administering the new drug they had been formulating, and were now testing, to one of the two still tied to the wall. The woman struggled against the hands attempting to hold her still. Fredrick yanked viciously on her hair, prying her head back. Her violent movements caused Fredrick to spill a good quantity of the liquid they were trying to get into her, and Gabriel shook his head.

He shoved the door open and descended the steps into the lab. He came to a stop next to Fredrick and looked down dispassionately at the gagging Valkyrie. "Is this the last one?"

"No, there's one left," Fredrick said. "The others are already starting to exhibit reactions. We wanted to stagger the times of this test run for observation purposes. We lost all the subjects during the first trial today all at once. It happened too fast. The cameras recorded everything, but now I want a firsthand account as it happens." Refilling his beaker, the doctor turned to the last Valkyrie.

Gabriel waved away the lab techs waiting to restrain the subject. A surge of adrenaline ran through him. At times like this he could feel again. Hot emotion breaking through the ice. And he craved more. He made eye contact with the captive.

The power. The wielder instead of the pawn. He shoved the memories that dared threaten back into their dark box and prowled toward the last subject, savoring the fear in the Hunter's eyes. The Hunter pulled at the length of chain attached to a collar around his throat and backed as far away from them as he could, frantically looking around. A smile stretched Gabriel's mouth, and he cocked his head, taking his time, prolonging the feeling. His hand skated along the wall, the captive's eyes following the movement, to the bolt that secured the chain. The cold metal of each link slipped slowly under his palm and he applied pressure, forcing the terrified Hunter closer.

He drank in the fear. The ability to feel. Almost an aphrodisiac. He smiled even wider when he reached the end of the chain and his fingers touched the silky lengths of dark hair. With a slight shift, his body lightly brushed against the Hunter's side. Soft pants echoed in his ears. He slipped his hand up, caressing the back of the clammy neck. The skin shivered under his touch and he continued to skim up under the metal of the collar. A sudden jerk pulled the band taut, choking the Hunter. Gabriel laughed softly as hands reached up, trying to pull the rigid metal away from his windpipe.

With a twist, Gabriel spun the desperate man against the wall and hooked his left arm under the wings to immobilize him, pressing along his back. He finally tried to struggle, and Gabriel chuckled in his ear before shifting his grip from the collar to continue the leisurely caress up the back of the man's head through his hair. The Valkyrie gasped in a ragged breath when the metal relaxed, his cheek pressed into the wall, and Gabriel swallowed the hunger that sprang up at the feel of the body against him.

Get to work. He's not one you get to take home. His hand cupped the back of the Hunter's head. With a curl of fingers, he clutched a fistful of hair and pried the subject's head back at the same moment that he put his foot into the back of his knees forcing him to the ground.

"Now hold still," Gabriel breathed into his ear. Nodding at Fredrick to come forward, Gabriel pulled back on the Hunter's head even farther, compelling the man's jaw to unclench. The scientist stepped up to him, reached out, and gripped the trembling man's lower jaw to open it farther, then he began to slowly pour the liquid down the lab subject's throat.

Holding tighter, Gabriel pulled his other arm out from under the Hunter's wings and slipped it around the man's chest to stop his arms from trying to bat away the drug. So close, Gabriel breathed in the Hunter's physical and psychic scent while he watched the Valkyrie's throat convulse, forced to swallow the vile substance or breathe the liquid in.

"You smell so good," he whispered in his ear, then finally not able to stop himself, he brushed the Hunter's cheek with his lips and captured the tears sliding down the man's face. The Hunter trembled and his arms fell limp at his side. Gabriel ran his hand up over his captive's chest to rest lightly on his throat, feeling the convulsive swallowing. He stroked the soft skin and pressed his body tighter into the captive's back, nuzzling the hollow of his neck. The man started to collapse, but Gabriel held him upright.

"There's no need for that you know," he commented, rubbing his cheek against the trail of tears, kissing the damp corner of his eye. "There's nothing you can do and you will be adding invaluable knowledge to the understanding of our fledgling species. Your sacrifice will benefit others."

The scientist finished and backed away, but Gabriel waited another moment before releasing the man to fall to the ground, coughing and shaking. He stared at the Hunter. Something about him...

He shrugged it off and stepped over the shivering man to join the scientist. Fredrick scribbled in his notebook. A moan drew Gabriel's attention, and he looked over at the other chained Valkyrie. She was lying on the ground clutching her stomach. He nudged the doctor's foot and nodded his head at her.

Pleased, the scientist waved his helpers forward then turned to Gabriel. "She's ready for a table. She didn't get as much down as subject B-Five here; I'm surprised she's responding so quickly. Thank you for restraining this one. He had already proven to be difficult during the check-in phase."

Snorting, Gabriel crossed his arms over his chest and watched the lab technicians get B Four unchained and secured to a table. "The fact that I'm intimately aware of their physical characteristics helps."

He watched the woman struggle feebly when they secured the straps, and he walked over, turning her face to look into it. Her eyes were glazing, so he dropped his hand and turned to pace with the doctor along the foot of the other tables, surveying the rest of the subjects. All of them had started to exhibit signs of pain and distress in response to the stimuli that the drug forced on them.

"What are the results so far?" Gabriel queried.

"The first trial this morning had no survivors. We're fine-tuning this next trial. We observed some interesting responses earlier, however it ended much too quickly."

"Send a copy of the video over to my office; I'll go over it sometime this evening. Unfortunately I can't stay now. We have an unscheduled event tonight. I need to get the coliseum ready for our visitors. Call me if anything interesting happens."

"Definitely, I will. Are you going to be fighting tonight?"

"No."

A scream, both mental and physical, tore through the air, and Gabriel spun to see subject B-Five gripping his head while trying to curl into a fetal position. The chains made the move impossible. The staff rushed forward to drag the Valkyrie to the last remaining table. When they unchained him, the Hunter took them all by surprise. He wrenched free and made a dash for the door.

Gabriel reached out with his mind and pierced the Hunter's weakened barriers, shouting, *Stop!*

The mental command felled the escaping man. Walking up to where he had collapsed, Gabriel stared down at him.

B-Five held his head, staring sightlessly as he rocked on his side, mumbling over and over, "Get out of my head. Keep them out of my head. Get out, get out, get out…"

Gabriel smiled and beckoned the scientist over. "He's a Seer. This one has promise, watch him." With a last look at B-Five, he waved to the research team and walked out the door.

He retraced his steps through the complex, startled a squeak out of Mary the receptionist, then stepped into the late fall sunshine. He stretched his wings, looking around. A few subdued Valkyries glanced his way before hurrying on to finish whatever task they had been assigned. Folding his wings neatly on his back, he strolled into the neighboring building. The small structure was deceptive. On the surface, its dimensions were only about twenty feet in diameter and contained surplus food storage on shelves.

Gabriel ignored all of that, and opening a locked door in the back of the building, he descended an elegant sweeping flight of stairs into a room much larger than the building above it could contain.

The reception hall of the coliseum always made him want to puke. Red velvet carpeting with matching upholstered walls, plush couches in gilt and ivory lining the room, making up cozy seating areas for waiting guests. *And in my opinion, I think it looks like a bordello. But no one wanted my opinion.* He walked past all the luxury and pulled a pass card out of his pocket. He swiped it in a reader, opening an elevator.

Descending to the arena floor, he got out and looked up. He scanned the multiple tiers of seats surrounding the oval of dirt in front of him. Nothing appeared to be amiss, so he continued to walk across the arena floor and swiped his card again to open the doors into the holding pens. *Don't know why they label them barracks, I mean get real.*

The cacophony within assaulted his ears. The door latched tight behind him and he strode over to the open practice area in search of the master of games. Not an involved search. The large, dark-skinned man stood over a prone Valkyrie. He approached and looked down at the heaving Hunter. "What's going on, Edward?"

Not taking his eyes off of the Valkyrie, Edward responded, "He decided he wouldn't fight. I'm convincing him otherwise."

"Ah. Well, chain him to the post for now. We have other matters to discuss."

The master of games kicked the reluctant fighter, then grabbing the collar around the man's neck, he pulled him over to a post on the edge of the practice arena. Pinioning his wings wide around it, he attached a chain to the collar to hold him up on tiptoe, not the most comfortable position, then lashed his hands so that they rested on top of his head but nowhere else. When Edward rejoined him, they both stood back to admire his handiwork.

"Good, that will do for now." Then indicating that Edward should follow, Gabriel turned down the rows of cells and started to slowly walk along them, dragging his hand along the bars. He watched the occupants and noted absently whether they cringed away or stood defiantly. "We need to assemble a list of events for tonight. The general is bringing a group in and wishes some entertainment. I don't think it needs to be elaborate, but you know how the general likes blood, so you'll need to get creative. There'll need to be at least one death. I think a two-hour program should be sufficient."

He stopped and reached through the bars of one of the cages, brushing the shoulder of a female Hunter. She just looked at the ground, not moving.

"Is this going to replace our regular schedule?" the games master asked.

"No, it's extra. So try not to maim our best fighters." Tangling his fingers in her flaxen hair, he pulled her up to the bars so he could look into her face. "He should be arriving by six tonight, so that gives you about five hours to get ready."

He stared into her cornflower blue eyes. Cowed but not broken, there was still a touch of fire in their depths.

"No problem. Are you going to participate?"

He looked over his shoulder at the Valkyrie chained to the post and smiled slowly. B-Five's scent still flowed through his body. "No, not tonight."

Then he turned back to the female in his hand and probed her mind, feeling an unexpected barrier. Intrigued he pushed a little harder until she gasped. Smiling, he released her hair and she backed away. "Prep her, Edward. She is not to be used for any fighting, but I want her ready when I call."

An appreciative gleam in his dark eyes, Edward nodded and they turned, walking back the way they had come. When they reached the practice area, Gabriel stopped in front of the Hunter chained to the post. He gripped the man's chin and turned his head so their eyes could meet. "I think I'll have a private party tonight."

He smiled and dropped his hand. A soft moan passed the man's lips, and Gabriel reached behind the post to pull a chain off the wall. When he stepped back around, he stretched it between his hands before he reached up and clipped it to the collar the Hunter wore. "I'll let you know when to come and collect whatever's left."

"No, please."

Unhooking the unfortunate Hunter's wings from the post, Gabriel lashed them together then unclipped the chain that held him suspended; the Hunter's knees buckled.

"Please, I'll fight, I promise," he pleaded.

"I know you will," Gabriel promised, smiling at him, then he tugged him along behind, still protesting as he left the hold.

♦ ♦ ♦

A kick to his foot woke Nickolas. He opened his eyes to Christoff peering at him. "Wake up, Nickolas. We're almost there."

He pulled his legs in and sat up, looking around. "What time is it?" he asked, yawning.

Jules, typing away on his computer, answered quietly, "One fifteen. The reports coming in are all quiet. There's been no sign of him trying to leave, though they've seen movement in his room recently."

"Jules, find out if he has any roommates or not. There's no way to keep this quiet in a dormitory, but the less commotion the better. And get a picture. Flynn, how far away are we?"

"Just a couple of blocks, Nick."

"Good, pull in near our watcher."

The van swayed to a stop. Nickolas unbuckled his seat belt, not sure of how it came to be around him in the first place, and tried to shift his wings a bit. He felt a touch calmer for the nap but expected it wouldn't last. He rubbed his grumbling stomach and glanced out the window. The driver's door of the black SUV in front of them opened and Scott got out. His brother reached over from his seat to pop the door open for him so he could climb in.

"Well, Nickolas, I see they pried you out of the Facility for this one."

Nick snorted a laugh.

Scott sat and leaned back. "My partner's watching from inside. Trying to keep a low profile in college territory's difficult. The target has stayed to his room, but he's still pretty wound up. He hasn't collapsed yet."

The ratcheting of the printer kicking on made Nickolas jump, and he looked over to see Jules swivel around to pull paper from it. Accepting the sheets from Jules, he shook his head at himself and scanned the printout. "Ok, it looks like he doesn't have a roommate. That's good. His name is David Marks; he's in his third year. He's twenty years old."

He passed the picture around and finished scanning the rest of the document before handing it on to the others. He stretched his legs out. "Well it sounds like he's still too active for an easy retrieval. We'll need to wait or we'll have a fight on our hands. And after our last retrieval, I don't think I could deal. Chris, you and I are stuck in here until then. Our wings would attract too much attention. But the rest of you can keep an eye on him."

Groaning, Christoff nodded his head. "You're right, of course."

"I'd like to stretch my wings too, Chris. Let's try to keep him isolated, that way he'll stay out of situations that could blow up in our faces. If we can keep him in his room and quiet, there's no need to disturb him until he's calmer. Do you know if he has any food in there, Scott?"

"We'll check, but I don't think so. At least I doubt it would be what he needs."

"True." Staring off into space, Nickolas chewed on his thumb nail. "It's probably going to be several hours still before he passes out, so you guys might as well go get in place. Phone us when there's a change."

Absently watching everyone but Christoff leave, Nickolas swiveled his seat to look out the front window. The sound of Chris rustling around behind him had Nick closing his eyes and waiting for the inevitable questions now that they were alone. The calmness he felt upon awakening evaporated like water in the desert.

"Nick, this morning..."

"Yes, this morning, Chris. What was going on that I needed to be bundled off?" He grabbed at his temper, mentally throwing a rope around it. The memory of events leading up to their departure marched through his mind, and he took a deep breath. "Somehow I get the impression it wasn't my lack of control that was the true issue. All of you, starting with Ian, wanted me gone. And in a hurry too. Why?"

Waiting, Nickolas stared out the window. The silence stretched and it became obvious that Christoff didn't plan to answer; he swung his chair back to face his brother. The reserved look in Chris's eyes caught his attention, and Nickolas pondered his Second's reticence. "What *are* the lot of you hiding? What good could it possibly be keeping me in the dark of whatever it is? There's obviously something, or we wouldn't be sitting here in the van *hours* early for a retrieval."

He felt sure the fraying edges of his temper must show in his eyes, but Christoff still refused to answer. In response to his frustration, Nick felt *something* start to surge within him. He met Chris's stare and let whatever it was loose; it pinned Christoff to his seat. His brother tried to move but could barely twitch a muscle, let alone look away. Mentally pushing harder, Nick felt the flow break open, like water that ran through a hole in the ice, and the ice suddenly gave, letting a torrent rush unrestricted.

Panic flared in Chris's eyes when he realized that he couldn't get free.

"Tell me, Chris."

Christoff's face twisted as he fought the compulsion, and he broke out into a sweat. "Don't...do this...Nick...pleeease."

The fear and pain he was causing Chris penetrated his single mindedness. Nickolas hissed and broke the contact. His brother slumped forward, grabbing his temples. Swearing viciously, Nickolas slammed his head into the back of the seat, clenching his fists. Unhappy with his lack of control, he tried to calm his mind. He thought of nothingness, then remembering what Chris had told him about the web, he spun a cocoon so thick about himself that he couldn't sense Christoff's presence anymore. Opening his eyes, he looked at his brother again.

"Nick, what have you done? I can't feel you anymore." He sat rubbing his temple, watching and waiting for him to gain control, the surprise evident in his eyes.

"That's probably a good thing." This time he just stared at his brother expectantly, using nothing more than his eyes to convey his desire for answers.

Still fidgeting, Christoff looked around the interior of the vehicle as if something would miraculously appear to get the topic changed, but then he took a deep breath and faced him squarely.

"Look. It's not us hiding stuff from you. It's us hiding you from stuff. Ok? Ian got warning that Gabriel was on his way to the Facility. We can normally keep you occupied somewhere out of his way, but not this time. Ian assured me that the moment Gabriel got close enough to the Facility, he would know you were no longer taking the drugs."

"You couldn't have just said this in the Hub? And how would Gabriel know? And what the hell? Keep me occupied? Why? So this is why I haven't crossed paths with him?"

"Were you really up for listening to anything in the Hub this morning? You looked one step shy of going feral. And I didn't have the luxury of time to talk you out of your tree. As for how he would know? I think that should be self-explanatory."

"Whoa, whoa, whoa. Ian? When...how did he find out?"

"Again, self-explanatory."

"Damn it, Chris. No, it's not. They would only know if they were not...on..."

Chris nodded his head.

He leaned his head back against the seat. "So the lies grow."

"Like weeds in a vacant lot."

He swiveled his seat to look out the window again. His growling stomach broke the silence. "Do you have a candy bar or anything? I missed breakfast thanks to you guys."

"What's with the sudden sweet tooth? And no, I don't."

"Don't know, just really tastes good." He folded his arms and closed his eyes. "Well, we might as well catch a nap. We won't be seeing any changes until dark, I expect."

"Just one thing more, Nicky; could you lower the shield just a little? It's really disturbing not sensing you when you're so close."

He reached inside and unraveled a bit of the cocoon, just enough so that he could hazily feel Chris's presence again. "There, how's that?"

"Much better, thank you. You rest, I'll keep watch."

Chris's voice roused him from a troubled sleep. Hot, gritty eyes tried to focus in the gloom. The nearest street lamp stood halfway down the block. Its light wavered as bare branches from the line of huge chestnut trees obscured it. He rubbed at his face and yawned, then stretched as well as he could in the confines of the van.

"Right, Scott, we're on our way."

His brother's silhouette sat across from him, phone pressed to his ear. Nickolas felt the weight of his gaze. He shook his head, trying to clear the cobwebs.

Chris tucked the phone into his pocket and sat up. "He's winding down. Time to move."

"Good. I want to get home and check on Jessica." He barely recognized his own voice. He cleared the gravel from his throat and slid past Chris when he held the door open.

They emerged into the shadows of the street. A deep breath filled his lungs and he stretched his wings out gratefully while Christoff locked up the van. "What time is it?"

"It's after eight."

What? I just slept for seven hours?

Stunned, he stared absently at their destination across the street, an old turn-of-the-century brick mansion. The building had been converted into small rooms for let, one of many on the street renovated for such purposes. He folded his wings.

The entrance to the building bustled with activity. Students wandered in and out, and packs congregated on the lawn and porch, talking or horsing around.

He followed his brother across the street. *I can't believe I just slept for seven hours. And almost four before that.* He wiped a hand across his damp forehead.

The sudden quiet caught his attention and he looked up. Dozens of startled eyes stared back at them. They ascended the steps; the intense scrutiny dug holes in his back. Chris held the door open for him and searched his face. He dodged the look and passed through the entry, then stopped cold, a shiver running down his spine.

The place was packed. The entry foyer they stood in boasted a tiny amount of open space; otherwise the maze of hall and doorways ahead contained a seething mass of humanity, shoulder to shoulder. Chris's hand at the base of his neck kept him steady. He drew in a shallow breath.

Their arrival caused a stir, and the dull roar of conversation dimmed as those nearest them stopped to stare before rushing to spread the word.

Gently, Chris urged him forward. Once moving under his own power, Nick felt the hand fall away, and they edged through the crowd toward the stairs at the end of the hall. His ears rang from the noise and fingers trailed all over his wings. Some just brushed, others pinched or tugged slightly. The press of bodies flowed around him. He kept his eyes fixed on the stairs. Halfway to his destination, an arch on either side of the hall led to adjoining rooms. The natural tide of movement forced him sideways into a large gathering.

He stumbled backward. Excited faces surged around him, the babble intensifying. The suffocation hit him and he fought the urge to drop into a fetal position as the room shrank. Smooth wall pressed into his back, and the sound of his name reached dimly through the roaring in his ears.

Anger surged and gave him the strength to push his weakness aside. He spread his wings, forcing a little space around his body, a low growl rumbling in his chest. His breath ragged, he struggled with his internal demons.

I'm stronger than this. What the hell's wrong with me? I've been off the drugs long enough that there's no way I'm still dealing with residual effects. I'm going to hurt these kids if I don't get it under control.

"Nickolas!"

His eyes snapped open. His brother shoved through the last of the college students to reach him. He latched onto Chris's green gaze like a lifeline.

"Leash it, Nicky. You can do it," he whispered.

Inch by inch, he dragged his wings down and furled them on his back. By force of will, he unclenched his fists and relaxed his stance. Chris nodded then turned to the crowd surrounding them.

"Space, boys. Never crowd a Valkyrie. Haven't you been taught anything?"

The excited group quieted and turned to look at the three males who were picking themselves up from the floor.

The three stared in awe at them as they regained their feet, the papers, dice, and books scattered at their feet forgotten.

"I've never met a real Valkyrie before," a tall, lanky blond said reverently. "We're having a gaming marathon this weekend. It just started, and we're running the new module, which includes Valkyries, so which do you think would win in a full-scale battle, an Elder Arrowhawk or Valkyrie Hunter? I think the Hunter would win."

The young man on the blonde's left whacked him on the shoulder and exclaimed, "Of course you think the Hunter would win, he's your character."

"You're just upset because he beat your anti-flight spell, Nat. Besides, why were you casting spells against your own team, huh? I don't see how someone with wings wouldn't win against an Arrowhawk."

"Shut up, you guys, and let him answer. I'm the game master and I want to hear what he thinks," the third kid spoke up.

At a loss, Nick looked at Chris for a moment, who just shrugged; neither of them had lived a normal childhood where they had friends and could play games, so neither one of them had a clue what the boys were talking about. Nick turned back to their avid audience and cleared his throat. "Well, in my opinion...I think the Valkyrie would win, of course. Um, you'll need to excuse us, we're here on business."

Chris grabbed his arm and towed him through the crowd to the stairs. Once at the top, it was much quieter, and Nickolas heaved a sigh.

"You ok, Nicky?"

"I don't know, Chris. I think so."

"I hope so. We still need to get you past the others. Let's get this fledge and get home."

They rounded the next flight and climbed a story. The rest of their recovery team and the watchers waited halfway down the hall. Nick gave his wings a shake and lengthened his stride. Christoff fell into his role as Second and flanked him.

"Anything happening?" he asked.

"Not anymore, Nickolas." Scott looked up at him from where he leaned against the wall. "He's been full of energy and argumentative all afternoon. The few times he tried to leave, we were able to get some of his friends to direct him back and get him settled. They were even able to get him to eat a whole pizza we had delivered. Everyone's stayed pretty calm. I don't think word's spread too far, yet. His friends were being pretty closemouthed to the others."

"Well that explains our reception."

"He finally fell asleep about half an hour ago. He should be prime for removal now."

"Good. Chris and I will handle the actual retrieval, the rest of you I need on crowd control. Unfortunately it's a mad house around here tonight, and we're going to need to take him straight through the middle of it."

Chris added, "Scott, Flynn, watch the kids downstairs closely. They don't understand Valkyrie etiquette. We don't need the massed hordes freaking the target."

"Right-O, boys."

Nick closed his eyes and took a breath, centering himself. He realized from the look Chris cast him that his brother was more concerned over *his* reactions than the fledgling's. "You ready, Chris?"

Grinning in answer, Christoff moved to the door and carefully turned the knob then pushed the door open. He stepped back to allow him to enter first.

The contents of the room had witnessed a hurricane from the looks of it. A brief scan revealed no movement, and he released a little of his tension. Their target lay on the bed in the far right corner. It took some work for the two of them to make their way over to him through the mess strewn all over the room. But they carefully cleared a path they could traverse.

"Sheesh, he was busy today, wasn't he?"

Silently agreeing with Christoff, Nick reached the bed and looked down at their sleeping target's slack face. "Well, he seems to be out cold."

He looked up to make sure Chris had made it into position at the foot of the bed before reaching out to rock the sleeping man's shoulder.

No response.

He sank down on the edge of the bed and tried again. This time the man surged up, but Nickolas was ready. He shackled the wrist that came swinging at him and pulled the man over onto his stomach. Chris grabbed his ankles.

The fledgling struggled against them; the savage noises he made didn't sound human. Nick pressed the arm he held into the bed and used his free hand to grab the back of the fledgling's neck to hold him down. "Hush, David. Settle. Quiet...we need to talk. Do you understand me?"

It took a few moments of coaxing, but he finally reached through and felt David nod his head. "Good. Now, we're going to let you go, and I want you to slowly turn over, ok?"

Again a pause, then the younger man nodded his head. He met Chris's eyes and signaled for him to let go first before slowly releasing his hold on David's wrist, then his neck. Standing up, Nickolas waited for the next move in the dance.

David rotated his wrist for a moment then shook it out before he rose up and turned over, bracing himself on his elbows. He looked down at Christoff then quickly up to Nickolas and groaned, falling back onto the pillow.

"Great, just great. I don't suppose you've made some kind of mistake?"

Nickolas cocked his head and turned to look at the wreckage David had made of his room, then turned back to look at the new changeling.

Rising back up on his elbows, David looked at his room as if seeing the destruction for the first time, and sighing, he fell back again. "I guess not. What now?"

"It's time for you to come with us. How are you feeling?"

"I'm really tired. What about my stuff? Can't I pack it up?"

"We'll have people come in and remove everything. You aren't in any shape to do it. Can you stand?" David flashed him a "what kind of stupid question is that" look, and turning, he swung his legs off the bed and stood up.

Or at least tried to.

Nick pressed his lips together so he wouldn't laugh at the shock on David's face when he found himself collapsing back onto the mattress. Nick shared an amused look with Chris as they waited for the fledge to find some balance.

"I don't understand," David said.

Nickolas caught David's dazed eyes and reached out to help steady him. "Your body is entering the second stage of the change. Up until this point the changes were subtle, all chemical and internal. Now the physical changes are joining them, and they will play havoc with you. We need to get you somewhere safe, with people who are experienced in dealing with the effects the change is about to cause in you."

"Oh...ok, I think. I don't know." He put his hand to his forehead and leaned on his knees. "It's hard to see suddenly."

Chris moved into position on David's other side. "Don't worry; we'll take care of you. You're one of us now. You're going to try standing again, but this time we'll be supporting you, all right?"

David grunted and wobbled to his feet. Both he and Chris grabbed his arms, quickly getting their shoulders under him before he collapsed again. They started making their way across the floor.

The rest of the recovery personnel scattered from the opening as they came through. Only Jules held back to keep them protected from the rear. Flynn and Scott ran ahead to hold the crowd at bay.

Nickolas ignored them, keeping his senses open to David's reactions. The residents of the building, alerted to the happenings by the two Valkyries' arrival, all waited along the halls, their excitement mounting. He listened to the snippets of conversations as he walked through the gauntlet.

"It's David."

"Who?"

"Which one?"

"The one in room fourteen."

"Whoa, wait till I tell Ellen. She's gonna freak."

The crowd on the first staircase hadn't been too bad, but at the landing of the second, he felt David tense and start to shake. His head shot up and he could understand the fledge's reaction. He had to clamp down on his own response to the huge crowd gathered at the bottom of the stairs staring at them.

The precarious hold on his calm slipped. The unfamiliar tide of energy building inside him swelled, prodding his emotions into turmoil. In an effort to siphon some of it off, he pushed a thread of power out, trying to use it to sooth David and hoping it would help himself as well.

Chris squeezed his arm and Nick looked across David's shoulders, taking strength from his brother's smile. "We'll be out soon, Nick, hold on."

"David? Ah crap, there goes one of our best gamers."

"Good luck, David."

Even with Flynn and Scott holding the crowd at bay, Nickolas found maintaining the calming influence difficult. A sigh escaped when they made it out the door. Careful on the steps, they slowly walked across the dark street to the van with their charge. Jules raced ahead and got the door open. Once they reached the van, Christoff ducked out from under David's arm and left him supporting the fledgling's weight alone.

"How're you doing so far, David?" Nick asked softly.

"How'm I suppose to answer that question?" The young man's heaviness seemed to increase to dead weight proportions. "I don' feel right."

His slurring had grown. They weren't going to keep him moving under his own power long. "David? I want you to lean forward; you're going to crawl inside with Chris's help. He'll get you settled, ok?"

"Sleep?"

"Yes, for a while at least. After you're in the van."

He lowered David to the floor of the doorway and helped the newly emerging Valkyrie coordinate his limbs into a crawl.

"Hello, David, my name's Christoff. Let's get you back here. There's a nice bench with your name on it for the drive."

His brother's voice faded as he walked away. He'd check the last couple of details off his list, then they could get out of here. And he could get home.

To Jessica.

He needed to see her. Needed the clear headedness he found when with her. Needed the calm.

He wrestled with the claustrophobia that had risen in the rooming house. *I've spent the better part of the last two weeks in a cell in the Hub and been fine, and now this?*

He rounded the hood of the van and found Scott.

"The team will be in here first thing in the morning, Nick, to pack up his stuff. I'll go and make sure the room's secure before we leave."

"Thanks, that's all that's left. I guess we're on our way then. Thanks, Scott."

"No problem, Nick."

He rubbed his snarling stomach and watched Scott cross the street before turning back to the van. He slammed the door and thumped heavily into his seat. His rioting emotions gave him a headache.

"You locked down, Chris?"

"We're set, Nick."

"Flynn, we're ready whenever you are." He leaned over to rest his head in his hands and pressed at the sharp pain in his eyes.

"The train is now departing from platform five, will all passengers please assume their seats and prepare for departure."

The van swayed as it pulled away from the curb. Flynn's flippant attitude pricked his temper. He took a long breath before he acted on his impulses, forcing it still. He'd come this far without alerting the others. He didn't need a rash desire to beat the Irishman's head into the steering wheel to destroy their chances. He sat back. *I'm hungry. That's all it is. Perfectly reasonable explanation for my irritability. As long as I don't look too close.* Now if only he could come up with a logical reason for sleeping the entire day.

He stared out the window, watching the fog line strobe past, and worried about his worsening condition, determined to remain awake this time.

Chapter Fourteen

Nickolas jerked awake when the van lurched around a corner. The seatbelt locked and pinned his chest, cutting into his neck. He fought the restraint before he woke enough to fumble with the latch and fling the webbing away.

How the hell did that thing get on me again? Fine tremors coursed through his body and he dropped his head between his knees before gasping in a long breath. Once he felt sure he had it contained, he sat back. The dim light from Jules's equipment fell across the tech's sympathetic face.

A growl formed in his chest, breaching the thin crust of control. His muscles tensed to spring at Jules, but movement caught his eye from the shadows in the rear of the vehicle and his focus snapped to it. His brother's intense stare challenged him; he had purposely drawn his aggression away from Jules.

Chris shook his head no.

He bared his teeth in response, and the growl grew louder.

"Not now, Nicky."

"Don't strap me in."

"Not safe. You would've rolled around like a loose watermelon. We're almost home."

That stopped him. He shot a look out the window just as the vehicle started to slow and the main gate for the Facility appeared out of the darkness.

He snapped his attention back to Chris. "Four more hours?"

The green gaze softened. "Closer to three. No traffic at this hour."

The van pulled to a stop under the overhang. Jules opened the door and the interior flooded with light. Nick squinted and took a deep breath. Chris tugged the straps from the unconscious fledge. The blood pounding in his head, he moved to help but stopped with a hiss as the pounding turned piercing for a moment.

"Nick?"

He ignored the concern and continued forward, unbuckling the last strap, then got a grip under David's knees. He slid the dead weight off the bench and waited for Chris to get him under the arms.

Hunched over, he backed up and they maneuvered through the interior of the vehicle. The jostling jarred the fledgling awake, and he started to fight them.

David, stop. We're trying to help. Nickolas sent. His grip firmed. *We need to get you out of the van.*

David whimpered but quit struggling. So he kept up a running mental monologue through the pain. Slowly, he backed out of the van.

"Quiet, Nickolas."

He slipped on the last step out and instinctively slammed his barriers up, cutting off his power. He whipped a look over his shoulder and saw Ian beside a wheelchair, staring at him.

His thoughts a maelstrom, he grabbed at David's legs as they slid out of his grip, missed, and they hit the pavement. The fledge grunted and Chris's eyes sought his as his brother grappled with the sudden weight. Backing away from the naked concern, he slowly retreated, aware of both Ian's and Chris's gaze following him while they settled David in the chair. The throbbing deepened.

"Flynn," Ian said. "Why don't you and Jules get the van checked in and go get something to eat. We'll get him settled."

"Yes, Doctor."

"Christoff..."

The van revved then pulled away, drowning out Ian's comments to his brother. He continued to retreat until his foot sank into grass. He had backed himself across the drive and onto the lawn.

Chris's voice telling him that Ian knew what he'd done circled through his shard-filled thoughts. He looked back at the building. Ian had turned his attention to David, taking him inside without a backward glance, he noticed with relief. The open sky beckoned and he lifted his face, the temptation to fly almost irresistible. Anywhere, it didn't matter. Somewhere else that didn't trap him inside shrinking walls. But then he remembered Jessica and his gaze lowered from the clouds.

Christoff stood where Ian had left him, his focus unwavering as he watched him, pity in the depths of his eyes, and Nickolas's relief fled as fast as it had risen.

"No, Nick. Don't make me chase you." The words whispered across the distance, and he held his hand out, pointing toward the door, waiting.

A shiver rippled down his wings. Only the thought of Jessica kept him grounded.

"Come on, Nick."

A step. Then two. He forced his feet in the direction of the building. Chris fell in behind as he passed. His steps slowed even further the closer he got, until the doors slid open and he stumbled to a stop on the threshold; the tunnel of hall froze the breath in his lungs.

His skin felt hot and tight. The shards behind his eyes sliced deeply.

He needed out.

Movement behind him. He twisted his head through quicksand and stared over his shoulder at Chris. The strength in the green gaze bored into him and he growled at the challenge from a Beta. The need to move became excruciating and he loosened his wings, the smell of the air calling.

Chris snapped his wings open, blocking his ability to back away from the threshold and take off. With a snarl, he jerked away, stumbling forward into the hall, and spun to face Chris as the doors shut with a whoosh, and a click announced their locking.

That sound reverberated through him with a finality that dredged up old nightmares. Chris advanced on him, one slow step at a time. Nick shook his head and backed down the hall to keep out of touching distance. Thrown by the challenge, the memories, and twisted by the pain. He spun on his heel and stalked down the corridor. At the first intersection he turned, intending to go to his suite, but Christoff blocked his way again.

Falling into a crouch, he barely held himself in check and growled, "Back off."

His brother stood his ground, his eyes never wavering. "Hub, Nick. Ian wants to see you."

Again, Chris pushed his space and he retreated away from physical contact. His brother played collie on his heels the rest of the way; he slammed the door to the Hub open and stalked inside, tossing a glare over his shoulder at the unrepentant herder.

Fully in the room, he cast an assessing glance that took in all activity. Ian had wheeled David up to the monitor island where Jays had a tray of instruments waiting. His explosive arrival had drawn their attention, and they stared at him before Ian murmured something to Jays, who quickly glanced from him to Chris and the door. That look sent alarm skittering through his nerves.

He turned back toward the door, but Chris leaned on the jamb, watching him. The alarm turned to panic, so he shoved it down, transmuting it into aggression.

"Jays," Ian said, though Nick noted that his keen eyes didn't cease watching him, "this is David. Let's get the preliminary paper work and initial tests done, ok?"

Jerking away from that gaze, he paced the long wall.

"Nick? Why don't you come sit down."

"No," he growled. His wings flared out behind him as he paced, and pain sliced through his head again. He pressed at his temples and took a deep breath. He wanted to see Jessica. But that would require getting close to the doctor.

With a snarl, he spun and continued to pace.

Ian and Jays kept on with David's exam; he stayed as far away as the space allowed, but that didn't stop him from feeling Ian's gaze fall on him repeatedly.

His stomach chose that moment to knot up. He doubled over; a gasp escaped his clenched teeth. Slowly raising his head, Nickolas zeroed in on Ian, who had paused taking

David's blood pressure. The doctor's look tangled with his and a gamut of emotions swamped him.

Anger, betrayal, lack of trust...fear.

The fear threatened to take over. Nickolas backed into the wall. He had seen that look far too often in Ian's eyes during his change. Ripping his gaze away, he shivered and glanced at the door. *I need to fly. I have to get out of here.*

Unfortunately, Chris still stood watch at the door.

You. Nick found an anchor in his brother's resolute green gaze. *You brought me here.*

He took a step.

Chris pushed away from the wall.

You brought me back to this hell.

Another step.

Not again. Never again.

Chris squared his shoulders and flexed his wings to loosen them.

His vision tunneled, focused on his target. Movement eased the pain but didn't eliminate it. The open air would fix it.

"Move."

"Nick..." Chris dropped into a defensive stance, barring the door.

"Nickolas." The shout came from behind him. He ignored it and surged the last few steps to engage Chris.

An explosive meeting. Chris held him off. Briefly. The two of them exchanged blows, and Chris succeeded in keeping him from the door, but at a cost.

He grabbed Chris by the throat and slammed him into the wall. The sound of glass breaking as things fell from the shaking went unheeded. All the rage that had been building boiled up. Chris's muscles tensed as he gathered to make a counter. Nickolas smashed him into the wall again, shattering the drywall, then squeezed until only a wheeze of breath could be heard. "Don't move, Chris, or I'll rip your throat out. So help me, I won't be able to stop it."

His brother's wide eyes latched on to his, but he wisely held still.

Nick concentrated on reining in the predator instinct before he did something he would regret for the rest of his life. Breathing, the wet rush passed over his lips, the slicing pain still eating away in his head. He still had one, fine, strand of spider silk holding his control. If no one pushed him...

"Nickolas, don't." Ian's voice echoed in his ears, and in his head.

As heavy as stone, his head pivoted to meet Ian's stare a foot away. The feel of his brother's pulse raced under his hand, and the quiet rasp of him trying to breathe filled the room. Fine tremors settled into his muscles, and he whispered, "What is happening to me, Ian?"

"Nicky. Let Chris go. Then we'll talk."

The strength in Ian's eyes surrounded him; he turned back to his brother's matching green, where understanding tried to cover the fear.

"You don't want to hurt him. You know that. Somewhere inside, you know. Now let your brother go."

His body reacted to the underlying steel in the command before his mind could process it. His fingers released and he took a step back. He shot a look at Ian, then squeezed his eyes shut and moaned. Through the pain he heard Chris draw in a ragged breath and slip away. Something wet rolled down his lip, and he wiped his hand across his face. Blood.

"Let. Me. Out." He turned his attention back to Ian. The doctor hadn't moved, hadn't taken his eyes off him. "Now."

"Christoff, go lock the door to the hall, immediately. Jays, get David into room two."

Watching both as they moved to do Ian's bidding, Nickolas backed up to the wall.

"Don't do this," he whispered. "Let me go."

Ian studied him for a moment before replying. "I'm sorry, Nicky. I can't do that."

He pushed farther into the wall, his wings flattened, and clenched his fists at his side, tipping his head to stare sightlessly at the ceiling.

Silence filled the Hub.

Jays cleared his throat. "David is settled, Ian."

Nick dropped his head in time to see Ian nod in acknowledgement, his mesmerizing gaze still firmly fixed on him. "When's the last time you ate, Nickolas?"

"I don't remember," he evaded.

"Jays, order food up for David and get extra for Nick. Christoff, did you bring the bag back from the van that I sent with you?"

"Yes, Ian. It's under the wheelchair."

"Good. Jays, get it unpacked, ok?"

"Understood, Ian," he said quietly.

"Come on, Nick. There's a few tests I want to run."

Frozen against the wall, he looked at his brother standing in front of the doors, arms crossed, face blank as he watched him. The beginning of bruises spanned his throat.

Jays had one eye on him from the telephone across the room. And Ian...

He stood waiting, a chair pulled out where the equipment they had used on David sat.

The effort it took to regain a modicum of civility left him shaking. He slipped away from the wall, dragging his feet, to where Ian waited for him.

"Sit." The doctor turned to his equipment and started pulling out some basic gear. "We need to talk."

He perched on the edge of the chair, every muscle tense for the expected physical contact. Ian roughly shoved his sleeve up and wrapped a pressure cuff about his bicep.

The doctor's gaze touched on his then went back to his work. "Your stomach is cramping, isn't it? Sharp pain in your head?"

"Yes," he hissed.

"The timing's right. You've been off of the arresting inhibitor for almost two weeks."

Arresting inhibitor?

"You likely won't remember the details of what I'm telling you." He pulled the Velcro and dumped the cuff on the table. Dictating the numbers to Jays, he started pulling electrodes out of the caddy. "Unbutton your shirt."

His fingers stiff, he opened his shirt. With brisk efficiency Ian slapped the electrodes to his chest, and Jays watched the monitor. "You've entered stage four. You are now in the process of completing the change that was chemically halted fifteen years ago."

Without thought, he grabbed Ian's wrist as he held an instrument toward his face. "What?"

Ian's sharp gaze pinned his. "The pills didn't just block your talents; they actually halted their natural development. All the symptoms, all the behaviors you experienced, will come back to haunt you, Nicky."

The truth of the situation stared into his soul. With an exclamation, he recoiled. The chair smashed to the ground and he ripped the pads from his chest. Breath labored, his wings fanned and he backed away from everyone in the room.

"Jays?" Ian picked up the chair but kept an eye on him.

"It was long enough. We got what we needed."

"Good. Nick, try and stay with me. It'll be harder for you than for any of the others."

Shaking his head, he desperately tried to get his thoughts and feelings under control. The memories of what Ian could do to him...

He shuddered and his back slammed into the wall. His gaze roamed the room, but he didn't see. All he saw was his cell fifteen years ago.

Alone. So alone.

"Nickolas."

His mind snapped back, and he stared at the concern on Ian's face. Then his head swiveled to the bank of screens, and like a rope thrown to him, he was pulled over. He barely noticed the other fledglings in their cells. Only Jessica. She paced the small confines. The sight of her settled the beast that had been set free inside.

"I need to see her."

"I'm sorry, Nick, but now is not a good time. You're in no condition to. You'll feel better tomorrow. Trust me."

Another flip in his equilibrium, and sudden rage poured through his system. He gasped at the pain that followed and his knees buckled. He caught himself on the edge of the desks with shaking arms. It took a moment but then he raised his head back to the screen. "I'll feel better if I see her."

"No."

He pushed away; a frustrated snarl tore from him, and he stalked around the island of screens to pace the length of doors. At her number, he pushed against the steel. No give. He started running his fingers along the seams.

"I will not unlock it, Nickolas."

He slammed his shoulder into it. A dull whump echoed through the Hub. But, not surprising, the door held firm. He rested his forehead against the cold metal. Not sure what Ian's plans were, besides not letting him out of the Hub yet, he closed his eyes and ground his teeth then spun away to stalk the perimeter of the room. If he couldn't get in...

I'll get out.

The clanging of the food trolley rumbled through the door. He tracked the sound then stared at the entrance.

They have to open it.

He loosened his wings and crouched in preparation for an extended leap across the large room.

Jays preempted his move by casually walking over to back up his brother, a trank gun in his hand and a second handed to Chris. Both sets of eyes trained on him. Fear of what Jays held twined with acute frustration. Unable to withhold a howl, he rose and backed away.

And if Jays hadn't been holding the trank gun, he would have attacked Ian in that instant for the slight smile he didn't bother to hide when he gestured to Chris to unlock the door and bring the cart in.

"Chris, Jays, let me know when you have the food ready." A challenging look in his eye, Ian moved away, walking over to the monitors, and picked up some paper work.

Getting out the door didn't look to be an option. At least not until Ian allowed it. Clenching his fists, he followed the doctor over to the desks.

"Either let me in or let me out, Ian. I can't take this."

A soft sigh passed the doctor's lips. "I can't, Nicky. Can you see yourself? Do you see what you're doing?"

"I..." He swallowed. "There's so much pain."

"I know. And it's only going to get worse for a while."

"She makes it better."

"I'm sorry."

He stared at Jessica through the glass of the machine. She kept casting expectant looks at the door. Almost like she knew he was near. *She's right. We need to get out. How do I get her out?* Out of the corner of his eye, he caught Ian nod slightly, and his focus shifted. Suspicious, he trained a look on each of them, but Ian flicked her screen off, which drew his attention back, along with a growl. He reached out to turn it back on.

"Don't touch it."

His hand froze at the tone. Anger simmered, but he couldn't force it to obey. Ian hadn't even looked up from his paper work.

"We're done, Ian," Jays said. He set a plate with a burger on it in front of Nickolas then turned and walked back over to Christoff and the trolley.

"We'll take David his in a moment, Jays. I need to finish this first. Eat, Nicky; you're hungry, even if you don't believe it."

The smell hit him and his stomach cramped. He licked his lips, staring at the food. Ian still ignored him in favor of the paper work he continued to fill out. The other two had relaxed slightly and held a quiet conversation at the door.

He looked under the bun. Cheese stretched and a drop of blood ran down to drip onto the plate. Everything else in the room faded from sight. His hands reached out and lifted it, so he took a bite. Warmth exploded on his tongue, along with the salty metallic taste of the rare meat. He bolted the meal in half a dozen bites.

As he finished off the last bite, his mind returned from the impulse it had fallen into; he caught Ian studying him out of the corner of his eye. He sought Jays and Chris, both watching and waiting. He snapped his attention back to Ian.

"You didn't."

"I'm sorry, Nicky, but you needed the food and the sleep. Your control is beyond shaky tonight, we can't risk it. You'll feel much better tomorrow."

"You know how much I hate tranks." He shoved away from the table and stalked around the room, pushing his body, trying to avoid the inevitable. "Why?"

"Nickolas, you're becoming a danger to yourself and others around you."

Flaring his wings for balance, he reached out to steady himself on the wall as he felt the drug start to kick in; shaking his head, he surged away, glaring at his brother as he passed. "Thanks a lot, Chris."

"It's for the best, Nick."

"I've heard that before." He turned away from his brother's concern. Rage made him want to lash out at them for what they had done, but they all wisely stayed out of his reach. A continuous low growl rumbled in his throat as he paced more and more unsteadily, frantic in his fear of being locked back up in one of the cells of the Hub. He shook his head to try and clear it but lost his balance and hit the computer desk with his hip. He managed to catch himself before he fell.

Across the desk, he met Ian's eyes. So many emotions skated across the green. He latched on to the understanding and he reached his hand out, hoping for help or comfort; he wasn't sure. Trapped in Ian's eyes, he heard the doctor's voice from a distance. "Chris, catch him, he's going down."

Floating, he barely registered Christoff's touch as his body gave in.

Ian's face swam into his view above. "Let's get him into the MRI. I need to see what's going on."

His vision continued to tunnel until it faded into the dark.

Christoff sat up and raked the hair out of his eyes. He looked blearily around, then heard the knocking again. Pulling the sheet off the bed, he wrapped it around himself before he stumbled in the dark through his bedroom doorway and across his living room. His stiff fingers fumbled with the knob, and he yanked the door open. The bright glare of the hallway lights made his eyes squint, and the silhouette in front of him laughed, brushing past.

"What the hell, Donald. You couldn't just open the damn unlocked door and come in?" He shoved it closed and turned back to his visitor, who walked the room turning on lights.

"Well your note did say to come and wake you up."

"You couldn't have done that from in here?"

"Did you really want that?"

Chris flopped into his chair, yawning, and tried to focus on Donald, who took a seat on the couch across from him. "I'll see *you* later in the ring."

Donald laughed, then sobered. "So what's up? It's important enough to have me wake you, but not important enough for you to wake me. Did something go wrong with the recovery yesterday?"

Ambushed by another yawn, he wrapped the sheet a little more securely. "Not exactly. That went smooth enough. It was after we got back that the difficulties started. Nickolas turned feral. Fortunately it was here, in a controlled environment, with Ian watching. He's sleeping off a strong dose of sedative right now. Ian doesn't expect him to wake until late morning."

Donald went still. "Any injuries?"

"It could have been worse." He lifted his chin to show the darkening fingerprints about his throat. "Nick almost didn't stop; it was close. He slept most of yesterday, and when awake, well you saw him when we left. He felt like a stretched spring about to snap."

He leaned his head back, clenching his fist on the arm of the chair. "It was my fault. I should have made sure he ate."

"Chris, look at me."

Opening his eyes, he looked wearily over at Donald.

"You know as well as I that he was building like a volcano; if not yesterday, then it would have been today or tomorrow. It sounds like the timing for his breakdown couldn't have been better planned. It wasn't in too public a place and the best individuals to handle it were available. You kept him in one piece, that's all that matters, Chris."

The sincerity in his Second's eyes helped. "Thanks, Donald. I need to hear that. It's just hard to see him like this. It reminds me too much of fifteen years ago. Anyway, Ian says we need to tighten the watch on him now. After we tranked him, Ian took the opportunity to get an MRI. His brain is ripping itself to shreds."

"Wha...what?"

"Yeah, fun, huh? Looks like we miscalculated. Turns out the 'anti-aggresion,'" he used his fingers to put air quotes around that, "pills are actually a different type of inhibitor. None of us have been allowed to complete our changes. So that's what we're up against. Ian expects Nick to continue to deteriorate for a couple more weeks before he's over the worst of it."

"You said Ian knew; why didn't he stop us?"

"I have no idea. He hasn't seen fit to fill us in yet. I am assured, though, that Nick's experience will be the worst. The rest of us won't be so bad. Those of us who are Hunters will get off the easiest. Anyone who turns out to be in one of the other castes will have a tougher time. Roughly, it can be judged on how difficult your original change was for you."

"Kieran."

"Ian is already making plans for him. He won't be as difficult to handle as Nick, but it'll be hard on him."

Donald pursed his lips in a soundless whistle. "So, what now?"

"Ian gave me a couple of trank pistols. We just need to keep them hidden from the Facility personnel. We'll set up a layered guard, two on his heels and two at a distance. And you and I will spend nights with him. Ian hopes we can keep him from needing to be placed under observation. You can guess what that would do to Nick."

"Fuck him right up."

"To put it mildly. Not to mention the attention it would draw to have him there. So we have to be the bars to his cage."

"Is there anything we can do to help him?"

"No. There's no way to relieve any of the effects. The best help we can give him is to try and make sure Ian doesn't have to confine him to a cell in the Hub." Resting his head on the side of the chair back, Chris closed his eyes. "Your first task is to get everyone up and to the gym within the hour. Ian assures me we can meet there en masse without causing too much notice among the rest of the Facility's staff. We need to get our plans in place before Nickolas wakes."

"What about Jessica?"

"At the moment, she's pretty safe under Ian's care. But Gabriel's already expressed interest in her."

"That's not good."

"No. For either of them. And unlike us, he's completely uninhibited. He'll be able to tell from a distance that Nick is off the drugs."

"But..."

"We'll handle that hurdle later. I'm sure Ian has some plan he's working from."

"Right. Then I guess we have a start, I'll go get everyone moving."

He opened his eyes and nodded to Donald as the Hunter rose and gave him a casual salute before letting himself out. The quiet settled around him and he stared into nothingness, remembering the past and comparing the present. *I wish I could spare you this, Nick; you've already been through so much.* With a sigh, he climbed to his feet. *Well, if I want to be awake to deal with this situation, I had better go take a shower and dress.*

Chapter Fifteen

One foot in front of the other. *Where were you yesterday?* Turn, stretching her growing wings until they hurt. One foot in front of the other. *I don't believe Kieran. There was something more than a recovery you went on.* Turn again at the end of eight steps. Drop into a squat and rise a few times.

The line on her thigh pulled a bit but held. She twisted to look at the red stripe; the dots from where the stitches had been removed were fading already. She rubbed her palm across it and continued her pacing. *Why didn't you come in last night?* The memory of raised voices and a large *whomph* on her door intruded. *I'm sure I felt you.*

She stopped and stared into the blank wall before her nose. *It's not so bad when you're here. And that's something I should watch out for. I need to get out. How do I get out? They don't present any opportunities.* She gave herself a shake then leaned her palms into the wall and stepped back. After several pushups against the wall, she turned to pace the opposite way again. *I had thought you were finally coming around and would help me get out.*

Snippets of their last conversation floated through her mind. And the luscious taste of the chocolate he had smuggled in to her as it melted on her tongue.

The door locks thunked in the frame and she jumped.

Breakfast? It must be morning.

She ground her teeth and glared when Jays walked through the door carrying her tray of food. He placed several plates on the table before glancing up at her.

Her wings spread before she realized what they were doing and she took a step toward him. "Where is he, Jays?"

He folded his arms and stared at her. "Sleeping."

"Really? Even I know he doesn't sleep this much."

He shifted his feet and flicked a glance at the camera in the ceiling behind her. "He has a lot of sleep to catch up on."

"Don't lie to me," she growled.

He rolled his eyes and uncrossed his arms, taking a step toward her. "You choose now to talk to me? Two weeks of nothing. But now?"

He took a deep breath and let it out slowly. "Eat. You didn't eat much yesterday. That's not good for your changing body."

And he turned and walked away from her; swiping his card, he left the room without looking back.

"As if you'd care," she mumbled, then scrubbing her face with her hands, she walked over to the bunk and sat. She pushed the meat cubes around with her finger. No fruit this time. *Guess they're serious about my meal today.* She sighed then tried to choke down a few chunks but had to stop. *I hope he's all right. I'm sure now, from Jays's reaction, that there's more going on.*

She tapped the thick plastic plate with her fingernail. *This could be useful.* Her fingers rubbed the cotton of the mattress pad she sat on then looked up at the ceiling vent. *Yes. That could work. I'm going to have to get me—us—out of here.*

She tried one more piece of the bloody meat, but her stomach turned and she spat it back out. Then, with quick moves, she combined all the food onto one plate and stacked the others before standing and carrying the full plate over to the toilet, where she flushed it enthusiastically.

She had barely managed to sit back down before the door opened and Ian walked in, followed by Jays pushing the exam cart. *Guess that one didn't get by them.* She leaned her elbows on the table and fidgeted with the stack of plates.

"So? Are you going to cooperate today?"

"Why should I?" She glanced up and met Ian's eyes.

He placed his hands on her little table and leaned down to her face. "Because if you want to see Nick today, you will."

She snarled and gathered herself to lunge at him, but his snapped, "don't," froze her in her seat.

"You won't win, Jessica. And I suggest you don't push me today. I'm not in the mood."

She glared but finally had to look away from the intensity in his eyes. He straightened and joined Jays at the cart, so she took the opportunity to slip the top plate from the stack and slide it under the pad of the bunk before they returned to her.

Jays cleared the table and folded it back down to the wall.

"Let's start with wing measurements. Against the wall, Jess."

Again, she met his eyes but couldn't hold his gaze, so with a curl of her lip, she crossed the six feet to the wall and placed her hands on it. She flinched when she felt his hand rest lightly on her shoulder. Then the two of them pulled, prodded, and muttered to one another as they recorded her growth for the day. The rest of the exam basics went by in a blur. Soon she relaxed against their touch, but something about the light caress of Jays's hand across her hair and his other hand brushing down her arm brought the tension back to her muscles. She started to spin away from the wall, but Jays dropped her faster than she could escape him. Her shoulder went numb as he simultaneously twisted her arm up her spine and slammed her knees into the tiles of the floor with his foot, bowing her back with the grip he had in her hair. She tried to struggle, but he had her balance in his control.

"Damn you to hell and back, Jays." Tears pricked her eyes as she stared up at the ceiling, her breathing harsh in her own ears. She pulled against his grip and succeeded in twisting enough to see Ian out of the corner of her eye, raising a needle and tapping it for air bubbles. Her growl turned into a gasp as Jays pulled her arm a bit more. She flailed her free hand, trying to get a grip on him, anything.

Ian stepped up, pulling the cart with him, and caught her free wrist, pinning it between his knees. He deftly inserted the needle into the vein in her elbow and started to draw blood samples. "Don't blame, Jays. This wouldn't happen if you would cooperate."

He changed the tube a third time, but this time she felt the burn from the inhibitor as he injected it and hissed. Then pressure from his thumb for a second before the sting of adhesive as he stretched a Band-Aid across the prick.

"Cooperate?" she gasped through her stretched throat. "You know as well as I do they don't use crap like this in Aurora. So why?"

"Ok, Jays, let her go."

Jays lifted his foot from the back of her knees then slowly lowered her arm and raised her head and back until she caught her balance. When he stepped back she stumbled to her feet, neither arm working properly. The burn in her veins started to spread; it already engulfed her hand and her fingertips, steadily working its way up her shoulder. Soon it would hit her heart and explode everywhere. It made the ache Jays caused in her other shoulder disappear. She stared at Ian, this time not dropping her eyes. "Why?"

"What they do in Aurora really has no bearing here. What would you do if I let you out?"

"Leave."

"And that's why the inhibitor."

Jays had finished packing up the cart. With a tip of his head, Ian saluted her, then swiped his card and held the door for Jays. Her body had started to shake. She couldn't make a play for the open door, and from the look in his eyes, Ian knew it. Cursing him, she stumbled to the bed and fell down on it. The drug pumped through her heart and she closed her eyes, praying that she could pass out before the rest of the effects grabbed hold.

Chris's hand at the back of his neck squeezed then shoved him through the doors into the Hub. With a growl, Nick spun and struck out halfheartedly at his brother, but Chris just grabbed his wrist and got in his face.

"You want to see her, right? Then get in here and knock it off."

The dark bruises around Chris's neck flexed, and Nick relaxed his arm, turning away as soon as Chris let him go. Jays held a clipboard over by the monitor island, waiting for them. Dragging his feet, he moved that way.

"He woke up in a mood, Jays."

"Not terribly surprising. How do you feel, Nick?"

"What do you think? Tranks suck."

Jays pressed his lips together, but his eyes sparkled. He proceeded to write a couple of things on the clipboard then handed him a heavily loaded tray. "Here. There's enough on there for both of you. She's hardly touched food since the last time you took in her dinner. So make sure she eats everything. Then we need to talk. As soon as Ian returns."

Not given a chance to respond, Jays hustled him over to her door and shoved him through it with a hand between his shoulder blades.

The door locks clicked behind him.

He swallowed and looked at her sitting on the cot. She raised her head out of her hands, her face still a little green.

"Thrown up already?"

"Yeah," she whispered, and her tongue passed across her lower lip, but she sat up straighter.

"Good. Then you should be able to eat." He placed the overstacked tray down on her table.

She made a choking noise and he glanced up. "They don't really think I can eat all that?"

He felt his face heat and he fidgeted with the plates. "Um, no. It's for both of us."

"I assumed that. It's still way more than what we normally get when we eat together."

"Jays said something about you not eating yesterday."

She exhaled and slid over, making room for him. "I just couldn't seem to stomach anything. It was like chewing cardboard."

"Why?"

She cocked her head and their gazes met as he slid behind the table next to her. "A little mad, mostly worried."

She knows, he realized as they stared, frozen. She blinked and turned to her plate. He pushed his own food around. Finally, he asked softly, "Promise me you won't do that again? You need to eat, Jess. If you don't…"

"You don't think they would use that stuff on me, do you? Not after the way I've responded to the other drugs?"

He shook his head. "But that doesn't matter. What matters is that you could cause yourself damage, you might not make it out.... Well, you could hurt yourself. A few missed meals can make a huge difference. Promise me."

"All right," she finally answered, but her continued scrutiny was a bit unnerving. "What about you?"

"What about me?" He started to eat, staring at his plate.

"What's wrong? What happened yesterday?"

He shoved more food in his mouth.

"Please don't lie to me like the others. I really doubt the recovery took that long. You would have been in here."

He coughed. "I wasn't. Lying, that is. I just don't know how to answer. Yesterday is mostly a blur," he finished softly.

He took a few more bites. "I hate not remembering."

Her hand slid up his shoulder and started to rub the back of his neck. He closed his eyes and chewed more slowly. "Chris has bruises all around his throat."

"And you don't remember doing it," she stated.

"No. But the thing is, before I came in here...I was almost willing to do it again." He shoved the empty plate aside and accepted the glass of milk Jessica handed him. She reached out and grabbed their second plates and plunked his in front of him. She dug into hers. They ate in silence for a while.

"Your favorite topic?" he said. "I think I agree now."

Her eyes darted a look over and he nodded. She glanced up to the opposite corner where the camera sat blinking at them.

"How sensitive..."

"Too much." They had both finished eating, so he leaned back and patted the mattress next to him. She scooted over and curled into his side. He brushed her hair with his cheek then whispered in her ear, "I'm not sure if they can pick this up or not. But if we aren't careful, they will get suspicious if they see us whispering a lot on the camera."

She shifted position, crawling into his lap, and wrapped her arms around his neck, pressing her cheek against his. He closed his eyes. Her breath tickled his ear.

"You really are willing to get me out now?"

"Us out."

"When?"

"It needs to be soon. I should feel Chris out. I'd really rather not leave them all behind, but I will if that's what it comes down to." His hands started to roam the skin of her back and flowed along the velvet of her wing membrane. She tightened her arms and rubbed her cheek against his. "I need to find you warmer clothes, and locating a place to hide will take some doing; especially if it has to be from my brother and the other lieutenants. The Facility will be hard enough, but the Hunters may well be impossible."

"I may be able to help with some of that." She sat back and looked into his face.

He cupped her cheek in the palm of his hand, his thumb brushing her skin. "We'll do whatever it takes."

He didn't remember choosing to lean forward and he really didn't care. All that mattered suddenly changed when, as soft as a dandelion wish, their lips brushed. And his brain felt as scattered as those same seeds on the wind. Their lips slid across each other before the tip of his tongue traced them ever so softly. She parted hers and the first brush of tongue against tongue tasted sweet. Just like his body craved. Her hands slid up into his hair and he sank deeper into the kiss.

His other hand came around, cupping both sides of her face, and they lost all track of time.

Breath labored, they pulled back for a moment; she studied his face, and he wondered what she looked for as he watched the hazel roam.

The door locks released. He closed his eyes, and Jess dropped her forehead to his chest. He thought he could feel the rumble of a soft growl reverberate through her back where his arms now rested. Wrestling with his own anger, he sent a slashing look at Jays, who waited near the door.

"Time to go, Nick. Ian's waiting."

"I'm not ready."

"Too bad. Lunch is over. You have duties you need to see to. Trust me, you won't like the consequences if you don't listen."

Jessica's growl became a certainty, and he stared into Jays's eyes. The grounded didn't flinch.

He felt his own growl try to form and shoved it down for the moment. *Damn it.* He realized this would only end badly.

He tugged on Jess's hair so she would look up at him. "I should go. But I'll be back as soon as I can."

The gold flecks in her hazel eyes flashed with a weak spark of power, even through the inhibitor. He felt his newfound power rise in answer. He leaned down and brushed his lips across hers once more.

"Nickolas."

This time he did growl, but Jessica slid off his lap. He stood then picked up the tray of dishes. And with a last glance at Jess, he stormed past Jays, who held the door for him.

Out in the Hub, he dumped the tray with a clatter on the cart. The noise would have drawn everyone's attention except he already had it, he noticed. *Great. I guess we were a popular peep show.*

Kieran and Dylan stood with Ian over Jessica's screen. The two Beta's made a valiant but ineffectual attempt to hide their smirks; Ian just looked grim.

"Nickolas, we need to talk."

"I don't feel the need to." He flared his wings and turned to prowl along the cell doors then along the wall.

"Nick, you almost killed your brother. We have to talk about last night."

He stumbled to a stop and stared at the ground.

"How much do you remember?" Ian's voice had gentled and drew nearer.

He raised his gaze from the floor to Ian's in front of him. "It's a bit blurry. I remember anger, I remember you drugging me."

He clenched his fists, but when Ian reached out to touch him, he shied away and started pacing again.

"I remember wanting to see Jessica."

The doctor sighed. "Jessica's arrival has set a train of events into motion. When you chose to stop taking the pills, it was because of her. But the pills didn't just block you from using talent that you already possessed. They froze your development at the end of stage three of your change. The reason you are having so much trouble controlling your mind is because it is changing again. You are in the middle of stage four."

Disbelief swept through him. "So many lies." He turned and stalked Ian. "Our whole life, a lie?"

Ian's gaze followed him, the swirl of power inside started to surge with a surf all its own. An answering light flashed in Ian's eyes and was gone so fast Nick doubted that he really saw it.

"Trust me," the doctor snapped, "if I had any choices, things would be very different. There are rules I have to follow. I didn't dictate the lies, but I tried to use them to my advantage. It was the only way I could keep you safe. I knew someday you would find out the truth or need to be told."

Ian leaned against the center island, his arms crossed, watching him like a bug under a microscope. A shiver racked his body, and he turned away from those green eyes.

"Nicky. I can't change the past. I can't change the fact that the rest of your isolation was delayed fifteen years. I can't take away your pain or your memories. But I can and will do everything in my power to keep you safe. Even against your will."

Nick stopped and turned to stare at the doctor.

"You almost killed Chris last night. Remember what your isolation was like."

"As if I could forget?" he snapped. "You made sure I wouldn't have that option."

"You can no longer remain unmonitored. I've arranged with Chris to take over your duties, not that you've been doing much with them lately anyway, and he and Donald have already talked with the Flight and Wing leaders and set up a rotation for you."

He backed away, his eyes flicking to Kieran and Dylan, now understanding their presence.

"Don't do this, Ian," he whispered. "I can handle it. I've been handling it."

"Not anymore. Last night was too close. I've given you as much rope as possible. But you're deteriorating too fast now."

He ran his hands through his hair and stalked the side of the island Ian didn't control. He raked a glare across Kieran, and the Beta pulled Dylan out of his way. He moved into the island and braced his hands on the desk, staring down at Jess. She did calisthenics in the middle of her cell. The feel of her lips lingered on his as he watched her. *How am I going to get her out now?*

"I'm sorry, Nick. This is the best I can do."

"And that's supposed to help?"

"I guess that's up for interpretation." Ian paused. "You've let your phys-ex tests slip. I need you to go with Jays and make them up, along with your agility."

"Now?"

"Yes, now. That should take you the rest of the afternoon. I'll see you back in here tomorrow morning."

"But her dinner?"

"Someone else will bring it."

With a snarl, he spun on his heel and stormed across the Hub, his two shadows hot on his heels.

Their footsteps, a quiet reminder of Ian's words, goaded his already tenuous temper as they made their way through the maze of halls. He slammed through the doors into the gym. All activity ceased as they turned to stare at him. He closed his eyes and took a deep breath. *Control. Get it under control.*

He ignored the concerned gazes and moved to the back corner of the large gym and started a quick muscle warm-up. Kieran and Dylan leaned against the wall a couple of feet away, their watchful stares grating on his self-control. He inched down the wall with each exercise, pushing for some breathing space, but they acted like he had an invisible tether attached and just followed if he got more than four or five feet away. The tension thrumming through his shoulders made loosening up his muscles more difficult than normal. Finally he spun at them. They fell back a step into a fighting stance; Dylan moved to bracket him.

"Back off," he growled.

Kieran took a slow, measured breath then shook his head before his eyes darted a look at Dylan, and together they stood up. "Sorry, Nick."

Jays chose that moment to arrive. He swept all three of them with a glance then flipped his notebook open. "Ok, Nick, let's start with the ropes."

A little of the snarl he tried to suppress escaped, and he plowed past his watchers, crossing the distance to the ropes, and vaulted onto the nearest. Swinging himself hand over hand, he ascended to the top. Upon reaching it, he kicked off from the wall, and doing a backwards somersault, he snapped out his wings to break his fall. He landed in a crouch. All eyes in the gym focused on him. The attention wasn't helping him regain his equilibrium.

"Again," Jays snapped.

He growled and threw a threatening look over his shoulder, but he leaped at the ropes again. He repeated each variation of the exercise to Jays's satisfaction then moved to the rings and continued. The damn doctor followed his every move, with Kieran and Dylan breathing down his neck, and the eyes of the entire clan stared at him, pushing him to his limits.

After the last circuit, he landed in a crouch and stayed there, breathing heavily and rumbling a growl at his escort. Kieran glanced around then slowly approached and held out a water bottle.

He didn't rise out of his crouch, but he did take the bottle, then ducked his forehead against his shoulder to wipe the sweat away. He drained the bottle and slowed his breath. And for the first time, he noticed the shards slicing behind his eyes; he pinched his nose and gave his head a shake.

"Let's move to the mats, Nick," Jays said softly.

He opened his eyes and met Jays's. The grounded didn't look away but just waited. Hissing, he lunged to his feet and smiled when Jays stumbled back a step. Kieran growled, and Nick slowly turned in his direction.

"Leave him alone, Nick."

He stared a moment at the Beta and felt Dylan move around him. Kieran's eyes flicked a look to the side, and Nick noticed Dev leaning against the wall twenty feet away. Nick turned and started walking to the mats, scanning the rest of the crowd. *There.* He found Aidan flanking him as he walked, also twenty feet out.

So it's double. Would Chris have posted a third circle on me?

At the tumbling mats, he dove into the first routine. He pushed himself in an effort to ignore the pain, but it continued to escalate. As did his visions. The talents growing within him wanted acknowledgement. Now that he no longer had Jessica helping to keep it in check, his power had started to build, the pressure growing uncomfortable.

He lost track of the time, and Jays pushed him through the tests, Kieran and Dylan always in his space. More and more eyes turned his way.

The pain ate away at what little self-control he could maintain, and the constant scrutiny finished off the rest.

He rolled, the movement taking him near the edge of the mat. But instead of rising from it then falling into the next move, he swept his foot out and forced Kieran into the air or get knocked on his ass.

"Stop smothering me," he barked at his escort.

Kieran dropped to the ground in a crouch but didn't answer. The pain sliced through and he touched his forehead to his bent knees with a groan. When he looked up, Kieran still waited but concern filled his eyes. Warm wet slid from his nose. Blood again.

"Nick," Jays said. "I think we'll skip the last set of evals."

He wiped the blood, smearing it across the top of his arm. The smell of blood drew more attention and others started to gather closer, not even trying to pretend that they were working.

Weekly evaluations? He shook his head again, trying to clear it and stood up, pressing his hand to his forehead. Too much pressure. *That's right. Sparring would be next.* That would help. Movement. He looked at Kieran and watched the Hunter's face blanch.

The workout had helped at first, but now it wasn't enough. *Fly. I need to fly.* He scanned the room. Too many to get through. The doors were too far away. *If I can't fly...*

He started to smile.

Spreading his wings, he did a somersault over their heads, landing outside the mats, then sprinted across the room.

I can fight.

He bounced on his toes in the middle of the large sparring circle. The tide of bodies that raced after him slid to a stop at the line painted on the floor. Kieran and Dylan split, pacing the circumference in opposite directions. His wings flared and his head swiveled, trying to follow both.

"Dev," Kieran yelled. "Go get Chris. Aidan, get Jays back, keep him protected. No one else move."

Out of the corner of his eye, he saw Aidan pull a white-faced Jays back away from the ring, but most of his attention had turned to focus on Kieran.

"Don't go too far, Jays. This is the last set of tests he needs, Kieran." He smiled. "He pushed me through the others, but I'll enjoy this one. Come on. I can take care of you two first, then Jays."

He held his hand out and beckoned the Hunter with his fingers. Kieran loosened his wings but continued to pace on the outside of the line, holding his attention.

"I don't think my crossing the boundary would be a good idea, Nickolas. I'm pretty sure both Chris and Ian would find that activity too dangerous. Think about what you almost did last night."

Ghost images started to flirt across his vision and he blinked. Mantling his wings, he feinted at the edge of the ring, trying to bring the Hunter across where he could do something...anything.

When Kieran wouldn't oblige him, he turned to baiting the rest of his audience and hoped someone would make a mistake and cross the boundary.

He heard a shuffled movement and snapped his focus over his shoulder. Aidan pushed Jays back and shoved him behind a larger onlooker to block him from his sight. Nick took a step in their direction, but Kieran raised his wings and he lost interest in the grounded for the moment.

"Come on, Kieran, come play with me," he said softly, but the Hunter shook his head and kept up his pacing outside of the circle. The sound of footsteps running broke through his trance, and he looked up to see Christoff race into the gym, Donald right behind him. Grinning, Nick called out to his brother, "Come to spoil my fun, Chris? Or do you have the balls to join me?"

His grin faded when he saw the black smudges marring his brother's throat, so he looked at the others instead. Donald had circled around behind him to the farthest quarter of the circle's perimeter.

"Kieran, Dylan, maintain your positions. Nickolas, look at me." Christoff's face was carefully neutral, and he stopped precisely at the edge of the circle.

Shaking his head, Nickolas turned away to continue toying with the crowd gathered around the edge, taunting them to join him. He spread his wings and gave them a vigorous flap then lunged at the circle's edge, laughing when a couple of the onlookers fell backward. His vision greyed out for a moment when the ghosts took on more definition, but he pushed the sight away and spun back to the center of the circle—only to double over, hissing from the sudden pain that ripped through his head. He tried to breathe through it, but he had to twist and fall into a crouch to forestall Donald's attempt to come in from behind.

He wove along the edge, assessing the four Hunters that kept him contained in the circle, frustrated that his control of the situation was gone. A new sound broke through his focus, and he started to growl as the rest of the Flight and Wing leaders arrived on the run. All of the most dangerous Valkyries were now present and accounted for. There were just too many.

Heat and force expanded in his center; the faces around him wavered like mirages on a sunny road.

"Chris!" Kieran shouted. "He's about to use his power."

"Nickolas. Look. At. Me."

Nick felt the breeze stir his hair, but the force of Chris's command drew his attention away from the seductive lure of power growing inside.

His gaze locked on Chris, who immediately started to move along the circle's boundary. Drawn to follow his brother's movements around the ring like he had Kieran's, the world started to narrow once more. Christoff gently directed the situation, taking control. "Nick, no one's going to fight you today. No one wants to see a repeat of last night."

He attempted a halfhearted lunge, but Chris didn't fall for it. "Don't worry, Chris. I won't try to kill you this time, just beat the crap out of you."

"I'm afraid that's not going to happen either. This isn't the way to deal with things, Nick."

The pain and the ghosts shattered his concentration. He couldn't dredge up the strength to force the welling power into an outlet; his world narrowed to the green of Christoff's eyes. That realization surfaced and he tried to pull away, but he couldn't break the eye contact with his brother. Trapped, he hypnotically followed the Hunter's movements.

"Relax, Nick. Don't panic. Remember? You asked for my help. You need dinner and sleep. Listen to me. Dinner and sleep."

The tide swelled but then receded. As it settled back down into its well, the ripples of his emotions evened out with it. A soft whine escaped his throat and he closed his eyes.

Chris's hand squeezed his shoulder now that he dared to cross the circle's boundary. He used the physical contact as an anchor.

"Come on, Nick, it's dinner time. Let's go eat."

Wearily, he opened his eyes and met Chris's protective ones. Chris squeezed his shoulder again, then turned him toward the doors and with a gentle shove, pushed him across the boundary line. He dropped his eyes to the floor as the crowd parted and the Flight leaders circled him. The image of a prisoner led off to the gallows flashed through his thoughts as they escorted him to the cafeteria. Dev and Aidan held the double doors wide so they could pass as a group from the Valkyrie section into the mixed corridors.

His stomach grumbled loudly and he sighed. Only a couple more minutes of this, then he could sit in peace to eat.

I can grab a table in the corner; Chris and Donald can tell me what I've been missing lately.

I wonder what they have for dessert.

He followed his escorts into the dining hall and started to scan the available tables, but Chris's hand returned to the back of his neck and propelled him toward an empty table in the center of the large room. He balked, but the hand tightened. Donald pulled out a chair, and Chris shoved him down into it.

"This is a little much, don't you think, Chris? I'd like to just sit over there, where it's quiet." He pointed to a small table at the far side of the room and tried to ignore the Wing and Flight leaders pulling out chairs from the surrounding tables to sit.

Christoff's eyebrows rose in an expression that said "you've got to be kidding me" then waved his hand at someone and took the seat across from him. Nick looked in that direction and felt the blood drain from his face.

"No." He started to rise and was shoved back down into the seat. Snarling, he turned and saw Donald and Kieran standing behind him. "I'm not going to be served like some child. I'm going up to get my own food from the buffet just like everyone else."

"You'll eat what you're served, doctor's orders."

"Not on your life, Chris. Not after last night. I'll pick my own meals." He shoved the tray of food aside and tried to rise again, with the same success as before.

His brother pushed the tray back in front of him, shaking his head. "We don't have to drug your food, Nick. There are plenty of ways to do it if necessary, you know that. Personally, I'd shoot your ass myself. Ian says you need certain things in your diet, and we're to make sure you get them. So eat."

He looked down at the tray of food. Rare steak and a metric ton of raw vegetables. The meat he could cope with, but the vegetables made him wrinkle his nose. And of course, no dessert. There was also one small grain roll and a huge pitcher of milk. He brightened a bit when he noticed the concession of chocolate milk.

He pressed the heels of his hands into his eyes. The anger haunting him for days started to resurface and settle into his gut, slowly simmering. He tried to push it away. But the crowding, the control, made it difficult. He looked up and met Christoff's gaze. Determination, covering fear, looked back at him.

Chris is afraid? Of me? For me?

Depression swamped and doused the anger. *Will I ever get this right?* He reached out and picked up a piece of broccoli. The relief surrounding him was palpable. Someone brought three plates to the table and Donald and Kieran dropped into seats on either side of him.

I just want today over. Get back to my room for some peace and quiet.

Muted conversations surrounded him. He picked at his food but eventually managed to choke most of it down then drained the dregs of settled chocolate out of the milk pitcher.

Everyone around him had already finished. He met Chris's scrutiny. "There, satisfied? Now I'm heading straight back to my room to go to bed. No detours."

Chris and Donald both rose with him; he closed his eyes and sighed but otherwise ignored them. He made his way out of the subdued cafeteria to walk the dreary halls to his suite.

"Look, Chris, I'm sure one day I'll appreciate all you're doing, but not right now." Arriving at the door to his suite, he stopped and turned to face them. "Right now, I'm worn and can't appreciate much. Hopefully tomorrow will be better. Good night."

He turned back to his door but was stopped by Christoff clearing his throat. His forehead thunked against the door and just waited for whatever shoe his brother decided to drop.

"Um, Nick, we need to come in with you," Chris said softly.

"No, Chris, I need the time alone. I've been hemmed in all day; I need the space."

The regret in his brother's voice didn't change his reply, unfortunately. "I know, Nicky, that's why it's Donald and I who will stay with you."

He spun around and backed Christoff up to the wall. "No, Chris, it's my room. I don't need you to protect me from no one. I'll be alone."

Chris's wings spread and he pushed back. "This isn't just about protecting you from making a mistake around the wrong people in the Facility anymore, Nickolas. You need to be monitored *at all times*. You heard what Ian said."

"Chris, listen to me. I will be fine."

"Hey, guys, we should take this into a less public venue. You're getting louder, and we don't need witnesses."

He turned to glare at Donald.

"He's right, Nick, we should take this inside."

"Fine," he snapped, and opening his door, he stalked inside, prowling around the furniture while the other two came in and closed the door. "Now that we are private, get out! All I've wanted all day was some space and to be alone. This is ridiculous."

Trapped, Nickolas ran his hand through his hair, gripping it at the temple, his mind whirling. Their low growls caught him by surprise. Already off balance, the push of aggression from the two Hunters sent him reeling. Christoff stalked him, Donald joining him.

He gave ground and backed away, attempting to keep the distance between them. The risk of his talent taking control if they touched him was more than he could cope with. The two Hunters maneuvered him into the corner, pinning him there with their presence. He flattened himself to the wall, his emotional rollercoaster running at full speed and headed for the first bend.

"There's no more arguing, Nickolas. No one is willing to take a chance. You will be monitored. We can do it here or you can stay in the Hub. Which is it?"

Memories swamped him of the nightmare he endured in the Hub during his isolation. He sagged against the wall and turned dazed eyes to his brother, sure in the knowledge that Chris was telling him the truth. Even knowing what such an action would do to him, they would still follow through with the threat. At a loss for what to do, his mind started shutting down.

Sadness, compassion, and a touch of fear flowed across Chris's face. "Nick, you need to sleep. We can discuss this more later. Come on."

They parted, giving him an opening to pass, then herded him toward the bedroom where he fell gratefully onto the bed and into oblivion.

Chapter Sixteen

Nickolas jerked upright, breathing hard, the tangled images of his confinement in the Hub twisting in his mind. Sweat cooled his body. The need to feel the open air beneath his wings was overwhelming. He rose quietly. His clock read 3:05 a.m. *This is probably going to be my last chance to get her out.*

He tiptoed out of his bedroom through the dark and paused to look down at Christoff sleeping on the couch. *I know you just want to protect me, little brother, but I can't go back there. I can already feel the claustrophobia closing in. It's not even a choice. I'm sorry. I really wanted you to come with us.*

He turned away and slipped through the rest of the dark living room to the door and stopped dead in his tracks. Donald slept on the floor, his body stretched across the doorway. Unbelieving, Nickolas stared at the Hunter, dumbfounded, trying to force his mind to reconcile the situation. The caged feeling from his dream engulfed him.

"Going somewhere, Nicky?"

He spun and stared wide-eyed at his brother. Propped up on one elbow, Chris watched him calmly. Donald woke at the sound of Christoff's voice and slowly sat up to lean against the door. He took a step back and looked from side to side, seeing no hope or compromise in their faces.

"Let me out," he rumbled. His wings opened and closed fitfully. Chris sat up and reached over to the lamp, flicking it on.

"You know what Ian said about disturbing Jessica in the middle of the night." His brother looked more intently at him. "Or *were* you going to the Hub?"

Nick looked away then glanced at the door. His muscles tense.

"Easy." Chris rose slowly.

"Let me out." He flexed his knees.

Donald slid up the door to a standing position. Chris held his hands spread low before him and took a step.

"Easy, Nick. Why don't you head back to bed?"

"You know what the dreams do to me. I need air."

"You can't seriously believe that you would be allowed to go for a flight?" Chris stared at him incredulous, then understanding dawned. "You never stopped. That's why you haven't lost any strength or agility."

He started to growl and looked at the door again.

"Nick, you can't be alone. Someone needs to be with you at all times until Ian says otherwise. He thinks it should only be about two weeks, then you'll be back to normal. Just two weeks. But until then, no more midnight flights."

"Don't do this to me, Chris."

"I'm sorry."

"No." He slammed into Donald with his shoulder. The door creaked and bowed outward but held in the jamb. He got his hand on the knob, but Chris grabbed him in a bear hug.

"Stop panicking, Nick. Easy." Chris dragged him away from the door. He struggled, but Donald joined Chris as soon as he got his breath back. Together they pinned him in a chair. "Stop."

He continued to struggle but couldn't gain any leverage.

"Nickolas," Chris snapped. "Let us help you."

"I don't think he hears you anymore, Chris."

"I've got him. Go call Jays."

Chris held his wrists tight to the chair arms, a knee across his thighs. Nick slammed his head against the back of the chair. "Let me fly, Chris!"

His voice broke and he turned his eyes to meet Chris's gaze. The green rippled, then he felt a tear slide down his cheek. He closed his eyes.

"I'm sorry, Nick," Chris whispered.

Exhausted, despair gained the upper hand and his muscles went lax. Chris quit pressing into him so tightly but didn't let go.

Eventually the door opened, then he heard the rustle of clothes next to him as someone crouched. He pulled his eyes open and met Jays's concerned expression.

The doctor reached over and brushed the hair out of his eyes then placed his palm on his forehead. "You're too hot. Ian thinks your body might be fighting itself like an infection."

Jays pulled a capped syringe out of his pocket. "Ok, Nick, I have something to make you sleep. Chris, turn his arm."

He flinched when the drug invaded his vein.

"I know. I hate using this sedative because it hurts," Jays commented soothingly. "But Ian specified I use this one for you; he said it should stop the dreams."

He put pressure on the needle mark then quickly applied a Band-Aid. "You shouldn't wake till midmorning, and you'll likely feel a bit groggy when you come to, so be prepared. Let's get him in bed, Chris, it moves fast."

His brother took his leg down then lifted away from the chair, releasing his arms. Now free, he tried to stand, but a wave of dizziness washed through him and his vision tunneled. Chris and Jays each grabbed an arm before he fell.

"I really hate tranks," he mumbled.

The two half carried him across the suite to his bedroom. He rolled onto his side after they lowered him to the mattress and looked up at his brother. "I wish you'd just let me fly."

Chris cocked his head and watched him a moment before responding. "Not happening, Nicky. Get used to it."

He felt another tear slide from his eye as Chris quietly pulled the door shut and let the drug finish claiming him.

"Rough night, Chris?" Ian asked as he watched the door to Jessica's room close behind Nickolas. Turning to look at Christoff and Donald, he noted the fatigue and strain in the young Valkyries' eyes. He motioned them to follow him over to the monitor so he could observe Nickolas and Jessica interact. "Has he eaten yet?"

"No. I thought I would get him straight over here."

"Jays, order up food for him and Jessica." He pulled his chair out and sank into it, pulling a clipboard to him then flipping through a couple of pages before he turned to face Christoff and Donald. "Tell me the details. I already got a report from Jays on what happened in the gym. How'd dinner go?"

They each pulled out chairs and joined him before Chris answered. "He wasn't overly happy having his food assigned for him. He tried to refuse, but we outnumbered him, and he eventually ate pretty much everything. He had a lot of trouble keeping it together though."

Ian chuckled. "Not surprising. I'm sure he was thrilled. He was always argumentative over his food."

"He did not take it well when he found out we were staying with him overnight."

Ian started writing. "Any particular reason? I would have thought the two of you would have felt comfortable to him."

"Maybe." Chris paused and he stopped writing to look at the Hunter. "I think I solved your mystery on why he hasn't lost any of his flight ability. He woke from nightmares and tried to get past us. I'm pretty sure he's been out flying most nights. Alone."

"Damn. I thought we'd broken him of that."

"Yeah, me too. Anyway, around three he tried to leave his suite and panicked when he found Donald across his door and we wouldn't let him go. That's when we called Jays."

He turned his head to look at his protégé and raised an eyebrow.

Jays folded his arms and leaned a hip against the desk. "You were right about the fever, Ian. The chemical rollercoaster was taking its toll. He needed relief. I think he was in massive pain, and not just mental either. He went under without a wave."

Ian flipped through some of Nickolas's previous records. "All of his responses seem to be in keeping with what I would expect. Any sign that he was having more dreams, Chris?"

"Not that I saw. He slept pretty deeply after Jays left."

"Good, that's what he needs. The MRI showed how much his brain is altering. His body is fighting itself because of the chemical buildup, which is a major factor causing his erratic behavior. Keeping him quiet, fed, and rested should help his body process and minimize the effects."

"It's the keeping him calm, sir, that is going to be the challenge," Donald added dryly.

Ian flashed a grin and set his pen down. "Right you are, Donald, right you are. We can't keep him tranked the whole time, so it's up to you guys to keep him on track."

"Ian. They're at it again." Jays sighed.

Ian swiveled his chair to the monitor that Jays stood over. The camera showed Nickolas and Jessica tight in an embrace, standing at the foot of her bed. The two Hunters stood and peered over his shoulders.

"Go, Nick," Chris cheered softly.

"Wow, I've never seen Nick kiss anyone. Let alone make out like that," Donald added.

"This isn't good." Ian studied the two carefully. His talent started to swirl and rise in his well, outside of his will.

"What do you mean?" Chris asked sharply. "Nick's finally showing a sexual interest, which is what you wanted."

"Keep watching, Jays." He turned back to the two Hunters, ignoring the rising currents for the moment. "That aspect is good, Chris. It's the timing that isn't. Neither is ready for what I suspect is to come. It's too early. They're both still at the mercy of their changing bodies."

"Looks like they're handling it just fine from here," Chris smirked.

Ian cast him a withering glance and the two returned to their seats. "This isn't just about sex, Chris. If it was, then we'd be overrun with little winged babies by now, don't you think? The sperm sample I took from Nick before the MRI shows that his reproductive tract is now processing viable sperm. I can assume that Jessica's eggs will be fertile as well. First of all, we can't take a chance on her getting pregnant before the coma; second, I think that it will take something more to make them able to conceive. I think it will take combining their power."

That caught their attention. He sat back and rubbed the bridge of his nose. "There's a lot you will all need to learn. I assume you've figured out that soon you'll have to leave?"

Chris and Donald exchanged a look, then Chris turned back and met his eyes. "We had wondered..."

"I won't be able to keep them safe, Chris. And this is too important a development to stop. I'm making arrangements for you to go and join the rebel Valkyries."

"But..."

"Aurora can keep you safe. They are stronger than the factions here at the Facility know. The Facility fears them enough already, hence the lies. They will be able to teach you what you need to know. But for now, I need you to trust me."

"Ian," Jays snapped.

He spun his chair back to the screen. Nickolas and Jessica now lay on her bunk, completely lost in each other and totally uncaring about how far they were going, considering the camera. But it was the haze of visible power growing around them that had him concerned.

"Are they...glowing?" Donald asked in a whisper.

"Ok. They have to be separated. Jays, get Jessica's inhibitor ready. Chris," he turned to the Hunter. "Nick won't go willingly; get Dev and Kieran. Hopefully that will be enough hands. I'd like to avoid tranking him again so soon after the last."

The Hunter picked up the phone and sent an announcement out while he turned back to the screen. The glow had definitely grown. *As long as no blood exchange has happened, we'll be in time. Thankfully, they are both operating on instinct and not knowledge.* Running feet drew closer, then the doors into the Hub flew open. He rose as Kieran and Dev skidded to a stop next to Chris and Donald. Their voices rumbled across the distance as they explained the situation. Jays finished drawing the inhibitor and joined him.

"Ready?" He looked at the assembled faces. "This isn't going to be pretty. Leave the door ajar so you can get him out."

He led them to the door and slid his card through the reader. The door popped, and Dev pulled it open for them. He entered, everyone filing in behind. A golden haze, like dust floating in a sunbeam, surrounded the two.

"That's enough, Nick. Time to go."

Nick's wings spread and curved down to cover the two of them; the Alpha turned his head to pin them with his gaze and snarled. A low rumble echoed from Jessica. She, too, stared at them. Both their eyes reflected the liquid sunlight.

"Let's go, Nick." He held that feral gaze, barely.

"No. Leave." The words were almost unintelligible mixed with the growls.

"Chris, Donald, remove him."

Nick's eyes snapped to the Hunters and he tensed.

"Don't touch him," Jessica snarled.

Nickolas sprang at Chris and drove him into the far wall; Donald grabbed him from behind, and Jessica launched herself at Donald's unprotected back, but Kieran caught her in midair. He and Dev struggled to restrain her writhing form, pinning her against the back wall.

Nickolas saw and went ballistic. Ian took the inhibitor, and he and Jays waded into the fray. "Jays, grab an arm."

As they immobilized Jessica, Nickolas fought the two Hunters. Blood ran down Donald's neck, and Chris favored his right side. Jessica's eyes never left Nick as she struggled against the two stronger Hunters. Jays held her arm still, and he quickly pumped the inhibitor into her vein. Her scream was heartrending.

Nickolas roared and almost succeeded in flinging Chris off. But the two Hunters took him to the floor. Ian backed up, pulling Jays with him. His skin tingled and his power flared. He shot a look at Nickolas.

"Chris," he shouted. "He's raising power."

Nickolas's brother didn't waste any time. He slammed a fist into Nick's face. Donald hooked his arms under the Alpha's wings and pulled back. Nick pushed off of the floor and rolled over the top of Donald, but Chris didn't let him get away with it. He dove across him, his weight flattening the feral Alpha to the tiles. He snagged an arm and twisted it up viciously between Nick's shoulder blades, pinning his wings in the process. Donald twisted the other arm and the two of them dragged him from the room.

Jessica writhed in Kieran's and Dev's arms like a wildcat.

"Jays. Out now." He backed to the door, holding it open. Jays rushed by. "Kieran. Dev."

The two Hunters tripped her so she crumpled to the floor and bolted at a dead run past him through the door. He slammed it shut. Her body smashed into it a second later with a resounding thud. The noise continued to repeat; he turned away from Jessica's rage to deal with Nick's.

The boys had Nick face down part way across the room. Chris had his knee pressed into the small of Nick's back, his arm still twisted up. Donald kneeled across his legs while Dev held the other wrist pinned to the carpet. Kieran had a grip on the back of his neck. And still he struggled against them, the sounds reminiscent of when Nick broke into the observation room so long ago.

Ian took a deep breath and grounded himself in his power, pulling its strength around him. Once he was settled, he walked around the snarling pile to Nickolas's head. He crouched and grabbed a fistful of hair, lifting. The eyes that looked back at him shot daggers. "Hate me all you want, it's just going to get worse. You have two choices. Either go to your room willingly and regain some control, or I'm going to lock you up in room three for the next two weeks."

Fear jolted through the blue, but it couldn't last through the rage.

"Make your choice, Nick. I'm not going to give it to you again."

He continued to snarl and struggle. *Damn, he's too feral.* He gripped tighter and pushed mentally.

Nickolas.

A glimmer in the blue.

He pushed harder, demanding submission. Cracks appeared. Then the briefest of eye flicks to the side. Grimly pleased, Ian held the contact. *Are you listening?*

His snarls had turned to a continuous growl, and stony eyes stared at him.

"That's better. Remember Jillian?" The emotions that cascaded through Nick's eyes assured Ian that he did.

"Not same." His voice sounded raspy from the strain. "Willing."

"The path the two of you were on isn't safe, Nick. She needs to finish her change. And so do you. Do you want to hurt her?" Nick recoiled against the hold in his hair. "I didn't think so. You won't be seeing her again until you're done."

"No," he rasped and pulled against his captors once more.

"Knock it off. The decision's made. Now make your choice. Room or Hub?"

His eyes rolled, trying to look around the room, and he gave another jerk. The Hunters bore down on him and he grunted. Finally he glanced up before answering, "Room."

Ian studied Nick's eyes, even though the Alpha wouldn't hold direct contact any longer. Awareness had started to return, along with pain and fatigue. On a sigh, Ian released Nick's hair and let his head lower to the carpet, then he looked at Chris.

"Get him to his room and confine him there for the time being. Kieran, make sure his food makes it to him. I'll send Jays when I can to check the two of you out. I don't think you need stitches, Donald, but get the blood cleaned up."

They nodded acknowledgment then hauled Nickolas to his feet and forced him out of the Hub.

As soon as the door had closed behind the Hunters, Ian turned and, with a glance at Jays, shuffled over to the nearest chair and sank into it, resting his head in his hands. The thumping on Jessica's door had diminished but not quite stopped yet. The inhibitor would take care of that pretty quick.

"Well, wasn't that exciting?" Jays quipped.

Ian sat back and cocked his head at his protégé. Jays turned some dials and watched Jessica's monitor.

"Sometimes, Jays..." He shook his head. "Guess my theory about them needing to blood bond will pan out. Though, what happened in there didn't look the same as what Marcus has shown me."

"So now what?"

"We have to keep them separated. If they exchange blood before they are strong enough, I don't know what will happen."

"As if things weren't challenging enough already."

He grunted. A beep sounded and he swung the chair closer to look at the room monitors. Some erratic readings from Jess's room, but that wasn't too surprising, all things considered. He glanced at the video display. She stumbled drunkenly around. It wouldn't be much longer before she passed out. "We'll have to go in this afternoon to complete her exam."

"I have Fourth Flight physicals this afternoon. I can break between Wing one and two, come in and help with Jessica's exam then finish."

"All right. Have Dylan and his Second come back with you. I don't know how much trouble she's going to be."

He watched her finally collapse on her bed, and he breathed a sigh of relief. Jays cleared his throat. He looked away from the monitor and gave him his attention.

"Did you get a chance to look at it, Ian?"

"Yes, I did. Marcus agrees that they think Gabriel is up to something. His Seers can't tell what, but something's not right. And not all of it seems to point to him. Too many fledglings are disappearing. I can't believe this is Gabriel; his orders are to take them from here and to secure the occasional new fledge that turns up near him. I have no idea where they are going. And we would never have noticed if I hadn't tried to contact Robert. I knew he was getting close to entering stage two, and I was surprised that we hadn't received a call from Jared to come and get him from the base yet. I can't find him; they aren't listing him as missing either. Jared knows nothing, he says. Marcus started quietly checking in with families he still has contact with, that he's sure would have new fledges, and several of them have recently disappeared as well."

Whistling softly, Jays straightened up. "No one knows that you can detect stage one, do they?"

"No. And we're going to keep it that way." He picked up a pen and started idly drawing on a blank sheet of paper while he organized his thoughts. "Now that we know to look, keep your ears open for any clue to the location of the missing fledglings. The rest of the message was pretty normal, Marcus is still scouting out sites for a new enclave to the north of Aurora. He's preparing quarters for an influx of new Valkyries, now that things are heating up here, and Nickolas has not tried to send anymore communications their way. Things are happening fast. We have to be prepared to get Nick and Jess out to safety. I feel like we're running out of time. It would be safer if two of us knew the details of how to find the rebels in case of an emergency."

"Ian, I'm not even a Valkyrie; they wouldn't trust me if I showed up"

Ian gave Jays an opaque look before he said sardonically, "That's not something you should worry about right now, Jays, just trust me. There won't be a problem with them accepting you."

He rubbed his eyes tiredly and went on. "There is an encrypted file on a card in the locked right-hand drawer of my desk. You will find the reader in the file cabinet third from the door in the store room of the pharmacy. You are the only one besides me who will be able to read and understand it once it's deciphered."

"Ian..."

"Look, Jays, I'm old. I know the risks and what we're up against. I have made sure you know, or have access to, everything necessary if things go bad. You are the only one besides me with the whole picture. Not even Marcus." Ian pinned Jays with a look, but his Second refused to yield, making him growl in frustration.

"Ian, you won't be able to pull off the same trick twice. No one will believe that you didn't have anything to do with another revolt..."

"I'm not planning to stage another revolt, Jays. Gabriel is already suspicious. And I would like to stay alive a little longer, which would not happen if the higher-ups come to understand just how much involvement I still have with the rebels. I'm just trying to cover all contingencies. All the paths are starting to converge and narrow into one outcome, an outcome which is getting harder and harder for me to influence. The pattern is setting."

"So what is our next move?"

Dropping his protégé's gaze, Ian leaned back in his chair. "We have the next shipment to get together. We need to get as much medical equipment as we can out to Aurora before the route is closed to us. Soon they'll have to fend for themselves, but until that time, I'll give them every help I can. We have three weeks still before they will expect to hear from us about it, which is good since we have no secure way of contacting them for a while. If necessary, we can contact Dustin, but I'd rather not."

Yawning, he rested his head in his hands.

"Ian, you're not getting enough sleep are you? You're not going to be much good to anybody if you fall over. You're here when I arrive in the morning and when I leave in the evening. When are you not here?"

"Honestly. I can't remember, Jays. There's too much I need to cover, I can't take the chance. And this is just not something that I can leave Michael to handle. He's not experienced enough. And with Jack gone..."

"He'll be fine, Ian," Jays said.

"I know. I just feel like I'm missing pieces." He raised his head up to look at Jays and sighed. He knew that look. He was in for it.

Jays was studying him closely, shaking his head. "Have you had your morning shot yet?"

Yep, in for it. Gritting his teeth, he answered his Second. "Not yet. Haven't managed to get around to it."

With an exasperated snort, Jays stomped over to the refrigerator and got the injection set up, then brought it all back over to Ian.

"You know," he berated softly, "at this rate, you're not going to have to wait for Gabriel to be your end." He pushed Ian's sleeve up, and finding a vein, he gave the shot. "All you have to do is keep forgetting to take your shots and you'll accomplish it for them."

Ian rolled his sleeve back down and winced at Jays's accurate barb. "You're right, there's just so much going on.

That's why I'm glad you're my assistant. Anyway, Marcus needs more antibiotics; we have three weeks to stockpile as much as we can in the way of drugs. I think that should be our primary focus this time."

After disposing of the used needle, Jays rejoined him at the console. "Right. Anything else I should try for?"

"Not specifically, anything available is always good."

The food cart rumbled into hearing then smacked into the doors to the Hub. The guy from the kitchen parked the full trolley next to them and left. Ian sighed. No wonder it had taken so long, apparently they decided to bring everyone's lunch early. "Call Kieran and tell him Nick's food is here."

Gabriel rolled over in the immense bed, stretching sinuously in the sunlight that bathed the room. The silk sheets slid against his skin as he propped himself up on an elbow and looked down at the foot of his bed. Petra lay curled, tangled amid a pile of silk cushions. Her wings slack and her thick fall of blond hair draped across her back, the glint of the collar that chained her to the iron bedpost peeked through. The dark crescent of her lashes rested against her cheek.

Reassured that she hadn't been part of the dream remnants evaporating, he smiled.

A puff of breeze from the air vents sent the multi-hued gauze that was hung from the bed canopy in a lazy billow. More relaxed than he could ever remember, he admired her sleeping form and remembered the games they had played.

Her fear. Her resignation. Her pleasure.

I'm not going to tire of her any time soon. I should look into better accommodations for her.

Pet curled tighter around a pillow, her naked flank pulled taught. His mouth watered at the sight and he slid out of the sheets; his wings loosened and the velvet rasp of the membrane slithered across his back as he crawled over to her. His fingers traced her ankle bone then skated up her calf to smooth his palm along her thigh and come to rest on her buttock.

She shivered and he felt her tense. He squeezed then continued to let his hand roam. She whimpered, so he leaned forward to place his lips under her ear and his hand slid up to span her throat over the collar. He traced her ear with his tongue then pressed her head back. He rubbed his cheek against hers. The fear in her eyes amused him, but there wasn't any time to play this morning. "Time to wake, sweet. The day is speeding."

He brushed his thumb across her cheek. Narrowing his eyes, he shook his head and rose up on his knees to tap in the code and unlock the chain at the top of the canopy. He gathered the links in his hand, and with a quick tug, had her scrambling to keep up with him.

An impatient hand thrust the gauzy curtains aside and he strode across the spacious room. Windows filled the entire wall behind the bed, flooding the suite with the warm glow of late morning. Large plants, hung in the corners of each glass bay, mimicked drapes, while more pots grouped throughout the room like a jungle created drifts of greenness that cascaded over the half walls leading into the living area of the suite. The effect was a stunning display of nature; except for the tropical feel, the line dividing outside from inside was blurred.

Pet struggled along behind him. Every time she tried to gain her feet, he would pull on the chain, throwing her off balance again. When they reached the wide arched doorway at the other end of the long bedroom, Gabriel pulled her through, then stopped. The bathing room seemed just as bright and airy as the rest of the suite but had even more plants adorning every surface if that were possible.

He tugged her over to the stone side of the empty pool. Her wings splayed and her breathing heavy, he reached down and unlocked the chain from her collar, coiling the length up and hanging it from a hook on the wall. Then he flipped the leavers that would start the water to fill the gigantic tub before stretching and spreading his wings out. The rushing waterfall sound of the pool filling soothed something in him.

Built to his specifications out of marble, the roman bath reproduction fulfilled his needs perfectly.

He took a hairbrush off of a shelf. After a quick run through his hair, he turned and sat on the smooth rim of the pool and pointed to the floor between his feet.

Pet raised her eyes enough to look through her lashes at him before taking a tentative step. She pulled her wings in tight, then presented her back and sank to the floor between his knees.

The rhythmic motion of the brush as he pulled it through her long hair lulled her and she fell back to sleep, leaning against his knee. Resting his hand on the top of her head, he savored the soft feel of her golden hair while he trailed the fingers of his other hand in the rising water. Once the level had reached high enough, he nudged her awake then gingerly stepped into the waist deep hot water. He shut the gushing faucets off and slipped under, fanning his wings like a manta ray, then broke the surface with a splash, the water streaming down his body as he folded his wings. Wading over to the side, he reached up and pulled a cloth and bar of soap off of a shelf and gestured her into the water, holding them out. "In. Come. Wash my wings."

The water lapped over the tips of her breasts as the ripples slapped into the marble of the sides. She took the supplies and he turned, spreading his wings out on the surface of the pool. At the soft touch of the soapy cloth as it rubbed across his wings, he closed his eyes and sighed.

She covered every square inch of his membrane, the circular massage freeing his mind to float like his wings. A soft pat and he arrowed forward to drag his wings through the warm water to rinse them. He pushed his wet hair out of his eyes and returned to her. He soaped the cloth then ran it down the length of her pinion strut, the soap curling in an oily stain on the surface of the water when he followed the strut down to her knees. He grasped the tip and forced her wing to extend, pulling the leading edge above the surface. He felt the shiver run down her back where it pressed tightly to his chest.

The discordant jangle of the alarm he had set on the door to his suite interrupted him. The instinct to growl surprised him and he dropped the cloth.

"Gabriel."

"Stay out," he snapped. Pet flinched.

He pushed her to the rim of the pool then climbed out and grabbed a towel. He dropped one on her, then quickly mopped at the rivulets running down his skin. He grabbed her chain off the peg, then stalked out, leaving her to follow.

Henderson stood near the desk, his eyes wide when he saw Gabriel. His gaze darted to the side, then he slapped a manila folder down on the desk.

"You wouldn't answer your phone last night or this morning. So the council sent me to deliver this in person."

Pet pressed into his back. He wanted the male out now. He snarled, and Henderson's face grew paler than before, but he didn't immediately leave. "You need to go through that, they've set up a meeting in an hour."

"Fine."

Henderson nodded, then left at a fast clip. When the door latched, he let his muscles relax and reached around to pull Pet from behind. He wrapped her tighter in the towel she still held, then pushed her to the floor at his feet when he took a seat at his desk.

He opened the folder. He flipped through the small stack, then returned to the first page and started to read.

The new fledgling brought into the Facility three weeks ago was Jessica Reuther.

Age twenty-five.

She worked in a bookstore at the local mall.

Daughter of Andrew and Jennifer Reuther. Deceased. Both of whom were fledged Valkyries.

One surviving brother, Robin. Location unknown, status unknown.

"Jessica Reuther. Now there's a name I haven't heard in a long while. You were probably six the last time I saw you." He sat back in his chair and recalled the last time he saw her parents...

"Gabriel? Hey, Gabriel?"

The nasal voice of the lab tech brought Gabriel out of his trance, and refocusing his eyes, he turned to look at the man who was trying to gain his attention. The exasperated look on the irritating technician's face made Gabriel want to smash it in. He had lost the trace thanks to him.

But instead of hitting the man, he replied, "We can finish up here in a bit. There's something I need to check out."

It felt good to walk out of the lab and leave the tech staring after him. In the hall, Gabriel slowly pivoted, searching. I know I felt something. Now where are you?

Sensing more than feeling the buzz in his head, he started walking down the hall, pausing now and then as he caught a whiff of a mental trace. Who are you? I know I've felt you before but not for a long time. Taking a right down the hall, he started to slowly make his way toward the Facility's computer labs.

A quick surge of power washed over him just before the Facility's alarms blasted. Clapping his hands to his ears, he raced for the nearest exit to the compound. A unit of guards rounded the corner and they fell in behind him. He stepped out into the night and probed his surroundings, hoping to narrow down the intruding Valkyries' presence, their clear mental signatures, unmuddied by inhibitor, compared to the control group maintained in the Facility.

The compound lights incandesced to his left. He twisted in that direction and watched two winged figures race down the tree-lined avenue. "Intercept them."

The guards surged ahead of him, and he followed the hounds. Bright flashes of gunfire blossomed in the night, and he watched in irritation as the feral Valkyries were shot out of the sky. He waved the guards back and approached the first downed Valkyrie.

He rolled the man over with his foot and recognized Andrew Reuther. One of the last of the Facility personnel to change before Marcus rebelled and fled into the mountains with the rest of the surviving traitors ten years ago. Crouching down, he checked for a pulse, finding none. Damn. Can't they aim better? Something stirred his other senses and he checked the dead Hunter's pockets. He pulled out the computer disks, and fanning them out, he clucked his tongue. Eight of them; whatever they were after was big. The hard plastic dug into his fist as he clenched and rose to look at the *second Valkyrie. Feeble movement stirred the gravel. Good, he wasn't dead yet.*

He walked over and recognized Andrew's wife, Jennifer. That observation made his mind race. Last time he had seen the two lab technicians, she had not fledged. And more, he hadn't realized that Andrew had been among the survivors of that night. I need a closer look at those records. Who survived the fighting during the escape and subsequent hunts. Apparently it was more than they had thought. If they can expand their population with new fledges, they'll become a threat.

He stared down at Jennifer and sent his mind out in a sweeping probe then blinked before he addressed her. "Hello, Jennifer. So, you turned out to be a Seer. I must say, that is a bit of a surprise. You shouldn't have come back. But rabid dogs usually return home. Marcus should have listened."

"We're not the rabid ones, you are," she rasped. *"Just because we don't want to live our lives doped up..."* She coughed and blood droplets splattered his boots.

"Well, it hardly matters now." *He smiled softly at her and held up the disks.* "Fortunately you didn't accomplish what you came for."

He studied her then bent down to wipe the blood from her lips with his thumb and whispered, "Who let you in, Jennifer? You had to have inside help. Tell me, and I'll get you to the medics."

"Never!" *she snarled, then spit in his face.*

Inside he stilled, then reached up and wiped the bloody spittle in streaks down his face. "Fine, bleed to death."

He rose and shook his hair over his shoulder. "It's not like I don't know who did it anyway. I will get proof, in due course. At least you can act as bait. We both know Marcus won't want to leave you behind."

He turned on his heel and gestured to the guards, who melted into the trees at his signal. Following in their wake, darkness returned as someone turned off the flood lights and alarms, and he prowled in the shadows of the trees, waiting impatiently for something to happen. Stopping in a good vantage, he watched Jennifer bleed out while he scanned the trees on the far side of the fence. He didn't have long to wait; soon Gabriel felt the telltale tingle that told him someone nearby reached out psychically. Come on, Marcus, come out into the open. I've got a nice cell with your name on it just waiting.

At the sensation of the connection snapping, he recoiled. *No.*

Then he yelled out to the guards. "They're not taking the bait. Get the lights back on! I want searchers in the woods now! Find Marcus! I want him."

The sound of running feet and vehicles revving did little to calm Gabriel, knowing the chances of capture dwindled fast. He lashed out with his own talents and tried to pinpoint the feral Valkyries' location without success. They must have a shield builder with them.

Snarling, he slammed his hand into the trunk of a tree. Mentally pushing, he tried to break through the shield, then felt the tickle of an imminent telepathic thread. Going stalk still, he heard, faint from distance, Marcus's mind voice. *I will have retribution, Gabriel. Someday. We will avenge Jennifer and Andrew and all who have come before and those who follow.*

You can try, Marcus. I'll be waiting.

His chair squeaked and Gabriel stared at the sheaf of papers in his hand. *Well, Marcus, it looks like you lose again. I will soon have Jennifer's daughter, and if things go right, your son too.* Well pleased with the circumstances, Gabriel picked up the phone and called the labs. "Fredrick, I need to move our meeting to this afternoon. What? Oh yes, I want to go over all the notes and tapes then. I have a good feeling that B-Five will prove out. No, probably about one o'clock. See you then."

He replaced the receiver in the cradle then dropped his hand to Pet's head, absently stroking while he read through the rest of the report. With a sigh, he glanced at the clock. Just enough time to get to the meeting. He would find out who was trying to yank his chain, and then they would see why that was not a good idea.

His fingers tangled in Pet's hair and he pulled back. A gasp escaped her lips, but she met his eyes. "Looks like they took away my play time, sweet."

He stood and pulled her upright then brushed a hand down her back. He shook his head and grabbed her chain, locking it to the collar, then he pulled her back to the bed, where he locked the other end of the chain to the iron bed pillar.

"Get some rest. We'll be busy later."

He walked into his closet, threw on some clothes, then stalked out of his suite.

He didn't lose much of his temper on the walk to the conference room, but he did bury the evidence. All the senior staff, except Edward and Fredrick, huddled around the table. Reserved looks turned his way, and he smiled. He shoved the door shut, then taking his seat, he laid the dossier on the table in front of himself. Before he rested his arms on the smooth wood, he looked at each person the council had placed in the compound. "Ok, I'm here. Why did this need to be an emergency?"

They all looked nervously at each other. *Good. They should be. Looks like I need to find whoever set them up and make an example again. The council knows better.*

One of them cleared his throat. "Did you read the entire report?"

He pinned the man with a stare and watched him gulp then start to fidget before he answered, "When am I anything less than thorough?"

"Yes, well..."

"I'm still not following what the emergency on this information is?"

The man coughed then shot a quick glance at his face before turning to fiddle with his own stack of papers. "Jessica Reuther's paper work isn't getting reported correctly. We don't have the proof yet, just word of mouth. But the rest of the Valkyrie control group is also acting strangely; they are much more secretive, and there has been little sighting of Nickolas. One of our people nearly compromised themselves trying to get close to him. Hopefully the risk was worth it. Nickolas's conduct isn't normal. But the descriptions of his behavior are vague, and we can't pin a finger on what it means. The council wants you to take a look and see what you think."

He shook his head. "I see your report, unlike myself, is not. Thorough that is. Where's the rest of this information?"

A new packet made its way down the table to him. He opened it and started to read. A frown grew. *What are you up to, Nickolas?* "I'm not sure what this means, either. Try to dig deeper. We need to know what's going on over there."

"The second item we need to go over," a mousy brown-haired woman added. She took off her glasses and nervously cleaned them. "One of our recon teams has located a little town up north near Bellingham that they believe to be a drop point for Marcus. All signs point to them trying to set up another colony."

"Really? I wouldn't have thought their population was that large. Do you have any idea yet how far into the mountains it is?"

"No, but they are working on it. The locals aren't very receptive of us. We'll have to be careful."

"Find their contact. Then get me the location. It's time to set up an ambush and get as many of the rebels into custody as possible. We can't have their numbers growing too large, the generals are uncomfortable and they want the troublemakers weeded out. Dead is better than loose, but I would prefer as many captured alive as possible."

He steepled his fingers and drifted off for a moment. "Back to the Nickolas problem; we need to get our hands on him. Ian will have conniptions, but possession is nine-tenths of the law. Once we have him in custody, it will be hard, if not impossible, for Ian to get Nickolas out of the compound. After we have more information about what is going on up in Bellingham, I want to set up Nickolas's recovery team to go out there. If we're lucky, we bring home a new subject. At the very least the exercise should prove insightful."

He gathered up his papers and rose. "Is there anything else?" Heads shook all around the table. "Good, then I need to grab a quick lunch and get over to the labs. If anything else urgent comes in, you can find me there."

Half an hour later, he stepped into the main laboratory. Fredrick stood over B-Five, stretched out on a table, staring vacantly. He waited until the scientist finished writing his observations before he asked, "So, anything?"

"I think so. We'll need to do a lot more tests and refining, but yes, I think we finally made a breakthrough," Fredrick said.

"Show me."

"Let's look at the tapes first. If I do anymore with him right now, I think he'll expire."

Gabriel followed Fredrick into an adjacent room, containing a table and video equipment. Fredrick grabbed the remote and planted himself in a chair and started it up. Sinking into another, Gabriel focused on the screen.

The analytical part of his mind kicked in, and ignoring the screams, crying, and pleading for mercy, Gabriel watched as Fredrick succeeded in forcing B-Five to do small movements and tasks against his will using voice commands.

"Yes, a definite breakthrough. We need the controlling to be seamless though. I don't care if it causes them pain, as long as they don't show it."

They continued to watch the footage of B-Five. He fought, both the drug and the doctor, but in the end complied stiltedly with the tasks given to him.

"It's going to be hard to use them if they are constantly screaming or mouthing off. He's also able to fight the control too much still. Does the drug cause a permanent change in the subject, or does it wear off?"

"It does wear off. But as long as you administer the next dose before your control wanes, it's fine. It does ultimately take a toll though. I don't know how long a specific individual will be useful before burnout. It might be that as we refine it, that issue won't be as much of a problem as it is now. So far B-Five has had the best results across the board. The voice commands are working, but I am really curious to see how he will respond to your mind commands. At the moment, I can control his movements against his will if I am there and pulling the strings, but we need to have them follow implanted commands at a later date. I think you might be the key for that phase of the work," The doctor said.

"Yes, I can see that. Has he had enough of a rest to continue, doctor?"

Fredrick shrugged. "Let's go find out."

They left the conference room and returned to the lab, approaching the bound Valkyrie. Eying them with fear and impotent anger, the captive pulled at the straps uselessly. Gabriel placed his hand on the side of the subject's face, holding him steady, and looked deep into his eyes. He pulled on a whisper of his power and probed the bound Seer and found all of his natural barriers stripped away. His mind lay completely open and vulnerable.

He formed the coercion and slipped it into B-Five's mind. "You cannot move unless I tell you. Understand? Just nod your head." Once he got a nod, Gabriel turned to Fredrick. "Take off the straps."

"What?"

"You heard me; take off the straps. It's not like I can't stop him, and I certainly can't test my control of him tied down, now can I?"

He watched the subject closely as the doctor removed the straps then grunted in satisfaction. As soon as he was free, the subject attempted to jump up, but his muscles only convulsed with the competing commands. Gabriel's won. Smiling down at him, Gabriel whispered, "I said don't move, didn't I?"

His breathing erratic, B-Five trembled trying to regain control of his body. "Now, subject B-Five, please swing your legs over the side of the table and sit up."

Slowly, fighting every inch, he obeyed. "Good, now stand and walk to the wall."

As the Seer stiffly walked the length of the room, Gabriel turned to the doctor and asked quietly, "Would you please have a female sent up from the holding cells immediately. I want to take this to the next level."

"Yes, sir."

Gabriel returned his attention to the experiment. "Now, B-Five, walk back over to me and kneel on the floor."

He observed the subject as he fought and lost against the combined force of the coercion and the drug. Dispassionate, Gabriel took mental notes on the responses.

B-Five worked his way back to him and fell to his knees at his feet. the Seer's head dropped to his chest. The sound of struggling came faintly through the doorway, then grew louder as Edward dragged a resisting brunette into the lab. "Good. Fredrick, have him chain her to the wall there."

As the games master dealt with the female Hunter, Gabriel lifted B-Five's chin with his hand. Looking down into his wild eyes, Gabriel said, "What is your name?"

B-Five's mouth twisted as he fought answering, so Gabriel gave a little push.

"Zachary."

"Very good, Zach." He smiled warmly down at him. "Now, this is what you are going to do, Zach. I'm going to give you a command word. It will release control of your body back to you—until I want it back. The catch is that before I release you, I'm going to give you a time-delayed task.

"Three minutes after I release you, timed by the clock on the wall, you will take the knife from my belt and walk over to the female Hunter. Then holding her down, you will carve your initials into each wing web on both of her wings. The release word is snowman." He reinforced his words with a mental compulsion then let go of the Seer's chin and stepped away.

Fascinated, he watched minutely every reaction B-Five had as he endeavored to stop the inevitable.

"Snowman."

B-Five, Zach, he corrected, jumped up and ran to the locked door at the other end of the room. In desperation he pulled and pounded on the metal, his voice hoarse.

"Tsk tsk tsk. You know you can't get out," Gabriel taunted softly. The Valkyrie spun around and put his back against the door, averting his face from the clock on the wall.

"Half your time is already gone," Gabriel added then stood back and watched the events unfold.

Raising his hands to his temples, B-Five fought the desire to look at the clock. The seconds ticked by, and shaking his head no, the tormented Valkyrie whimpered. The clock hit three minutes, and Gabriel held his breath.

Zach started to visibly shake, but he still refrained from looking at the wall. Unfortunately, after two more minutes elapsed, the coercion took hold and he couldn't pretend that the allotted time hadn't yet passed. His head slowly swung to look at the clock.

The effect was instantaneous, his body turned rigid and he started to walk toward Gabriel.

A smile spread at the stifled emotion Zach projected when he took the knife from his side. The desire of the Seer to use it on the knife's owner couldn't have been clearer.

But instead, the Seer followed the implanted instructions and approached the smaller female Valkyrie. She shrank back from him as much as the tether around her neck would allow. Begging her to forgive him and chanting that he was sorry, Zachary pinned her to the floor, splaying her wings, and proceeded to carve his initials into her wings while the blood flowed and she screamed until hoarse. Tears streamed down his face, and he kept chanting his apology; the moment he carved the last letter he quickly turned the knife on himself, attempting to plunge it into his gut.

"Stop!" Gabriel shouted and blasted the subject with a mental command as well. Shaking, with the point of the blade resting against his stomach, the Seer fought his compulsion.

"Drop it!" Gabriel snapped, and the knife clattered to the floor. Zach curled into a fetal position and stared sightlessly. "Well, that worked better than I had anticipated. Though I can see we are going to have to be careful about our instructions."

"I got it all on tape, Gabriel," Fredrick said.

"Good. That's very good." His mind took a mental snapshot of the whimpering Hunter and her bloodstained wings and Zachary rocking on the floor—and he let the satisfaction flow through him. They were on the right track. Soon the council would have what it wanted. The means to control the body, mind, and soul of any Valkyrie they wanted.

Step one accomplished, his thoughts returned to Pet. It was, after all, dinner time, and he highly doubted that she would bite the hand that fed her, at least not after last time. "Get this mess cleaned up," he ordered and walked out of the lab.

Chapter Seventeen

Jessica sat cross-legged on her bunk. Eyes closed, her breath whooshed in, then out after a pause. She continued the relaxation exercises as her mind geared up for the next step. *I hope it's late enough. I think it's the middle of the night. Damn it, Nick. You'd better be ok.*

The last sight she'd had of him, Chris and Donald had beat the crap out of him and forced him from her cell. They'd better hope not to cross paths with her for a while, or she'd rip their balls off and shove them down their throats.

If I'm right about the time, then only one watcher should be on duty. And likely not paying close attention. This is going to be my best opportunity.

She took another breath. This time, instead of grounding and centering, she tried pushing. The wall of inhibitor flexed around her mind like a thin balloon. She let it settle then tried again. After several attempts, a pinhole breached and allowed her minute access outside of her own mind. *Still no idea what I can do, but every weapon is useful.*

Her eyes opened. She slid off the bed and reached underneath it to pull out the plastic plate she'd hidden. Shooting a quick look at the camera, she set it on the floor and cracked it with her heel. She picked it up and pried the large shards apart then used a large sharp triangular piece to start hacking out strips of cotton from the futon cover. She worked quickly, tucking the strips into the waistband of her shorts. The shard joined them, then she moved to the corner directly under the ceiling vent. Warm air whooshed into her face when she looked up.

She rolled her shoulders and flexed her arms, then did a few squats to limber up. After a deep breath, she wedged her back into the corner and planted her hands and feet against the wall and started to pressure walk up the corner. Once she reached the ceiling, with her muscles quivering, she bashed the vent up with a fist, then shoved it over in the duct. Worried about the noise, she grabbed the lip of the duct and levered herself inside, squirming in on her stomach. Her breathing labored, she lowered her forehead to the dusty metal and rested a moment.

I don't know how long it will take to notice I'm gone. So get moving already. She took another deep breath and slid the cover back over the vent and started to slither. At the first juncture, she stopped. Indecision. She stifled a sneeze from the dust and peered into the dark down either choice. Faint light shone in places, marking vents to rooms.

The light breeze whirled around her. Something about it caught her attention and she let her mind quest out the crack she'd made in the wall of inhibitor. A tickle, like the wind wanted to play, pulled her in one direction. Without a better choice, she chose to follow. At each junction, she stopped and listened. Eventually it brought her to a vent over an empty hall where it spun around her happily and zoomed off.

She popped the vent off and lowered herself to the floor. No way to replace that cover. After brushing herself off, she pulled the cotton strips out and quickly wrapped her feet, tying neat bows at her ankles and took off down the hall. Probing past the wall, she reached out, trying to feel Nickolas. Like small bread crumbs left, she picked out the direction. Cautious, she stopped to listen at doors before she passed or peeked in.

A door to the outside beckoned, but she turned away with effort. She couldn't leave Nickolas. A sigh escaped and she moved on. The next door opened on to a darkened kitchen. *Oh yeah.*

She smiled and slipped into the room. It didn't take her long to pick out a long, sharp kitchen knife. Armed, she turned to the door then stopped.

A reluctant look over her shoulder. *It wouldn't take that long to look? Right?*

Licking her lips, she walked to the enormous fridge and started to rummage. The strawberries drew her eye, but then she found the jack pot.

"Chocolate cake." She moaned. And setting her knife on the butcher block island, she pulled the cake out of the fridge and started to dig in.

The incessant ringing broke through his exhaustion, and Ian reached out, pounding the nightstand for the phone. With a loud crash, he managed to catch the receiver as the rest tumbled.

"Yes?" he growled. He blinked and tried to bring the red numbers of the clock into focus. Four thirty.

"Ian. I need you back here. Now." Jays's voice sounded on the verge of panic.

"Whoa, slow down. What's wrong?" He sat up and started rummaging around on the floor for his clothes one-handed.

"Jessica. She's gone."

He froze. "Excuse me?"

Jays's voice rose an octave as he spoke at light speed. "She's gone Ian. Not in her room. I don't know…"

He cut his protégé off. "I'm coming. Cue up the archive."

He finished dressing and left at a run.

When he arrived, Michael sat with his head in his hands talking while Jays ignored him and searched through the recordings for her room. Ian made a beeline for the monitors and looked at Jessica's empty room on display. Shards of something littered the floor near her shredded mattress.

He narrowed his eyes then crossed to the terminal Jays used to review her room recordings.

"What the hell happened?" he growled.

"Michael was on duty. Ask him," Jays had calmed now that he had a direction.

He turned to the man in question. "Well?"

Michael shook his head but didn't look up. "I don't know."

"What do you mean you don't know? Why don't you? You should have been alerted as soon as her heart beat no longer registered on the remote monitors."

"He turned them off," Jays snapped.

"Off?"

"I'm sorry. I didn't think it would be a problem. The screens were all active and I just look at them. How would they get out of the room?"

"Jays? How far back are you?" He turned away from the junior doctor in disgust.

"An hour so far, and no signs of her yet."

"Move. Go call Chris and wake him up. Find out if Nick is still there."

"Shouldn't we initiate the lock-down procedures?" Michael asked tentatively.

"And lock us up inside when she could already be outside?" He took Jays's seat and continued to scroll through the recording. "Give me a break, Michael. Besides, after the last incident, I'm not too interested in dealing with Kratz."

He looked at the time stamp, two hours back and still no sign of her on the tape. *Damn it, Jess. How?*

Michael shuffled around, and he glanced out of the corner of his eye at the junior doctor. The man tried to surreptitiously close down the computer game he'd obviously been immersed in.

Ian growled. "Michael, head back to your quarters for the night. We'll discuss this sometime tomorrow."

"But..."

"No. I can't deal with you right now. Go."

On a sigh, he left, and Jays returned from his phone conversation with Chris.

"Chris says Nick is still there, but he's acting weird. The sedatives didn't keep him down tonight. He's up and bear-like. He and Donald have their hands full."

"Lovely. Get Kieran, have him get the rest of the Flight and Wing leaders in here."

"Yes, sir."

While he moved back to the phone, Ian kept scrolling through the footage of the empty room. Two hours fifteen minutes. Two hours thirty minutes.

"There."

Jays jumped, having just hung up the receiver, and rushed over.

Ian continued to scroll quickly so they could watch from the start of her activity.

"She got out at two a.m. Damn, Ian, she's had almost three hours. She could be anywhere by now."

"Maybe...but maybe not. Let's watch."

Kieran arrived on the run, and the rest followed in waves. "Holy...did she just do what I think she did?" Kieran asked as she finished scaling the wall.

"There's the fledgling who led us around by the nose for two days," Ian commented. "Yes. And we need to get those vents secured."

"Nick's the only reason we caught her the first time, Ian," Kieran said. "What are we going to do this time? We can try and scent track her, but I don't know how well that will work here. And it's going to be exceedingly obvious with all of us outside searching."

Ian rewound part of the recording and watched her enter the vent again. Something about it.... His strat talent started placing pieces on his mental map. He turned the sound up and listened to her mumble as she worked to free herself.

"Jays, bring up all the other terminals. Get the live camera feeds from as many of the hall cameras as you can from the Valkyrie wings. I don't think she's left."

Kieran started to help Jays type as they woke up all the computers in the bank. "That's nuts, Ian. She's only ever wanted to get away from here. She wouldn't stick around."

"She would if she was going after Nick. Think about it, Kieran. What's the last thing she saw?"

"Shit."

"Elegant way to put it, but accurate nonetheless."

The rest of the Wing leaders spaced out to start watching the various camera feeds as they came on. Ian rewound the recording again to the beginning and listened to Jays with half an ear.

"Kieran, get Dylan and Chelsea set up over there. On these two terminals, I'm bringing up the recordings from three hours ago. Come help me when you're done."

Silence fell as everyone turned their attention to their screens. Kieran called out first, and Ian joined him.

"She left the ducts in hall M near intersection nine."

"Ok, Jays, we have a start point. Trace her route. The rest of you, keep looking for her current location."

"What is she doing, Ian? Watch her," Jays called him back. He and Kieran had multiple camera recordings up so they could follow her from one point to another.

Ian watched her stop and pivot in an intersection, then stride purposefully down one. "If I didn't know any better I'd say she's using her talent. Through the inhibitor. She is tracking Nick."

"We've got her, Ian," Chelsea shouted. "She's in the kitchens."

Ian looked across the bank to Chelsea's screen. Jessica stood at a sink washing her hands and face.

"Here, Ian." Jays had brought up the camera feed from the moment she stepped into the kitchen.

Kieran swore. "She's armed."

"And full of cake. Crap," Jays groaned.

"Dev, call Chris and tell him what's going on and that Jessica is on her way toward them." Ian moved to an equipment locker and took out a couple of earpieces. Jays followed and readied two trank pistols then tossed one to Kieran. He handed Jays and Kieran the earpieces. "Divide up. Kieran take half the group and wait in Chris's suite. Jays will be in Donald's on the other side of Nick's. I'll keep watch here and be your eyes. Bring her back."

"Yes, sir," they all snapped, and a thunder of feet left the Hub. He turned back to watch Jessica feel her way down the halls toward her mate.

The stomp of boots as they ran through the hall sounded loud in Jays's ears. He slipped the comm into his right ear and got it settled. Static, then Kieran's voice, testing. "I've got you, Kieran. Ian? Can you hear us?"

More static, then Ian's voice whispered across. "I hear you both loud and clear. Keep moving. You have to get in place before she gets too near. And she's making faster time than I thought possible. She's definitely using some talent."

They rounded a corner and raced halfway down the hall before skidding to a stop. He ducked into Donald's room with four of the Wing leaders while Kieran passed Nick's room with the other three Wing leaders to hide in Chris's.

He stood tense at the door, Dev breathing heavy at his back. He readjusted his grip on the trank gun.

"She's a couple of corridors away," Ian said. Jays slowed his breathing and tried not to think about the next few minutes. "Be careful. Kieran was right. She's armed with a large kitchen knife."

He groaned at Ian's words and relayed the warning to the Hunters surrounding him.

"Ok, she's in the hall. Kieran? If you're near the door, back away now. She's wavering at Chris's door. Good, she's stepping up to Nick's. Kieran, bring your group out."

The sounds of snarls reached them through the door. Jays put his hand on the knob and looked at the Hunters.

"Ok, Jays, block the other end of the corridor."

"Now," he snapped to the Hunters, and they all surged into the hall. The sight that greeted him left him cold. The Hunters behind him stood shoulder to shoulder blocking, just like those behind Kieran. They all moved forward, shrinking the distance. Jessica faced off with Kieran, her knife brandished.

"Back off, Kieran. I don't want to hurt you."

The snarls Jays heard hadn't come from Jess like he thought, but through Nickolas's door. He could hear Chris and Donald yelling over the crashing. The door bowed as a heavy weight hit it. Jessica hadn't turned and noticed them yet, she was so fixated on Kieran.

"Jess, we need to take you back. You know that."

"Fuck you, Kieran. Let Nick go. You let them hurt him."

"That was your only warning, Jessica. Nick can't handle you this close, listen to him." He raised his trank pistol and fired.

She jerked back as the dart took her in the shoulder. The snarl of rage she let loose put Nick's to shame. She lunged and slashed Kieran. The slice opened his forearm as he blocked her, and the gun hit the floor as his fingers spasmed. All the Valkyries stiffened around him as the scent of blood hit the air. She hissed and drew in a huge lung full of air, then took a step toward Kieran.

Ian's voice shouted across the earpiece. "Kieran. Don't let her get your blood."

Jays raised his gun and fired a second dart into her back. She shrieked as the impact jolted her, and she turned a feral, malevolent gaze on him. Wobbling now, but still not down, she turned the rest of her body and charged him. He fired a third dart into her gut. It knocked her back, but she still managed the last few strides to collapse at his feet.

He let out his held breath.

Kieran, cradling his arm, approached. Jays knelt next to her, taking the wickedly sharp blade from her grasp. Her eyes followed his every move. She still had some muscular control because she flexed her fingers and her feet slid in slow motion.

"She's still awake?" Kieran asked.

"Yeah, this sort of trank doesn't always put them to sleep. Just takes away muscle movement and control."

"Damn, that's got to suck."

Jays pulled the dart out of her back then rolled her to her side so he could get the two in her front. "Doesn't look like she got hurt in the scuffle." A particularly loud crash made them look up at Nick's door. "Kieran, hand over your earpiece to Dylan. You need to come back with us to get stitched up. Dev, please carry her. The rest of you stay with Dylan until we get an all clear from Chris or Donald. It would be a disaster if Nick ran loose tonight next."

He helped Dev get her settled in his arms and made sure her half grown wings weren't bent funny. The impotent rage burning in her eyes was a promise. He brushed the hair off her forehead then kissed it before he whispered, "I'm sorry, Jess."

Robin leapt over the first attacker and barely missed the coordinated attack from the second. A wing beat into the air and he spun, lashing out with his foot and taking the other Hunter in the face. He dropped to the ground in a crouch and smiled at the first Hunter.

The first backed off and bounced, waiting for his teammate to shake off Robin's hit.

"Come on, Craig, give me a workout here." Robin laughed.

"Give *us* a break, Robin. Neither of us are Kelley. There's a reason you're Prime, for god's sake. And she's your Second."

"She's not my Second right now, so drop it."

"Bullshit and you know it." A third Hunter slammed him from behind. "Only because she's still in the infirmary."

Thrown forward, Robin recovered and dove into a roll. He sprang up and sent a backhand at Craig, then a spinning kick at the newcomer. "At least she can give me a workout all by herself. Unlike you pansy asses."

Kevin flashed out with his foot, but Robin saw it in time to not trip. They'd dog pile him if he hit the ground.

"Poor Robin. Doesn't get a real workout in the ring. And can't get a real workout in the air, either," Kevin taunted. All three men laughed. "No one to dance with. What'll you do for stress relief?"

Robin growled and dove at the Caster. But Ty took him in the side. Before he could recover, Kevin had an arm around his still bruised throat and his wings pinned. The Caster's breath tickled his ear. "I'll dance with you. Then let's see who can give you a workout."

He dropped his hip and tossed Kev over his shoulder. The other Prime just laughed as he rolled to his feet.

"Come on. You haven't had sex in almost three weeks, Robin. Give it up. Kelley's sending us out here because she's tired of your grousing. Pick someone to dance with already."

Robin! You're needed up at the tower immediately.

He froze. Thankfully the others recognized the signs of telepathic sending and didn't jump him. *I'm on my way, Nathan.*

"There's something wrong up at the tower." He turned to the Caster Prime. "Come on."

Kevin nodded and the two of them leapt into the air. They winged across the valley, slowly starting to climb altitude. The control tower came into sight at the top of the cliff, and he glanced at his wingmate. *Have I really been that bad?*

Kevin tipped his head and met his eyes. *There's no reason for you to pay a penance. Kelley earned the punishment, not you. It makes her unhappy to see you getting more wound up when you could pick a new dance partner for a while.*

He sighed. *Have I really been doing that to myself?* He watched the muscles along the Caster Prime's chest flex with the movement of his wings and realized he must have been doing just that. *I'll think about it, Kev.*

The Caster smirked at him, then they landed on the roof of the building.

Nathan waited for them. "There's a grounded demanding to see you. By name, Robin. He won't talk to anyone else until he's seen you."

They followed the Seer Prime down the steps to the first floor. A voice drifted up to meet them. "Better make sure my horse doesn't wander, Hunter, or I'll be pissed. I don't have fancy wings to get me home."

Robin choked and pushed past Nathan. "Adam? What the hell's happened? What's wrong?"

The man in question turned and clasped Robin's offered arm. "I have to see Marcus."

"Is Dustin ok? What's going on?"

"Marcus, Robin."

"Kevin, get a net and two harnesses."

He caught the harness Kevin threw him and buckled it in place. "All right. Let's go."

He led the way out then clipped his side of the net to his harness while Nathan showed Adam how to sit in the sling. The three of them walked to the cliff's edge and waited for

Adam to nervously get settled, then with a glance in Kevin's eyes, they stepped off. Adam let out a shriek that turned into maniacal laughter.

That was fun, Kevin sent to him.

He grinned back at the Caster but then sent his thoughts winging toward the longhouse. *Marcus? I have an emergency coming in. Adam's here.*

Dustin's cousin?

Yes. Kevin and I are flying him from the control tower. We'll be there in a moment.

They flew over the farm buildings then dropped lower once they had passed the trees scattered along the creek. He and Kevin back-winged and lowered Adam to the ground. He leapt out of the net and turned to watch them touch down.

Robin yanked the clip and tossed it and his half of the net to Kevin. Then he strode past Adam to lead him into the longhouse, unbuckling as they moved. He stripped the harness and shoved Marcus's office door open with his hip.

Marcus stopped his pacing and gripped the back of his chair as they entered. "What's happened, Adam?"

Robin pushed the door shut and dropped his harness on the floor next to it. He walked over to the corner of Marcus's desk and sat where he normally did.

Adam stood in front of the dark wood and fished around an inside pocket of his vest. He pulled his hand out and placed a micro computer disk down, then slid it across to his Alpha. "I don't know what's happened, but Jays looked harried and stressed when he brought this to Dustin. He said to get this to you now. I was there, so I was able to set out right away that afternoon. But it still took me two and a half days to get here."

"Thank you, Adam," Marcus said gruffly. He cleared his throat and opened up his laptop.

Robin moved around the desk so he could see while Marcus finished the maze of passwords, and Ian came on the screen.

"Hello, Marcus, I'm sorry for the scare. But with the mule out of commission at the moment, there was no other way, and this can't wait for Robin's next meeting with Jays. I know it will take a few days for this to reach you, that can't be helped. I need you to station a force at Dustin's. There have been some events that happened tonight. I won't be able to completely contain them. The wrong people witnessed and it's recorded on too many cameras for me to cover up. I may need to evacuate everyone on no notice, and I might need help. At the very least, they'll need a guide and escort to Aurora."

Ian sighed on the screen and closed his eyes before continuing.

"Jessica escaped. Before you panic—she's ok. She got out through the ceiling ducts. But instead of leaving the building, she went on a hunt for Nickolas. That gave us the chance to track her down and trap her. Took three darts to drop her. Then we needed to deal with the fallout of her outing. She managed to down an entire chocolate cake. The shock to her metabolism almost sent her into a coma. And not the one we're waiting for.

"And that gets us to Nickolas. I've had to confine him. He's gone feral and isn't doing well at all. He and Jess are trying to form some kind of bond. It's similar to the videos you've shown me of your people blood bonding, but not quite the same. When she got out, she headed straight for Nick, using her talent. Through the inhibitor. I've already had too many pointed questions lately about Nick. I can't believe that Gabriel doesn't already know. So I need you ready. If this goes down before Nick is fit, we're looking at a disaster. I know I don't need to tell you to tell your Wings to be careful. But please do. This is a dangerous, rocky time."

The screen went dark.

Robin scrubbed his face and Marcus sat back, clearing his throat. Adam shuffled, drawing their attention.

"Jays said to bring back any reply you had. But if a bunch of you are coming to the farm, you'll get there before me."

Marcus shook his head. "Actually, no. You'll make it home before we can finish getting organized. It's too late for you to start back today. Robin, go get him settled and get him dinner. Adam, I'll have my reply for Jays before you go, and a message of what to expect for Dustin. Thanks for taking the risk in coming to us."

"My whole family is behind you, Marcus. You know that. Gramps would tan my hide if I didn't do what I can."

"Please pass my regard on to him as well. I miss his company."

He nodded, and Robin touched his arm. As he led the grounded out into the dining hall, he saw Marcus turn to stare out the window, and Robin's heart ached for them all.

A week later, Chris yawned and sat up, leaning against Nickolas's door. Donald swung his legs over the side of the couch, exhaustion still plain on his face. He looked around the destruction in the room.

"Hear anything, Chris?" his Second asked him quietly.

Chris shook his head and started to fold up his blankets. "Not anymore. I think he finally fell asleep. The first night of weaning him off the tranks is down. I hadn't anticipated the withdrawals to be so devastating. I expect we're up for more lost sleep. His nightmares are brutal."

He set the blankets down on the back of the couch then slumped into the armchair and met Donald's eyes. "You all right?"

His Second grunted and leaned over to cradle his head in his hands. "I think so. I feel like a bruised melon inside though. We need to tell Ian that he's getting stronger. I'm really glad you were able to stop his mental attack Chris, it was most unpleasant."

"Good thing he has a hard head. I didn't really care for bashing it in with a lamp. Best I could think of at the time to get him to let you go, since Ian ordered not to trank him."

"And he'd been doing so well the last few days."

"I don't think he would have attacked you, if he hadn't had the added stress of the drug withdrawal pushing him. He's been able to bring himself under control several times in the last couple of days."

Movement came from the other room and he shared a glance with his Second. "I had hoped he would sleep a little longer. Why don't you call Kieran and get us all some breakfast up here."

Donald nodded and reached for the phone as a shadow-filled Nickolas edged into the room. Christoff studied his brother. Nickolas looked haunted and exhausted as he paced around the room, running his hands through his tangled dark hair, righting objects but otherwise ignoring them.

"You should have tried to sleep more, Nick," Chris said.

His brother shot a sharp glance at him and said resentfully, "I'd like to see you try, I really would."

"You have to try. Only you can beat this thing."

"Fuck you, Chris. Let me out to fly or trank me so I can sleep. And not that shit in the gun, the actual sedative."

He sighed. "That's up to Ian. You know that."

Still pacing, Nick looked at Donald. "How's your head?"

"It has certainly felt better."

"Yeah mine too. You guys should have just let me go."

Tired of the constant battle with his brother, Chris snapped, "Don't give me that, Nick. I'm not in the mood."

He took a deep breath and closed his eyes. "I'm not giving the Facility the chance to send Gabriel after you for going feral while you're still at a disadvantage mentally. Look, brother, whether you like it or not, we're doing this Ian's way, so learn to cope."

Growling, Nick kicked him halfheartedly. "Get out of my chair."

He flashed a grin and shifted over to the couch. There were any number of responses his brother could have had to last night. This was the best of them. A knock sounded at the door, and rising, Donald admitted Kieran pushing a trolley. He paused in the doorway; his eyebrows rose at the state of the room.

"Don't start, Kieran. I don't want to hear it," Nickolas stated flatly.

"Uh huh, fine." And he pushed the cart fully into the room. After setting the breakfast plates out, he sat down and took his own share. "Chris, Ian told me to tell you that he wants Nickolas in the Hub today after breakfast for an exam."

He shot a look at Donald then turned back to Kieran. "Is that wise?"

Kieran shrugged and finished chewing before he answered. "He understands and wants him there anyway."

Very quietly Nickolas interjected, "I want to see Jessica."

"No," snapped simultaneously from three throats. Glaring, Nick continued to eat.

Kieran took a drink before he elaborated. "Ian isn't going to allow you to, you know that, Nick. If it helps any, Ian has had me in to see her regularly since the last time you saw her. She's doing as well as can be expected under the circumstances."

Kieran's voice rumbled around the room, sharing his time spent with Jessica over the last week as they finished breakfast. Nickolas soaked in every word, and Chris dreaded the next hour they'd spend in the Hub. His mood swings were worse than any teenager he'd ever heard of, and the potential danger was deadly.

Nick finally pushed his plate aside, and Chris shared a glance with the other two Hunters. They both nodded. "Ok, Nick. Let's get you to the Hub."

Nick's wings fidgeted as they left his suite, thankfully the only sign of his irritation, as he marched in the center of their guard. Chris led the group through the halls; when they had almost reached the Hub, Kieran cleared his throat nervously.

"By the way, Nick, you'd better behave. Ian says he won't put up with you losing it again. He's already got enough trouble to deal with. He'll slap you in a room so fast it'll make your head spin."

Nickolas stumbled a step behind him, and he cast a glance over his shoulder at his brother's pale face. *Please hold it together, Nicky. I'll never forgive myself if I have to help force you back into that nightmare. This has been hard enough.*

They reached the doors, and he held them for the group to pass. He met Ian's gaze but remained by the door as guard. Nickolas made a beeline straight for Jessica's monitor. Chris's lips quirked up slightly as the doctor rolled his eyes at him before he walked over to meet Nickolas at the monitors. "So, Nicky, are we going to do the usual?"

"Just let me in, Ian, for a little bit. Please." His brother leaned over the desk, his head bowed over the monitor. "Please."

"Do you remember what happened to Jillian?"

"As if I could forget," he whispered.

"Are you sure that won't happen to Jessica? I'm not, so I will not take the risk. Please, sit down so we can get started." Nick slumped down into a chair in defeat and turned to face Ian. The doctor reached over to the tray placed next to the desk and got ready to draw Nick's blood. "So, Nickolas, how did you sleep last night?"

"Terribly, as I'm sure you know. Why wouldn't you send Jays over? I'm so tired."

"Nick, you've become addicted to the tranquilizer. You need to go off it."

"I would rather that than the dreams."

"Tell me about your dreams," Ian asked as he inserted the needle into Nick's vein. Nick ground his teeth, and Christoff wondered if he would talk about them or not. Anytime that he'd asked Nickolas about the details of his dreams, his brother just brushed him aside. Ian placed the vials aside then opened Nick's shirt and attached monitors to several places on Nick's chest, abdomen, and head then turned to look and see if the machine scrolled properly. "Would you really rather trade one drug dependency for another, instead of trying to come to terms with your subconscious?"

"They are worse than they used to be, Ian. It's not just replays of my time in the Hub, it's horrible images of deprivations committed on others. Some are on people I know and care about. They all get mixed up with my memories and I don't know what's real. I don't trust myself. Am I going to do something else like what I did fifteen years ago?" Nickolas asked uncertainly.

"Fifteen years ago was not your fault, Nick. And I don't think you're on your way to becoming a monster now. I do think you're having clairvoyant dreams though, but how much of what you see coming true will depend on the choices the different individuals involved make. But before we worry about refining and controlling that talent, let's get you stabilized, which means I can't allow you to develop a dependency on the tranquilizer. So, what other talents have you been exhibiting?"

Nickolas fidgeted in his seat. Chris narrowed his eyes waiting for him to mention his increasing strength.

"Nick," he warned.

His brother turned a glare on him then glanced at Donald and Kieran, who lounged against the opposite wall. "You don't have to."

"You're kidding me, right?" Chris turned to look at Ian's waiting face. "Last night he attacked Donald mentally, some form of coercion. He had almost succeeded in forcing Donald to let him out of the suite while I was occupied in the other room. You told us no tranks, so my only recourse was to brain him with the table lamp, which had the desired effect of getting him to release Donald. I've been on the receiving end of one of Nickolas's compulsions, and I think he's gaining strength."

Nickolas reached up to rip off the sensors glued to his body, but Ian grabbed his hand.

"Leave them; we're not done," he said evenly.

"I need to move around, Ian."

"I don't care. Sit." The doctor pressed a couple of the sensors back down and checked the others. "What did you think you were doing last night?"

"I just want to fly, Ian. I need out."

"And you don't think Jessica doesn't want that too?"

A soft sigh escaped Nickolas, and the fear and pain rang clear in his words. "I don't want to hurt anyone else, Ian. I just wanted to go away so I could keep everyone else safe from me."

Chris closed his eyes at his brother's admission. Ian's voice gentled, "One week, Nicky. You only have one more week, then you should be fine. One week."

Ian had almost finished going over Nickolas's test results when he felt Jays enter the empty Hub.

"What are you going over there, boss?"

He turned his chair to face his protégé before answering. "I had Chris bring Nick in for some tests this morning. You were right, he has become dependent on the tranquilizer. When you didn't show up last night, he attacked Donald. Fortunately, he doesn't have a concussion from Christoff bashing him in the head with a lamp."

"A lamp?" Jays exclaimed as he walked over to the coffee pot by the wall.

"Did you expect him to be reasonable?" he replied absentmindedly.

"No, I suppose not."

Ian looked back down at the papers while Jays grabbed a cup, and after filling it with coffee, he wandered back over to Ian. "How bad is the dependency? You know he won't get enough rest without it."

"We'll have to play it by ear. If his chemistry gets way out of balance again like it was last week, we may need to chance using the tranquilizer again, no matter his level of addiction, but not before then. Except for this setback, he's showing marked improvement. I think our original estimate of two weeks is really close. With one down, hopefully we can hold Gabriel off for another week." He looked up at the concern etched on Jays's face.

"And if we can't?"

"Then they fly free."

"Will Marcus get his people into place with Dustin in time?"

"I hope so. He should have gotten my message a couple of days ago. With any luck, they're already there." He flipped a page and studied the graph again. "Nickolas is showing strong talents in clairvoyance, coercion, and telepathy so far. If there is anything else, he's not talking about it. Trying to get him to talk about the talents we have identified is like pulling teeth. One positive sign of his improving condition though, he was much less obsessive while he was here, that was encouraging."

"Wish we could say the same for Jess." Jays sighed.

"She's tolerated Kieran's presence for the last week. And he's at least gotten her to eat. Has she asked you more questions?"

He shook his head. "No. She clammed up after the first day we had her back in her room. But I've listened to her grill Kieran."

Jays slid into the chair next to him, so he handed Nick's test results over. "Is she still scheming?"

"I can't tell. But at a guess, I'd say she's starting to seem frantic."

"That can be good or bad. On one hand, if she loses hope, it could impact her chances of survival, but if she's starting to resign herself to the fact that she's here to stay, maybe she'll start to cooperate." He waved at Jays to read, then rubbed his eyes. "Whatever she's up to doesn't change our course. Once Nickolas has himself in hand, we have to move on to Christoff's and Donald's withdrawal and resumption of the change. We need to get as many of the Valkyries cleaned up and through stage four as possible."

"I had a thought, Ian. For the Hunters, if we organized more frequent sparring matches, that could take a great deal of the aggressive pressure off of those changing. It might also work to hide the raised level of aggression to others in the Facility."

A smile broke out and he nodded. "Very good thought, Jays. When Nickolas is in a better frame of mind, I wanted to go over how he should handle the rest of this chaos. I'll recommend that approach."

He leaned back and stretched his legs out. "I'm estimating that it should only take the Hunters somewhere around five days to a week to finish their change. They won't have much in the way of brain alterations, if any. For them it really is just a matter of ridding their systems of the drugs and becoming used to telepathic intrusions. The Casters and Seers, I expect, will be somewhere in between how long it takes the Hunters and Nickolas's time."

He fell silent and closed his eyes, giving Jays some time to read through Nickolas's test results.

The squeak of Jays's chair brought him back to awareness. "These are looking really good. His blood work is showing elevations still, but not to the degree they were last week. Whoa, his brain wave patterns are off the chart."

"Yes. Chris said he was getting stronger. That just proves the point. I would love to see what a qualified grader would make of his power well."

Jays set the paper work down then leaned back in his chair before taking a drink of his coffee. "So now what? What's the next step?"

"We wait. There's really nothing else we can do. Either he gets it under control or he doesn't; either way, we still have to wait until his change is complete. After that we can worry about training." He gathered up the medical reports and put them into a locked drawer. Then he sat back and idly watched Jessica on the monitor and waited for his Second to broach what was on his mind; he could feel Jays collecting his thoughts.

Jays placed his coffee cup down with a controlled click before he asked, "So have you heard anything yet, Ian?"

Nodding his head, he swiveled away from the monitor to look at Jays. "Yes, finally. I was worried they had caught him," Ian said, feeling his relief return.

"It was his choice to go. He volunteered. He knew how unsuccessful we'd been in getting a spy into the camps," Jays said.

"That doesn't make me worry any less, and it's been a week. Jack hasn't been involved with us for long and doesn't know as much as I would like."

"It makes less for Gabriel to get out of him if he is caught."

"True. He was finally able to get a message out to me last night. Gabriel knows about Marcus's plan for the new settlement up north, and he is going to set a trap to capture or kill as many as he can."

"How in blazes did he find out?"

Ian shrugged and said, "Your guess is as good as mine. But I suspect *we* have a spy too."

"What about Michael?"

He froze and stared at the far-seeing, glazed look on his Second's face. Not wanting to break the tenuous trance Jays was hovering around, Ian asked softly, "What about him?"

Jays's eyes blinked, then he replied, "I don't know, something about the way he acts. What if he's a spy for Gabriel?"

Shock rippled through Ian, and he gasped as pieces started to fall into place. His head reeling, he saw patterns form from the new input and his mind skimmed through them at light speed. "Why didn't I see that? This just became too dangerous. We have to get Jack out. Now."

"What? Gabriel can't do much to him except question him. He's unfledged. Kratz tends to keep that much control on Gabriel, at least."

"No, Jays, he's not. He's about to enter the second stage of the change soon. And if he's there when the physical change starts, Gabriel will have all the control he wants. Normally if one of his staff starts to change, they get sent here to me. But if Gabriel knows he's my spy…"

"This is so not good."

Nodding at the dawning understanding on Jays's face, Ian said, "We need to do this by the book. Gabriel will know something's up if he requests a transfer out so quickly. Maybe Luther would actually help with this one."

He pushed to his feet, running a hand through his hair. "Jays, stay here and monitor the fledges. I'm going to my office to make a phone call."

Chapter Eighteen

Nickolas walked through the doors into the Hub and felt like himself for the first time in weeks. Christoff and Donald swung in behind, flanking him protectively. He laughed and just shook his head then caught Ian's eye as he sauntered over to the doctor. "Well, you've had your week."

Ian looked him up and down, smiling, his eyes twinkling. "Good to have you back, Nicky. Sit, we'll do a few final tests."

He straddled the chair and sat patiently while Ian drew blood then scanned him with a handheld device. His mind drifted while he reveled in the calm. Then his senses sharpened and zeroed in on a target.

Undisciplined spikes of energy flared when Jays walked into the room.

"David's exam is done, Ian," the younger doctor said. "Oh hi, Nick, you're looking good today."

He cocked his head and studied Jays as the power washed over him. It took a moment before he could respond. "Just waiting for the official go ahead, Jays."

Cloudy and disjointed images flooded him, and he had to work to control his expression. The realization hit him that the Frankenstein of scenes, pictures of Jays meeting with strange Valkyries, came from his friend's mind and not his own imagination. He pushed a little and they cleared, allowing a wider array of images, this time a disturbing sequence involving Ian. Concerned, he pushed at Jays a little harder.

Jays pressed his thumb and forefinger against his eyes. "Oh, what the hell?"

A wall came up between him and Jays, and Nick snapped his attention back to Ian.

"What are you doing, Nickolas?" the doctor asked him quietly.

What are you guys doing? Nick thought, then replied, "Have you noticed Jays lately, Ian?"

The doctor in question shook his head in confusion then moved to set up the cart for an exam. Nickolas looked back at him. "I can feel him."

"Stay out of his mind, Nick. And don't tell him anything. It's too disruptive to the new fledgling to know before they are well into stage two. I didn't tell you when your time was approaching for the same reason."

"I didn't know there was a way to tell when someone was in stage one," Nickolas said.

"It's not something that *is* known, Nick. And it would be good to keep it that way." He finished up the tests and removed the blood pressure cuff. "Well, Nick, you're good to go. Chris, Donald, please come over here."

He stood and stretched then gave his wings a flap before settling them on his back. At the relief that filled his brother's eyes, Nickolas grinned. "I told you, Chris. I could feel the difference this morning."

His brother snorted and said mockingly, "Forgive me, Nick, but after the last couple of weeks, I'm afraid your word on this subject was just a little suspect. So he's clear, Ian?"

Nodding, the doctor smiled. "Yes, Chris, he's clear. You and Donald are next. Don't take your pills in the morning. Since my estimate on Nick proved correct, I'm guessing it'll take around five days, give or take, for the two of you to clear the drug completely out of your system. Unless either of you prove to be in a different caste, though I don't think you will. I believe you both to be Hunters. It'll take about twenty-four hours before you start to feel the aggression take hold. Please...try not to kill anyone." He sighed. "It'll be hard enough to hide the injuries I'm anticipating. Nickolas, Jays had a good idea. Set up extra sparring practices now, focusing on those who are in the process of clearing out the drug. We might be able to channel most of the aggression, or at least cover up for it that way."

"Done. I'll work a schedule out with Chris today. Anything else, Ian?"

"No, I think we'll just have to play it by ear and see what happens."

He looked over at his brother and waved him off. The satisfaction of finally being able to get them to leave was childish, but he enjoyed it. "Looks like I don't need you guys anymore; why don't you take off for a bit and start to get things in order for the next week."

Chris laughed and waved while Donald snorted as they headed out the door.

His smile faded as the two Valkyries left and he turned back to Ian. "Can I see her now?"

Ian gazed at him, unblinking, then turned and walked away. He followed him over to the monitors and froze, the wind knocked out of him, as he stared at Jessica. She paced the short length of her cell. Her movements flowed, animalistic, less human. The sight pulled at something within him and power hummed. Her wings cascaded down her back in a dark waterfall. Not quite long enough for flight yet, but at the rate they were growing, it wouldn't be long. He couldn't help but wonder what else had changed since he saw her last.

Ian cleared his throat and Nick broke away from her image to find the doctor studying him closely. "That's something I need to talk to you about, Nickolas. How much do you remember of the weeks of your change?"

"Ah..." He shifted his feet and rubbed his hand down his thigh. "I'm not sure. I...well I mostly remember feelings I guess. There're some snapshots that are clear."

"That's much more normal. Glad to hear it. Your abnormal level of memory from your initial change came from the Xanthar." The doctor shifted over to a different computer and typed in some commands. A few seconds later, a recording of Jessica's room came on. Nick groaned.

Saved forever, he and Jessica lay sprawled on her bed. Heat filled his cheeks. "Ian..."

"Get a grip, Nicky. Just watch."

"It's embarrassing," he muttered. But he watched. A few moments later, he noticed a glow start to form around the two of them.

"What..." He swallowed and tried again. "What is that?"

"That's why you don't get to see her right now, Nick."

"I don't remember that," he whispered.

"I'm not surprised. Both of you were feral at the time and acting on instinct."

The scene continued on to show them getting broken apart, and he turned away. "What is it?"

"Not something that I'm willing to go into detail about. But you need to know that she's not ready and neither are you."

"Excuse me?" He flung a hand at the screen. "I think I have a right to know."

"No. You don't. You have no idea how dangerous you are. You don't know the first thing about your talents or how to control them. You walk in here and nearly compromise Jays without a thought. It is not safe here. You have to keep your talent locked down because if Gabriel comes near, he's going to know. And he has twenty-five years' experience using his talents."

"I..." *I don't even know where to step now.* He ran his hand through his hair and turned back to watch Jessica's room monitor. *What is it? The pull is so strong.*

"You need to let her finish her change, Nicky."

He nodded but continued to watch.

Ian sighed, then after a moment, changed the subject. "It's Wednesday."

He glanced over at Ian, not daring to let the hope start yet. He'd only just been cleared after all.

"How much wing atrophy have you suffered from the last two weeks? Spread."

He tried not to race across the room to the wall, and extended. "I can feel some, but every opportunity Chris gave me in the gym, I took."

Ian pulled and prodded. The smooth wall felt cool on his hands while he waited for Ian to decide.

"Well, without taking the time to hook you up to the machine, I think you'll be ok for a run."

"Yesssss." He nearly bounced and snapped his wings closed, then turned around.

Ian tried unsuccessfully to smother his smile. "Ok. You can go. We can bend the rules about an escort. Bring me back my usual. I figure you're desperate to get some wind. But keep low and don't over exert. Understand?"

"Sure. No problem," he called over his shoulder, already halfway to the door. Ian's laugh followed him into the hall.

The freedom to walk down the corridor without anyone breathing down his neck, coupled with the prospect of a flight, left him giddy. He shoved the nearest door out into the gardens open and stepped into the crisp late fall sunshine. He ran down the path, then without missing a step, jumped up onto the seat of a bench and leapt. With a huge downsweep, he sailed out over the bushes of the garden. He exited the garden at the water's edge and followed the twisting path of the slough, staying low like he promised.

Grounded too long. He thought as he pumped the soreness out of his disused wings and started evaluating how much strength and ability he needed to work on recovering.

Flying on autopilot, he made his way to the restaurant Ian liked. *So why is it that I am always the curry courier? Why not just order takeout like a normal person, and have them deliver it? Not that I really mind the excuse to get out and fly by myself every week, but still, I don't even like curry.*

He rose a little in altitude to get over the trees and buildings, keeping a watch on his muscle fatigue. He didn't spend long over the populated city sections before he dropped down in front of the tiny hole in the wall restaurant. The little bell on the door tinkled as he walked in, and he smiled when he was greeted warmly by the little old woman who ran the register. She called back Ian's usual before he could open his mouth, then he had to spend the time assuring her that, yes, he was just fine even though he hadn't been in on his normal schedule. Her obvious concern raised his spirits after the low of the last few weeks.

Her chatter kept him occupied until an unfamiliar feeling dimmed her voice in his ears. He absently took the little tied plastic bag from the woman and said good-bye as he tried to sort through the newness of his abilities. When he walked out the door, he paused on the doorstep, scanning the nearby rooftops, not quite sure what he was looking for. He had almost decided that he was imagining things when the watched feeling grew much stronger.

Movement caught his peripheral vision and his focus snapped to it, then he sucked in his breath. On the roof directly across the street, two feral Valkyries stood and made eye contact with him. One raised a little white carton in salute to him. Feeling a brush against his mind, he opened up.

So, Nickolas, it's good to see you out of the Facility again.

The shock of the unfamiliar telepathic touch rocked him. Feelings accompanied the stranger's sending, an overwhelming sensation while trying to shape his own reply. *Who are you? What are you doing here?* he sent.

The one with the carton raised it again. *Who doesn't like curry?*

Amusement laced the Hunter's sending. Not sure what to make of this encounter, Nickolas tensed when he noticed the other silent Valkyrie point a device at him. He reacted on instinct, liquid heat rising from somewhere inside him, and he got ready to defend himself, but the curry-eating one broke his concentration.

I see you've finally rid your system of the drugs. There's more to the universe than the two dimensional, black-and-white world that you've been living in, Nickolas.

And with that sending a slideshow of pictures slammed into his mind; his fingers clutched the bag in his hand as his thoughts blanked for a moment and the power that had coursed into him flowed back to where it came from. The images the Hunter sent to him of strange Valkyries, living, performing everyday tasks, seemed almost alien. Unable to think, he just absorbed the new information to process later. A feather light touch flittered through him. A flutter of sensation, barely felt over the crash of impression inundating him, and Nickolas became aware of the subtle intrusion taking place in his mind underneath. Slamming up barriers, he cut off access. *What the hell?*

Annoyed surprise, laced with a touch of amusement, circled his mental pathways. *Be careful, Nickolas, stay safe.*

And with that, the two Valkyries took off from the roof in a thunder of wings. Tempted to follow, Nickolas held himself back, remembering his physical condition just wasn't up to it. He launched into the sky, his mind full of questions about wild feral Valkyries, and Ian and Jays's involvement with them.

◆ ◆ ◆

Marcus paced in his office, shifting his wings restlessly. *Finally*, he thought as a knock sounded at the door. He moved behind his desk as he called out permission to enter. "You said he came to the drop this week. So how was he?"

Geoffrey, the Hunter from the team, shrugged his shoulders as he sat. "He looked a little run down and worn out but otherwise good. What did you pick up, Eric?"

The Seer cocked his head as he thought for a moment. "Geoff's right. He's had a time of it if his outward condition says anything. But he's strong in his power. Stronger than anyone I've had contact with before. I only got the most basic of a preliminary scan before he detected me and threw me out of his mind. He has incredible Seeing abilities; I was able to get that much. And we already know his telepathy has a huge range. Farther than anyone I've tested before. But other than that, my attempt wasn't terribly useful."

Eric gestured for Geoffrey to continue. "Since he's finished his change and is no longer inhibited, it was impossible for us to hide our presence from him. He sensed us, I think, before he even left the restaurant. He looked wary as he came out, scanning the rooftops. No way to download the chip without showing ourselves." He reached into his pocket and pulled it out.

Marcus accepted it, idly spinning the small piece of plastic in his fingers. "What was his reaction?"

"He seemed a little dumbfounded if you ask me. I tried to distract him with conversation and some images while Eric did the transfer and scan. It really wasn't very long, he caught Eric so quickly and threw us both out."

Marcus mulled over their observations for a minute then dismissed the two. "If you remember anything else of import, let me know. You're free to resume your duties."

When he was alone, Marcus inserted the chip. *Oh, Dad. You're looking awful.*

"Hello, Marcus. Nothing outward has changed since my emergency communication. But keep a presence at Dustin's. It's only a matter of time before they'll have to fly. As more come off the drugs, we won't be able to keep it contained. As you see, Nick has completed stage four. It's been hard on him. I've included a copy of his past and current records for Beth, but we were right; he's not a Seer. His scans and tests are off the charts.

"He's not forthcoming on what he can do. The talents I have been able to pinpoint are exceedingly strong. Telepathy, coercion, clairvoyance, possible precog. But he's not talking. It's going to take time to learn anything from him. You know how stubborn he is. I wonder where he got that from." Ian laughed, then the recording continued. "Chris and his Second are now taking the plunge. Hopefully that will keep them all occupied for a bit.

"Jessica's doing as well as can be expected. She's still not overly cooperative, but we've managed to avoid any more jail breaks. She's halfway through her metamorphosis, but condition-wise she seems farther.

"So here's the bad news. There's a spy somewhere. Gabriel is getting information he shouldn't have. He not only knows that you are in the process of setting up a new community of Valkyries, but he knows your drop town. It's only a matter of time before he has the exact location of your new site. It's less isolated than Aurora, so he'll find it. Warn Dustin and his family. Gabriel won't care if they are unfledged, Marcus, he'll bring them in. He's setting a trap for you.

"The next shipment is ready. I'll have Jays at the warehouse two days from now, at eleven in the morning. We focused on the more difficult drugs for you to obtain. I don't know how many more drops I'll be able to put together. Things are heating up around here.

"All my love goes out to you. Please watch out for Gabriel's trap. Clear skies."

The screen went blank and Marcus leaned back in his chair, absorbing all the information. After taking a deep breath, he mentally reached out. *Robin?*

Yes, Marcus?

Please come to my office.

I'm on my way.

He pulled the chip out and filed it with all the others he'd received over the years. After a preemptory knock, Robin strode in, not waiting for permission. Marcus automatically glanced at Robin's neck. Only a few red marks from the stitches remained to fade.

Kelley's recovery was, of course, much slower. "How's Kelley doing?"

"Good. Still a little discomfort breathing, but she can move her wings on her own now. Several weeks to go before they can support her weight though."

"Not being able to fly is always the hardest in a recovery. Well, I didn't call you in here to ask about your Second. The mule is back in the traces. I just received a message from Ian. Jays will meet you at the warehouse in two days. So you should join the Flight at Dustin's. But I want you to take a Wing of Seers and Casters with you."

Robin cocked his head and wrinkled his forehead. "Why?"

"There's a leak somewhere. Ian's looking, but we have to be careful. Gabriel has learned of our plans for expansion. I don't want anyone going out without protection. And that includes Dustin."

Nervous, Robin sat down. "How do you want us to play this?"

"Protect yourselves at all costs. If you have to hurt or kill someone, do it, but otherwise try to just get everyone out and run. I know that goes against the grain for most of the Hunters, but it's necessary. We don't need to develop a vicious reputation with the general public."

Thoughts swirled through Robin's eyes before he said, "I'll get my team together and meet with you tomorrow morning."

Marcus nodded his head. "That sounds good."

Nickolas watched the storefronts slip past and ignored Jays's chatter with the other two Valkyries sitting behind him. Control of his new abilities proved more of a challenge to learn than he'd expected. But he could almost overlook that, thanks to the relief of having his mind back under his own control. *I just wish I could remember more. It's been two days since Ian cleared me, and I still feel so raw inside. The drive to get to Jess...* Snippets wandered through his thoughts. Her voice, his. *Did I really think I could get her out?*

He tried to adjust his wings a little and took a calming breath of the air that blew in the open window. He had to remind himself for the hundredth time that he wasn't trapped, that he could get out and fly if necessary. *I haven't had this much trouble since I was first released from the Hub fifteen years ago.*

Then, most of his difficulties stemmed from the trauma of his isolation. Now, he still battled that trauma but in the form of memory. Shards that worked their way out of the abscess he'd created, that his resumption of his change had lanced.

He shied away from them. *I hope Chris and Donald are ok. It feels strange not to have them hovering. They're just getting in bad shape too. Anything could happen without me there to help stop it. Why did Ian insist that I had to leave now? Chris and Donald need me. He knows that. This resupply could have been done at a later time or without me. What's the point?*

Jays pulled up to the gate of the warehouse complex, and after opening the mesh, pulled up to the loading bay they normally used. He got out and stretched his wings, keeping tabs on the grounded as he unlocked the doors, then made his standard excuse about needing to go to the office and double check the paper work.

Suspicious, Nick watched Jays leave before he said in a low voice, "Kieran, you and Dylan get the truck loaded. I want to keep an eye on Jays. I'll be back."

He ignored Kieran's questions and slipped off to follow in Jays's wake. His suspicions were confirmed when Jays bypassed the stairs to the office and slipped out the rear door. He followed. Outside the back door, he flattened himself against the wall, then slipped behind a dumpster when his new senses warned him of several unknown Valkyries approaching. He wove a quick barrier, the kind he'd learned from Jessica, and hid his presence from the others.

From the protection of his hiding place, he watched Jays let a group of eight Valkyries into the building next door.

Still feeling out his abilities, he closed his eyes and dipped into that source of power he'd found the other day. Like a deep wide pool inside himself, he let the slippery warmth coat his "hand," then flicking his real world fingers, the droplets spread out in small tendrils. Something like a snake's questing tongue, the power wound through the group.

Knowledge poured in. *Half of them are Hunters; the other four are different. They must be Casters and Seers.*

He followed them up to the door and peeked in.

In the shadows of the interior, Jays clasped forearms with the dominant Hunter of the group. It took all of Nick's will to control his hackles. The Alpha aura surrounding the chestnut-haired male challenged him.

"You're looking much better, Robin. How's Kelley recovering?"

"She's not out of the infirmary yet, but she can move her wings on her own now. How's Jess doing?"

Nickolas froze. Jessica? What? *She said she had a brother named Robin, I remember now.*

"She's changing quickly. We aren't having as much trouble with her as we did at the start, but we still can't trust her. It's impeding our abilities to help her. She's having a difficult time as a result. And the added complication of her and Nick's reaction to one another has made it more tricky."

Robin shook his head. "She never did know when to quit. She's just too stubborn."

"She's certainly his match in that department. They've been separated for almost three weeks, and it's quieted down, thank goodness."

"So I hear he's pulled through and is now clean and in control of his talents."

Shrugging, Jays said, "Well, I wouldn't say control yet. Nick's still discovering his abilities, and they seem to overwhelm him at times. We aren't sure what all he can do. He seems to have the strongest talents in the Seers caste, but since he's not a Seer, we just don't know what to expect."

His lungs seized, and Nickolas's mind spiraled. Not a Seer? *What the hell am I?* He snapped back to the conversation and noticed the two wild Seers had stiffened and scanned the area. *Pay attention, Nicky, this isn't the time to lose concentration.* He rebuilt his shield and watched a confused look pass between the two, but they started to relax after he hid his power signature again.

"Is something wrong?" Robin asked them quietly.

They shook their heads, then one of them replied, "I don't think so. We both thought we felt something, but it was fleeting. Neither of us can trace it."

Jays scanned the building, his gaze pausing at the slightly open door, and Nickolas pulled back some; there was an edge to the young doctor's eyes that surprised him, though it shouldn't have. Jays wasn't stupid and he would suspect. And since he was getting closer to stage two, his instincts would be strengthening.

Still staring at the crack in the door, Jays said, "We should get you out of here. This is the stuff."

The doctor turned to pull a tarp back and Nickolas watched him show the group a rather large pile of stuff for them to take. "Same drill as usual. Make sure you lock up. I need to get back. They should be almost done. And I don't trust Nickolas's contentment to stay with the others."

"Thanks, Jays, hopefully we'll see you in a couple of weeks," Robin said.

He started toward the door and replied, "If things haven't blown to hell and gone by then. Stay safe."

Nickolas bolted and returned to the loading bay. He grabbed one of the last of the boxes and handed it off to Kieran at the edge of the truck

"Any trouble Nick?" Kieran asked as he took the load from him.

"Not now," he said and turned, taking the last box from Dylan as Jays walked up.

"Well the paper work all checks out," Jays said cheerfully. "It looks like you guys are all done here."

"Just finished, Jays," Kieran replied. "If you want to lock up, I'll get the back of the truck secured."

Climbing into the front seat of the truck, Nickolas watched Jays padlock the warehouse door. *What do you know, Jays? If I'm not a Seer, what am I? How do I get around you and Ian to find the information? Where would Ian keep it?* The magnitude of the deception coming to light astounded him. The truck dipped as the others got in, and Jays started the vehicle, pulling out and turning back onto the road leading home. The questions kept circling through his mind and he couldn't stop thinking about all the lies he had been taught about the wild Valkyries. What was the point? *Technically, I'm wild now too,* he thought as he stared quietly out the window.

"Hey, Nick, you ok?" Jays asked from the driver's seat. Not turning to look at him, Nick just shook his head. "What's going through that head of yours, Nick?" his friend asked softly.

"Trust me, Jays, you don't want to know." The shattered illusions and trust, his feelings of betrayal, warred with all the years of friendship and faith that Nickolas felt for the two men who had held all of their health, and more, in their hands for so long. Completely torn between that trust and betrayal, he didn't know where to turn.

Once back at the Facility, his frustration escaped briefly when he slammed the truck door and snapped, "Kieran, Dylan, we need to find Chris and Donald. Start in the gym, I'll check their rooms."

The two Hunters nodded and left the garage at a run. Nickolas turned to Jays.

"Is something bothering you, Nick?" Jays asked warily.

He stared at his friend, the tangled mixture of emotions that poured off of the first stage fledgling, concern and fear, directed at him. Anger that was aimed at himself, frustration about the situation. It all wrapped itself around Nickolas and triggered his instincts. The need to protect Jays, as a member of his clan, rose. This wasn't Jays's fault. The lies, the decisions; he had been too young to be involved in making them. He was just following orders. What Nick had to settle was between him and Ian. Nickolas shook his head at Jays. "Nothing that you can help with. I guess I'm just worried about having left Chris and Donald alone."

Relief filled Jays's blue eyes and his shoulders relaxed. "In that case, I should see about getting the truck unloaded then check in with Ian." Waving, Jays left him alone in the garage.

After the door shut behind the doctor, Nick looked up at the clock on the wall; the second hand swept by. Something in the back of his head tickled. The thought of using his abilities in some way to shorten his search for Christoff bloomed. His eyes unfocused, and he mentally turned inward.

A deep breath.

And he dove through blackness in his mind.

When his sight cleared, he found himself standing in a twilit landscape. Grey rocks pierced the ground and the soft blush of dawn bled over the jagged mountains when he looked up. Ahead on the short path was a small pool rimmed by the same grey boulders that punctuated the rest of the terrain. He neared the edge and knelt on one of the rocks to look down; he saw his reflection in the still water.

Puzzled, he studied his location, wondering where he was and what it meant. He reached out and trailed his fingers in the pool. The power hummed in his fingertips. As the drops plunked back into the whole, he felt the turbulence inside and sudden understanding followed. He stood in a mental visualization. This most likely represented his power.

With new interest, he looked around and saw the faint shimmer of threads suspended everywhere. Concentrating, he directed power into them and brought them into full view. The shimmering web was breathtaking. Thick strands and thin arched overhead and passed all about him; the largest sunk straight into the pool and he tried to follow their length, but they disappeared from his view. The pool was too deep to see the bottom. *This* is what Ian had tried to direct him to—what he had so far utilized was only a portion of his potential.

He pulled himself out of the trance and saw the second hand sweep by on the clock. Only a minute had passed. He plucked one of the small threads in the web of power and put out feelers in an effort to locate Christoff. The mental flares that held his brother's thought signature burst into view, and Nickolas left the garage, heading toward the gym, letting his power settle as he walked through the halls distracted by his thoughts. *I need to put the pieces of this puzzle together. But my hands are tied until Chris is clean. I hope Ian is right and that it doesn't take too much longer.*

Another power burst into his mind and he stumbled to a stop in the intersection of two corridors. His eyesight dimmed as the wash of cold smothered him. His power flared and pushed back against the sea cold current and Nickolas looked up. An unknown Valkyrie sauntered toward him.

Nickolas twitched but stood his ground as the other slowly circled him.

"So, the infamous Nickolas, at last."

Some part of him recognized the beautifully melodious voice.

"Why is it that they didn't manage to spirit you away this time?"

The weight of the other Valkyrie's presence pressed at his back as the older Alpha leaned close, taking in his scent near his ear before the voice said quietly, "Could it be that they have finally lost control of you?"

The man circled back around and caught his gaze, and his smile grew even wider before he pushed mentally. Instinctively throwing up a barrier, Nickolas took a step back, barely blocking the intrusion. The other laughed delightedly.

"You've slipped the leash. There's no way Ian doesn't know. I warned them this day would come."

Nickolas took another step back, shaking his head as visions and memories from fifteen years ago swam through his mind's eye.

He lay strapped to his cot in his cell in the observation labs, close to feral. The golden Valkyrie with the dark shadow consuming him hovered over his restrained form.

The pain. His screams as the voice and presence of this Valkyrie inundated his unprotected mind. His touch was enough to send Nickolas convulsing into unconsciousness as he mentally experienced the trauma of this other person's thoughts.

All of these memories cascaded through Nickolas, like a river whose dam had broken. Swamped, he looked into frozen blue eyes and tried to process what the man had said.

"Warned who? Who are you? You came to see me, in the cell." *Gabriel. This has to be Gabriel.* He caught the chittering chipmunk his mind decided to emulate and locked his mental fist around it. He would not give the Alpha the power of knowing how much he affected him.

"So...you do remember," Gabriel said softly and his eyes glowed.

The push came swift and sharp. Nick grabbed his head and reinforced his barrier. "Stay out," he growled, his hackles starting to rise.

Gabriel smirked and shook out his wings, then tossed his hair over his shoulder. "You're neither strong nor skilled enough, Nickolas. It will be a pleasure to find out what else you can do."

The echo of pounding footsteps reached them. Kieran rounded the corner and skidded to a stop, quickly looking from one Alpha to the other. Nickolas saw fear flash through his eyes before the normally calm and quiet Valkyrie snapped, "What are you doing here?"

Then he placed himself in front of Nickolas so he was between the two Alphas, and he asked again, menace clear in his stance, "What are you doing here?"

"Put your hackles down, Beta. He hardly needs your protection. And what I am doing is none of your concern." Gabriel met Nick's eyes again and asked, "So how is your brother doing?"

A jolt of fear arrowed through him, and narrowing his eyes, he growled, "Stay away from Christoff."

Gabriel laughed and brushed past them, calling over his shoulder, "This isn't over, Nickolas."

After Gabriel disappeared around the corner, Kieran swore and relaxed his stance. "That was Gabriel. We had no warning. Ian doesn't know he's here." The Beta Hunter looked stricken.

"What are you talking about?"

"Ian always warns us when Gabriel is going to be on the premises so we can stay out of sight. If we weren't warned, then Ian doesn't know."

"Calm down. We only just got back; maybe you didn't get the warning," Nick said.

He shook his head and rushed on, "No, that's what I came to tell you. Chris is out of control in the gym and they need your help before he seriously hurts someone. If there had been an alert about Gabriel, they would have told me there."

They turned in the direction of the gym and started to rush down the hall. "First things first, let's get to Christoff. Then we can deal with whatever comes from Gabriel."

He skidded to a stop in front of the gym doors, Kieran beside him. With a deep breath, he pushed through the doors. Inside, several Valkyries sat against the wall and tended to injuries. Donald lay among them, unconscious, with blood trickling from his temple.

His boots clicked against the polished wood floor and Christoff slowly turned away from the dozen or so Valkyries standing outside the border of the sparring ring to face him.

The feral light that glowed from Chris's eyes spawned an answering streak of his own. A smile lit up his brother's face, and Nickolas moved with predatory grace into the coming battle. "I guess the tables are turned, huh, Chris?" he drawled as he stalked the edge of the circle. The rest of the Hunters backed out of the way.

The boyish grin his brother wore held a blood lust that Nickolas understood well. "What was it you said to me, Nick? Come to spoil my fun, or do you have the balls to join me?"

He stopped at the edge of the ring and replied softly, "Oh, I have the balls all right, and the skill and training."

Without a second thought, he stepped over the boundary. Christoff lunged. Nickolas spun to the right then jumped into the air to do a somersault over Chris and land in the center of the ring. He snapped his foot out and landed a solid kick to Christoff's ribs. His brother exhaled with an oomph but didn't stop. Blocking two incoming kicks, Nick spun, just missing Christoff's head with his heel, then blocked a backhand Chris threw. He dove under his brother's wing then tumbled, coming up behind him and launching straight into the air about twenty feet. Folding one wing, Nickolas dove, leading with that shoulder, and slammed it into Chris as his brother tried to take to the air to follow. The move knocked Chris back onto the mat, and Nick snapped his furled wing out to land in a crouch beside his brother, delivering a backhand as Chris did a backward roll to try and escape. Slowly rising to a fighting stance, Nickolas watched his brother stand and wipe the blood from his mouth.

A grin stretched his mouth and he asked, "Are you about done, Chris?"

With a rough shake of his head, Chris lunged for Nickolas again; sidestepping, Nickolas caught him around the neck in a headlock, then hooked his other arm up under Chris's wings, effectively pinning the Hunter from behind. He drew his brother's body against his then forced Christoff to the ground by pressing his foot to the back of Chris's knees. Holding him there, Nick spoke softly in his ear. "Checkmate."

Chris made a futile attempt to struggle, so Nick squeezed, cutting off the blood until Chris sagged. "We don't have time for any more fun, Christoff. I need you to get some control. Gabriel's here."

"What?" he barely managed to say.

Nick loosened his hold and elaborated. "I ran into Gabriel in the hallway a few minutes ago. Just before Kieran found me."

He felt the shock run through Chris's body. "No. He'll know you aren't on the drugs anymore."

Slowly he let his brother go and backed up. Christoff rubbed his neck and rotated his wings as he turned to face him. "It's too late, Chris. He knows. And he'll be coming after me."

Ian raised his head from the eye piece of the microscope and rubbed his aching eyes. He reached for his pen and started to make notations on the properties of the blood sample he was working with. The pen slowed as his mind drifted off. He gave himself a brisk shake tried to refocus.

I was right, Jays. You'll be a Seer, and soon. I hope you were able to get to Robin and keep Nick occupied. Marcus needs the data I sent him. He turned the paper over then continued writing. *I know you don't understand why I needed you to go, Nickolas, that you wanted to stay here to protect your brother, but there's too much at stake to allow that. I have to get all of this done. I'm running out of time.* Papers finished, he slid them into a folder then pulled out some new forms and bent back to the microscope. *From the state of your blood, Jays, I'll be surprised if you last another couple of weeks. I'll need to discuss this with Nick soon. He already knows that Jays is changing.*

The shock of awareness jolted through Ian. Trembling, he raised his head. *No! Why wasn't I told? Thank god I sent Nick off already.* He stuffed the papers into the folder, grabbed the slide off the microscope and put it in with them, then shoved all of it into the first drawer of the file cabinet that he could. Just in time. The doors swung open, and Ian turned to watch Gabriel enter the Hub.

"What do you want, Gabriel?"

The Alpha sauntered over to the island and took a seat watching Jessica's monitor. "I'm here to do an evaluation."

"No. You have no jurisdiction here."

He swiveled the chair and smiled. "Oh I think that has changed, hasn't it, Ian?"

At the smug look on Gabriel's face, dread crept down Ian's spine. "What are you talking about?"

Spinning the chair in a circle like a giddy teenager, Gabriel stopped, facing Ian. "Guess who I ran into in the hallway today on the way here?"

The dread turned to certainty, but Ian kept his expression neutral.

"He seemed remarkably clearheaded for a Facility Valkyrie, though since I haven't seen him in fifteen years, I suppose I don't have much of a working knowledge of Nickolas's personality, now do I?" Gabriel rose and paced up to him; the softly spoken words did nothing to hide the steel underneath. "I am going in to see Jessica Reuther. Now, let me in, Ian."

His mind flashed across the hundreds of mental maps, but no moves countered this. He walked stiffly over to the door and swiped his card through. "Just remember, Gabriel, every word you say, every move you make, I'll have on tape." He watched Gabriel walk in then returned to the monitor and turned the sound up.

Jessica heard the door latch disengage as she paced in her cell. Her eternal hope that Nickolas would be allowed back got dashed when a tall, blond Valkyrie walked into the room. Full of resentment, she watched him make himself comfortable in her tiny domain. He lounged on her bunk, stretching his legs out and effectively blocking her into the end of the room unless she was willing to make an ass of herself by sliding along the wall. *Not on your life*, she thought. *I don't want to get anywhere near him.* Narrowing her eyes, she waited for him to make the first move.

He studied her for an uncomfortably long time before he spoke; his voice matched his looks, and Jessica shivered as it seeped into her. "Hello, Jessica. I'm Gabriel."

She stayed silent and just stared at him, waiting for him to continue.

Tsking, he shook his head. "Usually it's considered polite to reply when a conversation is started."

"So? Usually one chooses to initiate the conversation. Since I haven't chosen anything in weeks, I couldn't really care less about manners. What do you want?"

Brows furrowing, Gabriel sighed in irritation. "What is it with everyone demanding to know what I'm doing?"

He returned his attention to her and shrugged off the irritation. "Well, *I* can give you a choice. That's what I'm here for. I came to offer you the chance to join me; I can take you to the research facility I work with after you finish the change, or possibly before. You wouldn't need to be locked up in this tiny room. I have a lot of space. You could help immeasurably with the research just with your mere presence."

She folded her arms across her chest, hoping that he wouldn't see her hands tremble. "What research?"

He stood then started to pace in the small room, coming much too close to her for her liking. "Just as Ian does, we research the change and associated paths surrounding it. I feel you could make a valuable contribution."

"What if I don't want to?"

He stopped to stare at her, and she suppressed a shiver of fear. She felt like Jerry, with Tom pacing around her. "What would you do instead?" he asked softly.

"Make my own decisions. Everyone seems to want something from me. No one seems to care what I want, except Nickolas. So I'll take the known over the unknown."

Jessica flinched as something indefinable crossed Gabriel's face before he replied much too quietly, "Nickolas won't be here for long."

He started to stalk her, and she slid along the wall to maintain some distance, but soon she found herself trapped in the corner. His body heat seeped into her as he crowded in close, and she caught her breath when he reached out with his hand and forced her to meet his eyes.

"I lied," he said. "I wasn't going to give you a choice. You *will* be coming with me at one point or another." He was still holding her chin, and she was certain he was going to try and kiss her when, instead, she felt a strong presence try to force its way into her drug-shrouded mind. Panicking at the intrusion, she did what she could to protect herself. And raising her hands, she pushed against his chest while sending what energy she could muster past the drugs through her hands. It zapped into Gabriel, and hissing, he released her, stepping back, grudging admiration filling his eyes.

"You're strong. The drug level they have you at shouldn't have allowed that. Forget Nickolas," he said, and turning, he stalked toward the door. When he reached it, he looked over his shoulder, his gaze raking her. "You're *mine*," he promised.

When the door shut, Jessica slid down the wall, shaking from what had just happened and cursing the drugs that gave her no control over her own mind.

The inside of my head feels like its weighted down with lead and can barely move. I'm tired of being a pawn in someone else's game.

Chapter Nineteen

Nickolas flung the covers back and rolled off the bed to crouch in the darkness as he tried to sort reality from dream. Wet breath panted past his lips, and he pressed back against the wall as a bright flash of light burst behind his eyes.

He was in his cell; Gabriel reached out to touch him and he couldn't pull away. Another flash, this time a scene of carnage, strange Valkyries torn to pieces or screaming in pain. Nickolas grabbed his hair in his fists and pulled, trying to block the visions. Another flash, this time he relived the memory of breaking the neck of one of the people in the observation lounge.

He took a deep breath, fumbling in the unfamiliar exercise of trying to ground, and felt the power pulse inside before he brought it under control. When he opened his eyes, he was relieved to see only the vague outlines of his room instead of the bright pictures of horror that had taken over his vision. He rose unsteadily to his feet and made his way into the bathroom, squinting in pain at the bright light when he turned it on, then fumbled with the faucet. He cupped water in his hands then splashed his face a few times before leaning heavily on the counter. Nick looked up into the mirror, water beading down his face.

Another flash, but this time instead of a bad memory, or something horrible from Gabriel's mind, there was just the image of a storeroom. Then the pictures started to flip by, stills showing the room, several different file cabinets, and specific drawers. Then the clincher, his name circled in red on a paper that lay alone on the table in the middle of the small room. The vision started to spin around with the paper as the center, focusing his attention. Nick closed his eyes from the vertigo, and when he opened them again, the only thing he saw was his reflection in the mirror.

Does that mean what I think it means? Only one way to find out, I guess. It's not like I'll be getting any more sleep tonight anyway. I think I know which storeroom that was. I can at least start there.

He grabbed fresh pants, stuffing a few odds and ends into the cargo pockets, then slipped a dark green flannel shirt on up under his wings, reaching behind his neck to secure the Velcro as he left the suite.

His footsteps echoed in his ears as he walked the deserted halls, arriving at the locked storage room without incident. He rested his hand on the knob then reached out with his power and felt the locking mechanism, making short work of picking it telekinetically. He blinked at his second-nature use of his talent, then with a shrug, he slipped inside and relocked the door behind him.

His wings pressed to the door, he scanned the other three walls lined with file cabinets. A table filled the center space with barely enough room to maneuver around, as long as the file drawers remained closed.

A breath whistled through his teeth, and he clenched his fist then took a slow, deep, calming breath. He narrowed his focus and ignored the small space. Drawn to a cabinet, he let his feelings guide him and he started pulling out folders at random.

With his arms full, he hooked a chair with his foot, pulling it out to sit on. After setting the folders down, he took the top one and started to read.

A few hours later, he rubbed his eyes then looked at the papers and folders spread out across the surface of the table. His eyes sank closed and he leaned his elbows on the wood, his head pressed to his palms. *Why? Why all the lies?*

The lock clicked in the door behind him and broke his shocked contemplation. With the quick flash of a mental probe, he leaned back in his chair, folding his arms.

The door pushed open, followed by a second of stunned stillness.

"Hello, Ian," Nick said, then he slammed the door with his mind before looking over his shoulder at Ian's ashen face.

The doctor didn't stay frozen long. He shuffled forward and resignation entered his eyes.

"Why?" Nick asked.

With exaggerated care, Ian set the folder he carried on top of the nearest cabinet and pulled out the chair on the other side of the table. Looking old and tired, he sorted through which folders Nickolas had read. "You didn't miss much."

"Why? Why wasn't I told any of this? Why was I used like this? By you of all people." Nick took a deep breath to control the anger growing in his gut.

"I didn't have a lot of choice, Nicky. What was I supposed to do? Let Gabriel take you? What he is capable of stuns me sometimes; I couldn't chance it. I buried the knowledge of what I suspected you were so deep that nobody knew. I'm amazed that you were even able to find all of the files. I couldn't risk letting you finish your change earlier, you saw how fast Gabriel picked up on it. That couldn't have escaped you.

"And as for the camps? You would have balked in leading recoveries if you had known. And all that would have done was brought you right back into Gabriel's view—along with those who control him."

"After learning this," he flung his hand out, "I'm supposed to believe you?"

"Would you lie to Chris? If it was the only way to keep him alive?"

"This isn't about Chris."

"Isn't it?" Ian stared hard at him, and Nick looked at the tabletop as the doctor's voice pushed on relentlessly. "It's about you, it's about Chris, it's about every other damn Valkyrie in this new emerging species. And if I hadn't done the research I did, none of this would ever have happened."

"What are you talking about?"

Ian squeezed his eyes shut for a moment, then looked at the ceiling. "Your grandmother and I headed a research group studying ways to genetically help people with life-altering disabilities, in regards to their sight and hearing. We worked right here at the Facility for a private research firm, funded by a major pharmaceutical corporation. What we didn't know was how our findings were being used.

"Instead of trying to help people, they twisted our research, used it to try and manipulate the genetic structure of people for the sole purpose of cosmetic changes. They wanted something they could market. To athletes, say, so they could be stronger, faster. Or to the rich—give them enhanced hearing so they could eavesdrop without the use of traceable equipment.

"I had no idea what they had done until their experiment went rogue. Various potential clients had sent in guinea pigs. Some were second-string athletes, others were expendable employees to the rich. All had no clue how they were being used.

"We got called in as soon as it became apparent that something was wrong. My team did everything we could, but we were working blind. Gabriel was the only one to survive the experiment. But before they all died, the nightmare spread. *We* started showing symptoms."

He swallowed then took a deep breath before he continued. "They locked us up and did their damnedest to stop what they let loose...but they couldn't. It's continued to spread since.

"Your mother and father, along with a dozen others, were called in to help. They quickly realized that a virus had been used to carry the genetic manipulation, and that it was loose. I had recovered enough that when your parents' group started to change, I managed to get them what the first two groups didn't, freedom to change without interference. All of them survived.

"In one aspect, the original group's goal succeeded. They did give the people enhanced senses, but the wings came as something of a shock. After many years of research, it's become clear that instead of triggering dormant physical traits like they had hoped, the virus actually unlocked our genetic code and forced a jump in our species' evolution, a period of punctuated equilibrium.

"Unfortunately the virus has now spread too far. We see no way of containing it. It's just a matter of time, really, until Homo sapiens is superseded by Homo valkyrius. My fear for a long time has been that we were witnessing the end of our species. But with your change, we had new hope."

"Yes, my change." His brain reeled, trying to absorb the information, and he snapped, "The one most intimately involved in it, yet never told so things could make sense. No wonder I attacked Jillian."

"Yes, that was an unfortunate clue."

"Unfortunate? You don't have to live with it, Ian!"

"Now there you're wrong, Nickolas." Ian's voice cracked out, surprising him. "I have to live with everything you did and more than you will ever know. I was responsible for not just your protection, but every other Valkyrie that came through my hands. And so many I failed."

Ian's green gaze pinned him to his seat. "If lying to you for all these years was the price I had to pay to keep you safe, I would do it again in a heartbeat. I don't regret the lies, Nicky, but I do regret the pain they'll cause."

Not sure what to think, Nick's mind latched onto the first thought to float by. "Jessica; she's like me, isn't she?"

"Yes."

"But Gabriel knows about us now, doesn't he?"

"Sort of. He doesn't know about the new caste, he just knows that the two of you are different from any of the others. The original group of researchers, along with the parent corporations, still have a lot of power over us. But when the government stepped in to help try to contain the virus and quell the initial panic, we ended up with another faction to fight. They all have their own agenda's. I have to get you all out of here soon. But it's complicated. They'll be coming after you for all they're worth. What the two of you represent..." Ian shook his head.

"How can I ever trust you again?" His voice came out rough.

"The same way you have every day of your life."

Nick pushed away from the table and whispered as he turned to the door, "If only it were that simple."

"It can be as simple as you make it."

He shook his head and opened the door.

"Nicky."

He paused but refused to look over his shoulder.

"What you found? It was only about you. You've only touched the tip of the iceberg."

He fled into the corridor with those words rebounding in his head.

After a solitary breakfast, he stared at his brother across the table in the cafeteria.

Nick, you need to look at everything Ian told you objectively. It makes me angry too, but would you have made any different decisions with the knowledge he had? Knowing what the stakes were? I doubt it. I wouldn't have. His brother's eyes bored into him, willing him to understand, to forgive.

He glared at his brother for a moment, then sighed. *I know, Chris, it just hurts.*

That's a given. The question is, which would hurt worse?

You're a real jerk, you know that, Chris?

I know. I love you too, brother. Chris laughed through the link. *I like this. We certainly could have made use of this ability a while ago. Cell phones don't compare. This will make communicating in flight much simpler; we won't need to deal with you dropping your earpiece anymore. But, I can see why they didn't want us to have a secure way of communication though. There's no way for them to monitor us now.*

Don't rely on that, Chris. They may not know what we are talking about, but that doesn't mean they don't know it's happening. He shrugged at a table across the way. The grounded there kept casting them odd looks.

"Right. Out loud as much as possible," Chris said.

"Finish your breakfast. Then come meet me in the gym. I want to check Kieran out."

Donald's on him, Nick. Kieran's been off for five days, he's still got some time to go, according to Ian.

He pushed away from the table. "I know what he's going through better than any of you."

Chris nodded, his mouth full, then his eyes narrowed. Nick stilled, turning his head to look over his shoulder. Flynn pushed his way through the tables toward them.

"Come on, you two," the grounded puffed. "Ian caught me in the hall. He has a recovery we have to go on. Now. Let's move."

Nick?

He turned to face Flynn. "I should go and get the briefing then, Flynn."

The grizzled redhead shook his head vigorously. "He said to get moving. The stuff'll be in the van. Jules is already warming it up."

He looked at Chris. *Gabriel?*

Could be. He'd want you out of here. He shoved more food in his mouth and rose. *But I don't like it.*

"That isn't like Ian, Flynn." Nick pushed his chair in and they started to weave through the tables.

Maybe he knows how much you want to see him right now, Nick.

"Don't know, Nick. I'm just following orders." Flynn shrugged in front of him.

Still uneasy, he followed the grounded out to the garage.

An hour later, Nick stared at the skeletons of trees and brown dead vegetation as it skated by the window of the van. They'd been traveling north for most of that time.

I need to get a handle on these emotions. Chris is right. I likely wouldn't have done anything differently. Look at what I did to Jessica. If that doesn't prove the point, I don't know what would.

The blur outside let his mind drift. A tug of sorts caught his attention, and he brushed up against another presence. *Hello?* Nickolas sent.

Surprise jolted into him along the telepathic link. *Who is this? I don't recognize your voice.*

This is Nickolas.

Nickolas! What are you doing here?

The anxiety he received with the voice alarmed him. *We've been sent on a recovery, why?*

You're not going to Bellingham are you?

Yes, that's where we've been sent.

Can you meet with me before you arrive there? It's important.

He disengaged from the conversation for a moment to consider the ramifications. Talking to a sane and human feral Valkyrie had not been something he'd considered possible before a few weeks ago. *But look at me. Technically, I'm a feral Valkyrie now.*

All right. Where? he sent. Relief flowed down the mental connection and gave him something to think about.

There's a rest area about fifteen miles outside Bellingham. Does that work?

"Hey, Flynn? How far are we?"

"We still have about half an hour, why?"

"Are there any rest stops coming up? I really need to go."

"We just passed a sign for one in a few miles. I'll pull in."

"Thanks." *Yes, that will work. We're not alone. I have two grounded in my team, so stay out of sight. I'll fly a little ways into the woods.*

Gotcha. See you then.

The connection severed, and he sat back in his chair to wait. Flynn exited the highway and slowed to a stop, pulling into a space near the buildings. Nick popped the door and emerged, stretching his wings. "Hey, Jules, we still have a lot of waiting to do when we get there, don't we?"

The dark-haired comm tech stuck his head out. "Yep. Everything coming in on the radio says so."

"Ok. I'm going to take some time to stretch my wings then, before I have to sit in the van for hours. I won't be too long."

Chris snapped his wings closed and said, "Hey, Nick, I'm coming with you."

He shook his head no as he turned away and took off, but Chris took wing behind him. He looked over his shoulder in exasperation.

You know, Nick, I'm not dumb. I could tell you were talking to someone. Who?

I don't know. But I'm about to find out.

Not alone, you're not.

He sighed in resignation and circled the trees a few times, looking for a good place to land. A small clearing near a stream flashed by underneath, and he set down, Chris right behind him. He swept the area using his new senses and could feel his brother doing the same.

"Coming in from the north, Nick."

"Yes, I feel them too."

Eight Valkyries swept through the trees, landing in formation facing them. Both groups eyed one another for a moment before the leader of the rebels took a step forward. "I'm Robin, Hunter Prime of Aurora."

Eyeing the Hunter that he had seen talking to Jays at the warehouse, Nickolas shifted his weight. "From your reaction earlier, I take it you know who we are?" he asked.

Robin nodded, and a smile flirted with the corners of his lips. "You're very well known in Aurora. Your progress has been monitored for years."

He narrowed his eyes and growled. "Now why does that not surprise me. Everyone's interested in me." He looked the Hunter up and down then met the familiar brown eyes. "So, your Jessica's brother."

Shock flashed across Robin's eyes. "Now that does surprise me. Jess told you about me?"

"A little. I haven't been allowed to see her much for the last few weeks."

Robin blinked and looked away before he replied, "I'm glad she still thinks about me. I haven't seen her since I changed."

"She seemed to miss you."

The Hunter coughed then looked back at Nickolas; his attitude shifted rapidly and wariness suffused his posture. "You're walking into a trap."

Christoff tensed beside him and Nickolas's hackles rose. The Flight of Valkyries in front of them responded in kind and the tension levels spiraled up.

"Stand down!" Robin snarled to his Flight. "Don't be stupid, Nickolas. If we meant you any harm, you wouldn't be standing here."

"It would take more than the eight of you to take me."

"Especially with me at his back," Christoff replied menacingly.

The Flight in front of him loosened their wings, but Nickolas ignored them. Instead he watched Robin's self-confident expression as he held up his hand, stilling his Flight, before he shrugged and said, "That may well be, but it's not the issue at the moment. The trap you're walking into is."

"What trap?"

Robin shook the hair out of his eyes before he replied. "We just received word that Gabriel is in the region. He's been hunting us for quite a while. And we've been expecting a trap from him. A recovery in this region now is too coincidental. Ian knows this. Why did he send you out here?"

"Well, I have issues with anything Ian has been doing."

Robin's sharp eyes looked at him speculatively. "Something's not right. I would trust my life to Ian. Any of us would. You should think about that. Obviously your trust has been damaged, but there has always been a reason weighed against any decision Ian has made. The lesser of two evils sometimes. He has done the best that he could for all of us."

Tapping his temple with his finger, Nickolas said quietly, "I see that. It's just hard to resolve the lies so quickly. My head may say one thing, but my heart says another."

"Well, you'll need to figure it out quickly because you're running out of time."

"So what do you propose to do about this trap?" Nickolas asked.

"That depends on you. What do you plan to do about the fledgling?"

Nickolas shared a look with Chris. "With how unstable things are becoming at the Facility, I don't have any desire to bring him in."

"Her. The fledgling is female. So why don't we play it this way; you go in first, just like a normal recovery, but earlier than usual, before she passes out. You can get her moving, then we'll show ourselves, which will hopefully prod Gabriel into showing his hand. He won't expect any of us to be prepared for him. He especially won't expect the two of you to fight with us."

Nodding his head in agreement, Nickolas shook out his wings. "Sounds like a good start. We can play the rest by ear."

"Be careful sending to us. Gabriel will be able to tell we're communicating."

He glanced over his shoulder in the direction of the rest area and replied somewhat absentmindedly. "Thanks for the warning. We need to get back. Flynn and Jules are going to have a fit. Good luck."

"You too, Nickolas."

Chris launched into the air and he followed. They flew straight back, landing in a flurry of wings beside the van. Flynn leaned against the door, annoyance written plain on his face and barked. "What took you so long? Come on, let's go."

"Relax, Flynn, there's plenty of time," Christoff drawled.

The old man grumbled and got into the driver's seat. He started the van and merged back onto the highway, obviously irritated. Ignoring Flynn's temper, Nickolas swiveled his seat, gaining Jules's attention. "So, Jules, what do we have to go on?"

Jules typed on his keyboard then spun to the printer when it started spitting out pages, talking as he worked. "It seems we have a female, around the age of thirty. She's not local, so no one knows much about her. She checked into a motel last night, and this morning when the maids came by, she lost it on them and started trashing the place. She's registered under the name of Amanda Jones. Blond, blue eyes, average height. That's about it."

Nick exchanged a quick look with Christoff before he turned back to Jules. "How long ago was this? About four hours, you think?"

"That sounds right." He started typing quickly.

"I think we'll change our usual routine. I don't want to wait until she passes out; the damage to the business notwithstanding, I don't like the idea of her in such a public indefensible location. Even if we have to fight her, I want to take her in immediately."

"Nick, I don't concur," Flynn stated from up front. "There are sound reasons for the procedures we follow. We should wait."

The panic the grounded tried to conceal in his voice made Nick's suspicions rise. "No. I won't have a repeat of what happened with Jessica. I'm in charge, we do it my way."

"We are about six blocks away, Nickolas," Jules cut in.

"Park on the street not in the lot, that way Chris and I can get a feel for the situation."

"Nick, I really don't like this change in procedure," Flynn said, his voice rising slightly.

He cast a slashing glance at Flynn, who stared mulishly back in the mirror. "Then stay in the van. What about you, Jules? Are you in or out?"

The tech gave him an appraising look before he responded slowly. "You're the team leader, Nick. I trust your judgment."

He exhaled then nodded at Jules and followed Chris out the door when the van stopped. "Chris, stay alert. Go to the office and get her room number and a key. I'll do a quick scan."

As his brother strode off, Nickolas slowly turned in place, getting a feel for the location. He stretched his senses and reached out, studying the currents around the motel and parking lot. Somewhere to his right, Nick could feel the disturbance from the fledgling, but he bypassed it in favor of looking for more subtle signs of danger. *Robin's right. They're close. Something is out of place.* He refined his search, probing deeper. *Why can't I see them? It's like there's a blank space...* He pulled out of the trance when Chris returned and followed his brother to the woman's room; his eyes scanned the parking lot, still searching. They listened at the door. He could hear her stomping around and then a crash as she threw something against the wall.

Christoff looked at him to make sure he was ready, then he slipped the key into the knob. At his nod, Chris turned the lock and opened the door; both of them entered quickly and got the door shut before she managed to spin around to face them. At her first glance, the blood drained from her face.

"No!" she moaned. "I thought I was free." She slumped to the floor and burst into tears.

Shock rippled through him at her unexpected response. He approached her softly and rested his hand on her head then crouched down. "Shhh. It's all right. It's going to be all right," he murmured reassuringly.

"No. It's not," the woman sobbed. "I thought I had finally gotten out of that horrible place. Before, I at least had some protection. Now I'll be one of them."

Taking a stab at the meaning from her confused babbling, Nickolas asked, "Are you talking about Gabriel and his camp?"

She whimpered and nodded her head. "I wanted out, but they wouldn't let me leave. Most are military there, but I had seen too much, they said, so they wouldn't let me return back to my old life. I thought I had found a way to escape. I should have known better."

She hiccupped then continued with loathing, "A corporal I'd been friendly with offered me a ride out a couple of days ago when he went on leave. I jumped at the chance. That's how I ended up here. I just let him drive me until he got where he was going. I guess that was a mistake."

"Maybe not as much of one as you think." She looked up at him in confusion, and he brushed the tears away with his thumb. "How would you like to go to the mountains? The wild Valkyries are here hoping to get you out. At least it's a choice." Hope flared in her eyes and he smiled. "I'll take that as a yes?"

She wiped her eyes with the back of her hand and nodded. "What do you want me to do?"

He stood and held out his hand to help her to her feet. "This is a trap. What kind, I don't know yet. I want you to stay with Christoff and do whatever he tells you to. He'll make sure you get to Robin."

"Nick, I'm not leaving you undefended."

Raising his eyebrows at his brother's obstinate tone, Nick shook his head. "Give me a break, Chris. Do what I say for a change. You're no match for Gabriel."

Frustration filled Chris's eyes, and that let Nick know he would do what had been asked, though he wouldn't like it.

He pulled the door open a crack, scanning what he could see as well as doing a quick probe for trouble. That blank spot really worried him. "Chris, I still can't find them, can you?"

Christoff took Amanda's hand and they all stepped out of the room. "No, but the inside of my head feels like a bell tower with all the alarms going off in it; they're definitely here." His brother grasped Amanda's hand tighter and loosened his wings.

His own wings shivered, aching to spread and take to the air. To get out of the exposed, open parking lot they crossed. Nickolas stopped and looked around. Where were Flynn and Jules? They should be waiting. Christoff's back brushed his as they searched, and Amanda started to whimper.

Like the touch of butterfly wings, a mind brushed against his lightly, almost too lightly to notice, and Nickolas's spine went cold. He responded instinctively as he threw a physical shield up around the three of them; energy flooded him as his power shot a geyser up from his pool. The lightly shimmering barrier rippled a foot or two away from them. Just in time. Three soft puffs that were barely audible were followed immediately by three darts slamming into his shield; the sound of them falling to clatter to the asphalt of the parking lot resounded around them.

"Nice, Nicky. This wasn't on your list of abilities that I was aware of," his brother said from behind him.

"Amazing what you can discover under the right circumstances," he said. His mind was only half on the conversation. Slowly spinning around, Nick searched for the fleeting touch of dark he had felt. "I don't know what else I can do while holding the shield. When I tell you to, Chris, call Robin." There was a flash of movement out of the corner of his eye, and Nick swung to focus on it. "Here they come."

Eight uniformed men, all carrying tranquilizer rifles in their hands, swarmed out of hiding places along the perimeter of the parking lot and stalked slowly toward their bubble. Amanda stifled a shriek and started trembling so badly that his brother had to hold her up. Nick followed the direction of her panicked gaze and found the darkness.

Standing in the open doorway of the room adjacent to Amanda's was Gabriel. The Alpha wore a bemused expression on his face. He pushed away from the door jamb and walked forward, revealing a second man holding a video camera.

Gabriel stopped a few feet away from the shield and cocked his head. "You know, you shouldn't be able to do that, Nickolas. I'm surprised. I'm not often wrong. I thought you were a Seer, not a Caster." But then Gabriel looked thoughtfully into his eyes and blinked. "But then again, I'm not wrong, am I? No wonder Ian went to such great lengths to protect you."

He turned his attention to the woman and smiled. "Hello, Amanda. You did exactly as I hoped you would. I told you that you wouldn't get away from us, now didn't I?" Then he clucked his tongue. "As the saying goes, Nickolas, I've got you surrounded. You can't hold the shield forever."

"What do you think you are doing, Gabriel?" Nickolas snapped. "I'm here on official Facility business, performing a retrieval."

Laughing outright, Gabriel folded his arms. "No, I'm the one performing the retrieval, and not just Amanda, but the two of you as well."

"What are you talking about?"

Gabriel shook his head and sighed. "Oh, Nickolas. I have it all on tape. We had the room bugged. I know you were going to give her to those feral traitors. That, combined with your obvious increase in power," He waved his hand at the shield. "That gives me all the proof I need to support this move with the powers that be. It also gave me what I needed to finally take Ian down."

"We're not coming with you, Gabriel."

The Alpha looked pointedly at the soldiers surrounding them and smirked. "I don't see that you have much of a choice, Nickolas Sinclair."

"Now, Chris," Nick said. He felt the mental surge as his brother called Robin, but he didn't look away from Gabriel.

Gabriel's eyes snapped to look at Christoff in annoyance. "You too? I should have guessed you would have gone off the drugs as well. I don't want any of that."

Following his instincts again, Nickolas pushed back at Gabriel and blocked his attempt to douse Christoff's mind call. The diversion in his concentration caused his shield to start to waver, and he drew more power, slamming it into the shield before Gabriel or his men could get through.

Their gazes met as they locked power in a mental struggle to see who was stronger. Nick was barely aware of the arrival of Robin and his Flight. But the rebound on his shield from inside grabbed a portion of his attention, though he restrained the desire to look.

"Let me out, Nickolas! I need to help them!"

Gabriel's blue eyes bored into his, and he felt the power glow in his own eyes and tingle in his fingertips.

"Nickolas!"

"Amanda, get back into your room," Nickolas ordered as he dropped the shield, hoping she made it but not daring to look. He dove to the side and rolled, and Gabriel cut off a snarl. Then the hair on the back of his neck started to rise as he felt the gathering of power. He spun to face the other Alpha, ignoring the sounds of fighting as Robin's Flight battled the soldiers.

Gabriel had moved away from the center of the fighting and stood staring at him; tendrils of his blond hair lifted in a slight breeze that Nick couldn't feel. The flow of power built and shown through the other Valkyrie's eyes. Then Gabriel closed them, took a deep breath, and started to sing. The tendrils of power wrapped around Nickolas. He couldn't understand the words Gabriel sang, but it was beautiful; they drew him toward the other Alpha and he went willingly.

Slammed to the ground, Nickolas lost his breath as Robin landed on top of him and his head throbbed from the inside. "Shield, Nickolas! Damn it, put up a shield!"

Concentrating on Robin's words, he formed a crude shield around the two of them. His subconscious must have known what was needed because this shield differed from his last; it filtered sound somehow. He could still hear Gabriel's beautiful voice, but it no longer pulled him.

"He's a song weaver," Robin whispered, stunned, before he rolled off of him.

Nick rose stiffly and warily watched Gabriel sing. The Alpha had his eyes open and Nickolas could tell that he was working to match frequencies with the shield so his song could recapture him. A flash of light flared nearby, surprising Nick, but not as much as the person whose scream died quickly, and Gabriel's eyes narrowed.

"Kevin!" Robin yelled, then Nickolas felt the mental static that he was coming to associate with close telepathic communication.

A Valkyrie shot around his shield, and Gabriel was cut off midnote. Fanning his wings open, he took a step back, throwing up his own shield just as a glass ball exploded against it, sizzling across the surface in an eerie blue glow. Glaring at the Caster, Gabriel sang a note, but the Caster had thrown up his own shield.

"We've taken all of your men, Gabriel," Robin called out.

His eyes hot, Gabriel swept the parking lot. "But not me, Robin. Never me. We'll continue this at a later time, Nickolas." With his shield still protecting him, Gabriel launched into the sky.

Nickolas took a deep breath and turned to look at Robin, who clapped him on the shoulder, saying softly, "You can drop the shield now, Nick."

He pulled the power back into himself and the shield winked out of existence. Then he walked with Robin to help check the dead and injured. Christoff rose from checking the pulse of one of the attackers, and Nick caught his eye, jerking his head toward Amanda's room. His brother wiped the blood dribbling down his cheek and nodded, moving off to make sure the fledgling was all right.

"What's the count, Robin? Is everyone ok?" Nick asked. He joined the Hunter and the Caster who had thrown the ball at Gabriel.

"Mostly, we have a few bruises. Nothing major. Between using your shield and the shield from our Caster, Kevin, we were able to take down all the soldiers without anyone getting tranked. Of the soldiers, two are dead, three are injured and unconscious, and the other three are just injured."

"But they got at least one of your own team in your van, Nick," Kevin said.

Well, that would explain why they weren't here, Nick thought with surprise, then he noticed Christoff carrying Amanda out of one of the rooms. He met them and touched the blood at her temple. He sucked in a breath as the vision obscured his outward sight briefly. "Get Amanda out of here, Robin. She's only knocked out. The jerk with the camera hit her before he ran off. I'd just leave all the others if I were you. Let them explain this themselves. Chris, we need to get back to the Facility."

With a wave, they left Robin's Flight to their business and raced back to the van. He yanked the door then jumped back and raised his hands. "Whoa, Flynn, it's me. Nick."

"What the hell happened?" Flynn snapped, lowering the gun to continue holding an unconscious Jules.

"I'm not quite sure," Nickolas lied. "But we lost the fledgling to a group of feral Valkyries. We need to get back to the Facility."

Flynn gently laid Jules down and took the driver's seat. "Hang on."

He took his own seat and watched Christoff buckle Jules into the bench as the van swayed into motion. Staring at the sticky residue of blood clinging to Jules's temple, Nickolas contemplated how Gabriel's men had gotten to him in the first place.

Chapter Twenty

I guess they've won. I just can't do this anymore. Jessica sat listlessly on her bed and stared at the unfocused faraway point her tunneled vision contained. The thump of her heart, loud in her ears, slowed. Her breath passed her lips, drying their surface.

Her apathy must have been noticed, but she didn't care if they saw the downward spiral. Gabriel's visit five days ago had pushed the first pebble. And she could no longer cling to the crumbling edge. She just fell with the landslide.

She wouldn't get out of here. Nickolas had promised, but they took him too. Even Kieran. He no longer came to her.

The door to her cell opened and the cart trundled through, stopping near her full breakfast tray. She couldn't muster up the energy to eat it.

Silence echoed throughout the room.

After a moment, Ian's white lab coat swirled to a stop at her feet. She could feel him staring at the top of her head before he crouched down in front of her, waiting. It took all of her energy just to raise her eyes to meet his. Shadows gathered in the doctor's eyes as he contemplated her.

"Ian?" Jays's voice, hesitant and full of concern, shivered across her skin.

"I know, Jays, hold on." Still holding her gaze, Ian asked softly, "Jess, what's going on?"

A single tear slid down her skin; she closed her eyes to break the contact and rocked her head. Quicksand held her in its grasp; the simple act of stretching herself out on the bed for their exam took all her energy. She held her arm out, offering it to Ian. Instead of taking it, he withdrew to the far side of the room and held a whispered conversation in worried tones. Phrases reached her. Inhibitor, depression, despondency, the coma. She just let them wash by and instead let her thoughts drift through the shroud of fog that had taken over her mind.

It was soothing.

After a few moments, they came back and started the exam. Jessica tried to make herself pay attention to their requests as their gentle touches quickly took care of all the routine tests. She lay passively, drifting, as their voices floated quietly over her.

"Please stretch out your wing, Jessica. It's much too long for me to support easily myself anymore."

The muscles quivered as she held it out, and she felt Ian and Jays pass the tape measure around her wing then rotate the joints. She wished they would just be done and leave her to the silence. In the fog, all the pain and anguish no longer hurt, but Ian continued to talk to her, drawing her out of the soothing mist.

The look in his eyes let her know that he understood what he was doing, and a spark of anger flared, then died.

"I believe you've almost reached your full growth by the way," he rattled on. "Now it's just a question of exercise, building up your muscles enough for them to support you in flight. All the stretching and flapping you've done to occupy your time is a good start."

They folded her wing closed, and she held her arm out. For the first time since she had been brought in, she didn't care. The inhibitor would only help deepen the fog, so she welcomed it.

Ian crouched in front of her again.

She closed her eyes, and a slow shallow breath left her.

"Talk to me, Jess. What's happening?" Ian questioned.

She felt another tear leak out, but she didn't open her eyes.

"Come on, try," he coaxed. "This stems from Gabriel, doesn't it?"

Her eyes snapped open, and Ian trapped her gaze with his. "I won't let him take you. I promise."

She cleared her throat, but her voice still came out thin. "How can I trust that? Where's Kieran? Where's Nick?"

He stared at her, silent, and she tried to snort, but it came out as more of a strangled squeak. "Like you'll answer that. You haven't answered anything I've asked since I've arrived."

"You don't have the background for any answers to make sense. But more to the point, you don't need the knowledge right now. You have a lot of work cut out for yourself and some things can get in the way of that." He cocked his head but didn't release her gaze. "I don't like the readings I'm getting on you, Jess. You're slipping dangerously close to the edge."

"Why do you care? I'm just another fledge. I'm sure you see hundreds a year."

He nodded at Jays, who had packed up the equipment, and sent him out. She stretched out her arm more, but the younger doctor looked down and pushed the cart to the door.

"No," she gasped and rose on one arm, holding the other out.

Ian cleared his throat, and she jerked her gaze back to him. "Your systems aren't stable right now, Jess. Inhibitor would be a bad choice. And you aren't just another fledge. We've been waiting for you for a long time."

"You're nuts."

She collapsed back onto the bed and wrapped her arms around herself in an attempt to hold the fog, but Ian's conversation had tattered it to wisps.

"No, I'm not. I just have a clear picture. You want some answers? There are some I can give."

She tried not to look at him. She tried not to take the bait. But in the end, he held out longer and she couldn't resist. She raised her eyes and looked at him. A small smile flirted with the corner of his lips, and her blood started to rush through her veins. The anger finished off the fog and she growled.

"Like you pointed out, Jess, I've been doing this for a long time. And my talent makes me a past master at chess. I can counter any move you make. But my offer wasn't a ruse."

"Talent?" she said, shocked. "You don't have wings?"

He stood and shrugged out of his lab coat then pulled the hem of his shirt up to his shoulders. Small vestigial wings about the size of her hand rested flat against his back.

"But..."

He let his shirt drop and pulled his coat back up then leaned against the opposite wall, crossing his arms. "Care for a history lesson?"

She slowly sat up, pulling her knees to her chest. The mystery was enough to obliterate the last vestiges of fog, and she nodded her head.

"Twenty-five years ago, a private research group attempted to access dormant genetic traits in humans. They wanted to enhance sight, hearing, smell and reflexes by re-opening abilities that our normal evolution had deemed unnecessary. My wife and I led a team that had worked on research designed to help those with physical handicaps. We were manipulating their genetic structure in an attempt to give them back their lost senses. The other team took our research and twisted it. They locked it into a virus to act as a carrier and then they administered it.

"We knew nothing about the experiment until the twenty people in the test group started to react and they called Molly and me in to try and help. All of those injected went insane it appeared. Five didn't survive the first week. Then the rest started to grow wings.

"Of course they didn't tell us anything useful. So we lost another ten before the end of their changes, thanks to the lack of information. After the last five stabilized, we discovered the virus had gotten loose. My group started to show signs of changing, and we were taken into custody. The powers running the experiment felt they had lost control. That's when the military got involved. They came in with isolation equipment and attempted to contain the spread. At that point, Fredrick's group decided to try and stop what they had started. So they reengineered the virus and hoped it would halt the change once it had started in an individual. We were no longer people, but experiments. Out of all of the doctors in my group, I was the only one to survive. And that was barely. But they couldn't stop the second virus any more than they could the first, so now my life hangs by a thread they control. As long as I do what they say, I'm supplied with a different type of inhibitor that keeps the second virus suspended in my system. I need two shots a day of it. Otherwise, I'll follow my wife.

"The sad part is it was already too late. My son, Marcus, and his wife led the next group of doctors; they were brought in to care for us during our isolation. When their group started to change, Fredrick realized they had failed. At that point, thankfully, I was considered recovered as much as I would be and got myself put back on active status. I took over their care and was able to allow Marcus and Bethany and the rest of their team the opportunity to be the first to change in a more natural way. I'm pleased to say we didn't lose any from that group.

"But at that point, word had gotten out and people were starting to get scared. So far, the virus had been contained within a small group of people who had had prolonged, direct contact with the changing individuals, but then the first unrelated fledgling showed up. He was still nearby, within the Facility in fact, but he had not had any contact with the changelings. Directly at least. It turned out that he was watching Marcus's dog. And that was how we discovered that it could be transferred by blood. Fleas from his dog carried the virus and it started spreading. Everything was fumigated of course, and the scientists confiscated Marcus's dog and killed it for testing; let me tell you, that didn't endear them to Marcus, but of course by then it was too late. There's no way to completely eradicate all fleas, and we soon discovered that mosquitoes could also carry it.

"The number of fledglings appearing has slowly increased as the geographic circle of exposure grows. Someone who has been around the fledged Valkyries has a much higher chance of changing, themselves, but it's not necessary anymore. They just need to be bitten by an infected mosquito or flea. Geographically, fleas and mosquitoes can only travel so far on their own, so it takes some time for them to pass it a distance. For years now, we have seen the majority of cases coming from the family and friends of people who have worked for the Facility. The unrelated cases have all been close to here or to the homes of those who had been exposed. But the mutating virus is starting to spread faster. Now it is out in the general public, and people are carrying it farther away; it won't be long before we hear about a new fledgling appearing in a different state or even a different country. It also doesn't help that since the virus has escaped, it has changed. The incubation period has become extremely variable, some people who are exposed start to change within days while others, like you, were exposed years ago and have probably been infecting people the whole time."

"There's no way to tell when you're carrying it?" she asked.

"Not that we have been able to find yet. Back in the beginning, people didn't know how to treat us. How different our mental makeup really is from an unchanged human. So when fledglings started popping up, they were mishandled, resulting in people getting hurt and killed on both sides. So the measures to follow, when taking someone who has started to undergo the change, were drawn up and implemented. While a lot of the procedures the Facility follows are not necessary for the benefit of the fledgling, they do benefit their research. Not very nice for the individual, maybe, but the truth of the matter is that a fledgling must have help, or they will die."

"How does Aurora fit into that? What I've experienced here, and seen there…. It's like night and day." Her thoughts turned inward. Memories from her eight-year-old self crawled into the light. Her father's arms wrapped tightly about her as they flew through the night. Marcus or another Valkyrie holding her brother. Sitting on a rock in the grass while Marcus made magic with light to amuse her. Her mother scolding her before she could actually do the misdeed she was about to try.

"Life in Aurora is different." Ian sighed. "I wish I could give that to you, but it's just not possible here. What do you remember?"

"I remember watching the Hunters fight each other. It always seemed so scary, but they laughed like they were having fun. Marcus used to do these amazing things where light would come out of his hands, then he would do things with it. Usually to keep us distracted. And Mom knew things. Whether it was something Robin or I was going to do, or bigger things than children misbehaving." She hugged her knees tighter and looked across the room.

"So you have some rudimentary knowledge of the different castes and talents."

"Castes and talents?"

"You used the term Hunter, which is the most common caste, the one the general populace knows to refer to a Valkyrie by. But there is a small percentage of Valkyries that belong to different castes. Marcus is an example of one; he is a light weaver, which is a Caster talent; and your mother was a precog, which is in the Seer caste. There are several different talents in each of the two castes. But a general dividing line for determining which belongs where is in how a talent is used or manifested. Most Seer abilities reside solely within the person using the ability, in other words, nobody sees a physical manifestation. That would be talents like precognitive dreams or visions, clairvoyance and clairaudience, all of which have subsets within them as well. Then there is empathy. Empathy falls into a category of its own. It can be either receptive or projective. Depending on the type, one is a Seer and the other a Caster. So it forms the middle of the line when placing talents on the scale. Now Caster abilities are projective talents. They would include things like light weaving, telekinesis, teleportation, and pyrokinesis, among several other talents.

"That's three castes. And until recently we thought that was all there was. But your arrival changed that. The data collected from your tests and observations have proved beyond a doubt that you are in a completely different caste."

"Excuse me?" Her legs slid out to plop on the bed. She shook her head then cleared her throat. "What do you mean?"

"Earlier you asked why you mattered. Well this is why. Your body has changed in a new way. You are the first female to emerge with an intact operational reproductive tract. You are a Breeder. You have both Seer and Caster abilities, but you aren't either one. You are more."

"A what?" she squeaked.

He rubbed his fist against his mouth and coughed. She narrowed her eyes at him, daring him to laugh.

"Let me know if you come up with a better name for the caste, I guess," he said. "I have a theory that the reason the change is so hard for someone in your caste is because of how much you need to change inside, both physically and mentally, compared to the others. Then it's compounded by your extremely dominant nature. Your caste is born to be the leaders of the species."

"After telling me I don't need to know things, why the hell are you telling me this?" She got up and started to pace. "Wait a minute. If I'm the first, then how do you know that the change would be hard?"

"I said first female."

She froze midstep. After a deep breath, she looked over her shoulder at him. "Who?"

"Nick." He paused and his eyes flicked away. "And Gabriel."

She felt the blood drain from her face, and she groped for the cot. "This is my life. I'll make my own decisions. Not let some hormone-driven body system force me into this."

"You can try," Ian murmured.

"Ian." Jays's voice blasted from the ceiling. "You need to come out here right now. Jack's on the phone."

Her head snapped to look at the camera in the ceiling, then she jerked back to Ian.

The doctor's face had turned expressionless. "We'll finish this later," he said and swiped his card. The door shut with a loud click behind him.

Ian rushed over to the island where Jays held out a receiver for him. He took it in dread. "Jack?"

The clipped voice on the other end of the line spilled out, confirming his fears. "I don't have long, Ian. And yes, I know I'm screwed. But I didn't have a choice. Well, not if I wanted to keep any of you safe. They've sent Gabriel out. Something big is going down. I don't know the details, but I heard enough to know he's coming for you."

"Can you get out of there, Jack? Right now? Now that you've called me on an unsecure line, they'll be on you in no time."

"There's nowhere for me to go, Ian. I knew that when I made the call. Just get them out."

Click.

"Jack!"

The steady buzz of the dial tone sounded in Ian's ear and he slowly hung up the phone. At the question in Jays's eyes, Ian shook his head.

Jays slammed his fist into the wall and exclaimed, "Now what? What do we do for him?"

He narrowed his eyes at Jays's uncharacteristic display of aggression and replied quietly, "There's nothing we *can* do. He made his decision when he called. Get Nickolas in here. We need to start the evacuation. We can't let Jack's sacrifice go to waste. Gabriel is coming for Nick and Jessica."

Jays kicked the exam cart over then stormed around the room.

He reached out mentally and tried to soothe his young protégé. "Jays, I need you to get Nickolas for me. Jays. Focus."

The young doctor took several deep breaths as he calmed himself down before he said through clenched teeth, "Fine. I'll go find him." Then he stalked out of the Hub.

Could the timing be any worse? Ian thought as he opened one of the locked drawers in the file cabinets. He pulled out a folder and set it on top of the cabinet then fished around in the back of the drawer before he pulled out a small handful of flash drives. After setting them on the desks in the island, he proceeded to start emptying the file drawers and stacking the contents haphazardly.

Heavy footsteps heralded Donald arriving on the run.

"Jays said there was an emergency?" the Hunter inquired as he caught his breath.

"Where's Nick?" Ian snapped. "I sent for him."

"Where's..." Donald looked at him, confused. "He and Chris are gone still. They haven't gotten back from the recovery in Bellingham yet."

Folders slipped from his fingers as he twisted to face the Hunter. "No orders came from me. When did they leave?"

"About breakfast time, an hour or so ago."

"Damn. They're already making their move. We need to evacuate. I don't know if Kratz is part of what's going on, so don't trust anyone."

"Are you ready to tell us where we're going now?"

"Sorry, Donald. I'd hoped we wouldn't have to do this yet. The less people who know, the less chance of having the knowledge ripped from you. The safety of too many people is in the balance." He took a map from one of the file drawers and shook it out across the island. Donald moved to stand beside him as he smoothed his hands over the paper, taking out the wrinkles. "We need to alter course. My plans have been compromised and the safe house and guides I had set up for you are no longer safe."

He traced his finger along the map. "We can't have too many in the air at once. You'll need to restructure the Flights since Chris isn't here, and your Second is out of commission at the moment. Get one Wing out at a time, maybe fifteen- to twenty-minute intervals. That shouldn't look too suspicious. Hopefully it'll just be assumed that it's the return of the previous group, if they're seen at all. Follow the slough until you get to the river. Then follow the Snohomish River until it meets the Sky. Then take the Skykomish to here."

He picked up a red marker and circled a section. "This will work for a rendezvous point. It's a heavily wooded park on the river on the eastern edge of the city of Monroe. Regroup there. Stay below treetop height as you follow the water."

"How long do we have?"

"Not as long as we would want. I have files and some small equipment you will need to transport out. After that, take whatever personal effects there's room for. I'm afraid a lot will need to be abandoned. Let's get the first Flight in the air within the hour, if possible. But have everyone ready to scramble at a moment's notice."

"What about the fledglings?"

"If Jessica can go out in the third group, there will be a dozen or so people on hand to help control her. David can go at any time; I'll leave that up to you. Now, Jays is going to be more difficult."

"What do you mean?" the Hunter asked.

"Jays just entered the second stage today."

Donald dropped his chin to his chest and shook his head, muttering obscenities under his breath before looking back up. "You're right, that makes things more difficult. If you think he's becoming too erratic, let me know, and we'll take him in the next run. Do you think we should sedate Jessica and or Jays for the ride in the nets? If they struggle, it might cause the bearers trouble."

"I'll get you something. But don't use it unless you have to. Jessica's drug responses are too unpredictable. I've got a prepaid phone in my office to give you. Use it after everyone has reached the rendezvous. Dustin will be able to help get you to Aurora."

The door to the Hub slammed open and Jays stalked up to him and Donald. "When I found out where Nick and Chris went, I tried to get a hold of Jules, but we were cut short for some reason. I was able to tell him to abort, but as he was starting to reply, the connection went dead. I couldn't raise him again. What is going on out there, Ian?"

"I don't know. There're too many new pieces appearing. The matrix alters almost faster than I can keep up with. But some things are crystal clear, and our time here is done. Donald, make sure that everyone brings their pills. You don't need the added complication of forty-five Valkyries all coming off of the drugs at the same time. You're already going to have trouble with Kieran, Sara, and Ronny during the trip."

Growling, Donald shook his wings out and Ian gave him a sympathetic smile, then picked up a flash drive.

"Take these. Pick the most experienced computer users and have them quietly go around and upload the virus these contain. I want every computer wiped, including personal ones. Don't miss a single terminal in the Valkyrie section."

"Ok." Donald said.

Ian turned to his protégé. "Jays, you know which files and disks I want taken out of here. Please start gathering them up so the teams can each take what they can." Ian stretched before he moved over to the computer station. "I'm going to start wiping everything I can. Keep me informed as you both progress."

"Yes, sir," snapped both men.

Jessica paced her cell and fumed. *It has to have been at least two hours already. What's going on? I can sense something isn't right since my brain isn't so fogged up.*

Inside her, energy spiked and dropped, leaving her giddy one moment and exhausted the next. The pressure felt like it wanted to split her skin. She rubbed between her eyes.

The remembered panic underneath Jays's voice when he called Ian out left her worried. Her mind tumbled about, looking for why. Before her speculation could go too far, the door bolts disengaged.

Ian stepped through and beckoned her over. Shock nearly left her rooted to the spot. He hadn't pulled the door shut. She could glimpse through the opening into the busyness taking place in the Hub. With a jerk, she stepped forward and stopped in front of him, her eyes darting excited glances through the crack.

He reached out and cupped her chin to raise her gaze to his. "It's time we said good-bye. Things have happened.... It's no longer safe for you here. For any of you here. I just wish..."

Sadness crossed his eyes, but he hid it fast. "If you see Nicky...please tell him...I'm sorry."

He brushed a kiss across her forehead then reached down and took her hand to pull her from the room. After the weeks of silence in her cell, the noise in the Hub deafened her ears. She winced away, but Ian led her to a small group waiting for her. Relief whispered through her when she saw Kieran, but it faded fast after she got a good look at him. Pain lines etched his face and his body looked stiff enough to shatter if someone hit him.

Jays ignored her as he stuffed papers and folders into sacks then dumped them into a pile from which a steady stream of Valkyries loaded their arms. The doors to the hall swung back and forth as people entered and exited.

"Jess," Ian's voice drew her attention back to those in front of her. "Here, put these on."

He handed her a pile of cloth. When she shook it out, she found a pair of thick fleece pants and a matching hoodie, though the hoodie she just twisted around trying to figure out how the modified garment worked. Kieran took it from her and pulled the Velcro strips that held the split neck together, then pulled it up under her wings and her arms through it. He fastened the Velcro under her hair.

Ian gave her a sad smile. "Kieran and Aidan will take you to Donald; he's staging the evac. Please. Just for once, do as you're told?"

He brushed the tangles away from her face, then turned his back and started typing on the keyboards scattered on the desks of the island.

"Let's go, Jess," Kieran said, his voice hoarse, and she turned a concerned eye on him.

"What's wrong?"

He shook his head. Grabbing her hand, he started to tow her across the room. "Come on, Aidan."

The kid fell in behind her and she glanced over her shoulder while she pulled against Kieran. He didn't let up and dragged her through the doors someone held open for them. "Slow down, Kier."

"No. You need to get out of here."

They turned down a hall, leaving the stream of packing Valkyries. She started to dig in her heels more, but the teenager behind her just pushed between her wings and she stumbled a step. She whipped a look over her shoulder and a growl escaped. He grinned.

"Where's Nick?" she asked.

Kieran's fingers flexed against her wrist before he answered. "We don't know. He and Chris were lured away this morning."

Pain stabbed her, and then she remembered Ian's words. The unnatural strength of her fixation now had a reason. *I will not be some broodmare decided by hormones and fate.* She planted her feet again and jerked her arm, but all that did was stretch her shoulder then get her another shove between the wings.

"What is wrong with you, Kieran? You feel strange."

"You should try it from the inside," he muttered.

Her energy spiked again and she hissed. Each time a wave washed through her, she felt more of the inhibitor that remained in her system dissipate. Then she noticed Kieran's energy. Almost like looking into a mirror.

"Where are we going?" She tugged another time.

Aidan's voice, the deepness surprising for one so young, resonated behind her. "There's a garden outside where we can gather without too much notice. We've been staging there."

"No, not where are we going this minute, but where are we escaping to?"

"We're going somewhere called Aurora," Kieran said.

She planted her heels and succeeded in forcing them to stop for a second. Kieran stumbled back a step and Aidan ran into her back.

"That's what I thought." She tried to shake off Kieran's hand. Aidan planted both of his on her shoulders. *It's not fair that someone so young should be taller than me.* "I'll not go to Marcus willingly."

Aidan propelled her forward. Kieran still had her arm, but he'd sucked in a breath and used his free hand to press his eyes as they struggled down the corridor. Something surged around him and hot emotion licked at her; she gasped and her eyesight faded.

"Damn it, Kieran, what the hell is wrong with you?"

"Nothing time won't heal. At least it isn't anywhere near as bad as what Nick went through," he muttered. "Look, Jessica, I can feel how badly you don't want to go to this place, but it's the only safety we have."

Her bare feet stuttered on the tiles as they dragged her through a door. The weak December sunshine pierced her eyes as she found herself outside for the first time in almost two months. The brisk air filled her lungs with the promise of freedom. She quit resisting and tested Kieran's barriers with her mind and found them erratic as energy surged around him.

"Kieran, please let me go," she said calmly.

"Are you kidding me?"

She winced as they pulled her onto a gravel path. Aiden noticed because she suddenly found herself scooped up into his arms. She stiffened in response.

"Put. Me. Down."

The snotty teen had the gall to chuckle.

"I'll not ask nicely a second time."

He pulled her closer to his chest. She took a deep breath and felt her power swell. Kieran spun on the path to face them and she lashed out; a band of power wrapped around Aidan's ankles and he fell. She kicked free of him and rolled on the gravel. Kieran grabbed a fistful of her hair, then recaptured her wrist.

"Are you all right?" he asked her as he hauled her to her feet.

"I won't go without a fight, Kieran. Marcus has taken every member of my family." Another rope of light whipped around Kieran's legs and she tried to push free, but he held on and they both toppled to the ground. Aidan grabbed her ankle.

"I don't want to hurt you, Kieran. I really don't. Let me go."

"Where do you think you're going to go?" he asked calmly.

She twisted, trying to break away, but his hand completely encircled her wrist and she couldn't get the leverage. "I'm not going to Aurora. Gabriel will be following all of you assuming that I will be with you. So in some respects, I'll be safer."

"You're not thinking straight, Jessica. You haven't finished the change yet. There's a point where you must have aid, or you will die. Trust me. You need us. Don't do this." His gold-flecked eyes bored into hers, trying to make her listen.

"Jessica," Aidan said. "We won't let you go. You have to know that. Nickolas would kill us."

"Don't even get me started on him. I've made my decision. Now let go."

Kieran shook his head, refusing. "Let us up, Jess."

Frustrated, and having tried everything she could think of to get him to let her go, she cursed, "Fine, it's on your own head."

And she tapped into the power welling up inside of her. She pressed through his fluctuating barriers, invading his mind. He gasped in pain but still tried to maintain his grip, so she pushed harder, overwhelming his primitive hold to send his emerging gift out of control.

He shook and finally let go of her to clap his hands over his ears. She immediately turned her attention to Aidan, his expression half feral. His legs still bound, he had wormed his way closer and clamped his other hand on her ankles as well. His teeth tips shown as he snarled softly at her.

"Let me go," she snarled back.

"No."

She flung her hand out at him and a strand of light snapped around his throat and she pulled. His face turned red but he continued to fight to hold her. "I don't want to hurt you. Please let me go."

His fingers convulsed and she yanked her legs out of his reach, immediately releasing the wrap around his neck. A huge gasp filled the air. She coiled a strand around the rest of his body so he couldn't get up and follow her. Then she turned to Kieran, who lay in a fetal position with his hands clasping his ears, and did the same.

Only then did she get close enough to them to search their pockets and take what little money she found. Kieran opened pain-filled eyes, his breathing ragged as blood flowed from his nose. "You know, Jessica, we'll never let you go any more than Gabriel will."

She sighed then mumbled, "I'm not a possession, Kieran."

"Of course not. But you are a baby. An infant newly born into this world, knowing nothing of the dangers out there, needing protection and care until you can care for the rest of us."

Uncomfortable with the intensity of his statement, she backed away while they watched her. She shook her head to deny that truth and the responsibility that went with it. "No."

Both their gazes bored into her.

"I don't believe in it. I make my own decisions. Not destiny, or hormones, or fate, or...or..." She spun away from them and ran. The gravel dug into her soles and she embraced the physical pain. It overrode the mental.

She regained control after her moment of panic and slowed so she could keep watch for the others and avoid bursting straight into their gathering.

She made it through the gardens and down to the river's edge, where she rocked from foot to foot as she stared out over the water. The cold wet mud squelched between her toes, and she shivered at the thought of how cold the water must be. She threw a glance over her shoulder.

I don't know how long the energy holding them will last. Is there another choice?

She shivered in the damp air. The sunlight brightened the world but did nothing to heat it. Then the memory of Ian's explanation of her caste firmed her resolve and she stripped off her new fleece garments. Rolling them up as tight as she could, she tied them with some long grass so they wouldn't unravel, then waded out into the smooth, frigid water.

She held the bundle overhead and struck out for the far side with one arm, thanking her lucky stars that the channel was calm and narrow. The added difficulty of wings, and how to maneuver them in the water, ate up more of her time and energy than made her happy.

She angled for a large overhanging growth of willows planted at the top of the steep embankment. Their leafless whips undulated in the slow current of the river. Her teeth chattering, she kicked hard and surged up to grasp a strong branch, keeping her bundle up and mostly dry. Then transferring the cloth to her mouth, she pulled hand over hand, climbing the whip like a rope. Muscles quivering, she swung as close as she could and dropped into the sparse grass beneath the trees at the top of the bank.

That should help hide my exit. She sat spraddle-legged, trying to catch her breath. *No tracks up the bank. That'll keep the Hunter's busy. Not if it was Nick...* She pushed that thought away along with the memory of her tracking him in the Facility.

Shaking from the cold and exertion, she stripped off the scraps of cloth that had served as her clothing in the Hub and pulled on the mostly dry fleece. *Now what?* She wrung out the shorts and halter before wadding them up. *I need a plan. Actually, Kieran's right, I need help. Just not their help. Who?*

She picked her way across the grassy backyard of the old house. *May? I need a phone.* After slinking around the structure and looking in as many windows as she could, she climbed the steps to the back porch. She tried the door and wasn't surprised to find it locked. She wrapped her hand in the wet shorts and broke one of the small panes of glass in the door. Unfortunately, her arm slipped when she reached through to unlock it, and she sliced her wrist on a piece of the jagged glass. She gasped. The burning pain traveled to her fingertips and up past her elbow.

She crept into what she hoped was an empty house. Blood slid down her hand. She grabbed a kitchen towel as she passed through and wrapped it around her wrist. The old farmhouse didn't prove too large and thankfully the residents appeared to be gone, at work she assumed.

She found a phone in the living room and dialed her home number. The wall clock ticked, four thirty. No wonder the light had started to fade. She chewed her lip as the rings continued. Then a breathless voice picked up.

"Hello."

Jessica closed her eyes in relief. "May?"

"Yes?" The voice turned clipped. "Who is this? This number is private."

"May, it's me. Jess."

"Jessica?"

"Yes. I need your help."

♦ ♦ ♦

What the hell's going on around here, Chris? Nickolas waded his way through the tide of Valkyries that flowed from the Hub.

Something to do with today?

Nickolas pushed the doors into the Hub open then stopped dead. His head rose and he sniffed the air. Christoff growled and shoved by him and Nick snarled back. Jessica's scent floated on the air currents. He scanned the room. Chris's head lifted, the knowledge filling his eyes as he turned back to him.

She's unmuzzled. Where is she?

That's what I'd like to know, Chris.

Both of you get over here.

He and his brother swiveled to face Ian across the busy room. The doctor had his back to them, bent over, typing at one of the keyboards. He didn't bother looking up at them. He twisted to the next keyboard and continued whatever he was up to. Jays carried an armload of medical supplies from the lockers in the treatment alcove and stuffed them haphazardly into a sack, then returned for more. Nick raised an eyebrow at the looting, and he and Chris crossed the distance to Ian.

"What happened?" Ian asked, though he didn't look up from his flying fingers. "I'm glad you two made it out of that trap."

"How'd you know we walked into a trap?"

"Well, maybe because I didn't send you on a recovery, Nicky. Get a clue." Ian paused and glanced up at him; the cold rage suppressed in his eyes made Nick shiver. "I have half the clan evacuated. Jessica went out in the last run. There's two or three more Wings left to go. I need details."

"Flynn caught us at breakfast and told us you gave him the orders for the recovery. It seemed a little rushed, but after this morning…. Well, I figured we really didn't need to run into each other so soon."

Ian turned away, but not fast enough to hide the flash of pain in his eyes.

"If Robin hadn't been in the area, Gabriel would have taken us. As it was, with Robin's help, we got the fledgling out and managed to take out all of Gabriel's men, leaving him no choice but to fly off. They got Jules somehow though. He's over in the soldier's infirmary right now. They say he'll be ok. Maybe a concussion but that's it."

"So it was Flynn."

"Looks like."

"Damn it. I hope Dustin hasn't been compromised, but if Robin and his Flight were out..." Ian muttered. A crash resounded from the treatment area.

All heads swiveled. Jays swept another tray of instruments to the floor then grabbed the hair at his temple, breathing hard. After a moment, he groaned but returned to the job of packing up whatever supplies could transport easily.

Nick turned back to Ian. "Well, that complicates matters."

Ian sighed. "Donald already knows. He's going downhill fast. He'll need to go out in the next run, I think. Speaking of, here's the route to the rendezvous."

Before he could take the paper, an undisciplined surge of raw empathy blasted him, physically knocking him back a step. His eyes snapped a look at his brother, then to Ian before he stated quietly, "That was Kieran, Ian."

The doctor rubbed his temples from the blast and nodded. "Seems he possesses both receptive and projective empathy. I knew about the receptive, this is the first sign of the projective."

Anger and fear surged ahead of Kieran. Weeping started in the opposite corner of the room and Nick saw a couple of the newer Hunters curled up in balls on the floor, while a third held himself rigid and looked like he wanted to kill something.

The doors shoved open and Aidan helped a hunched-over Kieran in. The energy waves pouring off of him surged and pounded into the occupants of the room. His head throbbing, Nickolas imposed a shield on Kieran, cutting off the flow of emotion and enabling the rest of them to breathe easier again.

Kieran raised his head with a sigh of relief; dried blood streaked his face. "She smashed my shield, Nick."

The steely strength in Aidan's eyes as he lowered the fledging empath into a chair impressed Nick. The fact that the teen could withstand Kieran's leakage and still help him here proved Dev's arguments. He would need to sit down and discuss a few things with the kid before he got the crap kicked out of him for insolence.

Kieran accepted the damp towel Christoff handed him and started to wipe the blood away, muttering, "Of all the stupid, dumb, completely idiotic things for her to have done."

"I take it she got away?" Ian asked.

"Gloriously," Aidan replied.

Kieran threw the towel across the room when he was finished. He had nothing worse than a bloody nose. "She tied us up somehow. That's the closest way I can describe what she did. Then she blasted me, taking down my shields when I wouldn't let go of her arm. I could feel the emotions of everyone around and the flood made it so I couldn't tell what came from me, and what wasn't. What little control I had gained over my talent went out the window. Gods my head hurts."

Aidan cleared his throat. "She took off toward the slough. It took a bit before the energy she left us wrapped in dissipated enough to get free."

"She's a light weaver." Ian sighed. "How long were you down for?"

"Maybe half an hour."

Nick met Ian's concerned gaze. "Chris and I should go after her. We shouldn't take anyone away from the evacuation."

"Agreed." Ian pressed the folded map into his hands. "Catch up as soon as you get her."

Ian held his gaze, clouds of emotion scudded by, but the doctor didn't speak. He shoved the paper into the cargo pocket of his pants with a hand that shook, unwilling to examine anything in detail at the moment. He turned to Chris. "Get the two of us supplies. I'll meet you in the garden."

He turned and left the Hub. With each step, the predatory instinct he'd kept quiescent, waiting for Jessica to finish her change, surged and grew, stretching in anticipation for the hunt.

The need to see her had been a painful ache for weeks. One barely contained. He pushed through the exit and treaded the path, using his senses to locate the spot where Kieran was downed. The scuffs in the gravel reflected the remains of energy floating in the atmosphere. His mind quested out, reading the power, translating it into pictures in his head so he saw a progression of still photographs, saw what happened, which direction she went.

His brother's energy swirled and sent the currents eddying, distorting his pictures. He opened his eyes to Chris's, the worry obvious.

"Any luck?"

"Aidan was right, she headed to the water." He accepted the pile of gear Chris handed him and stuffed his numerous pockets full. "She's thinking awfully clearheaded for a fledge."

"And this surprises you? Besides, she's close to the coma, you know that."

He growled. "No one told her, did they? She wouldn't have run then."

"You know the policy is not to mention it. And do you really think that would have stopped her?"

He didn't dignify that with an answer. They strode down the path, following the route he saw in his mind and located the spot of bank to confirm she had indeed gone into the water.

With an oath, he leapt into the air, Christoff following him, and they started to track her.

Chapter Twenty-one

"Sweeting, what are you doing?"

Jessica curled her fingers in the phone cord. The sound of May's voice calmed her. "I need your help. Can you come get me?"

"Where are you? I suspect you're not where you should be."

That caused her to pause in her hunt through the papers scattered on the table for an envelope. She cleared her throat.

"Jessica? Where are you?"

"Where do you think I am?"

A sigh reached across the distance. "I know where you should be. And I know Ian wouldn't allow you use of the phone. Not yet. And certainly not to get picked up. What's happened?"

Shock rippled through her.

"Jessica Emily Reuther, answer my question."

After years of obeying that voice, the words tumbled out. "I don't know. Ian said he's evacuating all the Valkyries. He pulled me out of my cell and tried to send me to Aurora."

"So you left. Doesn't surprise me." Another sigh. "You don't need me, Jess, you need to go back to the others. Where's Nickolas?"

"I have no idea," she snapped, annoyed. "And I don't really care."

"That's not what I heard."

"What did you hear?" She growled then continued. "Does. Not. Matter. Not after what Ian told me. What I may have felt isn't real anyway."

"Don't be too sure of that, sweeting."

She rubbed her eyes, her anger suddenly threatened by tears. "You won't help me either, will you?"

"Of course I will. Your best interests have always been my number one priority. Where are you?"

She read off the address from the envelope she found then hung up.

I don't trust this. For the first time in her life, she felt heartbreakingly alone. She rubbed the back of her hand across her eyes then got to work. First she washed out her cut and tied a new bandage around it. The gauze discolored quickly. The bedroom offered up a pair of Birkenstocks in a size too big, but with two pairs of socks on, she could make due. Her feet shod and warming, she started to gather supplies. A wool blanket, rolled and secured with a belt, and a ladies London fog trench that did an acceptable job of covering her wings and keeping her warm. Then she moved to the kitchen. Her power surged and she pressed her wrist to her chest. After a deep breath, she started ransacking the cupboards. She threw anything edible that she could transport into a couple of bags, then she stopped and looked around. The déjà vu left her reeling.

Pushing it, and her suddenly pulsing power, out of her mind, she walked out the back door.

Chris trimmed his left wing and banked slightly to shadow his brother. Nickolas followed a trail only he could see. He angled up and skimmed the face of the willows across the slough and rose above them.

Are you sure she left the water here, Nick? I don't see any sign on the bank.

Why would she leave any? Just scale the willows.

You think she's capable of that?

Nick tipped his head and stared at him. The power glowing in his brother's eyes sent an uneasy shiver through his body until he looked away.

I'm sure she's in this house, Nickolas said as he gestured to the farmhouse on the other side of the willows.

Right. I'll land and get the net out. He touched down in the grass. Nick landed on the roof. He had just started to unravel the mesh when he heard the back door open.

Jessica stepped onto the porch. She froze when she spotted him in the grass.

"It's over, Jessica," he said.

Light flashed in her eyes. "Not yet, it's not."

She stepped off the porch and side-stepped away from the building, being careful not to turn her back on him. He smelled blood and stiffened. Her head tipped as she continued to move, allowing her a view of Nickolas on the roof. He crouched like a gargoyle, as still as stone, only the tendrils of his hair billowing around him to prove otherwise.

Chris swallowed. The air was still.

Jessica set the bags she carried down on the path, and his gaze shot to the red-soaked bandage on her wrist. They continued a slow dance as she maneuvered around them and the structures. He kept pace.

"I'll not go back. I refuse to go to Aurora."

"I don't know anything about the place, Jess." He shifted again; his gaze darted to Nick when he dropped to the grass with a soft thud. "Other than it's where Ian thinks we'll be safe."

She growled, her gaze pinned to Nick, and Chris's mouth went dry when he saw the power gleaming out of her eyes. Her hair swirled.

"Jessica." He swallowed as the power in the atmosphere hummed. He started again. "Jess, you're not through the change yet. You still need people to watch over you. Provide for you."

She shrugged the strap that tied a blanket into a roll from her shoulder and dropped it to the ground. Her steps took her farther away from the buildings, into the open space of the backyard. She still kept her attention on Nickolas.

I have my zip ties ready. It doesn't look like you'll have trouble keeping her focus, Nick. Just get her turned some so I can get closer to her. Nick?

Chris dared a glance at his brother and almost groaned. The feral quality in his movements matched those emerging from Jessica.

Nick.

His brother cast him a look out of the corner of his eye before returning his focus to Jessica.

Damn it, Nicky, we don't have time for this. Get it under control.

Chris tried to move closer, but she readjusted to keep them both where she could see them.

"So, Ian told me a few things today," Jessica said.

He shifted so she remained bracketed between him and Nick. Nick's wings flexed restlessly.

"Funny that. I learned a few things this morning too. I wonder if they're the same." Nick's voice came out rough, like it took all his will power to rise through the feral.

If the sun hadn't already sunk behind the house, Chris would have sworn that its light gilded a halo around Jessica. "Nickolas?" he asked uncertainly.

His brother ignored him and stalked Jessica.

"Shit," he muttered under his breath when he saw the same haze had grown around Nick, and he remembered the last time he'd seen it.

Jessica shrugged the raincoat off her shoulders and let it slip down her arms to puddle on the ground. She walked over it without noticing and stretched her wings. Nick froze at the sight, but Chris felt the power around him surge and start to pulse between the two of them.

"*My* life, Nick. I want to make my own choices, not let them be made for me."

"Who says you haven't chosen?"

"It doesn't feel like it."

"No, it doesn't. But answer me this? Did your power respond to Gabriel? Or anyone else?"

She stumbled a step and glared at Nick.

"Nick?" he whispered. "Remember what Ian said?"

Both of them ignored him now. Jessica focused solely on his brother. But the ability to get behind her still didn't present itself. The two circled the yard.

"I never agreed to be a broodmare," she snapped.

Nick flapped his wings then folded them with a snap. "We know nothing about it, Jess. And who said I want to be a stud? Studs are kept confined in a small stall, then used, and after a time, gelded. You think I like that picture? At least broodmares are well cared for. But really, we know nothing about what is happening. Just that we can't seem to stop it. I can't deny that I like you, that I admire your strength and mind. Is that enough for my subconscious to make a choice? We can make this be what we want. You're strong enough for that, aren't you?" he challenged.

She looked uncertain. The glow intensified and her hair lifted around her in a nimbus. She looked over her shoulder. "I just want to go home, Nick."

"None of us have a home. But we can make one." He took a step toward her.

Her wings moved restlessly and she looked back at him. "Only if you catch me."

During the conversation, she had worked her way close to the edge of the bank near a break in the willows. She spun and bolted, and before he could realize her intention, she dove off the bank in a graceful arc.

Nickolas snarled next to him and shot after her. Chris didn't have his feral instincts riding the surface, so her fleeing didn't trigger his chase reflex like Nick's. So he stared, dumbfounded, as she arced through the shadows of the trunks then snapped her wings out to glide the surface of the twilit water.

"Holy fuck," he breathed. "She shouldn't be able to do that yet."

Nick's shadow flashed several wing lengths behind. He shook some sense into himself, then ran at the bank and dove off after the two of them.

Jessica had already angled up and climbed. Her laughter rang back to him as he pushed himself to catch up. He knew she wouldn't have the strength or stamina to stay in the air long. Nick had dropped into the standard escort position below and a bit behind the probationary flier. As soon as he caught up, Nick gave the escort position up and immediately shot in front of her, attempting to herd her around and lower. For a maiden flight, she turned out to have a strong intuitive grasp of movement in the air. She slithered and slipped around every maneuver his brother put into play to force her where they wanted. The acrobatic flying took a toll on her unused wing muscles. With a critical eye, he watched the strain set in.

We need to get her down. She's going to damage her muscles at this rate, he sent to Nick, then he broad sent so both could hear, *Jessica, you must land. Before your wings give out.*

Her response was to fold her wings and dive under Nickolas then angle back up.

Nick's snarl whipped by on the wind and his brother showed his aerial skill as the two danced around one another. He attempted to remain close under them as he watched her wings falter. But the glow continued to grow brighter around each of them, making it difficult to judge when her wings would give out.

Jessica, please land. You're going to permanently damage your flight muscles, Chris pleaded.

I'll fly until I crash. That's better than going to Aurora.

Not happening, Jess, Nick snapped. And he barrel rolled in such a way that she had no choice but to clamp her wings and drop feet first, closer to where he flew below her as escort. He almost snagged her ankle, but she realized at the last second and shot up. Straight into Nick's arms.

Her howl echoed across the dark landscape. She writhed in his brother's hold, but Nick's years of experience on the wing let him gain the upper hand. With physical contact the glow brightened, and Chris squinted to look at them. Fear settled into his chest.

Nick! She hasn't finished changing. She's too close to the coma. Stop!

Too late now, Chris. Get to the ground. I can't stop it this time.

He hesitated. His wings pumped in a slow figure eight to hover underneath his two Alphas.

Back off, Hunter, Nick shouted. *Ground, now. Before it's too late.*

He folded his wing and dove over, arrowing for the ground. his mind full of the growing power igniting behind him.

♦ ♦ ♦

Nickolas felt his power rise to its full extent for the first time. And he joyously answered the call in his blood. In front of him, Jessica trembled. He held her immobile, her wings pinned to his chest, as her power mirrored his.

I'm scared, Nick.

He brushed his cheek against hers. *Me too. But can you stop it? I can't.*

She shook her head slightly. His left arm remained clamped tight about her waist and held her to him. He freed his right and slid it down from her shoulder to the bandage on her wrist, then brought it up to curve around his neck. She tipped her head back into his shoulder. His heavy wing beats kept them suspended high above the ground.

Everything's been leading to this, Jess.

I know. I just hate having no control.

Me too. He brushed his lips over the shell of her ear. She tilted her head and he nibbled down to the hollow of her neck. His heartbeat thudded loud in his ears, hers becoming a matching echo. The golden haze surrounding each of them grew stronger. If Ian hadn't shown him the recording from her cell, he might not have noticed it, so engrossed in her he became.

His tongue teased the sensitive spot where her shoulder and neck met, her fingers tangled in his hair, tugging lightly. As their heartbeats synchronized, their power twined together, and the haze each of them had on their own started to mesh and form a ball around them.

I'm going to turn you. Ready?

She nodded, so he slid his hand down her side and gripped her waist. With a light toss, he spun her in his hold, her wings snapped out. After a few moments, she got the rhythm and they hovered together. His hands rested on her waist, hers on his shoulders. They met halfway. Their lips brushed then nibbled, tongues twining like their power. And the golden cocoon pulsed with its own heartbeat.

The glow around them meshed, but their power continued to twine, like yarn as it's plied, spiraling around each other but still maintaining separate strands. Strands could be unraveled.

Nick pulled away with a gasp and rested his forehead against hers. *Something's wrong. I feel like I'm stuffed in a box that's grown too small.*

Her breath panting, she replied, *I do too. My energy reaches for you, but it's blocked.*

She moved her hand and brushed the hair out of his eyes, the smell of her blood on the bandage grabbed his attention. He seized her arm and pressed the cloth to his face, inhaling deeply. *I need...*

She shuddered but let him unwind the wrap. The cut still bled sluggishly. A little queasy at the thought himself, he let his tongue trace the thin line. Power arced through him and he jerked. If he'd been standing, he'd have gone to his knees. He pressed the slice and forced the blood to flow. He could feel her power wash through him physically and mentally, entwining itself irrevocably with his.

Instinctively, he knew after a couple of swallows that he'd had enough. He pulled her wrist away and felt his power hum in his fingertips as he closed them around the bleeding cut and stopped the flow of blood.

He met her eyes when she opened them. Knowledge penetrated the dazed look with an underlying thread of fear.

It's not so bad, he reassured, then pulled his knife and nicked the spot at the base of his wrist and palm. A thin trail of blood slid down his wrist. He held it up in offering.

The tip of her tongue brushed her lower lip and her gaze jerked away from the blood to his eyes again. His free hand rest on her hip and pulled her closer. She closed her eyes and leaned forward.

He understood the shudder that ran through her at the first touch; the power contained within their life's essence overwhelmed the senses. He gasped when she pulled and his power flowed into her. For an eternity they hung there, caught in the power as it mingled freely between them, binding them closer and closer.

The exhilaration as his power reached full potential crashed through him. It fountained up, spilling out to boldly trace every line in his web, burning away any barriers that might have still existed and leaving in its wake clear paths for his use. Breathing heavily, Nickolas turned his focus back out. He could feel Jessica just coming out of her own power at the same time. Following instinct, they wove the golden ball tighter.

Then in a blinding flash of light, it was done.

The binding was complete.

On the ground, Christoff fell to his knees as the power washed out across the landscape. He stared in awe at the small sun that had replaced his brother and Jessica as it hovered midair and pulsed rhythmically. The immense energy buildup reached out, flowing through everything, and he stared transfixed as *his own* power started to beat in time with it, attuning itself to the combined force. *No wonder Nick wanted me grounded, I could never have stayed in flight with this going on.* He mused. The feeling of witnessing something immense engulfed him, and he stared at the beautiful golden light that spilled out across the land.

Then with a blinding flash, the light was gone. Blinking the spots from his eyes, he rose, searching in the distance for Nick and Jessica.

The normal noise of bedlam prevailed during the dinner hour in Aurora. Marcus smiled and watched as people gathered at tables to eat or packed up baskets to take back to their cabins. He took another bite of rice and nodded his head at Beth in answer to her question before he shared an eye roll with her over Robin. His Hunter Prime looked harried thanks to Kelley. He and Kevin had just walked in the longhouse with the rest of the Flight that had been stationed at Dustin's, and he didn't appear to be in the mood to deal with his currently suspended Second. He found Robin's relationship with his Second highly entertaining, as did the rest of the table if the smiles were any indication. If Robin noticed their amusement at his expense, they would all likely regret it when they next met him in the ring.

The first shiver of power as it brushed across his mind took him by surprise, and he paused with his fork halfway to his mouth. He looked up, scanning the crowded dining hall, expecting to find one of his clan using their talent for mischief and prepared to reprimand them for disturbing dinner. But instead, he observed every person present freeze, adopting a listening pose. Eyes colliding with Robin as a psychic pressure built, Marcus caught a faint trace of the origins of the power at the same time Robin realized who it was.

"Jessica!" tumbled from Robin's lips, then all sight was cut off as a wave of power, the likes of which Marcus had never seen, rolled through their valley. In the darkness, a sun pulsed, drawing his power to it, tuning it to beat in time with the heart of that sun. He felt others join him in the darkness, their power opening like flowers at dawn as they set their own rhythms to match. Then in a flash, he was back in the common room, blinking dazedly at all those seated with him at the table. One look was all it took to know everyone in the valley had experienced the same thing.

The silence broke as a cup fell and shattered on the floor, then a murmur started as everyone turned to look his way, needing answers. He pulled his wits together and met Beth's and then Robin's eyes.

"We had better get ready. I expect we're about to receive close to fifty Valkyries." Nods all around the table agreed with him.

◆ ◆ ◆

Riding in the passenger seat of the troop transport, Gabriel stared out the window and watched the dark silhouettes of trees skate by—and wished he was in the air.

The annoyance over the failure of the recovery this afternoon dominated his thoughts. He obsessed over every move of the plans for the takeover of Ian's part of the Facility. Nickolas's power had surprised him earlier, but that wouldn't happen again.

This would be a lot easier if Nickolas and his brother were out of the way. Their leadership will make subduing the control group more difficult. He sighed.

My orders are clear. Jessica, Nickolas, and Ian. The presence of the control group is too valuable. But taking those three will cut one head off the hydra. It's a pity I have to break Ian. Such a brilliant mind. I'm going to miss him as a rival. But orders are orders. He knows too much. And they want it.

One slice of joy found its way to the surface of his thoughts. *I'm going to so enjoy Kratz's face when this goes down. I love being the instrument of discipline and Kratz really deserves this.* He smiled.

A wave of power slammed into him and jarred him out of his ruminations.

He sent his mind out, questing after the receding surge. The sun-like blast that caught him up took him by surprise and held him within it. The power reached through him and tried to force his energy into its own form. He fought the pull, altered his rhythm to counter the one from without, and gained some distance, which allowed him to recognize Nickolas's power signature and what must be Jessica's twining together. As he watched, the two combined and became exponentially stronger than they had been alone. Rage rose up, cutting him off from the wave of energy even more.

No! Gabriel screamed, sending out a burst of thought at Nickolas. The backlash of power when the binding concluded flashed through Gabriel and sent him to the grey area of almost unconsciousness. Wavering back into focus, he found that the panicking driver had stopped the truck and now hovered over his slumped form.

"I'm fine. I'm fine. Just get us to the Facility. There's no more time," he growled out.

Ian watched Jays rhythmically pound his fist on the table; it reminded him of a more violent imitation of drumming your fingernails. He finished corrupting another section of the computer system then sat back, and Jays pounced on him. "How long have they been gone? Donald only has a couple more groups to go. We're running out of time, Ian!"

Knowing better than Jays that they were running out of time, Ian probed his Second for the hundredth time in an effort to gauge his state. His deterioration had accelerated. It wouldn't be long before he passed out.

"Relax, Jays. There will be enough time for Donald to get the last of you out, barely. Nick and Chris have only been gone a couple of hours, and they have a map to the meet up."

Not satisfied, Jays spun away, then stopped. Intrigued by Jays's sudden stillness, Ian looked around, then he too felt the wave approaching. He rose and came up behind Jays, reaching out a hand to steady him. Ian smiled when he felt Nick's and Jessica's power signatures spiraling up like two birds in a mating flight. He opened himself up completely and welcomed the flow of energy as it coursed through him, reveling in the knowledge that he'd been right. His heartbeat, beating in time with the pulsing, grew stronger as his power fountained up, marching to the new music.

Hesitant flares of new power joined his, and Ian opened his eyes to look at Jays, who stood frozen in shock. Ian squeezed his shoulder reassuringly, and Jays slowly turned bewildered eyes on him. "What? I don't understand..." He trailed off.

"I do. I'll explain when it's over," he replied quietly. The pulsing waves gained momentum, reaching a crescendo, then, like a soap bubble, burst out over the land, raining sparkling golden dust to Ian's inner sight. Sighing in a mixture of relief and sadness, he turned his attention back to Jays.

The young man shook the dazed look from his eyes and turned on him. "What the hell was that?!"

He rubbed his tired eyes then smiled slightly. "Please sit. There're some things we need to discuss."

From his seat, he waited while Jays fidgeted around, eventually taking a seat. But even then he couldn't sit still, tapping his feet, drumming his fingers. Ian chuckled. "Ok, at least you're sitting. So, what was that? It felt like Nickolas and Jessica finished what they started a few weeks ago and confirmed my guess that they were trying to bind their power together. I hadn't expected it to spread beyond them though."

Jays's movements slowed as he listened, so Ian went on. "Did you feel the way the energy pulsed and the way something inside you matched it?" His Second nodded, so he continued. "I'm pretty sure that what we felt was a preliminary binding, a first stage. Our energy signatures were tuned to make it easier for us to bind to the pair if we choose. I can see the use in something like that. With the Alpha pair as the nucleus, a close knit group could form, with the ability to pool power and keep track of one another's health and safety, a huge benefit."

"Still, why...?" Jays asked, his eyes squinted in concentration.

"Why did you experience it?"

Numbly, he nodded his head.

"Have you noticed how you are feeling today, how you are behaving?" He paused, waiting for a glimmer of understanding; at the first kernel, he continued sympathetically, "You entered the second stage today."

Jays reared back like he'd been slapped then stood up and backed away. "No, oh no, no, no," he moaned, shaking his head in denial. "Not now. Not when so much is on the line."

The fledgling started to pace in front of the table and ran his hands through his hair in agitation. "How long have you known?"

"That you were changing? Or that you were going into the second stage?"

"Either, both, I don't know. Why didn't you tell me?" he yelled.

Ian sighed and pressed the heel of his hand to his forehead for a second before he answered. "You know the rules. We don't tell a new fledgling until they enter the second stage, which you did this morning. Donald already knows and he'll take care of you. You've done everything here that you can; I want you to evac in this next run. I need to know you made it out, Jays."

"You couldn't have made an exception this time? You have to have known for weeks..." Jays ranted, then stopped to stare at him a moment before he stated, "Wait a sec, what do you mean Donald can take care of me. That's your job, Ian."

Pain flashed through his chest, but he concealed it. "You of all people know how unlikely that would be, Jays. You know how long I can last outside of the Facility. Without a steady supply of my inhibitor, I'm dead, and they have gone to a lot of trouble to make sure I was never able to duplicate the formula. No matter how hard I tried."

"You just got this week's shipment. You'll have a week's grace, so maybe using Beth and Marcus's equipment, you can duplicate it."

He hated to kill the hope in Jays's voice. "They don't have that sophisticated of equipment, and I am tired of being a hostage, Jays. They use my presence to keep Marcus and the rebels under control, just as they use Nickolas and Christoff as a means to keep both of us under control. Besides, I still have too much to destroy. If I can, I'll join you guys later."
Donald, it's time for you to come and get Jays.

He stood and walked over to a cabinet, where he took out a small disk. "Here, take this. It will give you information on your gift. You'll be a Seer, and from what I can tell, your talent will have the same form as mine. This is everything I've learned over the years about myself." He pressed it into Jays's unreceptive fingers, then looked the younger man in the eyes. "They are going to need you, Jays. You know everything I do or at least how to access it."

The door to the Hub opened and Donald walked in to join them. "It's good to know Nick found Jessica," the Hunter said, then cocked his head at Jays. "So have you told him, Ian?"

"Yes. I just finished. And you need to combine the last groups. My talent is screaming; I want all of you to leave immediately. There's not much time left."

Nodding his head in understanding, Donald turned to Jays. "Come on, kid, we're pretty much ready. Is there anything you need to grab, Jays?"

The lost look in his eyes when he shook his head squeezed Ian's heart. Jays stood there, clutching the disk, not moving, so Donald took him by the shoulder and turned him toward the door. Halfway across the Hub, Jays pulled away from Donald and whipped back to him. "No, I can help you finish, then you can come with us. I don't want to leave you here, Ian."

He gestured for Donald to take him away and just shook his head. "I can't, Jays. I want nothing more than to be with my family and know all my Valkyries are safe, but they've made sure I can't have that. Clear skies." He raised his hand in farewell and watched Donald drag Jays through the door, then said under his breath, "My son."

"Donald, let me go!" Jays shouted.

He pushed Jays forward again then grabbed the new fledgling by the wrist and twisted his arm behind his back. "No. We need to hurry, Jays."

He clamped his other hand at the back of Jays's neck and forced the struggling fledge down the hall and out the door. He breathed a temporary sigh of relief once they were outside. The shouting was less likely to draw attention there. He kept him moving and wove through the paths to where they were staging the evacuation. Jays's voice broke and Donald hardened his heart. He was responsible for getting everyone out and that included Jays, whether Jays wanted to or not.

They reached the open garden, where he forced him into the center of the gathered Valkyries who immediately closed ranks, forming a wall. Only then did he relax his grip and let Jays have his arm back. The new fledgling immediately stepped away, rubbing his joints while his eyes darted around the group, looking for a way through the fence.

"Dev, is everyone here?" Donald asked as he watched Jays closely.

"We're waiting on the last two now," the Third Flight Wing leader said quietly.

"Get them to hurry. All three of our groups are leaving together, but we'll go as two Flights. Dev, I want you and your Second to head the other Flight. I'll take Kieran as my Second and we'll cart Jays. As soon as we have him netted up, I want to fly."

"Right, Donald," said Dev, and he turned away to issue quiet orders to his Second.

"Why am I your Second?" Kieran asked, irritated.

He looked at him in exasperation. "Why do you think, Kier? You're not in much better shape than Jays. There's no way I would allow you to lieutenant a Flight in your condition."

"I'm fine," he snapped.

He caught his cousin's gaze and pushed dominance with a hard stare until Kieran looked away. "I need to keep you close. You're my Second and that's final, now cope."

Kieran growled but kept his eyes averted and started to put on his harness. Heated voices reached Donald and he turned away from the fourth stage fledge to watch Dev's Second escorting the last two Hunters into the garden. One was empty-handed, but the other carried a huge black case.

"What now?" he muttered under his breath. "Kieran, keep an eye on Jays. And this time don't let go."

That elicited a snarl from his Second that he ignored, and he walked over to the argument. "No. Whatever it is, no," he said when he got close enough.

The Hunter holding the large case set her chin stubbornly. "I'm not leaving it behind, Donald. You let the others take things if they wanted and could."

Snorting, he looked at her. "I think that was a little different, don't you? Books, pictures, other small possessions. What is that thing anyway?"

"A cello," she mumbled.

"A cello?"

"Yes. It's been in my family for over a century. Jen agreed to help me carry it."

He could feel the battle slip away before he'd even had a chance to engage. Donald glared at the two and pointed a finger at them. "If at any time you can't pull your own or keep up, it's gone."

Smiles lit their eyes and he turned away, shaking his head to rejoin Dev. He started to tell him that he would get to keep an eye on the cello when Ian latched onto his mind.

Donald! You need to get everyone out now! Get into the air. Gabriel is almost to the gate.

Join us. We're still in the garden; there's time. We can have a net prepared and waiting, it won't delay us.

Regret flowed down the link, twisted through Ian's words. *No. It's not possible. Please go. I'm proud of everything all of you have done. And I'm sorry I won't be there to help any longer. Please tell Christoff and Nickolas I'm sorry. And...and take care of Jays.*

Sadness welled up in Donald and he choked out the last words. *I will Ian. Good-bye.*

Good-bye, Donald, the doctor whispered, then he felt the link cut.

"What's wrong, Donald?" Dev asked urgently.

Cursing under his breath, Donald looked at Dev, then over at Kieran and Jays. His voice rough, Donald snapped, "Ian said Gabriel's at the gate. We need to leave now. Get your Flight in order; Kier, get Jays into the net."

"What about Ian?" Kieran asked.

"He's not coming."

"Damn it, Donald, don't do this to him!" Jays cried, pulling away from Kieran. He then tried to push past the Hunters in his way. "You have no idea what Gabriel is capable of. He's going to tear him apart." He spun back to face Donald, fighting the hands that tried to restrain him.

The circle let him through, and he grabbed Jays by the throat and immobilized him. "Stop it, Jays. Ian needs to be free to do what is necessary, and he won't be if he has to worry about you. We all have our orders and we will follow them.

You're not helping him." He stared hard into Jays's blue eyes and could see the despair his friend tried to hold at bay. "Kieran, Dev, get the net." Jays's pulse beat steadily against the palm of his hand and the fledgling slowly shook his head.

"Please, Donald," he whispered.

"I'm sorry, Jays." He held him still as Dev draped the net over the fledge's head and Kieran pulled it around his body, then started lashing it shut. Jays's breathing took on a panicked hitch. Once the other two had him secured in the net, Donald released his hold so Dev and Kieran could pick him up and lay him out on the ground. He immediately started to try to fight the net. Kieran and two other Hunters secured the tether line clips from three corners of the net to their harnesses, while he quickly donned his own harness and clipped the last corner to his.

He staggered as he got pulled off balance by the struggling and snarled at the fledgling. "If you don't settle down, Jays, I'll trank you. Ian gave me some knowing you might need it."

The struggling stopped abruptly and Jays called, "Please don't leave him, Donald."

"I don't have a choice, Jays." With a nod to the others, he bent his knees, and on the count of three, they surged into the air. The sound of wings overwhelmed his ears as the rest of the twenty Valkyries followed them up into the moonlight. As they gained altitude, he looked down; a convoy of vehicles had pulled up to the outer gates of the Facility. *It looks like Ian was right*, Donald thought with sadness. Then Gabriel's golden head walked around the lead truck and looked up. He caught his breath as he watched the foreign Alpha follow their trajectory, then swore. It wouldn't be long before they had followers tracking them. Flashing through the moonlight, he pushed the two Flights of Valkyries into the night.

Chapter Twenty-two

Come on, Nicky, come on. There you are. Chris scanned the skies then launched toward the heavily flapping Nickolas. He immediately took Jessica's weight when he saw the fatigue etched into his brother's face. Concern swamped him at the limpness of her body. He looked for a suitable landing spot, then dropped to the ground in a shrubby, grassy wasteland.

Nick landed heavily beside him as he laid her body down on the prickly grass. With shaking fingers, he pressed the side of her neck and sighed in relief at the rhythmic pounding. His brother moved to her other side, blood dripping sluggishly from the tips of his fingers.

"You're bleeding." He reached into one of the pockets of his pants and pulled out a packet of gauze. He tore it open as he stood and reached out to wrap his brother's wrist. He tried not to look at Nick's eyes,—and the disconcerting power that surged through them. "What just happened? Is she ok?"

"I think so. The binding threw her into the coma."

"The what?"

Nick crouched and freed her hair from under her, laying it out over her shoulder.. "Ian mentioned something to me about bonding with other Valkyries, but this seemed...I don't know...more somehow? Our power mixed together." He shrugged. "I can still feel her inside."

"Well, that's good, maybe? Do you know if she got her last meal?"

"No idea."

"Can't do anything about it now." He sighed. "I left the net on the ground at that house. I'll fly back and get it, you rest. Then we can get to the rendezvous."

"No."

Chris froze midcrouch, his wings half spread for takeoff. "What?"

Nick stood and fished a piece of paper out of his pocket. When he opened it, Chris saw it was the map to the meet up. "Here. I need you to take Jessica and get to safety."

His muscles went lax and he stared at Nick in disbelief.

"I need to go and make sure everyone made it out of the Facility."

Fear lanced through his system. "No. Nick, you can't. I'll do it. I'm expendable, you're not."

His brother looked away. "You're not expendable to me, Chris. Besides, if there's a problem, I'm the one with the gifts to give me a better chance at getting out."

He paced and glared at Nick, but his brother just folded his arms and waited. Finally he growled, "Ok. But I want us to do that bonding thing you mentioned. I want to know that you're all right."

Surprise and uneasiness flashed through Nick's eyes.

"That's the price, Nicky. If you want me to let you take off on your own like this." He could see he'd pushed his brother into a corner, but he didn't care.

Nick glared, but he unwrapped his wrist and broke the light crust that had formed so the blood flowed again. Chris stepped up to him and looked in his eyes. "What do I do?"

"You need to take in some of my blood and the power it contains. It's as simple and as complicated as that."

"That sounds rather one way."

Nick ground his teeth then said, "Fine, have it your way."

He lifted Nick's wrist and licked the blood. Liquid lightning poured though his system. He dropped to his knees and convulsively clutched Nick's hand as the power wrapped itself around him, and he felt the same pulsing he had earlier, only a little different since he now found himself a part of that sun.

He drew away, blinking the spots from his vision. It took him a moment to realize that Nickolas held his knife out to him. Sluggish, he reached up from where he knelt at Nickolas's feet and took the blade, using it to slice his left wrist.

Nick pulled him to his feet, then he felt his power flowing out of him through his blood. His head swam and he barely registered Nickolas's withdrawal, then a burn.

He shook his head to wake himself up and noticed a faint glow fading from his brother's hands. Inspecting his wrist, he stared at the healed scab. His gaze shot over to Jessica's wrist, then back to his brother, who struggled to rewrap his wrist through the dripping blood. "You can't stop the bleeding?"

"Doesn't seem so. Not for myself at least."

Chris tied off the gauze for him then took a moment to poke at the new pathways in his head. When he looked outside of himself again, Nick had crouched next to Jessica, his hands held out over her still form.

"She seems to be doing fine, Chris. At least, I can't detect anything out of the ordinary. But I think you should bond to her as soon as you can." He unwrapped a foil blanket.

The two of them got her bundled and into his arms. Chris stared at him for a moment.

"You had better be careful."

Nick tucked a strand of her hair into the crinkly foil. "Just get yourselves to safety."

Spreading his wings, Christoff flexed his knees then gave himself more of a push than normal to get into the air, and pumped his wings to gain altitude. As he spiraled up, tucking Jessica in close, he looked back down at his brother; Nick stood where they had left him, staring up after them, his hand raised in farewell.

He shoved the crash of emotions flooding his system aside and turned east, then pumping harder, he flew through the moonlight into the unknown.

♦ ♦ ♦

The Valkyrie portion of the Facility was unusually quiet. Nickolas slipped through the door from the outside and paused to let his eyes adjust to the well-lit hallway. Silence stretched all around him, as did the feeling of emptiness. He turned in the direction of the Hub and carefully cast his senses out, looking for any sign of his people or...

Emergence

My home for three quarters of my life, and now I feel like I'm walking behind enemy lines.

He checked each room he passed, finding no trace, either physically or mentally, of any of his people. And the closer he came to the Hub, the more agitated he felt.

An air current wafted past his nose. He sniffed.

He continued down the hall, where he stopped at the doors to the Hub. The tendril hit him again and he frowned. He opened the door and his lungs expanded when he inhaled. He stepped through and took another deep breath. Fatigue fled and he looked around. All machinery and computers sat dead.

He checked all of the cells and alcoves. Nothing. He pushed his fingers through his hair and noticed the tingling and paused, then turned to the store room. The door sat ajar. He pushed it open and a wave of pure oxygen rolled across him and he heard the hiss. He backed up, dizziness already threatening, but he'd seen enough. Every tank in the room cranked out gas at full. He pushed the door back and hurried out of the Hub.

He moved with more speed through the halls and ignored the fatigue that descended with the absence of the O2, his talent pushing him to hurry.

This time, when he caught a whiff of a strange scent in the hall, he made more effort to track it. A sniff here, a sniff there led him to an access panel that had been jammed shut. The rotten egg smell exploded into the hall when he pried it open. He cursed. The gas main's piping spewed gas from a shattered coupling.

Very carefully closing the panel, he started running toward the older section of the Facility and Ian's infrequently used office. He passed more sections of broken pipe along the way and could smell the gas accumulating.

He slid to a stop on the tiles in front of Ian's office door. Through the window, Ian jumped back and forth in front of his bank of computers, his movements rushed. With a sigh of relief, Nickolas grabbed the knob, but it rattled in his hand. He shook it, then pounded on the reinforced glass.

"Ian, it's me. Let me in!" Pounding some more, he kicked the door in frustration. "Ian, open the damned door!"

The doctor didn't look up, but he did lift his hand, signaling for him to wait. Not having any of it, Nick focused his talent on the door mechanism. It was a challenge in his inexperience, but he managed to get the lock disengaged. Again, he tried to open the door. It didn't budge. He slammed his shoulder into it, then plastered his face to the window to see down the front. Blocked by heavy furniture. He didn't have the mental strength for that yet. He slammed it again. "Damn it, unblock the door."

Ian continued to type furiously at his computers.

Nick gave the window a last slam then spun away. He had too much adrenaline running through his system and couldn't stand still. Pacing back and forth in front of the door, he kept glancing through the window as the smell of gas got stronger. He returned to the window, pounding on it again. "Ian, come on, we need to leave. This place is going to blow."

Still ignoring him, Ian removed a small chip from one of the computers and placed it into a handheld device that he set aside. Then reaching down, he picked up a crow bar that Nick hadn't been able to see lying on the floor, and he bashed in all of his computers.

Nick watched, his forehead against the glass; one hand gripped the door knob and the other clenched in a fist above his head. He waited for Ian to come and unblock the door.

The sound of destruction reached him through the glass. Ian tossed the crowbar then picked up the portable device that lay amid the sparking remains and, making eye contact with him, he finally approached the door.

After pushing some buttons, he held up the instrument and pointed it at the door as he walked across the room. Nick rattled the door again. "Come on, Ian."

Sadness filled Ian's eyes and Nickolas froze.

"Nicky, we're out of time. Gabriel is already on the premises," he said and stopped on the other side of the door. "You need to leave now. It's going to be hard enough for you to get out on your own as it is, impossible burdened down with an old pinioned Valkyrie."

He shook his head in denial. "No, we can make it. The gas is building up fast, but the sparks didn't ignite it."

"I've blocked the door to keep as much out for as long as I can."

"Please at least try. I'm sorry I was so mad at you earlier, please don't do this."

Ian lifted his hand up to the window; a tear slowly started to track down his cheek. "I'm glad to hear you say that. I never wanted to hurt you. Please believe that. You and your brother have given me some of the only joy I have had since the first emergence. I am so proud of both of you. But there's no getting out of this one for me. I can't survive outside of the Facility, and I know too much to stay now. And I'm tired, Nicky, so tired. This place has taken everything from me, my family...my wife." He closed his eyes for a moment. "It's time I joined her, Nicky. My life was forfeit twenty-four years ago. It's time for that debt to be collected."

He stared hard into Ian's eyes and raised his hand, placing it over the one on the other side of the window. "Please, it doesn't have to be this way. They didn't take all your family."

A slight smile tugged at Ian's mouth and he blinked his eyes. "That's one regret I've always had. That I couldn't give the two of you a proper home. Living like this, we couldn't even have the normal family relationship that should have been ours. *They* always used you to maintain control over us. You were the leash to control the leaders."

Shock coursed through his system. "Us? How did they control Chris and me?"

Ian rested his head on the glass and clenched his fist before carefully flattening it out again. "That's the last lie, Nicky. Your parents didn't die during the escape like you'd been told. They lead the rebels. You were a means of control, on both them and me. I couldn't tell you. They made it quite clear what they'd do if I did."

Nickolas stared at him in shock, then said, his voice trembling, "Mom...and Dad...?"

"I'm sorry, Nicky, so sorry. This is definitely not how I would have liked you to find out." Lowering his hand, Ian wiped quickly at his eyes. "As much as I want to see my son again, I think the biggest regret I have is knowing that I'll never see my great-grandchildren. Jessica is beautiful. Now go, you don't have much more time. I broke as many of the gas pipes as I could, any stray spark out there could send this place up before the fire I've set to go off in the Hub does the job."

Then he backed away from the door and turned, walking back to his desk. After he sat, he looked at him again. "The people here never really understood what sort of enemy they made when they took my family; I never forgave them for killing my wife."

Nickolas swallowed hard when his grandfather opened a drawer and pulled a gun out. He handled it with expertise.

"No! Ian. Grandfather, please." He plastered both hands to the window and stared at Ian in horror. "No, don't," he pleaded quietly.

Ian cradled the gun in his hand and looked him in the eyes, the sadness and tears evident even from across the room. "I won't let Gabriel take me, Nickolas. Falling into his hands would be a fate worse than death, a fate worse than the last two decades. But more importantly, it would put everyone at risk. And everything I've worked for would be gone. At least now I know you'll be free. Please tell your mother and father good-bye for me. And tell Chris how proud I am of both of you. I love you. Now go please, Nicky. I don't want you to see this. Go!"

Mutely shaking his head, he started pounding on the door, trying to break it down. Not noticing the tears running down his face, he kept trying, futilely, to get the door open.

"Please go...," Ian said once more then raised the gun to his temple. "Good-bye, Nicky," he whispered, then pulled the trigger.

Screaming, Nickolas threw his body against the door again and again, the frame shuddered but held secure. The glass cracked, but the wire mesh held it together. Banging his forehead against the cracked glass, Nickolas stared unbelieving at Ian slumped over on the desk, the red stain spreading, then he slid down the door to the floor, sobbing.

The smell of gas finally penetrated his grief.

He pulled himself together and rose to look in the window one last time. Then wiping his eyes, he held his hand against the broken window, "Good-bye, Grandfather. I hope you fly in the next life," he whispered.

Turning his back on the man who had done more to raise him than his parents, Nickolas started to walk out of the Facility for the last time. With each step, he tamped down his grief. His senses ranging out for the enemy, violence swirled through him.

A warning screamed through his mind, and he jerked to a stop, his wings flaring. The door to the outside stood at the end of the hall. But an open side door fell between him and it. He took a step back, debating the wisdom of how long he had to take another route to the outside. The scuff of a boot ended it. Flynn stepped out of the room to block the hall, a gun raised and aimed at his chest.

"It would have been simpler if you had continued past, then I could have just taken you from behind," his teammate said quietly.

Nick growled and extended his wings as far as the hall would allow before he furled them with a snap.

"Stop. Any sign of you using those witchy powers of yours and I won't hesitate to pull the trigger. You blocked the darts earlier today, but are you faster than a speeding bullet, Mr. Superman?" Flynn waggled the gun at him. "Six thousand feet per second, Nicky. I make the distance between us about twenty. How fast do you think you can raise a shield? Now, where are they all, Nickolas? The Hub is deserted. We need Jessica back. Now."

The truth of Flynn's allegiance shone in his eyes, and the betrayal made him snap, "Too bad, traitor. She's gone."

"Traitor? I'm not the traitor here. You and the rest of your kind are the ones who have turned on all of those who've helped and cared for you," Flynn said.

"Helped and cared for? Don't you mean used and destroyed? Give me a break, Flynn, the people who started all this care nothing for us. We are all expendable experiments. We're treated no better than dogs. Worse, actually, since dogs have some rights protecting them." He took a step toward Flynn but paused when the grounded raised the gun a little more in warning. "So what are you going to do now, Flynn, shoot me? I thought Gabriel wanted me alive."

A savage grin spread across Flynn's face. "Sure enough he does, but he's not going to care if you're damaged. He understands the stakes and knows how hard you're going to be to catch. So unless you want a few holes poked in uncomfortable places, I would lie down on the floor if I were you."

He stared at Flynn and debated the wisdom of racing bullets. *I just don't have the experience yet*, he thought in disgust with himself.

"Why, Flynn?" he said, stalling for time, hoping an opportunity would present itself. "How long have you been Gabriel's man?"

"Does that really matter, Nick?" Flynn said. "You know nothing of the politics that surround you, boy, the different factions that vie for control. Gabriel put me in place at the start, but Ian was too careful, at least until the very end here." He motioned Nick to the floor. "Now get down, or I will shoot you, Nick."

Rage slipped into him and he stared at the gloating in Flynn's eyes, letting the other man know that he wasn't under control yet, and he sank to his knees, placing his hands behind his neck. He refused to be forced flat to the floor like a dog. The corners of Flynn's lips quirked and the man took a step toward him, his intention to kick him to the floor plain on his face.

A blur of red struck out of the room as soon as the grounded had his back to the doorway, and he crumpled to the floor.

Jules stepped out of the door, and the comm tech's eyes swept him as he set the fire extinguisher down next to Flynn's bleeding head and scooped up the gun.

Uncertain of this new development, Nickolas waited, smiling slightly when Jules hauled back and kicked Flynn in the ribs hard enough to force the unconscious man over onto his back. So he took the cue and lowered his hands to his thighs and stared at Jules's bandaged head, waiting to see where they stood.

Jules's eyes twinkled. "Had to do something to get the bastard back, since he's the one who bashed me in the van earlier. I really can't stand it when someone gets me by surprise like that." Jules's eyes grew serious. "I'm not Gabriel's man, Nick," he said softly, then he turned his back on him and shoved the fire extinguisher back into the room then shut the door.

Nick rose and shook his wings out, sniffing the air. "I'm glad to hear that, Jules. We need to get out of here. Ian's rigged the place to explode."

Groaning, Jules looked at him. "Is everyone out?"

"Everyone who matters," Nick said flatly and Jules flashed a surprised look at him as they turned and walked briskly down the hall toward the exit. "Did you know about Flynn?"

Jules glanced back over his shoulder at the downed man before he answered. "I wondered. A few things hadn't been adding up." And that was as far as he would take it.

They reached the door, but when Nick placed his hand on the knob, he froze; a cold chill ran down his spine.

"What is it?"

"Gabriel. He's on the other side of this door. I need to get out."

"How much time do we have?"

"Not enough. I don't think we can get to a different exit before the gas explodes."

"Go. Do what you have to do, I'll slip out behind you and find some way out of the complex. Maybe we'll see each other again sometime."

"I hope so, Jules, I really do." He took a deep breath and placed a skin-tight shield around himself before he pushed the door open and stepped out into the night.

Twenty feet away stood Gabriel, his dark wings spread slightly, his eyes glowing with power.

"Hello, Nickolas," Gabriel's voice drifted on the breeze.

He took a few steps closer to the other Alpha to allow Jules room to slip behind him.

"Gabriel."

A soft snarl sounded in the darkness and Gabriel leisurely stalked round him. "I told you this afternoon that you wouldn't get away. You and Ian are all I need. The others will come running when they feel your pain."

He moved with Gabriel, keeping out of reach as he gauged the interlaced tree branches and how far away he needed to get before he could get into the air.

"Don't count on it. I doubt Chris or any of the others will fall for that." He hoped at least. Knowing his brother and the others, they probably *would* do exactly what Gabriel hoped.

A ticking clock sounded in the back of his mind, his talent issuing a warning. He had very little time left before the complex went up.

He shifted to the side, but Gabriel kept him hedged with his back to the building. Raised voices reached them, then the flood lights flared on, blinding him for a second. In that moment of vulnerability, Nickolas heard movement and tried to spin, but Gabriel's hand clamped around his throat. Thankfully the skin shield kept him from squeezing. He pumped power into the shield and broke the hold by expanding it out several inches.

He would have laughed when he caught Gabriel's thwarted look, but he had his hands too full. Power battered his shield at the same moment as Gabriel spun low and swept his feet out from under him. He fell, just managing to tuck his wings and turn it into a backward roll, fighting to keep his shield intact. If he didn't succeed, the other Alpha's voice would take him down.

Gabriel's power stripped layer after layer from him, and he slapped new skins up as fast as he could, but Gabriel had so much more experience in using his talent. He skittered to the side trying to regain his feet, the combination of physical and mental attacks slowing him. *Out. That's my only option. He's going to get through at this rate.*

He dove under a sweeping wing and slammed against the brick wall of the building; his power bled out of him and left him dizzy. He pushed back harder with his thoughts. Reflexes, more than anything, got him back on his feet. He dodged, then clamped his wings down tight and leapt as high as he could, somersaulting over Gabriel's head, and hit the ground running. The growl of rage behind him pushed him on.

Racing down the tree-lined corridor, he focused on the end of the trees. The breath rasped in his lungs. The sound of others joining in pursuit penetrated his concentration. He shot past the last sentinel, and without missing a beat, he spread his wings and launched into the sky.

The psychic attack lessened a fraction as he shot straight up to gain distance with altitude, then it stopped abruptly when a hollow boom resounded. His wings faltered when his mind was freed. He slowed his assent and turned to look back at the Facility compound.

People swarmed out like a hive of bees that'd been kicked. Gabriel stood at the edge of the trees, talking to a frantically gesturing man. Shaking his head, he turned away from the grounded to look straight up at Nickolas. Even over the distance, Nick could feel Gabriel's eyes.

The arrow of thought slammed into him. *It's just a matter of time, Nickolas. You can't outrace us.*

There's no way to know if you don't try.

He still hovered in the air when the first fireball exploded out of the Facility. Apparently, the boom must have been Ian's detonator going off inside the Hub. Now the pockets of natural gas were igniting.

A billow of orange burst through a section of roof, raining debris across the gardens, and the alarms started to blare. Fire raced along all the arms of the buildings as more pockets of gas exploded here and there, pushing the devastation on. Black smoke poured into the sky and started to obscure the scene below.

Gabriel dove for cover as the building closest to him exploded glass all over the walk, and Nickolas shouted in joy. Grinning savagely as he watched the compound burn, Nickolas arrowed a thought at Gabriel. *Now you don't have anything. That's a big fuck you from Ian. He and everyone else here are beyond you now.*

Not you, the whispered thought skated through.

The last thing Nickolas saw as he dove away to start the harrowing flight out toward the mountains was Gabriel picking himself up off of the grass and the sound of the helicopters out on the helipad starting up.

General Rembrandt Harrison Luther Faulk read through the last of the reports for the night. He reached over without looking and picked up his cup of tea, his mind absorbed in the paperwork. The loose skin at the corners of his eyes creased when he read an amusing segment.

The door opened and he lowered the pages, his amusement tempered by steel. "Yes, Jared?"

His secretary, Jared Roberts, paced across the expanse of the office. Most people wouldn't recognize the danger held in the young man...most people.

Luther specialized in finding it.

He tapped his papers together and set them in his file tray, waiting to hear what news his boy brought at this hour.

"Carl's faction is making their bid," the lithe, sandy-haired man said quietly. "We got word that Gabriel attempted to take Nickolas, but that Robin prevented it."

"And?" Luther leaned back in his chair, folding his hands on the desk. Jared cocked a hip on the corner.

"Gabriel just took the Facility."

His eyebrows rose. "Well. I'm sure that hasn't gone over well with Ian."

A slight smile flitted across Jared's face and was gone. "You could say that. Ian got all of the Valkyries out, it appears. Either way, Gabriel has gotten nothing."

Confused, he stared at the amusement hidden in the depths of Jared's eyes. "Nothing? What about Ian and his research? Did he finally manage to break the code on the inhibitor?"

Jared shrugged. "I have no idea, General, but I can tell you, Ian was feeling pretty spiteful. The Facility needs to be replaced."

He sat up slowly, his mind shuffling through all the implications before he asked, "Replaced?"

"He blew it up, sir."

Blinking, his mind raced. "Well, that sure changes the game, doesn't it? I wonder what sort of hands the others were dealt with this. Now I'm doubly curious over May's call this evening. I wish I hadn't missed it." The pads of his fingers tapped a staccato on the desk as his thoughts turned inward. "Nickolas is now free, with no leash holding him; this could be good or bad."

"He's a wild card."

"The likeliest assumption for us to make is that Ian will take the Facility Valkyries to Aurora. Step up our surveillance; I want to know what's happening there."

"Done. What about Nickolas? Should we try to bring him back into the fold?"

He paused and considered his secretary's question. The young man's attention seemed focused on him and their conversation, but Luther knew how deceptive that appearance was. Jared's awareness of his surroundings made him indispensable.

He chewed his cheek then nodded. "Get the operator set up. If we get the chance to try and convince him to come home, we will, but otherwise let's see what he does with his newfound freedom."

Marcus sat back in his chair and tried to suppress his smile. The rest gathered around the large conference room table weren't quite as successful. Smiles stretched as they listened to Kelley and Robin argue in the doorway. Robin's cool, clipped tones seemed to infuriate Kelley.

"I'm your Second, Robin," she yelled.

"Not at the moment, you're not, and you know it. You're still Omega, and until you're flight worthy again, you stay that way. Now get out."

Marcus winced at the glare she flung at his Hunter Prime, but Robin didn't seem to notice. He just stared her down.

Growling with a promise of threat, she spun, her wings billowing, and stormed off. Robin's shoulders relaxed, then he turned back to the others in the room and raked them all with cold eyes. All smiles disappeared, except for Marcus's.

He waved his Hunter Prime into his seat next to Leslie, his acting Second, then did a quick count of the others assembled. "Is everyone here?"

Alex, the Seer Prime's Second spoke up. "Nathan said he'll stay up at the tower. He's called in four more Seers and is stepping up observations. That wave that came through here really has him nervous, Marcus."

"He's not the only one, Alex," Kevin said. Marcus shifted his eyes to the Caster Prime, silently asking him to elaborate, so Kevin turned to face him. "Everyone in the valley's concerned, Marcus. They're all congregating, waiting for you to tell them what's going on."

Well, that explains the level of noise out in the rest of the longhouse. He and Beth had retreated straight to the conference room as soon as the wave had passed, leaving Robin to gather all of the Primes and their Seconds for the meeting. "I wish I had answers for them, Kev, but all I know for sure is that the energy wave came from Nickolas and Jessica. What it means?" He shrugged. "I haven't a clue yet. But whatever happened to them created a backlash large enough to reach us all the way out here; and after needing to flee Dustin's this morning.... Something big has gone down in the Facility."

"I don't think Dustin and his family were compromised," Kevin added. "I'm pretty sure we got out in time. Do you agree, Robin?"

Robin toyed with a tea cup, stretched his legs out under the table, and nodded. "Yeah. Though whether Dustin'll stay that way.... If his family can keep his mouth shut and not let him near any of the Facility people. He's pissed and won't hesitate to tell them off."

Marcus shook his head. *He's almost as much a hothead as his twin.* "Did Amanda know anything?"

"No. She was just bait. I got her settled in the infirmary until a mentor can be assigned to her." Kevin yawned.

"Right." Marcus looked at all the ranking Valkyries. "I think it's safe to assume that Ian has evacuated the Facility. But to where? His escort is no longer at Dustin's, and we have to assume he'll know that. Ian knows where we are located, but he's never actually traversed the distance."

"Concentrate our search to the south?" Leslie asked.

"Only a couple are off the drugs, so it'll be like searching for a needle in a haystack," Kevin added.

"Our best resource will be the Seers," Marcus said. "Ian will have to have them moving fast. He's going to have his hands full with that bunch. Plus they've got two fledges. We need to get search parties organized, then finish clearing the south quad for refugee housing."

"What about Gabriel?" Robin asked.

"I guess we're going to have to hope that he stays focused in the north and they slip by him. But we can't count on that. The search parties need to watch for signs of pursuit."

A knock at the door interrupted him. A flick of his eyes had Robin rising to answer it. The woman who entered swiftly searched those assembled at the table and at Alex's welcoming gesture moved over to him before addressing Marcus.

"Sir, Nathan sent me down. The weather watchers report that we're about to take a turn for the worse. Snow is anticipated to start falling tomorrow afternoon or evening."

Closing his eyes, Marcus nodded. "Thank you."

"Well doesn't that just make things peachy?" Kevin muttered.

Marcus agreed whole-heartedly with that assessment. "We need to increase our defenses. They could be leading Gabriel straight to us."

Finishing off his tea, Robin set the empty cup down in front of him. "Kevin and I will go up to the tower and discuss increasing the numbers and rotation of our scouts with Nathan. After we figure out what we're doing, Marcus, I'll come let you know what we set up."

"And I'll get the infirmary set up for the two new fledges and for Ian and whatever equipment he's brought with him," Beth said.

"I'll come help you, Beth, after I'm done in the tower," Kevin volunteered. "I wanted to talk to Amanda anyway."

Raising his hand, Alex asked, "How many people are we looking at?"

Marcus brushed his hand over his mouth as he thought for a moment. "About fifty I think. So the south quad should house them all, I believe."

"I can help with that part, Marcus," Leslie said.

"Good. Anything else we need to cover this minute?" he asked, looking around. Everyone shook their heads. "Fine, you all have your assignments, report to me when you're done. Robin, Kevin, you're with me. We need to reassure the rest of our people, and you'll be able to get the search parties set up since everyone is already gathered."

The meeting broke up. Marcus, flanked by Robin and Kevin, left last. He led the way down the long wall of the common room and stopped in front of the fireplace. He gazed out over the sea of faces. *Kev's right. I suspect the scouts are the only missing bodies.*

Voices quieted. "Sorry, folks. I don't have a lot of answers. But I'm sure we'll get some over the next several days. What we have been able to piece together is that Gabriel's made a move on the Facility."

Murmurs rose at that announcement, and he raised his hand. "So we expect Ian has evacuated. Robin and Kevin will organize what needs to be done. I'll leave them to it."

He backed up and let Robin take center stage. "We have several tasks to start on. It's going to be a long night, everyone, so start drinking coffee. I want all scouts to gather by the other fireplace. We need to set up search parties to head out and look for the refugees and organize extra patrols because we expect they'll be pursued and we need the additional security."

Kevin stepped up next to Robin, and at the Hunter Prime's nod, started his own set of orders. "Everyone who still lives in the south quad, I want you to gather by the kitchen doors, and anyone else who would like to help. I know everyone's been slowly relocating from that section, but now we have to clear it out to make room for Ian's people."

As the room gained direction and started to shuffle into the asked-for groups, Marcus left them and made his way into his office to begin his own preparations.

Much later, Marcus stepped out into the hall and shut his office door. He rubbed his eyes then walked through the silent longhouse. The exterior door clicked shut as he walked outside into the soft grey mist and stretched his exhausted body. He stopped in the center of the flagstone courtyard and extended his wings out slowly, holding the position for a moment before closing them just as slowly. The cold forest air filled his lungs and he raised his eyes to the top of the mountains on the east side of the valley. The sun had just started to touch the jagged peaks as dawn brought them a new day.

Soft hands slid around his ribs from behind and Beth's scent drifted to his nostrils. She rested her head between his shoulder blades, nestled in the hollow of his wings. Pressing her hands into his chest with his own, he sighed.

"We should try to get some rest," her quiet voice whispered. It still sounded loud in the early morning solitude. "I just finished getting the infirmary set up. I hope Ian doesn't need anything too specific."

"Don't worry, Beth. He knows what we have. Probably better than we do." He chuckled. A yawn caught him by surprise. He took her hand from his chest and pulled her to his side to tuck her under his arm, where she rested her head on his shoulder. They watched the sun crest the mountains. "The first search groups have returned empty-handed. The second have just left." He could hear the concern in his own voice.

"Like you said to me, don't worry. Robin will find them."

"Robin." He sighed. "That reminds me, I just went over the last message that came in from May. She said that she's spent the last several weeks packing up the house and putting it into a storage locker. She says that when she's done, she expects me to come and pick her up. She's going to join her charges here. I nearly swallowed my tongue when I heard that."

He felt Beth's chuckle more than heard it. "Don't let her scare you so, Marcus."

"That old harridan. If she were a Valkyrie, she'd be an Alpha." He shivered.

This time, there was no doubt that Beth was laughing at him. "She was perfect to keep both Robin and Jessica under control while they were young. They were both so strong willed."

"Were?" Marcus said dryly.

Laughing softly, Beth said, "Point."

He hugged her tightly as streaks of sunlight flashed past the crags and shot out to illuminate the sky and countryside as the sun rose higher. Marcus tipped his head and placed a soft kiss on the top of Beth's dark hair. "Just think, my sweet. Our whole family is going to be back together soon."

"I'm so excited, but I don't know what to say to the boys, Marcus. I've dreamt about this for so long."

He could hear the joy and the fear in her voice. He understood it well, since he shared it. "We'll take it one day at a time, love. That's all anyone can do, one day at a time." Tucking her tighter under his arm, he turned her, and through the gilded mist, they made their way home.

ABOUT THE AUTHOR

Siana Wineland lives in the beautiful, but soggy, Olympic Peninsula of Washington State. When she is not writing urban fantasy or paranormal romance she is spending her time shepherding her young children, or the goats and sheep she raises on their little farm. For updates on her writing, please visit her website at sianawineland.com or follow her on Twitter at twitter.com/sianawineland.